HAVENWOOD FALLS HIGH
VOLUME FIVE
A HAVENWOOD FALLS HIGH COLLECTION

J.L. WEIL   CAMEO RENAE   AMY HALE

ABOUT THIS BOOK

Three novellas (books 14-16) in the young adult paranormal fantasy series Havenwood Falls High, Home of the Dragons – and vampires, wolves, fae, and much more.

Blood & Iron by Amy Hale

Born a vampire, from a situation deemed impossible, Miranda Saunders is an enigma to everyone. When a photo surfaces that brings up questions about her long lost father, she is determined to find the answers. That search lands her directly in the path of trouble —fellow vampire Kai Reynolds. Kai's prospecting for the SIN motorcycle club, and when he catches Miranda snooping around the clubhouse, he has to choose: turn her in and prove his loyalty to the club or help her find the answers she's looking for. Working together means taking risks far more dangerous than they understand. And the mystery surrounding Miranda's father is only the beginning.

Shadows & Spells by Cameo Renae

Sequel to *Bound by Shadows*—Rylan Gilles vows to never allow his past to interfere with his new life in Havenwood Falls. But when a psychotic shifter named Lars kills his old pack's alpha, they turn to Rylan to save them. Eris Blaekthorn has been working on growing her newfound magical powers, including nightmares that feel like premonitions. Horrifying images of Rylan being ripped to shreds plague her dreams. When she tries to discuss these with Rylan, he shuts her out. He's determined to handle Lars on his own, but Eris knows where this will end. But if Rylan doesn't face Lars, he risks losing everything, including the girl he loves.

Falling Deep by J.L. Weil

More than any other aspect of high school, Mallory Dorian

dislikes most the mean girls. Every school has them, and her new school, Havenwood Falls High, is no exception. Why they decide to make Mallory's life a living hell, she can't figure out. Maybe because she is falling for one of their boyfriends—the mysterious Torent Stark. But Mallory has bigger problems. From the moment she came to the quaint mountain town, something has awakened inside her. The mystic and dark waters call to her, beckoning her to discover her true self. But to find out what she is, Mallory must first survive her initiation into Havenwood Falls High.

HAVENWOOD FALLS HIGH BOOKS

Predestined by Valia Lind

Rediscovered by Morgan Wylie

Ashes of Fate by Apryl Baker

Stay up to date at www.HavenwoodFalls.com

BLOOD & IRON

AMY HALE

HAVENWOOD FALLS HIGH

Blood & Iron

AMY HALE

~ A Havenwood Falls Young Adult Novella ~

ALSO BY AMY HALE

Ulterior Motives

THE SHADOWS TRILOGY

Shadows of Jane

Shadows of Deception

Shadows of Deliverance

Overshadowed (A Shadows Trilogy Novella)

Catching Whitney

Letters From Jayson

HAVENWOOD FALLS HIGH

Somewhere Within

HAVENWOOD FALLS

Flames Among the Frost

To my husband John, for always encouraging me to dream big and think outside of the box. And for all the great trips on our motorcycle. I love and adore you.

CHAPTER 1

a bell rang. The loud clanging resonated from somewhere nearby. I was certain it was a familiar sound, yet at that moment, it seemed foreign. I couldn't register the meaning, only that it was annoying, and I wanted it to stop. I closed my eyes and rubbed my temples.

"What's wrong with you?" a grating male voice spoke near my ear.

I snapped to attention. "What?" I turned to find myself uncomfortably close to Gary Smithson, one of our notorious school bullies. His dark eyes stared back into mine. I placed a hand on his chest and pushed him away. "Nothing. I'm fine."

"You don't look fine. Are you on drugs or something?" He smirked, and I knew he'd just *love* to spread that specific piece of gossip around school.

"No, moron. I'm not on drugs. I have a headache. Now go away before I tell the entire school that you still sleep with a night light."

His eyes grew wide. "What? How . . ." He looked around and ran a hand over his brown buzz-cut hair. "You're suck a freak."

Then he strolled away, his stocky build shifting side to side as he pretended I hadn't just nailed his fear of the dark, which was common knowledge in vampire circles, or more precisely due to the vampires in those circles.

I sat at my desk a moment longer as the classroom continued to empty. I'd done it again. For the past several weeks I'd been having involuntary moments where my consciousness seemed to check out, like my body was present but my mind was elsewhere. Each time I found myself mentally transported, often surrounded by mist or fog, and I was always looking for something . . . or someone. I never found whatever it was, and it always left me feeling empty. I also woke from this odd trance with a headache.

I gathered my books and made my way to my locker, willing my head to clear before I had to face the rest of the day.

My best friend Zoey reached my locker about the same time I did. "I'm so glad it's Friday and only a half day. I'm already tired of this school year," she moaned.

I chuckled. "It's barely been a week."

"I know. I'm just over it already," she grumbled.

"One day you'll look back and wonder how it all went by so fast." I repeated the words I'd heard adults say dozens of times.

She rolled her eyes. "Hey, I've gotta help my dad at the shop for a little while after I leave here, but then I'm free if you wanted to watch a movie at my house or something." Her mood brightened significantly at the subject change.

"Uh, yeah. Sure." I dug through my purse, looking for my house keys.

"Are you okay, Miranda? You've seemed kinda distracted lately. And you look tired."

"Do I?" I glanced at myself in my locker mirror. I did look a little tired, although only those closest to me would have really noticed it. My shiny long blond hair was still perfectly in place. My makeup was flawless and accented my features impeccably. Looking amazing was just one of the perks of being a vampire. My eyes, though . . . the gold flecks that were scattered within the dark irises were usually luminous. Now they seemed dull and joyless.

"Have you been sleeping okay?" She placed a hand on my arm.

"Mostly. I seem to just randomly zone out a lot. And I've been having some strange dreams. Like I'm chasing something or being chased. For some reason, I've had a lot of anxiety off and on. It hits at weird times. I can't seem to shake it." It sounds odd, vampires sleeping, but my mom and I, we're not your average Gothic vampires. Truth be told, we're not average in any way.

I hadn't told anyone about the dreams, the anxiety, or the trances, but Zoey was my confidante. I could tell her anything. She knew my darkest secrets, like the fact that I was a vampire. And I knew hers, such as her being a dragon shifter. Those were the kinds of things you took to your grave when roughly half the population in your town was human.

"Want to talk about it?" She glanced at her watch, and I knew she needed to get to her dad's shop.

"We can later. I'll meet you at the store after I've dropped some stuff off at home." I gave her a quick hug.

"Great, see you in a bit." She dashed down the hall and out the front doors of the school.

I loaded my backpack with the books I needed to take home and slung it over my shoulder. It was a relatively nice day, and I was glad I'd left my old car at home. It hadn't been running particularly well, and I enjoyed walking, when the weather was nice anyway. The exercise gave me time to think, and this was a day I needed it more than ever.

I mulled over various issues as I walked, trying to decide which one might be the cause of the unsettled feelings I'd been fighting. I'd just celebrated my seventeenth birthday, but it wasn't a major milestone like eighteen or twenty-one. It didn't have the feeling of big changes and responsibility that I assumed would come with those ages. I hadn't seen a lot of my mother lately, but I assumed that was due to a heavy workload. Being a marketing analyst could be demanding work. Most of the time, she worked remotely, but now and then she had to travel to the main headquarters in Denver. I didn't even know what her company sold. It had something to do with computers or something. Whatever it was, it paid the bills. It was just her and me, and Mom worked hard to provide for us. I had no siblings, and I didn't even know who my father was. Mom didn't talk about him.

Nothing I thought of fit. I couldn't describe the feeling other than to say it felt like I'd lost something important. And that I only had so much time to find it before it was gone from me forever. It was ominous and frightening. Despite what the movies said, Gothic vampires couldn't see into the future or read minds. At least, I'd never met any that could. And although I wasn't a normal Gothic vampire, I still didn't think visions or trances were something I should be experiencing. It felt . . . wrong. So I'd been left with this void I didn't know how to fill, and disturbing episodes I couldn't explain.

I unlocked the door to my house and put my backpack on the kitchen table. I scribbled out a note for Mom letting her know I'd be with Zoey the rest of the day, then I locked back up and walked toward the town square and Simple Treasures Pawn Shop. I hadn't quite made it to Eighth Street when I heard a noise from behind me that sounded like thunder. I felt it as well. The ground vibrated beneath my feet, and before I could even turn around, my senses were telling me to be alert and careful. I looked back just in time to see three large men on motorcycles roar past me. They were wearing leather cuts with the Swords of the Infernal Night logo on them. SIN was their acronym, and it seemed to fit them to a tee. While they appeared to be ordinary bikers, something about them gave off a vibe that they were anything but. That ominous feeling intensified, and I was anxious to get to the pawn shop.

I reached the store and walked in to find Zoey dusting a shelf loaded down with various old junk. None of it looked very valuable on the surface, and I couldn't see why anyone would want to buy it. There were belt buckles, military patches, medals, watches, small trinket boxes . . . all of it appeared beat up and dull. I assumed they held some kind of historical value, so maybe that was the attraction.

"What's all this junk?" I asked as Zoey lifted a small metal box.

She quirked one eyebrow up at me. "Junk? It's not junk. It's . . ."

She waved her hand over it, as if that would somehow explain the purpose of the items before her. "It's . . . sentimental history."

"To who?" I crossed my arms. "The people that should care about it have pawned it."

Zoey opened her mouth, then shut it again. "Good point."

I laughed and nudged her side with my fist. Just being with her lifted my spirits. "How long do you work today?"

"Not much longer. I have to finish this shelf, then Dad said I had the rest of the afternoon free as long as nothing else came up. What kind of movie should we watch?" She pushed her raven black hair behind one ear, revealing some of the mother-of-pearl strands that ran through her tresses. Her hair was gorgeous, although she thought it was odd. I'd often told her it was a perfect accent to her stunning blue-gray eyes, but again she disagreed.

"Something funny." I didn't need anything scary or with major drama.

She glanced at me sideways as she continued to dust the shelf. "What? No campy slasher film? Blood and gore?" She turned to me. "Are you afraid it'll make you hungry?"

"No!" I nudged her again. "You know I'm not that kind of vampire."

"So if they were slaughtering woodland animals, you'd get hungry?"

I glared at her. "How do you like your humans? In barbecue sauce?"

Zoey laughed. "Sorry. You know I gotta tease you now and then." She dropped her rag on the counter and turned to face me. "Okay, well, what's the plan?"

"A funny movie. Or we could just hang out around town. See if there's anything new at Callie's . . . something like that."

Zoey shrugged as she picked up the rag once more and wiped down the last belt buckle on the shelf. "Sure. Any of that's better than doing nothing."

"Well," I sighed with dramatic flair, "I'm glad hanging out with me ranks just above 'doing nothing.'"

She put her hands on her hips. "Don't go all diva on me. You know what I meant."

I smiled. Someone in the hallway at school had once loudly called me a diva because I wouldn't hang out with her. While I was particular about my clothes, food, and who I spent time with, I was far from a diva. I was just very discerning where my tastes were concerned. That, and I wasn't your average vampire, so there were things about me I'd rather not divulge except to my closest friends. Spending time with me would ultimately bring those things to light. The biggest one was that I couldn't stomach human blood. I'd bring it back up every time. So instead, I fed on animal blood, which in my mind seemed cruel too, but it was better than starving to death. Human food was okay, and I'd eat it at times, but to really survive, vampires needed blood.

It was my turn to tease her. "Oh, you haven't seen a diva attitude yet. Just wait until I get my hands on Jordan. I'm gonna unleash the beast."

Zoey laughed. "Why?"

"Because I expected him to bring you one of those gorgeous flowered dresses from his vacation in Hawaii, and instead he brought you a T-shirt," I grumbled.

"Oh, you wouldn't. Besides, this is the first real vacation Jordan and his mom have taken since . . . ever. His dad wouldn't do things like that for his family. I'm glad they got to go. All I asked him to bring back for me was his gorgeous smile, tan buff bod, and photos from the island."

"I'm glad he went too, but still . . ." I crossed my arms in front of my chest. "I wanted to see you in one of those dresses like they always show people wearing on TV."

Zoey laughed. "Yeah, that wouldn't stand out on my super pale flesh at all."

"Hey, I'm the fashion maven of the two of us, and I'm telling you. It'd be perfect on you."

She waved me away as she put her cleaning supplies under a nearby cabinet. "Let me go see if Dad needs anything else. Maybe I can knock off now and we can grab lunch before we take off for the day."

I browsed around as she disappeared into the back room. The bell above the door rang, and I turned to see Zoey's grandfather, Lawrence Mills, slowly stroll into the room, his cane clicking on the hardwood floor as he moved. A young man with blond hair and an armload of boxes followed directly behind him, the pile teetering precariously every time he took a step. I recognized him as Glenn Williams when one of the boxes shifted and revealed his face. He used to go to school at Havenwood Falls High before he graduated last year.

"Miss Miranda. How are you today?" Mr. Mills smiled at me, but it never felt like he meant it. He had a tendency to creep me out.

"I'm well, thank you, Mr. Mills." I stood with my hands behind my back, hoping he didn't sense my discomfort.

"Glad to hear it." He turned to Glenn behind him. "You may put those on the counter."

Glenn did as he was told. Mr. Mills handed him some cash, and he scurried out of there as fast as he could. I didn't blame him. I didn't want to be around this cranky old dragon any longer than I had to, either.

"Please tell my son that I have some new items for inventory. He can keep what's valuable for the shop and toss the rest. I have an appointment, so I can't stay."

I nodded. "Happy to pass the message along, Mr. Mills."

"Thank you, girl." He turned and walked out of the store, not appearing to give me, or the business, a second thought.

Zoey and her dad, Tristan, came out of the back room a moment later.

"Was someone here?" Tristan glanced around. "I heard the bell, but I was on the phone."

"Yes, Mr. Mills dropped off those boxes for you. He said to keep the valuable stuff for the store and throw away the rest." I gestured to the boxes stacked on the glass countertop.

Tristan nodded. "Okay. Listen, girls, before you take off for the

13

day, would you mind sifting through the boxes and let me know if there is anything special that catches your eye? I have a few more phone calls to make before I can take a lunch break."

"Sure, Dad," Zoey replied.

I nodded in agreement. I was happy to be helpful in any way I could.

~

AN HOUR LATER, we'd just finished rummaging through the fourth box and still had one box to go. My stomach was growling. Tristan had ordered pizza for us. And while I was happy to help eat it, I'd soon need real vampire nourishment. I'd have to run by Sanguine Elixirs to pick up my own special blend.

We nibbled on the pizza as we sifted through the last box. I was mindlessly examining a small photo album, enjoying all the old photographs and wondering what kind of life each person led. Most of them looked to be taken sometime in the sixties or seventies. But one photo stood out from the rest. I removed it from its sleeve and studied it closer.

"This is weird," I said as I continued to stare at the photograph in my hand.

"What is?" Zoey leaned over to see what I was looking at.

"That's my mom. It's many years ago, but that's her." My mom was a vampire as well, so she didn't age, but it was obvious by the clothing style that the photo had been taken sometime in the nineties—a few years before I was born, at least. Her blond hair was a tad longer than it was in its current shoulder-length cut. Unlike me, she had bright blue eyes. Her slim five-foot-seven-inch frame wore a tight pair of stonewashed jeans and a tank top with what I assumed was a band name. She stood with a group of tough-looking motorcycle guys, her arm around one man in particular. He was a few inches taller than her, with sandy blond hair and dark eyes. His build was lean and athletic. He had more of a southern rock look going on, with his leather pants and tattered cowboy hat.

14

The smile on Mom's face was huge. She looked carefree and truly happy. I wondered why I'd never seen that side of her before. Sure, she smiled and laughed at times, but even then, there was a solemn sadness underneath. I could sense it, and it made me ache for her. Her most common mood was stern, serious, and worried. I'd never understood it.

"The back has names written on it." Zoey took the photo from my hand, flipped it around, and quickly put it back in my grasp.

I squinted at the faded names. They'd been written in blue ink, and some weren't legible, but I could clearly make out my mom's name. *Sade Saunders*. The name next to hers read *Baxter Morrison*. I studied him closely, noting that something about him seemed familiar, but not quite putting my finger on what it was.

"Hey, girls. Find anything good?" Tristan walked back into the room with a stack of mail.

"Yeah, a few things." Zoey picked up a few forty-five records that had been bundled together in the first box. "This vinyl will probably be popular, now that records are kind of cool again."

Tristan frowned. "Records were never not cool. You kids just didn't understand the value in vinyl until recently."

Zoey smiled. "If you say so." She winked at me and leaned forward to whisper. "Never argue with old people about nostalgia."

"I heard that, young lady," Tristan said, never looking up from his pile of mail.

We both laughed, and I held up the photo. "Should we ask him?"

Zoey shrugged. "I guess it wouldn't hurt."

"Mr. Mills? Can I ask you something?"

He turned his head to look at me. "Only if you agree to call me Tristan. Mr. Mills is my father, and since I can't disown him, I'd at least like to distance myself from him in whatever way I can."

I nodded. "Sure, Tristan." It was weird saying that out loud, even though I'd always thought of him that way in my head for the same reasons.

I stood and took the photo to him. "Do you know any of these people? Did you live here then?"

He studied the photo and then glanced at me. His expression turned from humorous to concerned. "Where did you get this?"

"It was in one of the boxes." I pointed at the photo. "That's my mom."

He nodded. "It is indeed."

"Who are these other people?"

He cleared his throat. "This is a motorcycle club."

"How do you think my mom knows them?" I had a hard time envisioning my prim and proper mother hanging out with bikers. It just didn't seem like her thing. But the proof was there before my eyes.

"If you want to know more, you should ask your mother. This isn't my information to share." His voice was firm in that no-nonsense tone that I'd heard him use with Zoey many times. Asking him further questions would be futile.

"Okay, thank you. May I keep this picture?"

He was silent for a moment, then nodded. "Sure, but don't flash that around. Show your mom, and only your mom."

I nodded.

"I'm serious." He looked at me, and then at Zoey.

She nodded. "We understand, Dad. We'll be careful."

He handed the photo back to me, and I tucked it into the back pocket of my jeans.

Zoey slipped her arm through mine. "Can we go now, Dad? We have plans for the afternoon."

"Sure, go have fun." He waved us away and turned back to the paperwork in front of him.

Zoey and I stepped outside, and I pulled the photo from my back pocket.

"Whoa, maybe you should put that away until we get somewhere private. Dad acted like the very sight of it would start World War III or something." Zoey was trying to shield it from view.

"I will, I just want to look at it one more time." I shook my head. "There's something about that guy next to my mom. He looks familiar, but I can't figure out how I know him."

She leaned closer and inspected the photo with me once more. "I've never seen him, but it's funny. He kinda looks like you."

I froze. *He looks like me.* Or rather, I looked like him. "Zoey, I think Baxter Morrison is my father."

CHAPTER 2

*T*he afternoon with Zoey was fun. We watched an old movie and made cookies. I got home around five-thirty and finished what little homework I had for the weekend. After straightening up my room, I sat on my bed and stared at the old photo of my mother and her biker friends. This was not the woman I knew. The woman pictured looked truly happy. No worries or burdens dimmed the glow in her eyes. The smile was bright and full of hope. It made me wonder what had happened that changed her so much, outside of being the freak vampire that got pregnant. I was sure that put a dent in her social life.

Our kind didn't reproduce. We were created from what's already living. But somehow I was born. A miracle, my mom called it. I didn't feel like a miracle. I felt like there was something wrong with me. While we didn't talk about it in public, my mother had called me a mostenit, a Romanian word that meant "inherited." Against all odds, everything I was came from my mother and absentee father. So that was technically what we'd been calling my specific species of vampire. As far as I knew, I was the only one.

From what I understood, Mom went through the pregnancy alone, dealt with a lot of mocking and whispers from a majority of the vampire community, and spent most of her time taking online courses up until I was born. She didn't care about having a social life or what others thought of her. To our species of vampires, she was unnatural. To humans, she was just another sad pregnancy statistic. She didn't let any of that bother her, and she tried to raise me with the same outlook. We stuck close together as I grew up. She allowed me enough freedom to enjoy friends and activities, but at other times I was sure she was afraid to let me out of her sight. Especially as I got older. Now that I was in high school, she was very protective, and the most unhappy I'd ever seen her.

Mom's voice called for me from down the hall. "Miranda? Are you in there?"

I stood and put the photo back in my pocket. I needed to find the right time to ask her about it, but when would be tricky.

"Yeah, Mom, I'll be out in a moment." I took a deep breath and mentally prepared myself to walk through that door and pretend like everything was normal. I stepped into the hall and shut the door behind me. When I looked up, my mom was standing there, staring at me. She looked haunted.

"Are you okay?" I asked.

She swallowed and clasped her hands in front of her. "I will be." She paused to take a breath. "Let's have dinner, okay?"

I nodded. Something was up, so maybe this wasn't the best time to bring up her past.

I helped set the table, which to many would seem like a useless step for two vampires. But it was part of a comforting routine we'd established when I was little, before I knew we were vampires. And even though we didn't need to, we did occasionally still eat human food during dinner hours, just to try to feel like we fit in with normal people.

We enjoyed human food more than others of our kind. We were a lot like the moroi vampires in that way, as they also needed human food as much as blood. This was yet another thing that we were mocked for by the Gothic vampires when they found out. They didn't understand my mother's desire for me to have a few basic human experiences. She still remembered what it was like to be human, and she wanted me to know what that was like, too.

She'd made a small batch of pasta with marinara sauce. She usually mixed blood in with hers, but tonight I didn't feel much like eating pasta or anything else. Mom ate slowly, while I picked at mine.

"Mom?"

She swallowed a bite of her pasta. "Yes, sweetheart?"

"What's going on?"

She took a sip of her water and stared at her plate. "I've not been feeling well lately."

"What? What do you mean? Vampires don't get sick." I looked her over. Now that she mentioned it, I did notice the slight dark circles under her eyes, and what little color she did have was gone from her pallor.

"Well, I don't seem to be your average vampire." She sighed.

"So, did you go to a doctor?" Even to my ears that sounded nuts. Did doctors know how to examine vampires? My guess was no.

"I talked to Dr. Underwood and a few members of the Court, but none of them have ever heard of such a thing. Just like they'd never heard of our kind getting pregnant."

Panic caused my voice to raise an octave. "So what do we do?"

"I'm not sure yet, but I know it'll be okay. We'll figure it out." She gave me a reassuring smile. "We have some brilliant people in this town. Someone will know how to help."

I nodded, trying to trust that she was right. Witches, fae, dragons, demons, angels, gargoyles, ghosts—we had it all in Havenwood Falls. Someone should have some ideas.

"I know this is bad timing, but in light of what you just told me, I have to ask." I pushed down the ball of nerves that rose in my throat, and pulled the photo from my back pocket. I placed it on the table between us.

She picked it up, and for a moment, a small smile played at her lips. Then her eyes met mine. "Where did you get this?"

I watched her closely. "I found it when I was helping Zoey go through some stuff at the pawn shop."

"I see." She looked the photo over once more, then handed it back to me. "What did you want to know?"

"Baxter Morrison. Is he my father?"

She pressed her lips together and closed her eyes, as if the thought pained her. I hated that my question may have brought her any heartache, but I needed the answer.

"Yes," she stated flatly. "Baxter Morrison is your father."

"Who are all these other people?"

She shrugged. "Just some friends I used to hang out with when I was young and stupid." She stood up and moved to the cabinet, retrieving a wine glass, then her favorite merlot. Bringing them to the table, she sat back down. "I think I'll need this if you're going to ask more questions."

"I don't want to make you uncomfortable. I just feel it's time I knew the truth." I prayed she'd understand why it was so important to me, although to be honest, I wasn't totally sure of the reasons myself.

"I don't like talking about that part of my past. I made a lot of mistakes. Mistakes I pray you never make. And there are some questions I can't answer." She poured a small amount of wine into her glass and took a sip.

"Can't or won't?" I felt her usual shields starting to rise.

"Both." She took my hand in hers. "Miranda, please try to understand. I'm just trying to keep you safe."

"What does that mean?" I was getting annoyed, despite trying to keep my calm.

"It means that I will answer what I answer, and you are not to worry about the rest." Her tone was firm, and I knew that she was not going to budge on the topic.

"Fine." I huffed. "So are you going to tell me about the other people? Their names are on the back, although I can't make them all out. How did you know them?"

"They were just friends that I met through Baxter. I don't really talk to any of them anymore. That's all you need to know." She sat back in her chair and took another sip of wine.

"Okay then. Where is Baxter now?" She didn't appear to want to refer to him as my father, so I'd go along with it. I didn't mind calling him by his name.

"I honestly have no idea, Miranda. He left town after he found out I was pregnant with you, and I haven't spoken to him since." Exasperation showed on her features. I knew she wasn't going to entertain my questions much longer.

"I thought he was the love of your life? You used to talk about how great he was when I was little. Then you just stopped talking about him completely." I didn't understand why it was so terrible that I wanted to know about my father.

She groaned. "Miranda. I was trying to give you a father figure in your mind. I thought he was the love of my life too, but you're old enough to know the truth. He was a scumbag who didn't give a damn about you or me when it was all said and done. He screamed at me, accused me of cheating, and then walked out on us forever." She put her hands on the table. "Now, I'm done with this conversation. It's been a long day, I'm tired, and I want you to burn that photo, do you understand?"

"Burn it?" I couldn't believe what she was asking. "But it's the only photo I have of him. He may not be a good man, but this photo is the only connection I have."

She raised her voice. "And it's more than he deserves."

I flinched. She rarely yelled at me. I didn't normally give her reason to. Talking about Baxter must have really upset her.

This time in a softer tone, she said, "Sweetheart, it's less than you deserve."

Tears filled my eyes. I didn't know why this old photograph meant so much to me in that moment, but I couldn't bear to part with it. Not yet. "Mom, please. Let me keep it."

"Burn it, or I'll do it for you." She put her hand out, and I put the photo behind my back.

"Okay, fine. I'll do it. Just let me do it with Zoey, since she was with me when I found it." One of Mom's perfectly shaped eyebrows rose above her lovely blue eyes. It was the look she always gave me when she didn't understand my reasoning on something.

"It seems only fitting. Technically, it's her dad's property anyway, so I should give it back to him or get permission before I burn it."

She frowned. "Fine. Give it back, or get permission to destroy it. Either way, you are not to keep it. Understood?"

I nodded.

"Good." She leaned forward and kissed my forehead. "Now, I'm gonna go to bed. I have a long day tomorrow, and I'm not resting well. Maybe tonight will be better."

"Love you." I hugged her, reminding myself that no matter how mad I was, she was ill and I needed to take care of her in whatever way I could.

"I love you too, sweetheart." She walked through the kitchen and into the living area that led to her bedroom.

I worked to clear the table and load the dishwasher, all the while attempting to push down the guilt in my chest. I'd never disobeyed my mother. I'd always been the kid that followed the rules, stayed between the lines, and never questioned that the adults in charge knew what was best for me. But for the first time in my life, I was going to willfully disregard my mother's orders. I wasn't going to burn or give back the photo. And she'd be angry if she ever found out. But that horrible feeling I'd been fighting recently had to do with Baxter, and for whatever reason, I couldn't walk away from that so easily.

CHAPTER 3

*S*aturday morning I got up early and went for a run. I'd worn my yoga pants, a T-shirt, and a light jacket to hold off the chill of the morning air. Fall was right around the corner, and in this Colorado box canyon, you felt it early. I'd put the photo of my parents in my jacket pocket, sure that if I left it at home, Mom would find it and destroy it herself.

After finishing my usual mile run, I sat alone in the gazebo in the town square to cool down. I'd been staring at the picture, just as I had been off and on since finding it, hoping somehow it would give me a clue as to why I felt so anxious and what connection Baxter had to it all. Despite Havenwood Falls being a small town, I didn't know everyone who lived there. Especially if they were supernatural. Some preferred to keep to themselves. Others only enjoyed the company of their own species. So it wasn't unusual for there to be people, especially adults, whom I wasn't acquainted with.

I felt the fog begin to roll around the edges of my mind. I couldn't stop it. My vision blurred, and everything surrounding me was muted and dull. I could just catch a glimpse of light in my peripherals, but no matter which way I turned, it escaped me. And there was a dull scream that sounded as if it were at the end of a very long tunnel. In my mind, I was running toward it, trying to find the person screaming, but no matter how far I ran, I was no closer to them than when I started.

My head began to ache, and I found myself still sitting in the gazebo, photo in hand. I closed my eyes and took deep breaths as I worked to interpret what just happened. I was worried these zoned-out episodes were becoming more frequent.

A familiar male voice said, "Hey, there," and startled me from my thoughts. I dropped the picture, and it fluttered to the floor. Before I could grab it, slender fingers connected to a strong pale hand had already picked it up.

I held out my hand as I looked up at him. "I'd like that back, please."

Kai Reynolds stood in front of me, smiling like a cat that had caught a mouse. His dark brown hair was perfectly combed, except for the one lock that always seemed to fall onto his forehead. The lighter brown highlights were easy to spot now that the sun was out. His golden-brown eyes twinkled as he held the photo high above his head, not bothering to look at what he kept from me. "I'm sure you would like it back."

"Seriously, Kai. I'm not joking. Give it back." I stood, and while he was only about four inches taller than my five-foot-eight-inch stature, I still couldn't reach it. But I wasn't going to back down. He was a vampire as well, and though others were intimidated by his arrogance and muscular physique, I wasn't.

"My, we *are* touchy today." He handed the photo to me, but not before snatching it just beyond my grasp one last time to annoy me.

"Thank you." I sat back down and glanced at the photo to be sure it hadn't suffered any damage before putting it back in my pocket.

"I saw you sitting over here by yourself. You looked like you needed some company." He sat next to me and stretched his long legs out in front of him. When he leaned back against the bench, he casually draped an arm behind me.

"Do I look so pathetic that I'd want *your* company?" I couldn't help but poke the bear a bit. He deserved it.

"You look like you needed something amazing in your life, so here I am." He smiled at me, and I rolled my eyes.

"You're so full of yourself."

He shrugged. "I'm confident. There's a difference."

"No, not where you're concerned, there isn't." I stood up.

He grabbed my hand. "Wait, where are you going?"

"I'm leaving to make more room for your ego. I don't think we can both fit in here." I pulled my hand from his and walked down the short steps that led to the concrete path.

He chuckled behind me. "You always were a chicken."

I stopped and whirled around. "A chicken?"

He had the nerve to smirk at me. I'd always hated that smirk. In the three short years since he'd moved here, I'd often wanted to smack it off his smug face.

I stepped toward him again. "And why am I a chicken? Because I don't like being around a pompous elitist who discriminates against those who aren't like him?"

He was on his feet and in front of me in an instant. "Now, wait a minute. You don't know what you're talking about."

"Oh, really?" I placed my hands on my hips and looked him in the eye. "So why is it you never associate with anyone other than your small group of vampire friends? Why is it you don't attend parties you're invited to unless they are specific vampires? Why are you so opposed to interspecies relationships or even friendships, for that matter?"

He glared at me, but said nothing.

"Yeah, that's what I thought." I turned to walk away.

"You don't understand anything." His tone was low and angry.

I didn't give him the satisfaction of looking back to acknowledge his answer. I kept walking until I reached Coffee Haven and went inside. I ordered my usual white mocha and chose a table at the back of the shop. I needed to think, and my mind was muddled. My thoughts kept whirling between the odd trances, finding Baxter, and the irritating interaction with Kai a few minutes earlier. I didn't talk to him often, but when we did speak to each other, it always seemed to end in a verbal joust. One I didn't always win.

The bell over the door rang, and I looked up to see Zoey's aunt Jetta walk in. She was kind of known as the town bad girl, although if you really knew her, you learned that she was a great person. She'd been in some trouble in the past, but that wasn't all necessarily by choice. She'd run with the wrong crowd once upon a time. She did look the stereotypical bad girl, though. Short, spiky silver hair, multiple piercings and tattoos, and she wore tight clothing like she'd invented the look.

I kind of envied her free spirit. I've always worn the latest styles and was known for setting a few trends in our little town, but everyone expected a certain kind of behavior from me. It's all my own fault. Since I was little, I'd found myself working hard to please everyone. I was that poor little girl without a dad and with a mother who worked all the time. I'd heard the judgmental whispers about Mom and me from an early age. Later, when I learned the truth about myself, I discovered I was viewed as the odd vampire that defied the nature of our species. I battled both of those stereotypes with everything I had. I overshot it a bit. To the human world, I was this upstanding young citizen getting good grades and volunteering when I had time. To the supernatural world, I was still a freak of nature, but considered well-behaved, and I never stepped out of place. And while I did generally enjoy being viewed as a respectable young woman who set standards to be proud of, sometimes it all felt forced. I wanted to break loose now and then, but I feared doing so would only start the whispers of "I told you she was no good."

Jetta was a rocker by trade, so if she got rowdy and loud, no one batted an eye. It was just all part of who she was, on and off the stage.

She grabbed her coffee, saw me, and came over to sit down. "Hey, chick, how ya doing?"

"I'm good." I took another sip of my mocha. "How about you?"

"Same." She smiled and leaned forward with a conspiratorial

whisper. "Conrad keeps asking me to pick a date for the wedding, but I'm enjoying making him sweat a little."

I laughed. "You are so bad."

She pointed a finger at me. "Hey, always keep a little mystery in your relationship. Give your man a reason to keep digging and learning about you. It keeps things interesting."

I shook my head. "Well, that would require a man first."

She took a sip of her coffee. "What about that Kai fella? I saw you two talking in the square a bit ago."

"Oh." I laughed nervously. "Oh ho no. He's not at all my type."

"Really? What type is he?" She smiled behind her cup.

I frowned a bit. "He's arrogant. Condescending. Elitist. Reckless. Bossy."

"Hot," she interjected.

"Well, yeah, but that's superficial," I amended.

"Maybe, but he might be good for you." She winked at me.

"You've got to be kidding me." I couldn't hide the disgust in my voice.

She shook her head. "I'm totally serious."

"Have you forgotten what he did to Zoey at the ball?" I couldn't believe she was suggesting I date Kai Reynolds, of all people.

"No, I haven't forgotten. But he was being pushed into those shenanigans by my father. You know how persuasive the almighty Lawrence Mills can be when he wants something. He didn't want Zoey dating a human, so he pushed Kai into trying to steal her away from Jordan. I don't hold it against Kai for doing what his elders told him to do, even if it was stupid."

"We can barely stand the sight of each other," I stated flatly.

"Hmmm . . . that's not what I witnessed in the gazebo," she said in a sing-song voice.

My eyes shot to hers. "Then you misread the situation."

"Oh, I don't know. I think I know sparks when I see them. I am marrying a lava dragon after all." She winked at me.

"Eventually," I retorted.

"You got me there, kiddo." Jetta reached across the table and took my hand. "Sometimes you have to take a chance in life to find what you're really looking for. What you need isn't always what you think it should be. Happiness rarely shows up in the package you pick out for yourself."

I felt sure Kai wasn't it, but her words did strike a chord on another matter. "Can I ask your help with something?"

"Sure." She sat back in her chair and twisted one of the skull rings that adorned her fingers.

"I found this photo of my mother, from a long time ago. Do you know any of the other people?" I pulled the picture from my pocket and slid it across the table.

Jetta picked it up and studied it for a moment. "Wow. This was a while back."

I nodded. "Do you know anything about the people she's with? Or Baxter Morrison?"

Jetta lowered the photo. Her eyes were full of a sadness I felt deep within. "Oh, honey. This isn't a road you want to go down."

I felt tears prick the corners of my eyes. "Why does everyone keep saying that? He's my father. I have a right to know about him."

"I understand, Miranda, but this isn't the way to learn. These people . . ." She hesitated, like she was choosing her words carefully. "They aren't the kind of people you want to cross."

"Are they murderers or something? Was my dad a criminal?" Even if I hated the answer, I needed to know.

"It's not as simple as that. The situation with them . . . it's very complicated." She handed the photo back to me. "What does your mom say?"

"Nothing. She tells me nothing." I wiped away angry tears. "She wants me to forget about all of this and burn the picture."

"Well, I can't say I blame her. She's just trying to protect you. If I had a daughter, I'd do the same." Jetta closed her eyes briefly. "I can tell you that he hasn't been back in town since he left in 2001. No one has heard from him or contacted him, and he's never coming back."

"Did you know him?" I couldn't hide the small hint of hope in my voice.

"Not very well. I'd only talked to him a couple of times." Jetta downed the last of her coffee. "He was a wild one. He liked to party. He had a reputation of sorts. He was good at getting into trouble. But that's really all I should say." She took a deep breath, then exhaled. "Now, if you need me, you call me anytime, sweetie, but be careful with this." She tapped her finger on the picture still sitting on the table. "There are people in this photo that might not appreciate you digging into their business."

"Sure," I said, as I worked on finishing the last of my drink as well.

"Okay, I need to run. I've got rehearsal and errands before my show tonight. Are you good?"

I nodded and forced a smile. "I'm good."

"Aww, you're lying, but I appreciate the effort." She stood and kissed the top of my head. "You're a great girl. Don't let anyone change that, no matter what happens in your life. Stay true to what's in here." She poked her finger at my chest as she spoke. "Your heart will never steer you wrong."

"I will. Thanks."

She winked at me, grabbed her cup, and walked to the front of the shop.

Once again I was alone with my thoughts, left wondering what awful thing my parents had been so mixed up in that no one will talk about it. Jetta said to be true to myself. And that sometimes we had to take risks to find what we were looking for. I'd never really been a risk taker, but that was about to change. I wasn't a child anymore, and this aching in my soul would never cease until I had the answers I needed. I would have to be careful, but I would find out the truth.

CHAPTER 4

I only knew of one motorcycle club in town—the notorious SIN club. While there was no proof they were doing anything illegal, there had been whispers of nefarious activities for as long as the club had existed. I had only just started hearing the rumors in the last couple of years. The adults in town had been very careful about what information was passed on to the kids, but secrets tended to get around once you were in high school. We'd all heard talk about the club full of big scary guys with equally scary reputations. No one ever came out and accused them publicly, but the whispered rumors often connected them to various disappearances and other questionable activities. Some people claimed that SIN did the less-than-desirable deeds for the Court. Others had said they operated outside of the law when not in town. And there were those who believed that SIN did whatever they wanted because they were untouchable. Who really knew what was fact and fiction?

Was Baxter a member of SIN? It was hard to comprehend. Visualizing my mother hanging out with, let alone dating, a member of such a disreputable group seemed ludicrous. Yet the proof stared back at me right there in the photo—she was standing with a whole group of them. She'd said herself that it was when she was young and stupid. I didn't know if her reasons for not telling me were more for my safety or because she was ashamed of her past. Maybe it was a mixture of both.

I decided the only way I was going to learn more about Baxter was to learn more about SIN first. So my plan was to start at the beginning. Or rather, the only beginning I knew of anyway.

That evening I waited until my mom was asleep before I left the house. It hadn't taken me long to locate the clubhouse, since I'd heard it was right next to the Cerberus Delivery building.

The clubhouse turned out to be a red brick building with a thick wooden door guarding the entrance. Above it hung a sign with the logo for SIN. It was a sword-impaled skull with roses wrapped around the hilt. I sat outside of the building for about thirty minutes before I finally worked up the nerve to sneak inside.

Music could be heard filtering through the front door, so I made my way around back to see if there was another way inside. I found a back entrance, so I slipped through the door, which thankfully didn't squeak, and pressed my back against the wall. A wall that did not feel clean. I cringed and tried not to imagine what kind of nasty things I might be rubbing off on my new blouse. Music came from the opposite end of the hall, and the stench of cigarette smoke and alcohol was strong. I wrinkled my nose, determined I wouldn't let anything deter me from my mission. It was dark, apart from the glow of neon coming from somewhere near the front of the building. I assumed that must have been the main part of the clubhouse. The shadows would help me sneak around a bit, but also made it difficult, since I didn't know the layout of the club. I stopped and took some deep breaths, trying not to cough when the smells hit me stronger this time.

I listened carefully, trying to ascertain where all the voices were coming from. It was a little hard to tell over the music. I hoped that with any luck, they were all in the room with the neon and music, so I could snoop around a bit. I took a careful step to the side, wanting to dislodge myself from whatever nasty substance had me temporarily stuck to the wall, but worried any bigger movements would alert someone to my presence.

My eyes were adjusting to what little light there was, and I could see several doors on either side of me.

I took several more cautious steps until I was almost at the door leading to the noisy room. I thought it might be good to know what I was facing. I peeked around the door to see several burly men and a few women in a very large room. I quickly pulled back. My mind started to race, and the hairs on the back of my neck felt as if they were standing on end. *What am I doing? I don't even know what I'm looking for. This may not be the best idea after all. I'm in way over my head, and I should leave while I can.* Nerves caused my stomach to do somersaults. I listened to shouts and laughter as I took one step backward to disappear back into the hallway.

The sound of several bottles tipping over and spinning on the hardwood floor suddenly echoed through the building. Despite the music, I was sure I'd just sent an alarm up to the entire clubhouse. I froze. I'd kicked the stupid bottles. That was it. I was dead.

I held my breath as I heard the rustling of bodies near the doorway. Then a hand clasped over my mouth, and someone pulled me deeper into the hall. I struggled to get free, but whoever had me was very strong. Much stronger than me.

He pulled me up against him and hissed into my ear. "Shut up and stay still if you want to live."

I stopped moving, hoping I was making the right decision by obeying his commands.

He pulled me with him as he moved closer to the hall doorway, then leaned out slightly, keeping me against him but out of sight. "Sorry, guys. I just tripped over some bottles."

Kai? Why is Kai here?

Mumbles and groans came from the main room, with one gruff shout of "Clean that crap up." Then it sounded as if they resumed their previous activities.

Kai pulled me back down the hall to the end, and out the back exit, keeping his hand over my mouth the entire time. Once outside he shoved me away from him.

"What in the . . ." He clenched his fists above his head in what appeared to be frustration. "Are you out of your mind?"

I had just been asking myself the same thing, but I ignored his question for the moment. "Don't you ever grab me like that again. Do you understand?"

I brushed off my sleeves and jeans, hoping that if there was any grime from the building still on me, I could sweep it away.

"Miranda." He stepped closer, his tone giving away his irritation. "I just saved your neck. How about a little gratitude?"

"Saved my neck?" I knew he was right, although I wasn't sure how he'd done it. And I didn't want to give him credit for anything that might give him a hero complex.

"Yes. If they had found you in there . . ." He shook his head. "It could have been really bad."

He ran his hands through his hair, and I noticed they were shaking. He was truly rattled. I'd never seen Kai Reynolds upset by anything.

"Are you okay?" It felt weird even asking him such a question. I shouldn't care. I didn't care, I told myself.

"I'm fine." He put his hands in his jeans pockets. "Let's get out of here. We need to talk somewhere less likely to get us in trouble."

I nodded. "Sure."

I would normally argue with him just for the chance to put him in his place, but seeing Kai so concerned caused me more anxiety. It was eerie to see him that way.

I followed him around the building until we reached a motorcycle that looked brand new.

He pulled an odd-looking key out of his pocket just before throwing his leg over the seat. Kai looked back at me. "Hop on."

"What?" I knew nothing about motorcycles, except that they were dangerous if you didn't know what you were doing. I'd never seen Kai on one.

He sighed, then spoke slowly. "Get. On."

"Are you nuts?" I looked around. "I'm not getting on that death machine with you. We were lucky enough to get out of the clubhouse, but stealing one of their motorcycles is just stupid."

"*You* were lucky to get out. And I'm not stealing anything. This is my bike."

I felt my mouth pop open. "When did you get a motorcycle?"

"I bought it late last year when the 2018 Fat Boys rolled off the assembly line." He smiled and rubbed a hand over the metallic blue tank with pride.

"Fat boy?" I raised an eyebrow.

"This is a Harley Davidson Fat Boy."

"Oh, I guess it's obvious I know nothing about motorcycles." I put my hands on my hips.

"It is, but you are part of a large group, so don't feel bad about it." He smirked at me in that condescending way that always made me want to throw something at him.

"I don't feel bad about it." I huffed. "I don't care about motorcycles, so there's no need for me to have any knowledge on the subject."

"Well, lucky for you, knowledge isn't required to be a passenger. So quit stalling. Get your butt on this seat so we can get out of here."

"Wow, you are such a jerk." I crossed my arms. "Do you even know how to drive that thing?"

"I do." He didn't offer any further explanation.

"Fine." I climbed on behind him, letting my feet rest on the pegs behind his legs.

"What do I hold on to?" I tried to sit upright and pushed myself as far away from him as I could without sliding off the back of the seat.

"Me. You hold on to me."

That did not appeal to me at all. I pinched a bit of fabric from his shirt between my forefinger and thumb on each hand.

"I'm not gonna bite you, Miranda. Not unless you ask me to."

I smacked his shoulder.

He chuckled. "You will need to wrap your arms around me and scoot closer if you don't want to fly off the back and land on your butt."

I groaned.

"Fine. Have it your way." He started the bike and revved the engine a couple of times before pulling into the street.

I immediately wrapped my arms around his chest and pressed myself against his back. It felt like we'd gone from zero to a hundred miles an hour in seconds.

I yelled over the rumble of the engine. "Slow down! You're going too fast!"

"Calm down. I'm doing the speed limit." He shook his head at me.

I gripped him tighter and closed my eyes. I didn't want to see whatever it was that we'd eventually run into. Another weird quirk about me: I could heal myself, but it was a slower process than for most vampires. And I didn't like pain, so I preferred to avoid it whenever possible.

I felt the wind whipping my hair around my face as we sped down the road. If I was being totally honest, it was a tad exhilarating. Not that I was going to say any such thing in front of Kai. He'd just spout something conceited and pat himself on the back.

We'd only been moving a few minutes when I felt the bike slow. I cracked open one eye to see we were nearing Danzan Lake. He pulled off the road and parked in a patch of grass.

"Why are we here?" I looked around at the peaceful setting. The moonlight reflected off the still water and made the lake resemble a large sheet of glass. Trees dotted the shoreline on the opposite side, and I could hear crickets everywhere.

"I figured this was a safe place to talk." He sat still for a moment. "Um . . . you can let go now."

I looked down to realize I was still clinging to him. "Oh. Sorry."

I released my grip and slid off the seat, happy to have my feet on solid ground again.

He stood and dismounted the bike, then walked to the edge of the water. I followed, and once at his side, he turned to face me.

"What were you doing sneaking into SIN tonight?" His frown and eyebrows angled severely downward.

"I . . . wait. You tell me why you were there first." I wasn't sure I wanted to share the news of my father with him. I expected him to mock my existence and lack of a proper two-pure-vampire-parent household.

"No, I asked you first. Why were you there, Miranda? If anyone had caught you, the consequences would have been serious. Why would you put yourself in danger like that?" He sounded angry.

"I have my reasons, and they are none of your business." If he wanted to be angry, I could be angry, too. "What were you doing there? You were in just as much danger." I poked at his chest.

"No, I wasn't." He crossed his arms.

"Oh, really? And what makes you so special that a bunch of badass bikers wouldn't beat the crap out you for being in their clubhouse?"

"Well, I'm a member, for one." He smirked at me again.

"What?" My voice did that high-pitched squeaky thing I hated when I was caught off guard.

"Okay, not a member yet. But I'm a prospect."

"And why would you do this?" I was now the one trying to find logic in *his* actions.

"Because I want to. My buddy Jack Peters is prospecting soon. He lives there since his dad is president of the club, so it's fun to hang out with him." He paused. "And that's all I can tell you. We aren't allowed to talk about the club." He put his hands on my shoulders. "Now, back to the question you keep trying to avoid. Why where you there?"

I didn't know what to tell him. The truth would be easiest, but Kai was a snob. His parents had brought him to Havenwood Falls to rub elbows with the rest of the rich people and turn him into one of the town elitists.

"Now, out with it." He looked into my eyes, and for a moment, I didn't feel annoyance toward him. He truly seemed concerned.

"I can't talk about it, Kai. It's personal." As hard as I tried, I couldn't keep the tremble out of my voice. All the emotions from the night had started to crash in on me. I closed my eyes and took a deep breath while I worked to steady myself.

He put one finger under my chin and tilted my face up so his eyes could search mine. "I know you think I'm a jerk. And sometimes I am. But I would never do anything to purposely hurt you. Despite the opinion you've formed, without getting to know me, I might add, you can trust me." He paused and waited for me to answer, but I couldn't move words past the lump in my throat. He put his hands by his sides. "Maybe I can help you."

It was then that it struck me. Maybe he actually could help. He was welcome among the members of SIN.

"I was looking for information . . . about my father." I tried not to outwardly cringe while I watched his expression. I was expecting disgust at the mention of my absentee father. Instead he looked confused.

He stepped back and put his hands on his hips. "Why would you think the club would have information on your dad?"

"Because of this." I pulled the worn photo out of my pocket and passed it to him.

He looked at the picture. "Is that your mom?"

I nodded.

He continued to study the photo. "You assume one of these bikers is your dad?"

"No, I didn't assume anything. My mother confirmed it. The man next to her, Baxter Morrison, is my biological father."

He handed the photo back to me. "Wow. That's a lot to take in."

"Yeah, it is."

"So you think he was a member of SIN, and you hoped to find something about him by snooping around the clubhouse." He spoke it as a statement, not a question.

"Something like that."

"These are not the kind of people you mess with. Or steal from. The leaders are hellhounds, for crying out loud. Have you ever seen a hellhound?"

I shook my head. "Not as far as I know."

He scoffed. "Oh, believe me. You'd know."

"I have to do something, Kai. I can't explain it, but I need to find my father. It's important." I once again felt the tears threatening to fall. But I'd rather swallow my tongue than cry in front of Kai Reynolds.

"Miranda." He pinched the bridge of his nose. "This is a suicide mission."

"Forget it. Just take me home." I stomped back to the bike and waited for him to follow.

His voice was directly behind me in seconds. "You're gonna do it anyway, aren't you? No matter what I say, you're gonna poke around and get yourself hurt."

I didn't answer.

"I'm so gonna regret this," he muttered.

I turned to face him. "Regret what?"

"I'm going to save you from yourself. I'm going to help you get the information you're looking for."

"I don't think—"

He cut me off with a wave of his hand. "On one condition."

"What would that be?" I eyed him with suspicion.

"You have to promise to let me handle this. And if we don't find anything, you drop it."

I shook my head. "No way. You have no stake in this, so it doesn't matter to you if you find anything or not."

"No stake? If they find out I'm helping you, they could kick me out . . . or worse." He shook his head. "I'm putting my future on the line for you here. I promise to do my very best to find what you are looking for, but in return, you have to let me do this my way and not stir up trouble. You have to stay out of the way."

I thought on that for a moment. I might have to have him clarify what he meant by "stay out of the way." This was my father we were discussing, after all. But for the moment, I agreed. I did need his help. Tonight had been a close call, and I did not want to find myself face to face with a hellhound.

"Agreed, for now."

He sighed. "I guess I'll take what I can get."

CHAPTER 5

J didn't sleep well, and the following morning I had very little appetite. I sat at the breakfast table but had barely touched my usual morning smoothie. I found myself so preoccupied with the events of the previous evening that I almost jumped when my cell phone rang.

"Are you okay?" Mom's voice held concern.

"Yeah, I'm fine. Would you excuse me? I should take this." I pulled my phone from my pocket and walked down the hall to my bedroom. I quickly closed the door behind me and turned on my MP3 player in case Mom was attempting to listen in.

"Hello?"

"Miranda, it's Kai."

"Oh, hi. I didn't expect to hear from you so soon." I sat on my bed. My stomach was in knots.

"Well, I hadn't planned to call you this morning, but you need to know there's been a slight change of plans." His voice sounded odd, like he was nervous.

"A change? How?" I bit my lip.

"When I got back to the club last night, Liam Peters asked me where I'd gone. He's one of the founders of the club and the president. One of the hellhounds you need to avoid." Now I knew the tone of his voice wasn't just in my head.

"And what did you tell him?"

"He saw me leave the club with you. He could smell you in the club. He knows you were there, Miranda."

"Oh, no." I gasped.

"I had to make something up on the fly to save both our butts. The only way this works is if you go along with it."

"Okay, so what's the plan?" I had a feeling things were going to go from bad to worse.

"I told him that you were my girlfriend."

"What?" I screeched.

"Hear me out." He sighed. "I told him that we'd been dating a few weeks, but that you thought I was lying to you about being at the club. You thought I might be cheating on you. You got jealous and were hanging around outside, trying to catch me in the act, or at least in a lie about being there. When I saw you, I took you home, we fought, made up, and now all is good. I assured him you won't be repeating that mistake again."

"And he believed that bull?" I stammered.

"He actually did, for the most part." Kai chuckled softly.

"I can't imagine why. And thanks for making me look like a jealous harpy." I thought that irritated me more than the girlfriend lie.

"Well, it didn't hurt that I told him who your mom was. He remembers her and Baxter. He figures like mother like daughter, I guess."

"I don't know if I should be insulted or flattered by that." I huffed.

"Probably both." He laughed again.

"This isn't funny, Kai!"

"Aw, come on. It's a little funny."

"It is not," I growled between clenched teeth.

"Well then, you are really not gonna like this part." I could almost hear that smug smirk of his.

"And what would that be?"

"We're gonna have to sell it. We have to make it public so he doesn't doubt any aspect of our story. And so he doesn't question if I bring you around now and then, or ask about Baxter."

"Um . . . absolutely not." I couldn't believe what I was hearing. There was no way I was pretending to date Kai Reynolds.

"Fine." His voice went hard. "Then enjoy watching your back for the next several years, while I skip town."

"Seriously?" He had to be exaggerating.

"Seriously. If they find out I lied . . . I don't know how bad the consequences could be. You don't cross SIN." He didn't sound like he was joking. And Jetta had said the same thing to me yesterday. We were in deep trouble, thanks to me.

"Ugh . . . crap on a cracker. Fine. I'll do it." I sighed, resigned to the fact that this was going to be a horrible experience.

"Crap on a cracker?" Kai laughed.

"Shut it. We make this the shortest relationship possible, got it?"

"I got it." He reverted back to sounding annoyed.

"So what now?" I wasn't sure I really wanted to know.

"I'm going on a run with the club later, but how about we do something tonight? We could grab dinner or see what's on the schedule at the Annex. Something so we are seen in public. I'll let you choose."

"Oh boy. Okay, I guess we could get dinner. We both need to eat anyway, so we might as well be at the same table and kill two birds with one stone."

"How logical." I swear I could hear that smirk again. He was mocking me. "I'll pick you up at six-thirty."

"Not on the death machine," I replied quickly.

He laughed and hung up on me.

"Ahhh," I moaned into the air. "He makes me so crazy sometimes."

THE DAY SEEMED to drag on, and I couldn't focus on any one thing. I was really nervous about my fake date with Kai. I knew it wouldn't take long for word to get around that we were together, which was both good and bad. Good for our particular purpose, but bad because I disliked the thought of my friends believing we were really dating. I couldn't tell anyone the truth, except maybe Zoey. She'd keep our secret, even though she wasn't Kai's biggest fan.

I dressed in my favorite jeans and a white long-sleeved top, with the addition of some silver jewelry and white boots. I pulled my hair back at the sides, allowing the rest to hang down my back.

At exactly six-thirty, I heard the rumble of Kai's motorcycle pulling into the driveway. I'd been sitting on the sofa, hoping to intercept his arrival. My mom had just walked in and heard the noise as well. I hadn't told her I was going on a date, let alone who it was with. I'd really wanted to sneak out before she had the chance to ask any questions, but Kai just screwed that all up. I was sure I'd end up killing him before this was all over with.

"Who's here? Are you expecting company?" Mom walked to the door and opened it.

Kai stood on the other side, his smile wide, and as usual, he was dressed impeccably. Even I had to admit he looked good in his black slacks and snug blue polo shirt. "Hello, Ms. Saunders. You're looking lovely, as always."

Mom smiled at him. "Why, thank you, Kai. That's very sweet of you to say." She stepped aside to allow him entrance.

Suck-up.

He turned to face me. "Hello, Miranda. You look beautiful."

He held out a small bouquet of daisies—my favorite. For a moment, I was speechless. He was really putting on quite a show to convince people we were dating, and we hadn't even left my house yet.

"Thank you. These are lovely." I held them awkwardly, unsure of what to do with them.

Mom came to the rescue. "Let me put those in water for you." She gave me a look that said *What is going on?*

"Thanks, Mom."

She stepped into the kitchen, and I turned my attention to Kai.

"Daisies?" I whispered, again trying to ensure Mom couldn't hear our conversation.

He stepped closer. "They're your favorite, right?"

I nodded. "Yes, but how did you know that?"

He shrugged. "I remembered hearing it somewhere. You probably told me at some point during school or something."

I raised one eyebrow. "I can't think of a single social situation that required my discussing my flower preferences."

He simply shrugged again. "Lucky guess then."

"Uh huh." I didn't believe him for a moment. I was sure he'd asked someone about that tidbit of knowledge. I guessed that was the sort of thing a boyfriend should know about his girlfriend, fake or otherwise, but that didn't mean I had to like it.

Mom reentered the room, and we quickly stepped apart. "So do you kids have plans for the evening?"

She was trying so hard not to ask the obvious question.

Kai didn't give me a chance to answer. "Miranda has agreed to a night out with me."

He flashed his perfect white teeth once more. I almost groaned out loud. He was too happy about all this and was overselling it. She'd get suspicious if he didn't tone it down.

"We're just gonna grab dinner and hang out for a bit. I won't be out too late."

She nodded. "All right then. You two have a good time."

Kai opened the front door for me, and I stepped through onto the front porch.

When the door shut behind him, I whirled to face him. I gestured to the motorcycle in the driveway behind me. "I told you not to pick me up on that thing."

"Yes, you did." There was that smirk, combined with his right eyebrow cocked at an arrogant angle. I was now convinced he did this just to irritate me.

I put my hands on my hips. "But you did anyway. Why?"

"Because that's my main mode of transportation at the moment. Besides, it's fun."

I rubbed my temples. "Only to crazy people."

"Call me what you like, but at least I know how to loosen up a bit."

I narrowed my eyes at him. "Are you calling me rigid?"

"I'm saying you're so terrified of relaxing and bending the rules that you never truly enjoy anything." And cue the smirk.

I released a very unladylike snort. "Let's go. The sooner we eat, the sooner this is over with."

I walked over to the bike, thankful I hadn't worn a skirt.

He threw one leg over the seat and settled in. I climbed on behind him and remembered that I had to hold on to him tightly to keep from sailing off the back like a cup left on the roof of someone's car.

"Could you maybe take things a little slower this time? It'd be great if my eyeballs weren't completely dried out by the time we got to the restaurant."

"Sure." He started the engine and pulled out of the drive.

I didn't have to grip him for dear life this time, so the ride was a little more enjoyable. I was able to watch as the modest little homes of our neighborhood gave way to the buildings in the town square. Soon we were driving out of town and picking up speed. I wrapped my arms around him tighter, willing myself to keep my eyes open and take in the view of the landscape.

The green of the blue spruce and pines was sprinkled among the quickly changing leaves of the sugar maple and sycamore trees, as well as the gold of the quivering aspens. The contrast was gorgeous. I could look to either side and see rocky outcroppings and peaks that stretched far past the clouds. Even at sixty miles an hour it was breathtaking. The air was so clear and crisp that I found myself wondering how people in crowded cities could stand to breathe. I'd never been outside of Havenwood Falls, but I'd heard awful stories about the air pollution in some of the bigger cities. Zoey had experienced a bit of it herself.

We pulled into the parking lot of Fallview Tavern & Grille at the top of the waterfalls. I released my grip on him, and he helped me off the motorcycle.

"It's turning out to be a nice evening. I thought we'd eat on the patio. Is that okay with you?" Kai motioned for me to lead the way to the doors.

"Yeah, that's fine." I looked around, once again taking in the majestic view of the mountainside. Once we entered the establishment, the ambiance was quite different. I always thought of a dungeon when I stepped through those doors. It was kind of cool, and I supposed the dimmer lighting was romantic for real couples. But I wasn't interested in being in a dark corner with Kai. As he'd suggested, the seating outside suited us much better.

We were shown to a table on the patio and given menus. I scanned the list of great food, but once again those butterflies were pushing out any thoughts of eating, despite the fact that I'd been starving earlier. It made no sense to me. I had nothing to be nervous about, unless you counted the fact that we lied to a hellhound. And that if we didn't pull this entire scheme off, not only would we be in hot water with the club, but I may lose my only chance at learning more about my father or why I'd been feeling so weird. No, nothing to be anxious about at all.

"What sounds good?" Kai asked as he looked over his menu.

"Honestly, I don't know. Do you even eat human food? I've seen you pick at stuff at school, but I don't think I've ever seen you really eat a full meal."

He flipped to the back of the menu. "Sometimes. It's not horrible, most of the time. Don't expect me to eat kale, though. That's never gonna happen."

I laughed. "Yeah, me neither. Who looked at grass and thought 'Yeah, let's eat that?'"

He smiled. "Someone who hadn't yet discovered steak."

I nodded, still laughing. "Preferably rare steak."

Kai put down his menu and leaned forward. "Oh yeah. Now that's good. All that blood . . ."

We both stared at each other for a moment.

He broke the silence first. "Honestly, that's the only thing that sounds good right now."

"Steak?" I asked.

"No, blood." He looked around, assuring no one was sitting close enough to overhear our conversation.

"Yeah, it does," I agreed, except we were on different pages with that. Like most other vampires, he drank human blood. I drank animal blood. Many thought it was an ethical thing for me, and I allowed that to be my publicly known reasoning, but in truth it was a little more complicated than that. Human blood made me ill, and I didn't know why, but I couldn't keep it down.

"Would you . . ." He paused and seemed to be searching for the right words. "Do you want to go . . . get some?"

"I don't think that would work well, Kai. I only drink animal blood. Besides, isn't the whole point of this exercise to be seen together in public?"

He nodded. "We've been seen here and on the bike. And there are things we can do later as well. We don't have to do all our convincing in one night. That wouldn't work anyway."

"My supply is at home and—"

Kai cut me off. "Let's hunt for it." His voice held a tinge of excitement.

"What?" I'd never hunted. Ever.

"Get it fresh. It's amazing that way." When I frowned, he groaned. "C'mon, Miranda. Live a little. It's easy. I can teach you."

For some reason, his earlier assertion that I didn't know how to enjoy myself had poked a sore spot. And now he'd poked it again. "What about you? I'm not going to watch you hunt humans."

He shook his head. "You won't have to. I'll hunt animals, too."

"Really, you don't have to do that just for me."

"I'm not doing it for you. I drink animal blood, too. I switched to it about a year ago." Ugh. He smirked.

I had to look like a fish out of water, with my mouth gaping open like a trout. I wasn't sure what I was hearing. Kai and his buddies were the kind of vampires that mocked others for not drinking what they called "real" blood.

"Excuse me? I must have something in my ears. I thought I heard you say you drink animal blood."

He nodded. "I do. Almost exclusively."

"Why?" I managed to stammer.

"You don't have the market cornered on ethics, you know. Others can decide to be more humanitarian." He crossed his arms.

I wondered if I'd actually offended him. "I didn't say I did. I was just surprised. What do your parents say about that?"

He frowned. "I'd rather not bring them into this. I've been having a good time so far and would like to keep it that way."

"Okay then." I was once again at a loss for words. Why all the hostility toward his parents? I thought they were a close family.

"So, are we gonna hunt or not?" There was that excitement again.

"Well, I guess. I don't think I'm properly dressed for it, though."

He smiled and stood, reaching his hand for mine. I placed my palm in his, and he pulled me to my feet. Nikki, our waitress, walked up to us at that moment.

"Sorry, we've had a sudden change of plans." Kai released my hand and pulled out his wallet. He dug out a twenty dollar bill and gave it to her. "That's the tip I would have given you if we'd stayed."

She smiled. "Thanks!"

He took my hand in his once more and pulled me through the building and back out the front doors. We reached the bike and were seated in moments. He drove us farther up the mountain, and all the while, I wondered what I had just gotten myself into.

CHAPTER 6

*W*e were moving farther up the mountain and once again picking up speed. I closed my eyes this time. I couldn't believe what I was about to do, and who I was about to do it with. Hunting animals with Kai Reynolds. Nothing about that seemed sane.

He eventually pulled off onto a small dirt road, and once we'd traveled the dusty path several feet back into the trees, he parked.

After we'd both dismounted, he turned to face me. "So here's the thing about hunting. You have to be calm and steady. It takes a few tries to catch something your first time out."

"How many times have you done this?" I was surprised he knew how to do any of this. And how did he expect to catch them? We easily moved faster than humans, but I'd never raced a wolf or a bear. Could we outrun those? A terrible thought occurred to me, and I gripped his arm. "Kai, how will we know if an animal is just an animal and not a shifter?"

He squeezed my hand. "Don't worry, you'll know. Shifters give off a different smell. There is a slight tinge of human. Just enough that you can tell the difference. The tattoos help us identify each other as well." He pointed to the magic infused tattoo he had to get when registering as a supernatural being in Havenwood Falls. We all had one. It was necessary to keep track of everyone and assure the rules from the Court were being upheld.

"Oh, yeah. That's good." I was relieved to hear that. I'd never forgive myself if we attacked a local.

"Just follow my lead. I think you'll find certain parts of it come naturally." He quietly stepped into the tree line, and I followed.

I highly doubted any of this would be second nature, but I'd do my best.

The forest floor was already showing the telltale signs of fall. Colorful leaves scattered here and there, still mostly damp from the abundance of rain we'd had in August. Twigs and branches intermingled with weeds and wildflowers. Crickets chirped as the sun began to set. Squirrels scampered up the trunks as we passed by. The beauty of nature was serene, even as the darkness descended on us. It seemed a shame that we were about to disrupt that calm with our activities.

I focused on walking as quietly as I could, tracing Kai's steps exactly. Thank the stars for vampire night vision. We'd traveled a good distance from the original trail when he put his hand up to stop me. I froze, listening for any sign of . . . something. I wasn't sure what I was supposed to be doing. He put his finger to his lips, then motioned for me to stand beside him.

I did as instructed, allowing my eyes to roam the vast forest around us. All I could see were trees. We were engulfed by them.

He pulled me in front of him and pressed his chest against my back. With his lips at my ear, he whispered instructions to me.

"Do you hear that?"

I shook my head.

"Just take some calming breaths and listen."

I took several deep breaths, allowing my body to relax and my mind to clear. That's when I heard it. The sound of something walking in our direction. It had a light step, but I was sure it had four legs.

"Do you hear it now?" he whispered again.

I nodded, afraid that if I spoke, I'd scare whatever it was away.

"Keep your mind clear. The closer it gets, the more you can hear."

I focused on the sounds I was hearing, trying to drown out any other senses, which was complicated with Kai touching me so much. The closer it came, the more I heard. In moments I could hear minute things—like the breath from its nostrils and the pounding of its heart. I felt my own adrenaline kick up a notch in response.

Kai must have sensed my reaction, or more likely he knew what I was feeling because he felt it too. "Do you feel that excitement? That's our instinct. We know prey is near."

I wanted to ask why I'd never felt that before. I'd been around animals plenty of times and never wanted to attack them. Why was this different? But I'd have to save that for later. Right now I could only focus on the task at hand.

"Now start adding your sense of smell to your tools. Are you picking up on that musk?"

"Yes," I whispered. "What is it?"

"A buck."

I felt my eyes go wide, and I turned my face to his. "We're gonna take down a buck?"

He smiled. "Yes, ma'am."

I wasn't sure I was ready for this, even with all the adrenaline spurring me on.

"We'll tag team this one, since it's your first time. When he gets close, I'll grab the rack and take him to the ground. You go for the jugular."

"I've never done that before!" I could hear the panic in my own voice, despite being able to keep it at a whisper.

"More instinct. You'll know what to do when the time is right."

I groaned. "You'd better be right, Kai."

He patted me on the shoulder. "I'm never wrong."

"That's a debate for later," I murmured.

We both stood very still as the buck neared the tree we were standing behind. In an instant, Kai had jumped out and grabbed the large deer's rack. He was so fast that the buck didn't have time to register what was happening before he tried to escape.

Kai's vampire strength kicked in, and he wrenched the animal's large head to the left, causing its body to twist in response. The buck went down hard, and as Kai had said it would, my instinct kicked in. I lunged, landing on top of the beast. I felt my fangs extend from my gums, and the only thing I could hear was the blood running through the buck's veins. It called to me. I could almost taste it. And without having to think about it, I sank my teeth into its neck.

It was euphoric.

It was satisfying.

It was delicious.

And for a few moments, I was immersed in the feeding.

But then the more human side of my brain began to slowly filter back in. What I had just done ran like an instant replay in my mind. A sob escaped my throat, and my heart sank as I pulled back. Without even thinking, I ran my hands over my face and then down my pants. Blood dripped from my chin onto my clothing. Blood also ran from the wounds on the buck's neck.

Kai growled. "You're wasting it!"

Then he jumped to the other side of the buck and fed from the spot I had just vacated.

I fell back on my butt, my hands behind me and supporting my upper body. I watched in terror and fascination as Kai finished draining the life of the animal we'd just hunted. I saw the buck's breathing slow and then stop. I heard the heart beat for the last time.

A tear ran down my cheek, cutting a trail through the blood that still covered the lower half of my face.

Kai looked up, a satisfied smile on his face, until he saw me. "Are you okay?" He moved closer and crouched in front of me. "What's wrong?"

I couldn't speak. The tears just kept flowing.

"Miranda, I didn't mean to yell at you for wasting the blood. I know this is all new to you." The look he gave me was genuinely apologetic.

I shook my head. "It's not you." I took a deep breath, trying not to let a sob escape. "I've just never taken a life before. I didn't expect it to be this hard."

He nodded. "Yeah, that takes some adjusting to. But look at it this way—if we didn't, some hunter would have come along and got him. Or a mountain lion. This way we feed, and then leave the carcass here for the carnivores to feed on as well."

"Yeah, I guess." I wiped another tear away.

"Miranda, it's the cycle of life. For something to live, something else has to die. Plants die and feed the buck. The buck dies and feeds the carnivore. The carnivore dies and feeds the soil. The soil feeds the plant. Full circle." He gave me a small smile.

"Except in this case, the carnivore doesn't die. We've cheated nature."

"Well, true. But who knows what's ahead? I'm sure it all balances out somehow." He stood and offered me his hand.

I took it, and he helped me up. "So we just leave it here?"

"Yeah, it won't take long for the other animals to find it. I imagine by now they are already closing in. The smell of blood draws them in quickly. They'll come out of hiding once the more dangerous predators leave."

"More dangerous predators?" I asked.

"Us." He smiled.

We started to walk back the direction we came. I focused on the logic in his explanation to help control my emotions.

"So," he said, "aside from the sad part, did you enjoy hunting?"

I nodded, surprised at my answer. "I really did. There was something exhilarating about it. And it tasted . . ."

"Better than the bagged and bottled stuff, right?"

I chuckled. "Yes, much better."

"I knew you'd love it." He turned and started walking backwards so he could face me while we walked. "Although, we're gonna have to get you a huge bib if you continue to be so messy."

I glanced down at myself. It looked like I'd barely escaped a horror flick. "Oh, crap. This was my favorite shirt, too."

"Well, I'm gonna say that's a goner. You might as well use the rest of it to clean off your face."

I stopped and turned my back to him, using the bottom of my shirt to wipe my cheeks, mouth, and chin. I faced him again. "Did I get it?"

"Meh, enough. You still look like a psycho Barbie doll." He turned back around and started to jog away.

"Hey! You aren't insulting me and then leaving me behind, mister!" I hurried to catch up.

CHAPTER 7

*W*e'd only been back in town a few minutes when Kai tapped my leg.

I leaned forward.

"We're being followed."

I looked back to see a dark-clothed man on a motorcycle a few car lengths behind us.

I again leaned forward as much as I could and tried to speak to Kai without having to scream over the engine. "Who is that guy?"

"I'll introduce you when we stop. Just follow my lead, to the letter. Got it?"

I nodded. "Got it."

I looked down and remembered I was a quite a mess. Blood stained my white top in several places, and there were random splatters and streaks on my jeans. *Kai's right. I'll have to trash the shirt. There's no getting that mess out.* I then remembered that SIN members weren't likely strangers to blood. It wouldn't faze them a bit.

We pulled in front of the club, and the other biker pulled up next to us. Kai shut off the engine and turned to face the man.

"Hey, Monte, what's up?" Kai kept his face impassive, but I could feel the tension in him as he helped me off his motorcycle.

Monte wasn't an imposing figure, with his tall, slight frame and scruffy features, but I caught myself wanting to hold Kai's hand for reassurance.

"Just takin' care of some business." He gave Kai a pointed look.

"Cool. Miranda and I were just up in the mountains doing a little hunting." He gestured to my blood-soaked shirt. "She's a little new to it, so she's still getting the hang of a clean feed."

Monte looked me up and down, and this time I did move closer to Kai and grasped his hand. He squeezed mine in return.

He chuckled. "She's a messy eater."

I fought back the urge to say something rude. Instead I held my tongue.

Kai put his arm around me and squeezed. "We'll fix that, right, babe?"

I looked up into his face and did my best to paste on a sweet smile. I could feel my teeth grinding together. "With your help, I'll be a pro in no time, stud."

Kai's eyebrows drew together in warning. "You know I love it when you talk dirty."

I continued to smile at him, hoping Monte would buy our horrible acting so we could go.

He turned and took a few steps toward the front door, then stopped and looked back at us. "Well? You coming or not?"

Kai nodded. "Sure, I just need a moment alone with my girl, if you don't mind."

"Sure." He opened the door and stepped inside the club just as Kai pulled me close.

There was a moment when I was sure Kai was actually going to kiss me. I was totally unprepared for it. And then I found I was even more unprepared for what happened next.

He put his forehead against mine. "Okay, we are expected to go inside. I'm supposed to introduce you to the guys. Be cool, pretend you're having fun. I'll take care of the rest. And don't cringe at anything you hear or see. They get kind of . . ."

"Debased?" I finished for him.

"Something like that," he muttered, then released a deep sigh. "I'll get you out of there as quick as I can."

I stepped back, putting some distance between us. "You forget, I've seen the inside before."

"That's when the lights were down and you only got a quick glimpse. This will be different."

I was starting to rethink this whole plan of his. Surely I could find information about my dad some other way. Did I really need Kai or the club's help? The reality of it was that I absolutely did. They were my best shot at getting answers.

I straightened my spine. "Okay then, lead the way."

Kai put his arm around me, and we walked through the door together.

We entered the busy clubhouse. There was a big guy sitting at the bar quickly downing a beer. He appeared to be all muscle and had long, dirty-blond hair with a beard that matched. He turned to face us.

Kai moved his arm from my shoulders to my waist in a more intimate, possessive gesture. "Hey, Crusher, this is my girl, Miranda."

Crusher smiled, lifted the bottle a bit and gave a small acknowledgment with two fingers, then swiveled his seat back to facing the bar.

Kai lowered his lips to my ear. "Let's hope they all go that easy."

"Yeah," I whispered. Having him that close was disorienting.

He guided me toward the middle of the room and surprised me with an announcement. "Hey, everyone! This is my girl, Miranda."

Several beers rose in greeting, and a couple of the women sitting on the laps of two of the men smiled and nodded, although I wasn't sure how genuine those smiles were. I was already uncomfortable, and we'd been inside less than five minutes.

Kai pulled out a wooden chair, which looked to be the cleanest spot in the room, and motioned for me to take a seat. "I'll pick some music."

He walked to the jukebox and stood next to Monte. They chatted quietly while I assumed they looked through music. Kai finally picked a song, and some Five Finger Death Punch poured out of the speakers.

Kai sat next to me on a sofa that looked pretty nasty. Monte sat next to him and looked me over.

"You seem like a nice girl. Why you datin' a jerk like Kai?"

Kai flipped Monte the bird. "I'm not all bad."

Monte snorted. "You sure ain't all good."

"Stop busting my chops, dude. You're making me look bad in front of her." Kai turned his attention to me. "Don't listen to him. He's just jealous that I have such a gorgeous girl all to myself."

I knew it was all part of the act, but dang it all . . . I actually blushed. I felt the heat rise to my cheeks. I didn't even know vampires could blush, but there it was. Kai noticed it, too. He looked at me and for a split second seemed to lose his train of thought. Thankfully, he recovered quickly.

"I'll admit, she's too good for me. And it's getting late. If I don't get her home soon, her mother may never let me take her out again."

A loud snicker came from Crusher at the bar. I had a feeling Kai was gonna catch a lot of crap over this visit later.

"I'll bring her back when we can stay longer." Kai nodded at Monte.

Monte shot him another look that I couldn't decipher, then took a swig of the beer in his hand. "Yeah, I don't think her momma would be too thrilled to learn she's hangin' out with us."

My eyes shot to his. "You know my mom?"

"Not really, but any self-respecting parent would have a coronary if they learned their little girl was seen in this club."

I wanted to remind him that I'm not all that little, and in a year or so would be making my own decisions, no matter what anyone else said. Kai didn't give me that opportunity.

"I'd appreciate it if you kept her visit here just among the group. It'll be bad enough when people realize I'm part of SIN."

Monte slapped Kai on the back. "You can count on us, bruh." He turned his eyes to me. "Have a good night, Miss Miranda." Then he found a seat at the bar and left us to show ourselves out.

We made it to the motorcycle, and I put my hands on my hips. "What just happened in there?"

He raised one eyebrow. "What do you mean? We got lucky. We didn't have to spend much time with the crew tonight."

"No, I mean all the 'she's too good for me' stuff. How does that help them believe we're an item if we don't seem like a good match?" It didn't make sense to me.

"That's just it. We aren't a good match. Everyone knows you're Miss Goody Two-Shoes." He jerked his head in the direction of the club. "Even those guys. So I have to make it look like I'm winning you over slowly. Getting your mom's approval. Wearing your perfect persona down a bit, so that we'd eventually make a better pair."

"That just sounds . . . weird. And I am not Miss Goody Two-Shoes!" I wasn't a troublemaker, but still, I wasn't perfect or even pretending to be. I couldn't help if that's how people perceived me.

"Uh huh. You just keep telling yourself that." And there was the smirk. I wondered if he'd think I was so innocent if he knew how much I wanted to rip his lips off in that moment.

"Take me home." I was tired and ready to get out of my bloody clothes. And I still had to come up with an excuse for my appearance. Mom would not have approved of my hunting.

Kai drove to my house slowly, which surprised me. I assumed he was as ready to end this false date as I was. But instead of his normal kamikaze speed, it was actually a pleasant, almost relaxing ride.

We pulled into the driveway, and I quickly hopped off the motorcycle.

"Wait." Kai was right behind me. "You can't just run in."

I turned to face him. "And why is that? The night's over, right?"

"Yes, but this isn't usually how a date ends." He hitched his thumbs in his belt loops.

"You expect a kiss?" I didn't think I could've been more surprised if my teeth had sprouted wings and flew out of my mouth.

"Not a real one. It just has to look like it."

"You think they have spies in my neighborhood? You are really paranoid, you know that?" I was starting to wonder about his sanity.

He stepped forward, closing the gap between us. "Miranda, we can't be too careful. I don't know who may or may not be keeping tabs on us. You don't have to be a member of SIN to be reporting in. They can afford to pay average people to share information."

I looked up at him. "Do you really believe that?"

"I'm afraid not to. We can't take any risks."

"How long do we have to play this game?" I didn't know how long I could keep up the ruse.

"Until we find the information you need. Or, if you decide you don't want to know more, we can end it early, once we are sure we've convinced them it wasn't a lie to begin with. We can stage a big fight or something." He shrugged. "I'm sorry it's come to this."

"It's not your fault. I'm the one that got caught sneaking into the club." I sighed.

"Oh yeah, it is all your fault."

I smacked his arm. "Don't push your luck."

He laughed.

"Okay, so what do we do to fake a kiss?" My palms were a little sweaty just thinking about it.

"Well, I guess we just put our faces close to each other so it looks like our lips are touching."

"You guess?" For someone with all the plans, he sure was uncertain about some parts.

"Well, excuse me. I've never had to fake a kiss before. Up to this point, all my dates have actually wanted to kiss me." His tone gave away his annoyance. Could his ego have been hurt a smidgen? I couldn't muster an ounce of sympathy for him.

"Well, mark this down as date number one that definitely does not want to kiss you. At all."

His jaw clenched a little. I was getting to him. I shouldn't have enjoyed it so much, but this was a side of him I'd rarely seen. I couldn't let it go just yet.

"In fact, I can probably think of several other people I'd rather be kissing right now instead of you."

That must have been too far.

He put his face close to mine. "Well, let's get this horrible experience over with then, shall we?"

I nodded.

He pulled me against him and pressed his lips to mine. I was caught completely off guard. I grabbed ahold of him to keep from falling backward, and at the same time, his hands slid around my lower back and pressed me close. I wasn't sure how to respond. The pressure of his lips started out almost punishing, but quickly changed to something more gentle. It didn't take me long to realize that there was nothing fake about this kiss.

I couldn't decide whether to push him away or melt into the warmth of his arms. Seemingly against my own better judgment, I'd given in to the kiss, allowing my lips to relax under his. My senses were a little hazy when Kai finally pulled away.

He looked down at me and smiled. "I hope that wasn't too disgusting for you."

It took me longer than I would have liked to register that his intent was to prove me wrong. I felt the anger build, and I balled my hands into fists.

"Why you . . ." I started to stammer, unable to find the right words to express my feelings.

He placed a finger on my lips. "Don't say or do anything you'll regret later." He turned and got on his motorcycle. As he started the engine, I finally found my voice.

"I already have," I growled. Then I turned on my heel and disappeared inside.

Once the door shut behind me, I leaned against it and took a deep breath. *What was that? Why did I enjoy that? Why am I admitting I enjoyed that?* I was sure I was losing my mind. Kai was not my type and never would be. My mind flashed back to my conversation with Jetta at Coffee Haven. She'd said she sensed sparks between us, but even if that were true, it didn't mean we were good for each other.

Mom walked into the living room. "Miranda, you're home. How was your date?"

I shrugged. "It was okay." I didn't want to talk about it.

She looked down at my clothes. "What happened? Are you okay?" The alarm caused her voice to raise an octave.

I looked down at my shirt. "It's not my blood."

She crossed her arms. "Then whose is it?"

"No one's." I wasn't sure how to explain this.

"Miranda, it has to belong to someone. Blood doesn't come out of trees."

I rubbed my hand over my face. "Well, it belongs to something, not someone."

I'd heard it said that the truth will set you free. I was about to put that to the test.

She motioned to the sofa. "Sit. Explain."

I moved next to her and sunk into the cushions, exhaustion from the day starting to catch up with me. "Kai and I were at the restaurant, and nothing sounded good, so we went on an impromptu hunt up the mountain."

Her eyes went wide. "You hunted? Animals? With Kai?"

I nodded but didn't answer otherwise.

She looked at my clothes once more, then back at my face. "Did you actually get any in your mouth?"

"Mom!" I snapped.

She started to giggle. "It looks like you hit a major artery, and then it shot around like a runaway fire hose." She started to wheeze between even deeper laughs.

I was shocked she wasn't chastising me, but also relieved. And she was laughing. Something I didn't witness nearly enough. I started to laugh, too. "It does look pretty bad, doesn't it? But I did get full, so it wasn't a total loss."

She put her arms around me and pulled me in for a hug. "Well, that had to be a new experience. I'm not really sure how I feel about it. What did you think?"

"I'm not sure myself. Parts of it were exhilarating. Other parts were very sad. You're not mad?"

She shook her head. "No, I'm not mad. That's how I figured

you'd feel. I hadn't suggested you go before because I wasn't sure you were emotionally ready for a kill. You love animals so much . . . and taking a life isn't easy, especially the first time."

"Did you ever hunt?" I felt the sting of tears prick my eyes, the vision of the deer taking its last breath as Kai drained the life from it still vivid in my mind.

She cleared her throat. "Yes, a few times."

"How did you handle it?"

She pressed her lips together. "It's not a time I'm very proud of, sweetheart. I wasn't the person I am now."

Baxter. She was talking about when she was with my father. Another thought pushed through my mind. She didn't take to animal blood the way I did. She drank human blood. She'd probably hunted humans. I suddenly felt a little ill.

"I'm pretty tired. I think I'll get to bed." I stood.

"But aren't you going to tell me about Kai? I didn't even know you were interested in him."

"Neither did I, Mom." And that was a truth I wasn't sure how to deal with. "I'll talk to you about it in the morning, once I've had some sleep, okay?" *And I've had time to make up a backstory.*

"All right. Good night, sweetheart." She kissed my forehead.

"Good night, Mom." I quickly made my way down the hall to my bedroom, the need to be alone driving me forward. Tonight was quite possibly the craziest experience of my life. I'd hunted, helped kill, and fed on my first live prey; sat in the den of the most dangerous men in town and survived; learned my mom used to hunt humans; and scariest of all, I discovered that I'm physically attracted to Kai Reynolds. This was not good. Not good at all.

CHAPTER 8

 he next day was Labor Day, so we had the day off from school. I hadn't made any plans and spent most of my time catching up on some chores for Mom around the house. Since she'd been sick, she hadn't been able to keep up with her part of the cleaning list as easily.

Mom had planned on working, but woke up that morning feeling pretty bad. She was actually throwing up—something I'd never seen before. She couldn't keep blood or food down. When I wasn't cleaning, I stayed by her bedside, helping her in any way I could. She didn't need me often, but I didn't feel comfortable leaving her alone. At my insistence, she'd given me the number of Dr. Underwood so I could reach him in case of an emergency. She was sure a day of rest was really all she required. I worried she was in need of so much more.

The entire day had gone by before I heard from Kai again. I was starting to wonder if the kiss we'd shared had repulsed him so much that he didn't even want to look at or talk to me. I hadn't gone on many dates, to be perfectly honest. I'd always been very careful. Some guys were nice enough, but didn't hold my interest. Others had reputations that kept me as far away from them as possible. So far I hadn't found anyone that interested me both intellectually and physically. Kai ticked that last box, as I'd realized the previous evening, and I knew he was a smart guy. That didn't mean we meshed on a psychological level, but he did have both attributes in his favor. When it came down to it, how I felt about Kai didn't matter. We were acting a part to get information, then we would go our separate ways.

The doorbell rang around nine-thirty p.m. I'd just finished giving Mom some water and putting a cool cloth on her head.

When I opened the door, Kai was standing there.

"Hi." He looked tired.

"Hello." I looked like a wreck. My hair was falling out of the bun I'd put it in earlier in the day, and I was wearing an old T-shirt and sweatpants. Seeing Kai brought out a self-conscious side I didn't know I had. I caught myself trying to shove my hair back into place.

"Can I come in?" He gave me a nervous smile.

"Oh, yeah. Sure." I stepped aside and allowed him to walk past me, then closed the door behind him.

"I may have some news for you."

"Okay." I was ready for anything that might move our plan forward and get it over with quicker. I motioned for him to sit at the kitchen table while I rushed to Mom's room to make sure she was asleep. I shut her bedroom door, hoping to muffle our conversation even more.

Kai cleared his throat as I took a seat. "I was sitting in the conference room, sorting some stuff for Liam, when I overheard him ask Monte about our visit yesterday. Of course I was on high alert then, trying to catch every word I could. Liam didn't seem to mind that I'd brought you with me. He was more interested in your mom."

That caught my attention. "Why would he be interested in her?"

"I didn't get that part. But I did hear him say that he felt bad about all Baxter had put her through . . . and was still putting her through."

"That doesn't make sense. He's not been in her life since before I was born." It felt like I was ending up with more questions than answers.

"He also kept mentioning someone he called Doc, but it didn't sound like Liam liked him very much. There were other names he called the man that were not things you'd say in polite company."

I shifted in my chair. "This just gets weirder and weirder."

Kai nodded. "I don't understand the connection either, but it's a start."

"Yeah, I guess."

We sat in an awkward silence for a few moments. I tried to think of something to say that wouldn't bring up last night.

"My mom's been sick today."

"Sick? How is she sick?" His voice held the same confusion mine did when I first received the news.

"I don't know. We're trying to figure it out. I'm sure you've heard the stories . . . about my mom and me." I glanced at him quickly, then looked away. "How we aren't like other vampires."

"I'm sorry to hear she's not well." He didn't acknowledge the stories surrounding my birth. He just leaned back, acting as if I'd never brought them up. And while I wasn't looking directly at him, I could feel his eyes on me.

"I should go check on her." I stood, trying to appear calm despite the butterflies in my stomach.

"Please tell her I hope she's feeling better soon." He stood as well. "Before I go, I wanted to talk to you about something."

I groaned inwardly. I did not want to have this discussion right now. Maybe ever.

"I wanted to apologize for last night. I honestly didn't intend to kiss you like that, but you'd been insulting me and . . . I guess my bruised ego took over."

I shook my head. "I owe you the apology. I was being rude."

He smiled. "So we're even then? Your rude cancels my ego trip?"

I couldn't help but return his grin. "I guess that works."

"Great. Go check on your mom, then call me in the morning. I'll let you know what else I've found."

"I have school in the morning, so it may be after three before I can call. You're going back to look for more info?" I was starting to think we should quit while we were ahead.

"Sure. To be honest, I'm pretty curious now. And lately there hasn't been a whole lot for me to do around the club, besides clean up after the parties. It allows me to snoop a little."

I frowned. "I don't know, Kai. Mom is sick, and SIN is watching our every move. Maybe it's best if we just call the whole thing off."

He crossed his arms in front of his chest. "Are you chickening out on me? After all I've gone through? I never took you for a quitter."

"I'm not a quitter. I'm just concerned." I glanced back at my mother's bedroom. "She's really sick. I've never seen her this way. I'm scared. Dr. Underwood hasn't found any answers yet."

He pulled me in for a hug, and I didn't push away. I needed the comfort he was offering in that moment. "I'm sure it'll be okay. Someone will figure out what's going on."

AROUND MIDNIGHT I checked on Mom one last time before I went to bed. Her fever had broken, and she seemed to be sleeping better. Kai had left around ten p.m., and my mind had been racing ever since. I tossed and turned for a good hour before I decided to get up and read. I went to the small bookshelf in my room and ran my fingers over the spines, searching for a book that would take me away from the mess my mind was in. It would suck tomorrow when I was exhausted at school, but better to keep my mind occupied than lay there and worry about the worst possible scenario.

I settled in on the window seat across from my bed with a well-worn copy of *Sense and Sensibility* when a loud knock on the glass next to my head almost made me scream. My reaction was to toss the book and fall off the seat, landing hard on the floor.

My heart raced as I looked up to see Kai tapping on my window. My fear turned to annoyance.

I got up and turned the latch, then pushed the window up. "What in the world do you think you're doing?" I whispered in anger.

"My parents kicked me out." He tossed a duffel bag past me, and it landed on the floor with a loud thud.

"Why?" I couldn't take my eyes off the bag sitting in the middle of my bedroom floor.

"They don't like some of the things I'm doing." He climbed through the window and sat on the floor. I joined him on the floor, facing him.

"Like what?" I couldn't imagine him committing any offense that would push his parents that far.

"They found out I'm part of SIN."

"Oh." That did make sense.

"Oddly enough, that wasn't what they threw the biggest fit over." He leaned back against the foot of my bed and rested his forearms on his knees.

"What's worse than joining a notorious biker gang that may or may not be involved in unspeakable acts?"

He raised his eyes to mine. "Apparently, dating you."

I swallowed hard. "Me?" I felt my heart break a little. Not that I'd expected his parents to like me. We weren't even really dating. But to know that anyone thought so little of me, especially when I'd worked so hard to develop a respectable reputation—it hurt. "What's so wrong with me?"

He sat forward and put his hands on top of mine. "Absolutely nothing. Nothing is wrong with you. It's them. They're . . . terrible people." He sighed. "During our fight, I learned a little more about your mom and dad."

"That's good." I pushed down my self-consciousness so I could concentrate on this new information.

"Well, it is and it isn't. I think we have to see this thing through. Your mom's life may depend on it." He gave my hands a squeeze.

I took a moment to soak that in. "Continue."

"Mom said I'd regret being with someone like you. When I

asked her to clarify, she said that you're not a true vampire and that we'd never be happy together. That your dad ruined your mom's vampiric purity. Dad jumped in and told her to shut up. He said that no one was supposed to talk about that, and it was just gossip anyway. So I pushed further." He dropped my hands. "Mom pulled me aside as I was packing my bag. She told me that I really needed to understand what I was getting into. To ask the club about Doc and his experiments. That's all she'd say."

"So maybe whatever is making my mom sick has something to do with this Doc guy?" I was worried and hopeful at the same time.

He nodded. "That's how I took it. Maybe he's the one we need to find. He might know how to help her, since no one else around here seems to have a clue yet."

"If that's the case, then we definitely can't give up." I couldn't walk away if it would help my mom, no matter how uncertain I felt.

"I'll see what I can learn about Doc. Maybe Liam or Savage will be willing to talk to me about it." He ran a hand through his hair, messing it up slightly.

The thought of him approaching the very people we were warned to avoid made me nervous for Kai, but I didn't know if we had any other options. "Okay, just be careful. The more we dig into this, the worse I feel about the whole situation."

"It'll be fine, Miranda. We'll figure it all out and find help for your mom. Maybe we'll even learn about your dad as well, just like we'd intended."

"I hope you're right." But I had my reservations.

He picked up his bag and tossed it back out the window. "I'm staying at the clubhouse for now. Not sure if I'll try to get my own place yet. I'll have to get a job first. No more freeloading. Gotta stop living the good life off Mom and Pops's money." He grinned, and I got the feeling he didn't mind that one bit.

He moved to climb out the window, but I stopped him. "Kai, can I ask you something personal?"

He turned and sat down on the padded seat. "Sure. Can't promise I'll answer."

I smiled a little. "I know they aren't your real parents. I mean . . . you weren't born into this, like I was. You were turned, right?"

He nodded. "Yeah."

"So, when were you turned?" It had just dawned on me that his family wasn't actually family.

"Shortly after my seventeenth birthday." He looked down at his hands, and I worried that my questions made him uncomfortable.

"If you don't want to answer . . ."

"No, it's fine. It's just . . . weird." He looked up at me. "Susanna and Zeke were turned in the early 1900s. They traveled a lot, always looking for the next best thing to elevate their status among other vampires. Money, power, status—that's all they care about. Then one day they found me. I'd run away from an abusive father, quit school, and was living on the streets. I guess they decided they needed a son to complete the perfect family picture. So they turned me and trained me to be the ideal mini Reynolds."

"How long have you been with them?"

He thought about it a minute. "Well, let's see. I moved here two and a half years ago, so . . . just a little over that."

"So you would have been nineteen, had you lived?"

"Yeah, but I'm technically seventeen forever now." He smiled. "On my last birthday I baked myself a huge cake and invited them into the dining room for a toast."

"That was nice," I said.

He chuckled. "No, it wasn't. No one knows this about me, but I appreciate a good prank. I knew they weren't going to touch the cake, since they don't approve of human food anymore, so I explained that it was a symbolic celebration of my new birth and life with them. They seemed to fall for that, so once we were all in the room, I lit the candles." He put his hand over his eyes, and his shoulders were shaking. "They weren't really candles. They were firecrackers, which were connected to even more firecrackers inside the cake." He laughed openly now. "There was cake and icing everywhere. They were so pissed."

I laughed, too, as I envisioned his stuffy parents with icing and cake all over them.

"But what were they gonna do? They made me immortal. It wasn't like they were gonna kill me. Then who'd they get to be their errand boy and do the dirty work for them? I'm just so sick of it all."

"What do you mean?" I knew I was prying, but I wanted to understand this side of Kai's life.

He shrugged. "I'm tired of pretending to be like them. The night of the Cold Moon Ball, I told them I thought Mr. Mills's plan was a horrible thing to do to Zoey. I didn't want any part of it. We argued for almost an hour, until Zeke physically hauled me to the Annex." He shook his head. "It's always like that. I'm expected to do everything they, or anyone in their circle, asks of me. Even if it's despicable. When you have that many people pushing you, it's hard to say no." He laughed. "It's funny—as much as I hate them, they did me a favor. I was hungry, dirty, and sick when they found me in that alley. They promised me a good life, and they've given it to me. I just didn't understand the costs at the time. But I'm making the best of it. And it'll be even better now that I'm out from under their thumb."

"Are you really out?" The break seemed too easy. Too clean.

"They'll demand I come back. They always do this when I step out of line. They kick me out, then they decide their reputations as fabulous parents with the perfect, conveniently obedient son are more important and try to lure me back in. I'm not going back this time."

"Well, if you need anything, I'm here to help. It's the least I can do after all you've done for me."

He climbed out the window then leaned the upper half of his torso in through the opening. "There is one thing you can do."

"Sure, what is it?"

He crooked his index finger in a come-hither motion. I stood and moved close to the window.

"I need to know something." His voice was barely a whisper, so I leaned closer.

He looked down, and I couldn't see his eyes.

"Kai?"

When he raised his face to mine, he was wearing that smirk that I hated. Correction—used to hate. It was starting to grow on me. "Did you really hate my kiss last night?"

I felt the heat rush to my cheeks once again. "Umm . . . I . . ."

"Glad to hear it." Then he backed away and was gone.

Nope. I take that back. I still hated that smirk.

CHAPTER 9

School the next day was excruciating. I tried to concentrate on my first two classes, but I couldn't get Kai's conversation with his parents out of my mind. Waiting until school was over was going to kill me.

The bell rang, and I put my books in my locker, grabbing what I needed for third period. I'd just passed one of the janitorial closets when a hand wrapped around my mouth and pulled me inside. The door slammed behind me. I lashed out, trying to hit whoever it was that had grabbed me.

"Stop it, Miranda. It's me," Kai hissed. He removed his hand from my mouth and stepped back.

The closet was dark, so I searched for the light switch. Once I flipped it on, I glared at him. "You gotta stop grabbing me like that! You couldn't say 'Hello' like a normal person?"

"I'm not a normal person. And no, not for what we're about to do."

I raised my eyebrows. "What are we about to do?"

"You're ditching school for the rest of the day." He beamed as if he'd just learned he'd won a prize.

I shook my head. "No, you're nuts. That's not a good idea."

"It's perfect! You do something out of character, which shows

74

SIN I'm rubbing off on you, and we get a chance to do some research on Doc." He pulled a sheet of paper out of his pocket.

"You found something?"

"Sort of." He wiggled it in front of my face. "But we can't discuss it here. Are you coming with me or not?"

I sighed. "I . . ."

I wasn't sure what to do. Skipping school might go on my record. And what would my mother say?

"C'mon, Miranda. Take a chance. Live a little before you die, in a manner of speaking." He winked at me.

I groaned.

"You know you want to." He poked me in the ribs, which was a ticklish spot for me.

I jumped. "Stop."

"You want to go, and you can't say no to me." He poked me again.

"Kai . . ." I warned as I jumped away again.

"Stop playing hard to get."

I froze. I wasn't sure how he meant that. "I'm not."

He crossed his eyes and tucked his upper lip under where I could see his teeth and gums. He looked ridiculous. "No one says no to this gorgeous face."

That did me in, and I started to laugh. "All right, you got me."

He relaxed his face and flipped off the light. "We'll wait until the bell rings and the hall clears, then we'll take the back way out."

I waited quietly behind him, trying not to hyperventilate at the very idea of skipping school.

In less than two minutes, the bell rang and everyone hurried to their classes. Kai cracked open the door and stuck his head out, looking around to ensure the coast was clear. He waved at me to follow him, and then we shut the door behind us. Just as we reached the small entryway that led to the exit, we heard voices. He grabbed my hand and pulled me the rest of the way out of the building. We ran all the way across the campus and to a spot near the street, where he'd parked his motorcycle.

"What do you do when it gets too cold to ride this thing?" I asked, knowing that winter weather was just weeks away.

He shrugged. "Haven't worked that out yet. I guess I'll buy a car or something."

"With what?" I asked as I climbed on the seat behind him.

"Oh yeah. I need a job." He chuckled.

"Is your entire life plan to have no plan?" It seemed to be the way he operated lately.

"No, I have plans. But the most important parts are still in development." He fired up the engine.

That had me curious. I yelled over the engine. "What are the important parts?"

"Someday you'll see." He didn't say another word.

I held on tight as he sped away from the school and toward the clubhouse.

When we got there, he wasted no time getting me inside. He quickly pulled me into the hall and down past several doors. We reached one on the left, and he opened it, dragging me in behind him. The room was mostly empty, with the exception of a bed, a chair, and a bookshelf. It appeared Kai still had all his belongings in his bag on the floor.

Once the door was shut, I whirled on him. "Why are you shoving me around?"

"Sorry, just trying to get through this without you being seen." He ran a hand through his hair.

"What's the big deal? They think we're dating, right?" Sometimes I didn't understand him.

"Yeah, but . . ." He frowned. "It's just easier if we don't have to explain anything at all."

"And what if they catch me here?" It seemed like we'd better have a cover story.

"We tell them you're skipping school, and we're in here making out."

I pushed a big puff of breath past my lips. "My reputation is not going to survive this, is it?"

"I'll do my best to make it right. I promise."

I needed to focus. "Let's just get this done. What did you find?"

He pulled the paper from his pocket and sat on the bed. "Here's a membership list from when Baxter was here. There was a member who went by Doc."

Well, that was something. "Any other info on him?"

"From what I could find, it looks like he and Baxter were banished from the club at the same time."

"Banished?" That had an ominous sound.

"Yes, when you screw up big around here, you don't just get kicked out. Banishment is the merciful punishment. Dead is the other option." He looked back down at the sheet of paper in his hand. "Baxter and Doc were doing something they shouldn't have. It's the only way they would have been banished."

I tried to imagine what would have been even beyond SIN's code of ethics.

"Miranda, there's a chance your dad didn't run out on you. He may have been forced to leave. Banishment makes life tough here in Havenwood Falls. The smart thing is to move on and start a life somewhere else, if you aren't already forced into it."

I gave that some thought. "Really? Then maybe it wasn't because he didn't want us?"

Kai shrugged. "It's possible. I'm not saying that's the absolute truth. He could still be a total scumbag, but it's possible."

"I need to find him, Kai. I have to know what really happened. I have to let him know that mom is sick." The need to find him felt more urgent than ever.

He nodded. "We will."

"How? How do we find someone who was banished?" It felt kind of hopeless.

"We ask for help." He stared at the paper in his hand.

"Who? The club?" That still sounded like a horrible idea. What if they decided Kai was a traitor for helping me and they banished him?

"We don't know until we ask, right?" His face appeared sure, but his voice was less confident. "I'll talk it over with Monte. He'll tell me straight up if it's a bad idea."

I felt a little better knowing he'd check first, although asking a lesser member of the club seemed just as scary. "When this is all out in the open, will they be mad that we lied about dating?"

Kai drew his brows together. "I think we need to keep that one going. There's no reason they need to know about that. As far as they know, I'm helping my girlfriend find info on her dad and Doc to save her mom. I think that would make sense to them."

I nodded. "Yeah, I guess you're right. It'd be hard to understand why you'd go through all of this for some random girl." It hit me then. Why was he going through all of this for me? I knew he covered for me at first, but he had gone above and beyond at this point.

He studied the paper while I studied him, allowing myself to piece together all I'd learned about Kai in the last few days. It was obvious he wasn't who I once thought he was. There was a depth to him that I didn't see until I really got to know him. And I'd bet even then he had willingly opened up and let me see those vulnerabilities.

"What are you looking at?" He looked at the front of his shirt, ensuring there was nothing on it.

"You," I said softly. "I owe you an apology."

"No, you really don't." He adjusted the way he was sitting so he could face me better.

"I do. When we were at the gazebo Saturday, I said some unkind things about you. You said I didn't know what I was talking about." I sighed. "You were right. I didn't understand at all. I'm sorry."

He shrugged. "Honestly, it's okay. It's my fault people see me as a spoiled snobby elitist. That whole act is how I've been trained to behave." He chuckled. "It's not really who I am, or who I want to be. I'm not exactly an extrovert by nature."

I smiled. "You sure have everyone fooled. Maybe you should go into acting?"

He shook his head. "That'd probably be my worst nightmare. The jerk act has kept a lot of people at arm's length, which I like, for the most part. Sadly, it's kept the people I wanted to get to know better away from me as well." His eyes met mine, and there was something there that made my heart leap in my chest.

I felt that increasingly familiar heat rise in my cheeks. "I—"

A loud commotion down the hall halted anything else I might have said. Kai jumped up and ran to his door, cracking it open enough that he could see what was happening. He turned to face me. "It's just the guys. Looks like they're celebrating something, but they're coming this way."

He quickly shut the door and ran to the bed. He shoved the paper behind me and then pushed me on top of it. The next thing I knew, he was half on top of me, his face not even an inch from mine.

"They're coming," he whispered. "They can't find the paper until I talk to Monte."

"Then I guess we need to give them a show," I murmured. I pulled his head down to mine, and our lips connected. A jolt of exhilaration ran through me as he relaxed against me. I tried to keep my senses about me and listen for whomever was coming down the hall, but I was slowly disappearing into one of the most amazing kisses I'd ever experienced. His lips moved over mine as his hands began to roam down my torso. I moaned into his mouth and ran my fingers through his hair. Kai deepened the kiss.

The door flew open and banged against the wall, but I was so lost in the feelings Kai was stirring that I didn't let it concern me. A voice said, "Oops! Sorry, dude!" Then a loud laugh was followed by the door closing and the distant yell of "Kai's gettin' him some!"

I pulled away just a little, and Kai did the same. He stared down at me, his breathing fast and erratic.

I took a deep breath. "Do you think we convinced them?"

He continued to look down at me. "You sure convinced me."

There was no smirk or attitude in his statement. He actually looked confused.

"Oh, well. I guess I'm getting better at this." I didn't think it was

AMY HALE

smart to admit that I was kissing him because I wanted to. Not if he didn't feel the same.

He sat up and finger-combed his hair. He cleared his throat a couple of times, then stood.

"Kai, are you okay?"

"Yeah, I'm fine. I just need . . . a minute." His voice was raspy, and I worried I'd upset him.

"Did I do something wrong?" He wouldn't even look at me.

"No," he said quickly. "You were perfect. Absolutely perfect." He groaned. "And if you keep being so perfect, you are gonna be the death of me."

ai and I grabbed lunch at Napoli's, looking over the list for any other possible clues. Nothing of note stood out. He gave me the impression he didn't want to talk about kissing, so I didn't bring it up again. I was nervous about running into my classmates since it was so close to our regular lunch time, but what few students were there only waved and went about their business. He drove me back to the school to get my belongings, then dropped me off at home a little after two p.m. When I walked through the door, Mom was waiting for me.

"Where have you been?" She was angry and looked exhausted.

"What do you mean?" I was going to claim innocence for as long as I could.

"I got a call from Principal Friske. He was worried because you disappeared after second period and never came back." She tapped her foot on the carpet. That was a bad sign.

"I left with Kai." Why not try the truth again? Sort of. I wasn't going to tell her we went to the SIN clubhouse. I wasn't that delusional.

"Why is Kai encouraging you to skip school? This isn't like you at all, Miranda. What is going on with you?" She was obviously disappointed in me.

"I just needed a break. I've been anxious and having a hard time focusing. I'm worried about you . . . I just needed to get away, Mom." I moved to her and wrapped her in a hug. "I'm sorry. I tried to call, but you know how terrible the cell service is here." I felt bad about that lie, but I knew she wouldn't be okay with the real reason I skipped school.

She hugged me back. "Well, anything is better than just running off. Mercy, girl, I was about to go nuts with worry. Next time leave a note, at least."

"I promise I won't do that again." I kissed her cheek. "If I have another problem like that, I'll be sure to keep you in the loop."

"Good. Thank you." She sighed. "We need to discuss your punishment. But for now, let's get something to eat. I'm starving."

A moment later, my world changed. Mom took two steps into the kitchen and collapsed.

"Mom!" I shouted. "Are you okay?"

She didn't respond.

"Oh no!" I grabbed my phone, remembering the emergency number Mom had entered the day before.

"Hello! Dr. Underwood! It's Miranda Saunders. My mom just collapsed. I don't know what to do." I did my best not to cry, but the tears were pushing through every syllable.

"Try to stay calm. Are you at home?" His voice was soothing and was one of the reasons he was such a great doctor. He was also fae and one of the few medical experts in town we could trust with mom's situation.

"Yes," I answered.

"I'll be right there. Meanwhile, make sure she's breathing."

Breathing—another one of those oddities we shared that other vampires didn't have to deal with.

I hung up the phone and crouched next to mom. She was breathing, but it was labored. Silent tears rolled down my face. I couldn't lose her. She was the only family I had. If Mom died . . . I couldn't even finish the thought.

I took her limp hand in mine. "Mom, I don't know if you can

hear me, but Dr. Underwood is coming. He's gonna help us. I just need you to hang in there for me, okay? Please don't leave me."

I squeezed her hand, hoping, praying for her to squeeze it back. I needed a sign that she was still with me. I got nothing.

I sat by her side, talking to her, begging her to wake up. As the minutes passed, her breaths became harder to detect.

I heard the front door open, and I turned to see Dr. Underwood rushing toward us, his medical bag in hand. He was wearing jeans and a dark blue button-down shirt that almost matched his eyes. He must have had the day off. I stepped aside as he checked her vital signs.

"She's dehydrated." He opened her eyelids and checked her pupils.

"She was throwing up a lot yesterday," I informed him.

"She didn't tell you to call me?" He seemed surprised and ran a hand through his salt-and-pepper hair.

"No, she said she just needed to sleep a little. She'd been running a fever, too. It broke late last night." I clasped my hands together, needing to keep them occupied so I wouldn't give in to the urge to grab her and hold on.

"I need to get her to the med center." His words were calm but they created a panic in my chest.

"Is she going to be okay?"

"We'll take good care of her." He dialed a number and went outside.

I kneeled next to Mom and hugged her. "You have to get better. I'm going to find out what's going on, Mom. I promise. I don't care what it takes."

Within minutes, two men with a stretcher arrived, and they loaded Mom into an ambulance. I stood at the door watching as they secured her inside and began running vitals.

"Miranda, I'll call you as soon as we have things set up. I have someone preparing a private room for her right now. I know this is unusual, but this isn't a usual situation. Do you have someone who can be with you or somewhere you can go?"

Zoey's family would take me in without question. But oddly enough, Zoey wasn't who I wanted to see. I wanted to call Kai. "Yes, I'll be fine. I'll have my cell on me when you're ready."

He nodded, got in his car, and followed the ambulance down the street.

~

I PULLED up in front of the SIN clubhouse and parked Mom's car. Kai's motorcycle was two spots down, so I knew he was there. I wasn't sure if I should knock or just walk in. I opted for walking in. I pushed open the door and entered the clubhouse. Crusher was just about to enter the hallway.

"Crusher, hi. Have you seen Kai?" I tried to seem confident, as if I belonged there.

He jerked his thumb in the direction of a door toward the back of the room. "He's in the conference room." Then he disappeared down the hall.

I hurried to the door, once again not sure how to proceed. I was about to knock when I realized the door was partially open. I could hear Kai and a voice I didn't recognize talking inside.

"This is the last address I had for Doc. We've been trying to keep tabs on him for years, to make sure he doesn't cause trouble for us again. But I can't guarantee it's current. He's a crafty creature, and he's slipped our grasp a few times." The voice was deep and clear.

"Thanks, I'll check it out." I smiled when I heard Kai's voice.

"I need to warn you, Kai. Doc is dangerous. You'll need to be on your guard. He did some unspeakable things back in the day." I frowned at that bit of news from the unknown voice.

"All the info about him is in here?" Kai's voice was determined.

"All that we know."

Kai coughed. "Holy crap."

"Yeah, it's bad." A brief pause, then I heard, "Are you going to tell the little lady?"

"I guess I have to." Kai chuckled. "Since she's eavesdropping outside the door."

"But otherwise you would have kept it from me?" I pushed open the door. "And I wasn't eavesdropping, I was just trying not to interrupt."

The man standing next to Kai was huge. One glance at his jeans, leathers, and tattoos, and I recognized him as one of the bikers that passed me on my way to school the day I found the photo of my mother and Baxter. He tilted his head at me slightly, and his sandy hair fell over his dark sunglasses just a bit.

Monte had been quietly standing near the back of the room. At this point, he grabbed his stomach and laughed. "Oh, you are so whipped, bruh!"

Kai looked at the larger man. "Liam, this is Miranda."

Liam nodded his head in my direction, and I smiled in return.

Kai held his hands up, one of which contained an envelope. "Miranda, I wasn't going to keep this from you."

I glared at him. "So if I hadn't been standing here, you'd have told me everything?"

He sighed. "Yes . . . eventually."

"Sounds a little sketchy to me," Monte interjected.

Kai turned to scowl at him. "Not. Helping."

Liam smiled at me. "Keep him in line, sweetheart. Don't let him do anything stupid."

Kai rolled his eyes and stuffed the envelope in his back pocket.

Monte and Liam walked past me and out the door.

"Good luck, you two." Liam turned and faced me. "Be extra careful, Miranda. If you meet Doc, don't tell him you're Sade's daughter. Not that he won't figure it out on his own, if his memory is intact. You might be careful what you tell Baxter, as well. At least until you're sure he's on your side."

I nodded. "I will. Thank you."

He looked at Kai. "We have your back."

Kai slapped his palm against Liam's. "Thanks man. We appreciate it."

My cell phone rang. "Sorry, I need to take this." I turned away from them and answered it. "Hello?"

When I looked up, Liam had disappeared out the front door.

Dr. Underwood was on the other end. "We have her in a room and stable. When you're ready, go to the front desk and ask for me. I'll come get you."

"Okay, thank you. Be there soon."

I hung up, and for a moment had forgotten my frustration with Kai.

He stepped closer. "What's wrong?"

I looked up, fighting the urge to cry yet again. "Mom collapsed. She's in the hospital."

He pulled me into his arms, and I buried my face in his chest.

"I'm so sorry." He kissed the top of my head. "Is she at the medical center?"

I nodded, then pulled back to look at him. "Dr. Underwood put her in a special room. That was him on the phone. He said we could come see her now."

"We?" Kai asked.

"Well, if you want to go with me. You don't have to."

He didn't respond.

"I don't really want to do this alone, but I can call Zoey if you—"

He cut me off. "No, I want to go. I'm just surprised you want me there."

"I do." I needed him there, no matter how annoyed I was with him at times. He'd become important to me. I could deny it to myself all I wanted, but it didn't make it any less true.

"Let's go see her then." He put his hand on my lower back and guided me out of the club.

I held up the key fob to my mom's red Hyundai and pushed the unlock button. It beeped, and the lights flashed. "I'm driving this time."

"After you." He followed me to the car.

We drove the short trip to the hospital in silence. I wanted to see her so badly, but I was also terrified of what I might find. Once we reached the front desk, I did as Dr. Underwood instructed, and he joined us within minutes.

"Miranda, I want to prepare you for what you're going to see." He put a hand on my shoulder as we stopped outside an unmarked room. "It looks pretty scary, and honestly we don't yet know what's going on, but I have hope we can figure it out."

I nodded, and he opened the door to the room. I grasped Kai's hand as we walked in side by side.

Mom lay there, still as a stone, tubes and wires seeming to come from everywhere. A machine next to her monitored her heartbeat and oxygen levels, which again was a weird thing to witness with a vampire. I walked to the side of the bed and touched her arm. "Is she breathing on her own?"

"Thankfully, yes," Dr. Underwood said. "That being said, you need to know that she hasn't woken up yet."

My eyes flew to his face. "Is she in a coma?"

"We aren't ready to call it that just yet. We're still running some tests." He scratched his head. "It's odd. She's having some strangely . . . mammal-like medical issues."

"Mammal-like?" What did that even mean? It made no sense at all.

"Yes, like her blood pressure dropping rapidly, then spiking. Heart palpations. Hypoglycemia. Very erratic stuff. It doesn't make sense."

I frowned and looked at Kai. "Do vampires have blood pressure?"

He shrugged. "I don't. Our circulatory systems work differently than humans'."

"We are doing all we can to ensure she's getting the best care. You are welcome to stay if you like. There's a recliner in the corner if you'd like to rest. The kitchen just closed, but I guess that doesn't matter much to either of you. I'll let the front desk know you are allowed to come and go as you need to. As before, I'll contact you if

I learn anything new." Dr. Underwood looked at my mom's chart one last time and left the room.

Kai and I sat quietly by her bedside for the next hour, the beep of the monitors the only sound breaking the silence. I held Mom's hand as Kai clasped my other hand in his. It was comforting to have him there with me. He turned out to be the strength that was holding me upright when it felt like my whole world had collapsed. I laid my head on the bed and closed my eyes, trying to clear my mind of any worries. I just wanted to think happy, healing thoughts and send them to her. I hoped that somehow they'd leave my mind and enter her body.

My eyes closed, and suddenly I found myself surrounded by a fog. I was running through a forest. I was being chased, but I couldn't see what was chasing me. I looked behind me, but all I could see were glowing red eyes. Terror struck me as I continued to flee, looking for anything I could use as a weapon, should I need to fight. Then the screaming began. That faint sound of misery and fear welling up from somewhere ahead. I battled the urge to turn around, now caught between whatever was screaming and whatever was chasing me. The voice ahead was getting louder, and it caused my head to ache. I felt something behind me, and there was an odd odor in the air. I turned in time to see the eyes right behind me.

I woke with a start. I must have been exhausted, as sunlight was beginning to peek around the window shades. I'd slept all night. I heard the faint sound of Kai's voice, but didn't see him in the room. The door was ajar, and when I walked over, I saw him pacing the hallway just outside as he talked on his cell phone.

I stepped out and leaned against the door jamb. I gave him a little wave.

He waved back, but walked farther away, still talking in hushed tones. Something was up.

I went back into the room and checked on Mom. Her condition appeared to be the same. I leaned over and kissed her cheek, then brushed some stray hairs from her forehead. That's when I noticed something odd. Mom's usually shiny blond hair, very much like my own, was starting to turn gray. I ran the strands through my fingers.

"What is happening?" I whispered.

I pulled the chair closer to the head of the bed and sat back down. I studied her face. Her perfect skin was now showing the beginning of crow's feet. Her normally full lips were thinner and chapped. I picked up her hand and inspected it closely. The skin seemed more translucent, and her wrist felt fragile.

I stood up and rushed to the door just in time to run into Kai. He looked angry.

"Kai, I think I know what's happening. At least part of it," I blurted out.

He frowned. "What do you mean?"

"With mom. I think she's aging. Quickly."

Kai pushed me back into the hospital room and shut the door. "It's a little more complicated than that."

"More complicated than an immortal aging rapidly?" I frowned at him. "And how do you know it's more complicated?"

"I just got off the phone with Liam. I read something in that information he gave me that I wasn't sure I understood, so I called him to verify." He sat down in the recliner and put his head in his hands. "This is bad."

I pulled the other chair close to him and sat down. "What are you talking about?" The terror I was feeling was steadily coming through in my voice.

Kai clasped my hands in his. "Okay, so you are partially right. Your mom is likely aging rapidly." He shook his head. "We have to find this Doc guy and find a way to make him fix this."

"Does he know what's happening?" At this point, I was willing to take answers from anyone.

Kai's anger was barely controlled. "According to Liam, he's the reason it's happening."

CHAPTER 11

*D*r. Underwood walked into Mom's room just as I finished scanning the information Kai had on Doc and Baxter.

I looked at Kai. "Can this be reversed?"

"I don't know, but Dr. Underwood might."

The doctor looked up at the mention of his name. "What was that?"

"We think we know part of the problem." I said. "According to records we got from . . . a reliable source, my father was mixed up with an Unseelie fae who went by the nickname of Doc."

Dr. Underwood frowned. "Yeah, I know of him. He considered himself some sort of a scientist back when I knew him. The guy wasn't all there."

"He and my father were dealing. My dad didn't know that Doc had been messing with the chemical composition of the drugs. Doc thought addicts were useless sores on society, so he decided he would attempt to transform the poor souls into other creatures. Creatures that would look to him as their god."

Dr. Underwood shook his head. "Sounds like him. He had some crazy ideas."

"My mom and dad were addicts back then, Dr. Underwood." It

was hard to admit that out loud. I knew my mother would hate her past being brought back out into the open.

He glanced at the frail shell of a woman slipping away from us. My proud, beautiful mother. "I'd heard the rumors, but I didn't know if they were true."

"She beat her addiction when she found out she was expecting me."

I watched him putting the pieces together in his mind. "I see. This may explain a lot."

"It seems that way," I said.

Kai spoke then. "If we find Doc and haul him back here, can you make him fix this?"

"I don't know. I can try. But he's not going to be easy to persuade. And he's probably dangerous." Dr. Underwood checked mom's pupils. "Be very careful. Get help to do this, and make sure you're prepared, but do what you need to do as soon as you can."

Kai nodded, grabbed his phone, and went out into the hall again.

I moved to Mom's side and leaned over her. "Mom, I'll be back soon. We're gonna go get help." I kissed her forehead and left the room to find Kai.

He was standing near the door, the phone to his ear. "Yes, got it. Thank you. I owe you one." He hung up and shoved the cell in his pocket. "Let's go."

"Where?" I asked, as Kai led me to Mom's car. I'd just pulled my keys from my pocket when he swiped them from my hand.

"I'm driving."

I didn't argue as we buckled in. I was too upset to drive. "Where are we going?"

"We're meeting your dad." He put the car in reverse and quickly backed out of the parking spot.

"What?" I squeaked. "You found him?"

"Sort of." Kai pulled onto the street, squealing the tires. "Agatha Temple did a location spell for me."

I was confused. "The chubby, dark-haired woman who drives the shuttle?"

He nodded.

"I didn't even know she was a witch." There was so much I didn't yet know about our little town.

"She's pretty chill about it."

"When did she do this? What did she find?"

"While you were sleeping, I asked her to see if she could do it. I sent her a picture of your picture, since we had nothing else to go on. I didn't even think it'd work since you usually need a personal item of the person you're looking for, but we didn't have anything to lose by trying. And Agatha's good." He pulled the photo out of his pocket and handed it to me. "I took it while you were asleep. Anyway, Baxter is living in a cabin about fifty miles from here."

He pointed the car west and steered us down County Road 13.

"He's only been fifty miles away? All this time?" I couldn't believe what I was hearing. "Why didn't he check on us? Call? Write a freakin' letter? He had twenty-eight days before the memory spell kicked in. He could have at least let mom know what was going on before he forgot about us completely."

Kai focused on the road. "He couldn't come back, so maybe he felt like it was pointless."

"Pointless?" I could feel my anger rising. I couldn't direct it all at Baxter. He was only part of the reason we were in this mess. Mom was partially responsible, and Doc carried the biggest load of the blame. It was Doc I wanted to scream at and throttle.

The more I thought about it, the angrier I got. I started to literally see red. I closed my eyes and placed the palms of my hands over my eyelids. My head began to hurt.

"Are you okay?" Kai's voice sounded distant and slightly muffled over the almost deafening sound of screaming I heard in my ears. I didn't understand what was happening or what I was feeling, and I worried that some of the things in my dreams were pushing through to reality, but intuition told me I needed to calm down.

I blew out a shaky breath and looked at him. "Yeah, I'm just . . .

I've never been so angry in all of my life." I balled my hands into fists.

"Really?" His lips pulled to one side. "Huh. I would have thought I'd made you furious at least a time or two."

I smiled. "You've come really close."

The closer we got to the cabin, the antsier I became. I couldn't keep from tapping my foot on the floorboard or drumming my fingers on the armrest. I could tell Kai wanted to say something, but he didn't, and I appreciated his understanding. I was sure my one-man-band act had to be annoying.

We pulled up to a small gravel road, and Kai turned and followed it all the way to a dead end. Sitting before us was a modest cabin. It looked no bigger than what most would consider a hunting shack. It was surrounded by trees, and hidden well. Kai turned off the engine, and we sat quietly for a moment, just staring at the dark wooden door. It was a typical log-cabin-style build and looked like it probably started as one of those do-it-yourself kits.

"Whenever you're ready." He didn't want to rush me, even though we really needed to hurry.

"No time like the present," I muttered.

We opened the car doors and stepped out, when the cabin door opened and a middle-aged man with a shotgun stepped forward. He pointed the barrel directly at us.

"You've got the wrong house, kids. Turn around and go back the way you came." His voice was raspy and low.

It was Baxter. He looked older, and I assumed he was aging, similar to my mother, but his features were distinct. His blond hair was shaggy, and he was thinner than the man in the photo. He wore a faded pair of jeans, black button-up shirt with the sleeves rolled up to the elbow, boots, and the tattered cowboy hat he wore in the picture.

"Are you Baxter Morrison?" I asked.

He lowered the gun slightly. "I don't know anyone by that name."

He wanted to play dumb? Fine. "Do you know a Sade Saunders?"

"Nope," he answered.

"Can we just speak with you for a few minutes?" Kai asked.

"No need. We have nothing to say to each other." He raised the gun again and continued to point it in our direction.

"I'd say we do," said Kai. "And that gun isn't gonna do jack to us, because we're vampires."

Baxter narrowed his eyes at Kai.

"But better than that," continued Kai, "this beautiful young woman is your daughter. You wouldn't want to shoot up your own baby girl, now would you?"

Baxter scoffed. "Vampires don't procreate."

"Our kind doesn't. Not normally. But you're not normal, are you, Baxter?" Kai took a step forward. "You're aging, and you're sick. Just like Miranda's mother."

"Miranda?" Baxter lowered the gun and slowly walked down the steps. He looked me over slowly. "Your name is Miranda?"

I nodded.

"That was my mother's name, a long, long time ago." The hard lines of his face softened just a bit.

"I guess that's why Mom chose the name." I wasn't sure why she'd chosen it. I'd never thought to ask, but I'd run with that if it would get him to listen to us.

He frowned. "I don't understand any of this." He looked around. "Hurry. Get inside."

He shooed us up the steps and inside the cabin. When he locked the door behind him, I noticed odd symbols painted on the door and other spots inside the cabin walls.

"What are all these?" I took a closer look at one.

Baxter placed his gun to the side of the door. "Those are wards to keep undesirables out."

"Undesirables?" Kai asked.

"Fae," he answered. Then he pointed to iron hanging on the walls. "Iron helps, too."

Kai and I looked at each other.

Kai spoke first. "You wouldn't be avoiding a specific fae, would you? One called Doc?"

Baxter stiffened. "What do you know about Doc?"

I decided to take over. "We know that he likes to play god. We know that he was experimenting with a combination of drugs, DNA, and magic. We know that you and my mother were addicts and ended up with Doc's drugs in your system. So he cursed the drugs you were stealing. In the meantime, it altered your DNA just enough that you got my vampire mother pregnant. Then you and Doc got caught by the leader of your motorcycle club and were banished from Havenwood Falls."

He pulled his eyebrows together in a disbelieving expression. "Havenwood Falls? Never heard of it."

"That's because once you left town, the memory spell slowly wiped all that from your mind," Kai answered.

Baxter rubbed his chin. "I don't know if I believe any of this."

"Can you account for how you got here? In this cabin? Hiding from Doc?" I asked.

He looked around. "Actually, no. All I recall is that Doc was after me. He kept saying I took something from him and I ruined everything, but I didn't know what he was talking about. After a few weeks, I'm not sure he knew what he was talking about either. He kept vowing revenge, though. I've been battling the little jerk ever since." He sighed. "But I'm getting too weak to keep it up."

I passed the photo I carried to him. "That's you, standing next to my mother."

He studied the photo. "She does kind of look familiar." He raised his eyes to mine. "You look a lot like her."

I nodded and smiled.

"We need to find Doc," Kai said. "He knows how to heal Miranda's mother . . . and you."

Baxter looked at Kai. "You think so?"

He passed the picture back to me.

"We know so," I said.

"He's crazy. And dangerous. Do you know what you're getting into here?" he asked.

We both nodded.

"Okay then, what's your plan?" Baxter was warming up to us.

Kai ticked the points off on his fingers as he spoke. "We need to lure Doc back into Havenwood Falls. Once he's there, we have people that can handle him. They'll figure out the cure, you and Sade can get better, and you won't have to worry about Doc ever again."

Baxter thought on it for a moment. "What have I got to lose? If I stay here, I'll eventually die anyway. Might as well take a chance or go out in a blaze of glory."

Kai smiled. "I like your style."

I smacked Kai's arm with the back of my hand.

"Thank you," I said to Baxter. "I can't tell you how much this means to me."

He gave me a small smile. "No problem." He tipped his old hat in my direction. "Just glad I'm useful for a change."

WE MAPPED out the plan for drawing Doc out, which included making a few calls back home. We ensured the right people were prepared for plan A, plan B, and plan C. We'd get Doc there one way or another. Plan A was that Kai would drive my mom's car back to Havenwood Falls, and I'd ride with Baxter in his truck as he followed Kai. I knew that once Baxter got into town, his memories would likely start to return. He might change his mind, so I wanted to be with him when we crossed the town's border. If he flaked out on us, I was determined to bring him back to reason. Kai wasn't happy about leaving me alone with Baxter, but I wasn't budging on the issue.

"It could be dangerous, Miranda. Doc could attack before we get home." Kai gripped my shoulders.

"It's possible. And if he does, that's what plan B is for. I'll be there to protect Baxter, and our friends will help us get him home safely," I countered.

"What if you get hurt?" Kai's frustration was loud and clear.

"I won't. You'll be right in front of me. It'll be fine." I smiled up at him, and he rolled his eyes.

I crossed mine. "C'mon. No one can say no to this face." I mimicked the way he'd said those very words to me the day before.

He smirked, but didn't say anything.

"Really. I've got this. What can I do to convince you to trust me?"

He stared at me for a moment, then stepped closer. "Kiss me."

My goofy grin faded. "What?"

"Kiss me. I can't let you out of my sight until I've had one sincere, heartfelt kiss from you. One I know, without a doubt, you really mean." He didn't smile, and there was no teasing tone in his voice.

"Is this one of your practical jokes? Because it's not funny."

He shook his head.

"You really want to kiss me?" I thought I might be dreaming.

He framed my face with his hands, one thumb softly stroking my cheek. "I do. I've wanted to ask you out for years. And if there is any chance that this is the last time I might have to tell you how much I care about you, I'm not wasting it."

He pressed his lips to mine, and this time I didn't allow my mind to think up horrible scenarios or wonder what his motives might be. I just kissed him back and enjoyed knowing that it was something we both wanted.

He pulled back and looked into my eyes. "When this is over, we need to talk."

I nodded. "Sure."

He lowered his hands and took one of mine in his. "Be careful." He raised my hand to his lips and kissed it. He dropped it as he backed away and got into the car.

Behind me, Baxter started up his truck. "Ready?"

I turned. "Ready as I'll ever be," I said. "Let's set the hook."

CHAPTER 12

*W*e followed Kai with only a few car lengths between us. It was close enough that he wouldn't lose us, but far enough that if Doc were to strike, Kai wouldn't get caught in the crossfire. Baxter looked relaxed as he drove, but every now and then, I caught him checking his mirrors and monitoring the landscape around us. I didn't know if he sensed something, but I did. It was that feeling I'd been fighting since this all began. The ominous apprehension was stronger than ever.

We were only about two miles outside of town when the truck was hit with a blast of something invisible. The force felt like what I'd imagine a cannonball would feel like if it'd hit us broadside. For a brief moment, I saw Baxter's arm shoot out toward me in an effort to protect me, much like my mother did when I was little. Then the world around us spun out of control, with trees and mountainsides blurring together before my vision. The sickening sound of metal meeting something solid filled my ears as we landed hard in a ditch.

Baxter reached over and touched my arm. "Are you okay?"

"Yeah. What was that?" I sat up, attempting to pull the too-tight seatbelt away from my chest.

"I'm not sure." Baxter tried to open his door, but it wouldn't budge. "My door's jammed." He unbuckled his seatbelt and rolled

98

down the window. After quickly poking his head out to look at the door, he turned to me. "There's a huge dent in my door."

I looked ahead on the highway to see Kai turning around. I tried not to panic, but whatever hit us might hit Kai next. He needed to keep going.

Another blast hit the truck from the front and shook it violently. I screamed as the windshield cracked and caved in, while the side windows shattered and littered the inside of the cab with small pebble-like glass. I could feel fragments of it clinging to my hair.

It was then that I heard a menacing male voice. "I knew you couldn't hide from me forever, Baxter."

I looked up to see a youngish-looking man with dark hair and dark eyes walking toward us in the middle of the highway. He was decked out in all black clothing, right down to his boots.

I looked past him and couldn't see Kai anymore. I tried not to panic. *What had he done with Kai?* I tugged on my seatbelt, but it wouldn't budge.

Baxter reached across and handed me a knife. "Here, cut the strap."

I did as he instructed and moved closer to him.

"We may be in a pickle here. He's a lot stronger than me. I don't know what you can do, Miranda. Let's hope we can hold out until Kai can get help." Baxter rubbed his temples.

"Are you okay? Did you hit your head?" I worried he might have a concussion.

"No, it's just . . . I'm getting these weird flashbacks."

"The memories. They're starting to return." I gasped. "That means Doc's probably are too. We have to get out of here."

I tried to open my door, but it was stuck as well. I turned my back to Baxter. "I'm gonna brace myself against you. Push against me."

He leaned himself into my back, and I kicked the door as hard as I could. It gave way just a little, but not enough to open.

"Let's try again," I said through labored breaths.

Baxter leaned in again, and I adjusted myself to where I could kick with both feet. This time the door shot off its hinges. I grabbed Baxter's hand. "Let's go!"

"Where are we going?" he said, as he grabbed the small bag from the floorboard and scooted toward the passenger door.

"Plan B. We're going to play a little game of hide-and-seek with Doc." I pulled out my phone and hit the pre-programmed text message I had set to go. All it said was "Plan B." It went out to several friends. They all knew what to do.

We ran just a few feet into the trees when we heard Doc yell for us. "Do you really think you can hide from me among a few trees?"

He laughed, and it echoed around us.

If we could just make it a little farther, I knew a great hiding spot to kill the time we needed. We heard branches break behind us, and a sound that roared like a mighty wind rushed to meet our backsides. We hit the ground and covered our heads as we felt another blast of invisible energy move over us. It came a little too close for comfort.

I could see the tree we needed. It was just across a small clearing. We'd have to make a run for it.

"Baxter, we'll have to run for that tree. The one with the huge trunk. Do you see it?"

Baxter was staring at me. "You look just like her. I can't believe it."

I nodded. "We can talk later. Right now we have to focus on not dying."

He looked at the tree and then back to where we thought Doc was. "I'm ready."

"Go," I urged.

We sprinted across the open space, branches and leaves crunching beneath our feet. We'd just made it when we heard Doc again. "I can sense you. No matter where you hide, I'll find you. Why don't you make this easier on all of us and just give up?"

We crouched behind the large tree and opened the small bag we'd brought along. I grabbed an iron rod and chain. Baxter grabbed an iron dagger.

"Stay here. My friend Conrad will be along soon to get you. He'll take you to Mom." I paused. "Don't freak out if he's naked. He's a dragon and probably didn't bring any clothes with him for shifting to human and back."

He nodded, but looked a little concerned by that. He reached for me. "But what about you?"

"I'll be fine. I'll distract Doc until you're safe. Then we'll get him into town so he can be dealt with." I tried to sound more confident than I felt. Sure I was a vampire, although not exactly like the others. But I'd never had to fully put my skills to the test.

Baxter frowned. "Be careful, Miranda. I don't want to lose you now that I've found you."

"You won't. Now stay down and quiet."

I knew Conrad was close. I could smell the pungent odor of sulfur that followed him when he was in his lava dragon form. He was currently using his camouflage, or we could have easily picked him out among the trees surrounding us.

Sulfur. I now recognized the smell from my dream. Was the thing chasing me a lava dragon? I didn't have time to analyze that, so I filed it away to examine later.

I glanced down at the new message on my cell phone. The SIN club found the truck and were almost in position. Jetta was looking for Kai. It was time.

I stepped out from behind the tree. "Doc, how about we talk? I don't think all this violence is really doing anyone any good."

"Oh, I don't know," he said, his voice still seeming to come from every direction. "I'm rather enjoying it."

"It's a waste of your time. Baxter is already gone. He's safe in Havenwood Falls. Of course, you could always go after him." I smiled.

"Do you think I'm stupid? I know what happens if I step foot in that town again. Liam doesn't forgive or forget. I have Baxter to thank for that. But you know all that, don't you, Sade?"

I chuckled. He thought I was my mother. Which meant he didn't know she was sick. I tried to use that to my advantage.

I tried to mimic something my mother would say. "Yes, we know all about the mess you made."

"I was creating!" he bellowed.

"You were playing with things you shouldn't have," I yelled back.

He laughed. "Want to know a secret? I still am."

He stepped out into the clearing. I could see him well now. His nose was sharp, and his features were angled. His black eyes narrowed. "There's something different about you, Sade. I wonder what it is." He stepped closer.

"Stay where you are. You are surrounded, and I suggest you cooperate if you want to live."

He shrugged. "You won't touch me."

"And why is that?" I asked.

"Because I have a hostage." He reached out and pulled Kai out of thin air.

"Miranda, don't do anything he says!" Kai choked out.

"Miranda?" Doc replied. "So you aren't Sade, yet you look very much like her." He studied me a moment, then his face lit up. "I did it, didn't I? You are one of my creations!"

"Let Kai go," I demanded.

He shook his head. "Oh no. That's not going to happen. Not when you have me boxed in like this. I need leverage."

He must have sensed everyone I'd called in, despite any spells or cloaking abilities.

"If I tell them to leave, will you let Kai go?"

Doc thought about that a moment. "I'll need one more thing."

"And what is that?" I asked.

"You," he stated.

"No!" yelled Kai.

Doc hissed at Kai. "Shut up."

"I'll make you a deal," I said. "My friends back off, and you let Kai go. Then it's just you and me. If you can catch me, I'll go with you. No arguments. But if I catch you first, you go with me and help me find a cure for Baxter's and Sade's sickness."

Doc shook his head. "Oh my. Sade's sick too? Such a shame."

"Do we have a bet?" I was working to hold my temper.

He smiled. "We do indeed."

Kai yelled. "What are you doing?"

"I'm doing what I have to, to save the people I love." I hoped he caught what I was saying. I wanted him to know that he was included in that group.

Jetta uncloaked herself, her twenty-foot-tall stature an impressive figure, even among the tallest trees in the forest. Her bluish-white scales reflected the light as she moved toward us. Her large blue eyes narrowed as she bent her head lower to the ground, getting a closer at Kai and Doc. Doc stepped back, but pushed Kai in her direction. "Take him, dragon. Get him out of here. This is now between Miranda and me."

Kai pleaded with me. "Miranda, please . . . don't. You don't understand—"

Doc snapped his fingers and cut off Kai's voice. "Quiet, boy. I'm tired of hearing you talk."

"It'll be okay, Kai. I promise." I hoped my voice didn't betray the doubts that came with such a flimsy promise.

Jetta vanished with Kai. Conrad was long gone with Baxter. Most of the SIN club had left, but Liam and Savage had stayed behind. I couldn't see them, but somehow, I knew they were there. Doc didn't say anything, so I didn't know if he sensed them or not. He had a crazed look on his face and was starting to babble to himself. I was suddenly very thankful I wasn't doing this alone. This man was truly mad.

"So," he said. "Do you want me to give you a head start?"

I shrugged. "I was going to give you one."

He pointed a finger at me and laughed. "You are a sassy one."

"Oh, you have no idea," I said, my words laced with venom.

"Well . . ." He looked at his hands, and I took that moment to run, the iron weapons firmly in hand. I ran faster than I'd ever run before. Hopping over logs and dodging low-hanging limbs, I managed to avoid crashing while keeping up a decent rate of speed. My plan was to circle around and get behind him. I still sensed Liam and Savage. They were alongside of me, keeping up with me, but far enough away that they were outside the hearing of most creatures. I couldn't hear them. I felt them. However it was happening, I wasn't going to complain. It gave us the advantage.

I heard Doc's movements, but it was hard to tell just where he was coming from. He was overconfident and wasn't as cautious as he should have been. That was a flaw I was counting on. I quickly climbed a tree to get a better vantage point, and I saw him moving a couple hundred yards behind me. I stayed perfectly still and waited until he passed me.

I jumped down behind him. "Got ya! I win!" I felt sure it wouldn't be that easy, but I had to try.

He laughed, then flicked his wrist and flung me backwards into a tree. I hit my head and landed in the dirt face first.

"Ow." I pushed myself off the ground, spitting out dirt and leaves. "You dirty cheat."

He chuckled. "I'm Unseelie. What part of that do you not understand, little girl?"

"I don't care if you're the devil himself, you are going back with me," I growled.

I ran toward him, and he almost dodged me, but my fingertips managed to grab his shirt, and I jerked him off his feet. He landed on his knees.

I stood over him. "Now, let's go."

"Fine. You win." I backed up, and he stood, then dusted himself off. He bent to wipe dirt from his knee, and when he rose back up, he produced a dagger. He lunged for me and caught my left shoulder. Pain and blood saturated the area. I grabbed my iron chain and swung it in his direction. It hit his hand, and he dropped the knife. He grimaced as he clutched that hand to his chest.

He smiled, but it was one of pure evil. "I'd hate to have to kill you. As your creator, that'd make me very upset. But if that's what it takes, so be it. I can always dissect you, learn your biology, and make another."

I gritted my teeth. "I will die before I go with you," I hissed.

He pulled out a syringe. "Oh, no. I think you'll cooperate."

At that point Liam and Savage stepped out into the open. "You will not lay a hand on her, Doc."

His eyes went wide. "No. You left."

"Did they?" I taunted.

Then once again he pulled Kai out of thin air.

"Impossible! You already let him go!" I yelled.

He threw my own words back in my face. "Did I?" He shook his head. "No, I let a duplicate of him go, which disintegrated once it got to town. I bet that freaked your dragon friend out." He smiled.

"I'm warning you—"

"No, I'm warning you. I'm calling the shots here. Speaking of shots—" He jabbed the needle into Kai's neck.

"No!" I screamed as Kai hit the forest floor.

Doc laughed, and Kai held his neck as he writhed in pain.

I started to shake, and as before, red clouded my vision. In my peripheral vision I could see mist rolling in around us. The screams I'd heard last time were there, but much louder, as if they were right beside me. Then they morphed into the sound of a heartbeat and blood rushing through a maze of veins. There was a throbbing pulse calling to me, right at the base of a neck nearby.

It was Doc's neck. I saw nothing but the outline of Doc's body and his circulatory system pulsing through him. There was also the faint wisp of something dark hovering within him, but I was unaware of what that might be. All I could focus on was the blood.

I lunged, grasping his head and spinning him in the air. He landed on his back with a thud. The wind had been knocked out of him, and I sat crouched on his chest, making it even harder for him to breathe. I held the iron pipe to his throat. He looked up at me.

"You . . . you . . . your eyes . . . ," he stammered.

A deep, beastly growl escaped my lips, and even to my own ears, it sounded wrong. Then, from somewhere around me, I heard a sorrowful howl. I smelled sulfur again. I assumed it was Liam or Savage. It made sense that hellhounds would have that sulfur scent on them as well.

Kai moaned, and my anger peaked. I pushed Doc's face to the side, smashing his cheek into the dirt. It was then I noticed steam rising from my skin, like waves of heat from the pavement on a hot summer day. I refocused on the pulse that beckoned me. I bit into his neck and drank just enough to make it hurt. When I pulled back, his blood dripped from my fangs. I grabbed his face and made him look at me as I allowed his own blood to land in droplets on his cheek.

"I would love nothing better than to finish feeding on you. And then, when there is nothing left but your desiccated corpse, I would personally drag your soul to Hell." I lowered my face a fraction, so we were nose to nose. "But sadly, your sorry life is needed elsewhere. So we are taking you back to town and you will cooperate. You will fix this mess you created. Or I will hunt you to the ends of the earth and finish what I started."

He nodded, and his mouth moved but no voice came out. I growled at him one last time, and then there was another howl. He promptly passed out.

The iron must have wounded him more than I realized. I stood and wiped my mouth. The blood tasted awful, so I spit out what I could, then ran over to check on Kai. He glanced at me, then closed his eyes.

Liam and Savage moved to Doc and put his arms and legs in iron shackles.

"Are you okay?" I touched Kai's neck at the site of the puncture wound. My vision had quickly returned to normal, for which I was thankful.

"I think so." He groaned. "I have no idea what he jacked me up with, though. I think I might be hallucinating."

"I don't know either, but we'll find out." I helped him to his feet, trying to ignore the pain in my shoulder. I hated that I healed slower than most vampires, but I did take comfort knowing that it would be healed soon. "Where's the car?"

"It's on the other side of that hill. I tried to come at it the back way, but he knew I was there." Kai dusted the grass off his clothes.

"Let's get this jerk in the car." I walked toward the unconscious body of Doc.

Kai looked down at him. "Can we drag him by his feet?" he asked.

I laughed. "He deserves it, but no. We need him to be able to think later."

Liam touched my shoulder. "Are you okay?"

I nodded. "It's sore, but it'll heal."

He shot Savage a look, then the two bikers picked Doc up and carried him through the trees, up the hill, and to Mom's car.

Kai put a gag over his mouth, and they tossed him in the trunk. He sent a text message to Dr. Underwood letting him know we were on our way.

I decided to drive us back just in case Kai had any side effects from the injection. Liam and Savage followed on their motorcycles to assure we didn't have any issues with Doc.

I'd just pulled on to the highway when Kai put his hand on my back.

"Miranda?"

"Yeah?" I answered.

"Are you okay?"

"Yeah, it's healing slowly, but it is healing. It sucks not being a pure vampire like you are." I smiled at him.

"Good, but I mean . . . what happened to you back there? Did I imagine that? Was it the injection?" He sounded concerned.

"Honestly, I'm not sure what happened. But you didn't imagine anything." He couldn't have been more concerned than I was. Some very bizarre things happened to me in that forest, and I wasn't convinced they had anything to do with being a vampire.

CHAPTER 13

Savage split off and went to the club to inform the other members of the mission's progress, while Liam followed us to the hospital and parked next to our car.

"We did it!" I said as I got out of the car.

Kai just nodded.

"We sure did." Liam looked at Kai and then back at me. He studied me a moment, then turned his attention to the trunk. "Well, let's get this monster inside."

I popped the trunk, and Liam and Kai pulled Doc out. The angry fae glared at them both. When I walked around to face him, he started yelling under the gag and tried to get away from me. *I must have really scared the crap out of him.*

Liam gave me another odd look, then he and Kai dragged Doc into the hospital.

I sat outside for a few minutes, catching my breath and trying to think. In a matter of a few hours, I'd met my long lost dad, saved him, found out the guy I loved cared about me, too, got the bad guy to the hospital to help heal my sick loved ones, and I had an odd moment in the forest where something new happened when I fed. What a strange week this had turned out to be. I'd never been on a vacation, but I was pretty sure I was overdue for one after all this.

I went straight to my mother's room. When I got there, I found Baxter sitting next to her bed, in the same spot as I had the day before. He was holding her hand as tears ran down his face.

He looked up at me. "What's happening?"

"Mom's been having health problems the last several weeks. She passed out yesterday and hasn't woken up since. She's aging quickly, much like you." I sat next to him in the recliner.

"Why is she more advanced than me?" He sniffed.

"We aren't sure," I admitted.

He bowed his head. "Dammit Doc!"

"Do you know exactly what he did to those drugs?" I asked.

Baxter stood and paced. "He sold a lot of different crap. And each drug had a different experiment with it. He thought of himself as a scientist." He chuckled. "More like a mad scientist. He was messing with DNA and all other kinds of biological stuff. Tricking people into shooting it up by mixing it with the drugs."

"What was in the stuff you and Mom took?"

He looked me in the eye. "I'm not completely sure. When he found out I'd been stealing from his supply, he was really angry. Only he didn't tell me right away what he'd been doing, or that he knew. Instead he made the mixture stronger and then cursed it with his dark fae magic. He left it where he knew I'd take it. I swear, I had no idea your mom was using my stash, too."

"Dr. Underwood will figure it out. He's gonna make Doc fix it." I tried to reassure him, although I wasn't so sure myself.

"As far as I know, everyone else he'd experimented on died quick deaths a long time ago. My curse was that I'd suffer slowly. Before the memory spell kicked in and wiped all recollection of Havenwood Falls, I'd planned to just die in that cabin alone, hoping he'd never find out about you and your mother." He sighed. "But you came to me instead." He rubbed his temples. "Do everyone's memories come rushing back so quickly like this? It's killing my head."

I shrugged. "I've heard it's different for everyone. You were protecting us?"

"Yes. He didn't know your mom was using. I found out about

her pregnancy about the same time he told me what he'd done. I couldn't risk him learning that his idea of creating a new species might have actually worked, even if it wasn't directly the way he'd planned. He would have taken Sade. He'd have taken you. I couldn't allow that. So I admitted everything to Liam and requested that he banish us both. If I wasn't tempted to come back, then I knew you were safe because Doc wouldn't learn about you."

Knowing my father didn't abandon us, but sacrificed his happiness to protect us instead, was heartbreaking and humbling. "Thank you. I can't imagine how difficult that was."

His voice cracked. "Hardest thing I ever did was walk away from you and your mother."

Dr. Underwood walked in. "It will be a little while before we have answers, but he's cooperating reluctantly. At this time, he swears he can't remember exactly what was in the drugs he gave you, Baxter. He does remember that he cursed them, though. We'll keep working on it."

"Thank you, doctor," I said. "Did you find out what he stuck Kai with?"

He nodded. "It was just rubbing alcohol and a flu virus. Thankfully he isn't human, so it won't hurt him long term. He'll be fine very soon. He just needs to rest."

I shook my head. "I don't know what Doc was thinking."

"He probably wasn't," said Dr. Underwood. "Some things he's still a genius at, like DNA splicing, but the simple, common sense stuff seems to have fled his mind years ago. Otherwise, he'd have known jabbing Kai with that wasn't going to do anything."

Baxter broke into a coughing fit, and I put a hand on his back. "Are you okay?"

He nodded. "Yeah, those are just getting more frequent."

I looked at Dr. Underwood, and he frowned. "I'll be back as soon as I can."

After he left the room, Baxter released a deep sigh. "I don't know what's going to happen, but thank you for bringing me home,

Miranda. If I have to die, I'm glad I've gotten a chance to see you first."

"You're not gonna die." I refused to let another tear fall. "It's gonna be fine."

He gave me a tired smile. "Sure."

He looked at Mom, and I could see the love he still had for her. It was as if he'd never left us. And I guess for him, it probably felt as fresh as before he'd forgotten. He hadn't had time to grieve or let his feelings fade. Bitterness hadn't had a chance to set in. For Mom and me, it would take a little time. We had seventeen years to make up for. Eighteen, if we counted Mom going through her entire pregnancy alone and her being a pariah of the vampire community. That one was going to be hard to forgive. But I was sure once she heard the reasoning behind Baxter's disappearance, she'd slowly come around.

He stretched and leaned back in his chair. "I think I'm going to rest a bit. This was an exhausting day."

I glanced at my watch. It was later than I'd realized. I stood up.

"Here, take the recliner. It's more comfortable." I grabbed a blanket from the small dresser on the opposite wall and draped it over him as he settled in. "Get some rest, and I'll be back a little later to see what kind of progress they've made."

He nodded and yawned. Before he closed his eyes, he touched my hand. "Miranda, I'm so proud of you. You've become an amazing woman. Just like your mother."

"Thank you." I patted his hand and left the room, shutting the door firmly behind me. Then I let the emotions hit me. I couldn't count all the times I'd wanted to hear my father say he loved me or that he was proud of me. Many of my friends had fathers cheering them on at events and attending daddy-daughter dances, but I was always the girl who stood alone, not even sure who her father was.

I didn't even bother to wipe the tears as I went in search of Kai.

~

I LOOKED in the waiting area, but Kai wasn't there. So I started asking nurses if he'd been admitted to a room. He wasn't on the admissions list either. It wasn't until I passed Dr. Underwood in the hall again roughly twenty minutes later that I learned Kai had left shortly after we'd arrived.

"He let me examine him, asked me if Doc was secure, and then left with Liam." He checked his clipboard, then looked me over. "Are you okay?"

"It's been a weird day. I think I could use a good meal and a shower." That wasn't my first priority, but it sounded believable.

"Well, do that and get a little rest, too. You know I'll call you as soon as I have anything new." He patted me on the shoulder, then continued down the hall.

I slipped out into the parking lot and went to the car. I'd hoped Kai would have at least left me a note, but there was nothing.

I started the car and took off toward the clubhouse. When I pulled up, Kai was sitting on his motorcycle.

I quickly got out and walked over to him. "Going somewhere?"

He shrugged. "I just thought I'd take a ride and clear my head."

"Want some company?" I smiled.

He didn't return it. "I need a little alone time."

"Oh. I see." I did not see. Something had changed. "Did I do something wrong?"

"No, it's not you. I'm just trying to shake off today's events and relax. Ride off the stress."

"Yeah." I stepped back and leaned against my car. "Well, be safe. Don't drive the death machine too fast." I wanted to give him a smile, but I couldn't make it happen.

He stared at me for a moment. "I'll see you soon, okay?"

"Sure."

He started the motorcycle and pulled away. I watched his taillights disappear into the dark, along with my heart.

"He just needs a little time." Liam walked out of the shadows.

"How long have you been there?" I was a little put off that I didn't notice him there, considering I'd felt his presence earlier in the forest. My mind and emotions were so muddled.

"The whole time." He put his thumbs in his pockets. "He's coming to terms with some things. He'll be okay. And he's in love with you."

"Okay." I didn't know what else to say. I was glad to hear he cared. Liam even said the word love, so I should have been ecstatic, but I didn't understand what he needed to reconcile with.

"He saw you transform in the forest when you subdued Doc. It's not something he expected."

"Transform?" I knew my anger had pushed through at that moment, but I didn't realize there was any physical transformation.

"You didn't change shape, so to speak, but your voice deepened to a beast-like growl and your eyes turned red. You threatened to drag Doc to Hell." He stepped closer, leaning against the car next to me.

"Well, I was really angry. And I did see red, which I didn't think could literally happen. I was so angry. He was hurting people I love."

"You called in mist as a defense mechanism and you howled . . . twice." He grinned.

"Don't be silly. I didn't howl, that was one of you guys. The howling, the sulfur, all of that."

He shook his head. "Nope. It was you."

I was confused. "How could it be me and I not know that?"

He shrugged. "It can feel like an out-of-body experience when you start to shift. You were on the verge, I think."

I looked at him. "What do you think happened to me?"

Liam turned to face me and lowered his sunglasses. This was the first time I'd ever seen his eyes. They were dark with a reddish-orange tint. He pushed them back up his nose. "I wear these because it's dangerous to look into the eyes of a hellhound. Mortals, and some supernatural creatures, see their own death. You showed Doc his fate. The red is probably your version of night vision. Being half vampire, you probably experience things a little differently than I do."

I couldn't quite comprehend what I was hearing. "Are you saying I have similar traits to a hellhound?"

He shook his head. "No, I'm saying you are hellhound and vampire. You got the vampire DNA from your parents and the hellhound DNA from . . ." He gestured to the club. "Likely one of us. Doc was grabbing samples from everyone right under our noses. Whatever he put in your parents' dope, I'd bet the entire club it was stuffed with hellhound DNA."

I slid to the concrete in shock. My life just became a lot more complicated.

CHAPTER 14

J went home and attempted to sleep. In between short bouts of rest, I had nightmares of being chased by huge violent dogs with vampire teeth. Or there were scenes of myself attacking everyone I knew because my rage had gotten out of control. Now all those weird dreams and visions were making more sense.

At six a.m., I gave up on any further sleep and took a shower. I managed to take down half a smoothie before I lost my appetite again. I tried not to think about Kai as I drove back to the medical center. I needed good news. Something to help me see the light at the end of a very dismal tunnel.

When I walked into Mom's room, she was sitting up.

"Mom!" I ran to her side and hugged her.

"Hi, baby." Her voice was raspy. "Are you okay?"

I pulled back to look at her. "Am I okay? You're the one that's in the hospital. Are you okay?"

"I've been better." She smiled and pushed a strand of hair behind my ear. "You look tired. Are you taking care of yourself?"

"Yes." I grasped her hand. Now was not the time to get into any details of my situation. There'd be time to talk when she had her strength back.

"Where's Baxter?" I looked around the room.

"Baxter?" Mom frowned. "Why would Baxter be here?"

Oh no. She hadn't seen him yet.

"Miranda May Saunders. Why did you ask that?" Her tone was as stern as it could be, under the circumstances.

"Because he's back," I said.

She blinked several times. "That's impossible."

"It's not." Baxter's voice came from the doorway. He held a cup of coffee in his hand.

"When did you wake up?" I asked her.

She couldn't take her eyes off Baxter. "I'm not sure. It wasn't that long ago. I've been drifting in and out a bit." Her mouth popped open, and she tried to say more, but words failed her.

"I'm gonna let you two talk. You have a lot to catch up on. I need to find Dr. Underwood." I slipped out of the room and shut the door behind me. I wasn't sure I wanted to hear the conversation coming next. Mom would need to get her anger out before she calmed down enough to listen to him.

I walked to the lobby in time to see Dr. Underwood coming through the main entrance.

I ran up to him. "I'm so glad I caught you."

"Good morning, Miranda. What news do you have for me?"

"Mom's awake."

"That's great news. I'll go see her now." He started for the wing containing her room.

"There's more," I said quickly. "I know what Doc did to my parents."

He stopped. "Also great, talk to me on the way."

"Hellhound DNA. He did whatever crazy spell he did with hellhound DNA," I blurted out.

"That would explain some of the odd things they are experiencing. How did you learn this?"

I sighed. "Let's just say I learned it the hard way. I'm part hellhound."

He gave me a sideways glance. "Well, that's interesting."

"To say the least," I muttered.

"I'll give your mom another checkup, then we'll talk to Doc about reversing it."

"Do you think he'll remember?" I asked.

"I hope so." He took a deep breath, then pasted on a smile as he opened the door to my mom's room.

THE NEXT COUPLE of days were touch and go. Mom and Baxter were both getting experimental treatment. Liam, Savage, and I all donated blood, since it seemed the hellhound element was needed to strengthen their immune systems. The vampire genes were failing, thanks to the curse Doc had put on the drugs they'd stolen, and there were no healthy cells to replace them. Mom and Baxter were both regaining strength in small strides. It was encouraging, but they still had a long way to go, both physically and in their relationship. But I was starting to see Mom smile more when Baxter was around, and I had a feeling things between them were going to be just fine.

I'd also started to understand why Mom was as cautious as she was. She'd made a lot of decisions in her life that didn't turn out so well for her. She was terrified I'd go down that same path, so she'd overcompensated with rigid rules, hoping to protect me. But we were both learning a lot of lessons. I couldn't learn from her mistakes if she never told me about them. And she couldn't help me with problems I faced if I never confided in her.

On the scientific front, Doc was working under the supervision of Dr. Underwood and a few other Seelie fae who were tasked with making sure the nasty little man didn't make a misstep. Most of the time, all it took was the threat of a visit from me to keep him motivated. It was odd, but I was glad he was that scared of me. It was a comforting feeling knowing I had some control over something in this crazy situation.

I still hadn't heard from Kai. I tried to remind myself that no matter what else happened, we'd never agreed to anything more than a temporary arrangement. He'd said he cared. And he'd sure kissed me like someone with feelings for me. But the heat of the moment can make a person do funny things. Maybe that's all it was—fear, adrenaline, and the uncertainty of the future. I could see how that could be mistaken for love when everything was on the line.

I didn't call him either. You couldn't make someone love you, no matter how much you loved them. And if you could, that wouldn't be real love, would it?

I was ready to turn in for the night when there was a knock at my door. It was almost ten p.m., and I wasn't expecting anyone. Zoey had brought my missed homework over so I could prepare for school Monday, but that had been hours ago, and I was pretty sure we'd covered everything.

I opened the door to see the biggest bouquet of daisies that I was sure had ever existed. Kai poked his head from behind them. "Can I come in?"

I nodded and stepped aside.

He placed the flowers on a side table, and I noticed he had a couple other things in his hands. "I come bearing gifts."

"You didn't have to." I wasn't sure I wanted them.

"I know, but I'm a nice guy so . . . here they are." He smirked, but I didn't respond. "Are you okay?"

I shrugged.

"Are you mad at me?"

"No," I said. "I'm just . . . disappointed. I thought we were friends."

He cleared his throat. "I thought we were more than that."

"I was starting to believe that, too, but then you ran off when I needed you most." I walked to the living area and flopped down on the sofa.

He followed me over, placing the wrapped gifts on the coffee table. "Listen, I'm really sorry about that. I had to work some things out. Not things about you, but about me."

"You couldn't pick up the phone? Ask how I was doing?"

"I wanted to, so many times. But I was afraid if I heard your voice, I'd come running back to you. I knew I needed to figure things out before I spoke to you again."

"What was there to figure out, Kai?" The heartache of seeing him again, fearing he didn't feel as I did, was breaking me. "Did you need to see if there were better options for you than a vampire-hellhound hybrid?"

"No. God no. That's not it at all." He pulled one of my hands to his chest. "This heart may not technically beat, but it still belongs to you. I'm pretty sure it was yours the moment I saw you walk into the cafeteria on my first day of school."

"So you're not bothered by what you saw in the woods?"

"It surprised me at first, but no, it doesn't change anything." He raised my hand from his chest to his lips and kissed my palm.

"What took you two days to figure out?" I still didn't know what to think about his absence and silence.

He lowered our hands to his lap. "I had a talk with Liam after we dropped off Doc. He gave me some good advice. I needed time to reflect on the future." He looked me in the eyes. "Do you remember when we left Baxter's, and I told you that we needed to talk when this was all over?"

I nodded.

"This is that talk." He cleared his throat. "You once asked me if my plan was to live life without a plan. I told you I had one, but I had to wait for the important parts to fall into place." He took a deep breath. "You are the most important part. I had to make peace with myself that if I couldn't convince you to give me a chance, I was going to move away and never come back."

"Kai . . ."

He shook his head. "Let me finish. I honestly never thought I had a chance with you. Then I saw you in the club, and I worried about what would happen to you. When Liam asked about you, I blurted out we were dating. It was a great cover, but a part of me was really glad I had an excuse to be with you. To pretend you were mine, even if it wasn't real. I have to be honest. Things weren't quite as dire as I made them out to be. Liam isn't as much of a tyrant as it seems. We still shouldn't cross him, but . . . I wasn't one hundred percent honest. I wanted a reason to spend time with you." He chuckled. "The day you kissed me in my room. Wow. I thought I'd just become the luckiest guy in the world. But I didn't know if I was kissing the girl I'd always wanted, or the girl that just needed me to find her father."

I looked at my hand still clutched in his. "I'm not that good of an actress, Kai."

He bit his bottom lip and smiled. "I hoped that was the answer. I know you have to finish school, and there are a lot of things ahead that are uncertain. But I'll be here through all of it, if you want me. I'm willing to wait, if you need time. I'll quit the club, sell the motorcycle, get a job in an office—whatever it takes to take care of you. Because, so help me, I'm in love with you, Miranda. I have been for a long time. I've always wanted you, but I knew you deserved better than the Kai Reynolds everyone thought they knew. I wasn't sure I could really be myself and stay here. You've shown me I can." He took another deep breath. "But if you don't see a future for us, just say the word, and I'll stay out of your way. I'll let you find someone who will make you happy, and I'll move on."

"You make me happy. I'll admit I never thought I'd say that. And Zoey is gonna faint when I tell her, but it's true. You make me very happy."

He pulled me to him and kissed me.

"I don't know what the future holds for us, but I'm happy to give us a try."

He bounced off the sofa and stepped backwards. "Speaking of the future, you need to open my gifts."

I eyed him suspiciously. "Okay."

He handed me a small box with a bow on it.

I pulled the top off the box, and inside was a folded piece of paper. When I unfolded it, there were a bunch of scientific-looking scribbles on it. "I don't get it."

"It's the formula to the cure for your parents. Dr. Underwood figured it out. It's requiring some more DNA shenanigans that I don't understand, and probably more fae magic, but who cares. They're gonna be okay."

I jumped up and threw my arms around him as I released happy tears. "Oh, Kai, this is the best news ever!"

"I thought you'd like it." He kissed the top of my head.

I wiped my eyes. "So what's in this one?" I reached for the other package, but he snatched it away. "Uh, it's nothing."

Now I was getting suspicious. "Then why did you bring it? Wrapped."

"Well, it was kind of a gag gift. Something to make you laugh. I thought you'd be in a better mood when I got here." He cleared his throat. "I didn't realize how much I hurt you when I took off."

"I can take a joke. Hand it over." I placed my hand out, palm up.

"Are you sure?" He was wearing that smirk I now had a love-hate relationship with.

"Yes, I'm sure."

He handed me the package. I sat on the sofa and unwrapped it. For a moment I just stared at the contents of the box, then I slowly raised my eyes to his. "Seriously."

He was snickering. Like a ten-year-old boy.

"So this is how it's gonna be between us, huh?"

He was now in the throes of a full belly laugh. "C'mon, you gotta admit it's funny."

I grinned. "I will admit that." I stood and put the box of dog treats on the coffee table. "But you need to know that I am fully prepared to pay you back for this."

He wiped his eyes. "I deserve whatever you do to me. I just couldn't resist that."

I patted his cheek. "You just wait."

He pulled me against him and kissed me again. "For you, I'll wait forever."

I smiled as I thought about how shocked he'd be when he learned I'd decided to buy my own death machine, and that Liam had promised to teach me how to ride.

AMY HALE

ABOUT THE AUTHOR

Since childhood, best-selling and award-winning author Amy Hale has been creating exceptional stories that summon a whirlwind of emotions and inspiration unto the reader. She loves creating characters and worlds from nothing but her imagination and a few glasses of wine. Her love of the written word has not only resulted in her writing some of her readers' favorite adventures, but has also manifested itself in the form of book hoarding. She's convinced it's not a sickness.

She debuted her first fiction novel in 2015 after retiring from thirteen years of nonfiction writing for various online entities. For the last couple of decades, she's also carried the titles of Laundry Goddess, Chef, Butt Wiper, Soother of Temper Tantrums, and in more recent years, Moderator of Sarcastic Eyerolls and Sass. She resides in Illinois with her husband, as well as two grown children who claim they are never moving out. Regardless, they are the center of her universe, although her cat believes otherwise.

If she had any spare time, she'd love music, photography, watching Mystery Science Theater 3000 with her family, and long rides on the back of her husband's motorcycle.

Learn more at authoramyhale.com

ACKNOWLEDGMENTS

There are times when "Thank You" never seems to say enough. This is certainly one of those times. I dearly love and appreciate everyone who has devoted time and energy into helping me make Miranda and Kai's story come to life. Without the help and support of such an amazing team behind me, this book would have never seen the light of day.

Many thanks to God for His grace and granting me patience as I stumbled and cried and wanted to throw my laptop across the room. I went through some big life upheavals while working on this book. And while they were good changes, they really messed with my writing mojo. I had to learn a new process, and there were moments when I wondered if this story would ever happen. Thankfully, it all came together on time.

My husband is my rock, and without him, I would never have attempted writing fiction. So if you see him at a signing (he's pretty much always with me) be sure to tell him thank you for supporting me. His support is why you have this book in your hands today.

Many thanks to my Havenwood Falls Family! Love to Regina for the gorgeous cover! And to Kristie Cook and Liz Ferry for making the book look amazing on the inside, as well as making sure my words make sense to all of you. They make sense in my head, but they don't always come out on paper that way. Kristie and Liz have the fun job of steering me back on the right path when my mind starts to wander off without me.

Thanks to my Havenwood Falls siblings for loaning me their characters. I appreciate you allowing them to pop in now and then!

A huge hug goes out to my beta readers Ashley Longcrier, Amber Peterson, and Felicia Thorn. You ladies helped me work through the plot, and I appreciate it so much!

As always, thanks to you, dear reader. You are the reason we keep telling these extraordinary stories of a town we all wish we could live in. I hope these books help you all keep your own little piece of Havenwood Falls with you wherever you are.

SHADOWS & SPELLS

CAMEO RENAE

HAVENWOOD FALLS HIGH

Shadows & Spells

USA TODAY BESTSELLING AUTHOR

CAMEO RENAE

~ A Havenwood Falls Young Adult Novella ~

ALSO BY CAMEO RENAE

Hidden Wings Series

Hidden Wings

Broken Wings

Tethered Wings

Gilded Wings

Wings of Vengeance

Midway Series – Hidden Wings Series Spin-off

Guarding Eden

Saving Thomas (Coming Soon)

After Light Saga: Arv-3

Sanctum

Intransigent

Hostile

Retribution

In My Dreams - Duet

In My Dreams

In My Reality

To all the Havenwood Falls Authors.
Because of you, my characters have the coolest places to hang out, and the most awesome peeps to interact with. Thank you! You all rock!

CHAPTER 1

ERIS

*I*t was after midnight when Rylan pulled his motorcycle into the vacant parking lot of a small motel. There was one flickering streetlamp, which added to the already eerie vibe in the air.

But just down the road, an illuminated grocery mart sign gave away his location. He was in Montrose.

I sensed something dark, menacing, and evil nearby. My eyes scoured the area, desperately searching for something I could feel but couldn't see. Then, I saw them—a pair of blood-red eyes, lurking in the shadows. Watching Rylan. Stalking him.

Rylan slid off his bike, his attention on a small piece of paper—the one the girl Keira had given him a few weeks ago at the Festival of Lights. It was the location of the rest of the pack.

With Rylan's attention averted, I heard a faint guttural growl that made the hair on my body stand on end. The wolf was downwind, which was why Rylan couldn't smell him. Sneaky bastard.

The beast was large and crouched in an attack position. I could see the want in his wicked eyes, hear it in his terrible growl.

"Rylan!" I screamed, as the wolf bounded toward him.

Before Rylan could figure out what was going on and shift, the huge wolf pounced.

Sharp teeth sunk into Rylan's neck. Then, a sickening crack shattered the air.

"No!" I wailed, running toward him.

Rylan lay on the ground. His throat was gone, torn flesh hanging in its place, while blood pooled around him. His eyes—those beautiful hazel eyes—were wide open but unseeing.

He was dead. Rylan was dead.

"Rylan!" I sobbed, shooting up, soaked with sweat.

Darkness enveloped me. It wasn't real. It was a nightmare like no other I'd experienced before. This one was so real. So vivid. My heart was still hammering hard against my chest, and I was breathless. I stood from my bed, my body trembling, and peered out my bedroom window.

Rylan's bike was still parked in its usual space next door. Thank the gods.

There were two quick knocks at the door before the knob twisted and it opened.

"Eris, are you okay?" my dad asked, his brow furrowed with concern.

Camden poked his head in right behind him, sniffing the air, his eyes almost glowing gold.

"What are you doing?" I exhaled.

His narrowed eyes met mine. "Checking to make sure there isn't a dog in your room."

I growled at him. "There isn't. I just had a bad dream."

"About Rylan?" Camden asked with a raised brow.

"Yes. And it's not the kind of dream you're thinking of."

I proceeded to tell them about the nightmare and how real it felt.

"It could be a premonition," my dad said. "Your mother used to get them all the time. A foreseeing of the future."

"Did they ever come true?" I asked.

"Yes," he sighed. "She rarely got them, but every time she did, she'd wake up crying or screaming. They were burdensome for her. She didn't like that part of her gift."

I only needed to know one thing. "Can it be changed?"

"I don't know. I guess it's possible, depending on the circumstances."

"Just talk to him in the morning," Camden said, stretching his muscular arms over his head. "I'm going back to bed." He started walking away. "And please, don't yell a dude's name like that again. I was about to pounce in here and bite someone's head off."

"I love you, too!" I hollered after him.

"If you have any questions about the premonitions, maybe you should call your grandmother. She has them, too," my dad said softly.

I was shocked, but shouldn't have been. "I will. Thanks."

"Good night, sweetheart." My dad smiled and closed the door.

I fell back into my pillow and stared at the ceiling. The dream was probably triggered by the visit from a girl named Keira, who was a member of Rylan's old pack. Somehow, desperate and alone, she found him to tell him about a psycho shifter named Lars, who was hunting down and killing off the members of his old pack. There were only six left—of the twenty they originally had.

Rylan had told me a little about Lars. How he suspected he was the killer of both his parents, and now, he'd murdered their pack's current alpha, Axel. Rylan was their last hope . . . their only means of survival. They were running for their lives, and I'd overheard the girl, Keira, tell him those remaining members were in Montrose, over an hour away.

They'd been there for a few weeks now, while Rylan decided whether he wanted to take on the new role as their alpha. I knew he was conflicted. From what I knew about Rylan, after spending almost a month with him, he was torn. I could see it on his face and the way he stiffened after he had the discussion with Keira.

He'd grown up with them. They were his family, and I knew he wouldn't leave them out there alone to fend for themselves.

Especially when that psycho was out there, murdering for whatever sick, twisted pleasure he got out of it.

I knew Rylan was going to leave. I just didn't know when.

I'd tried to talk to him after the Festival of Lights, but he was tight-lipped. He didn't want me or my family involved in his past issues. He wanted to deal with Lars alone.

After the dream . . . I was worried as hell. I had to find a way to convince Rylan that our pack, the Blaekthorn Shadow Pack, was his pack too. We were his family now, and any one of us would do anything to help him. But convincing him of that wouldn't be easy.

CHAPTER 2

RYLAN

*S*leep evaded me. I watched rays of moonlight stream through cracks in my curtains, one of them illuminating the new tiger's eye amulet Eris's dad had given me. An amulet like other members of the Blaekthorn Shadow Pack wore that kept them from being forced to change by the moon's phase.

Before Eris's mother died, she'd searched for the spell, and when she'd found it, she cast it over the stones so her family wouldn't have to live with the curse. She also planned ahead, spelling extra stones, knowing the family would inevitably grow.

Then, they eventually found Havenwood Falls. The town seemed to call to supernatural beings, drawing them in so they wouldn't have to be alone. Those who weren't completely human—like me.

In Havenwood Falls, the Court of the Sun and the Moon governed the supernatural residents. They had rules to ensure every supernatural being was able to control their gifts, and to keep the humans in the town safe. Each supernatural resident and visitor was given a tattoo, and the tattoo meant something different for each supernatural being. The Blaekthorns' tattoos allowed them to change at will, so within the town's wards, they didn't really need the amulets Eris's mother had spelled.

But should any of them leave the magical town, the amulets

were a must. Which was why I wondered why Piers had given me one.

Maybe he knew I was about to leave.

Grasping the stone in my fingers, I couldn't help but wonder what my life would have been like if I hadn't wandered here and met Camden. And now, as fate would have it, I was part of the Blaekthorn Shadow Pack and family. A pack where Eris's father was alpha.

Seeing Keira a few weeks ago brought back every horror I'd tucked away—memories from the past that haunted me. And now the horrors were following me, just when I thought my life was taking a turn for the good.

Was I damned to live a life of running and fighting for my life? Because I was tired and didn't want to run anymore.

Hell, I wished I could close my eyes and have it all be a terrible nightmare. But it wasn't. Lars was out there—so close to my new home and the people who helped mend my shattered life. A life I thought was irreparable.

I couldn't let Lars set foot in this town, and wouldn't allow the Blaekthorns to get injured or killed trying to help me.

The bastard murdered both of my parents. And although we didn't witness him do it, we all knew it was him. His scent was always there, lingering around the gruesome scenes.

Lars had coveted everything my father had, especially my mother. He was infatuated with her, and believed she was supposed to have been *his* mate. When she refused him, he completely snapped and went on a killing spree, leaving nothing in his wake but chaos and bloodshed. Starting with my father.

Although I wanted to, I knew I couldn't ignore Keira's plea. It was an enormous weight pressing on my already heavily laden shoulders. A weight I never wanted to bear.

Hell, I was graduating high school in a few months and just wanted to start my life over. To work and have some semblance of a normal life. Was that too damned much to ask?

I now had a good life, with people who actually cared for me and took me in, who gave me a job and a roof over my head. I was thankful for them. They were a close-knit and loving family, and I knew they would do anything for each other. Which was why I didn't want any of my old pack's baggage to be dragged back here.

And then there was Eris, my half-witch, half-shifter girlfriend. She wanted me to open up and involve them in that part of my life. But it was too dark, and I knew she could get sucked up into that darkness if I let her in.

The burden was weighing heavier with each passing day, but there was only one right choice. I'd been avoiding for it too long already. I had to go. I had to leave Havenwood Falls and find Lars.

CHAPTER 3

ERIS

*T*he sun had finally risen, and I was already dressed and ready to head over to Uncle Garrick and Aunt Vera's cottage. I had to let Rylan know about the dream. Maybe it could convince him to stay, or even ask for some help.

After being in Havenwood Falls for almost a month now with my childhood memories restored, I felt like I'd known the Blaekthorn Shadow Pack my entire life, even though I was still a newcomer to our pack. They were family, and they treated me no differently than they did Camden, who had never left. I knew they'd do anything for Rylan, now that he was also a part of the family.

I still couldn't get the nightmare out of my head. It was times like these I wished my mom were here to help me understand these new gifts. If she had premonitions, like my dad said, maybe she could have helped me understand them better. But since the Festival of Lights, I hadn't seen my glimmer—my secret ball of light that brought me so much hope and light whenever my world was dark. The light I found out was my mother, who had been with me all along.

Maybe she left because I was now old enough to stand on my own, and had found out the truth about her death. Maybe it was because I was back with the family in Havenwood Falls and had reconciled with my grandma.

I could call Grandma Gertie, but it was much too early in the morning. The last time I'd talked to her, when we went back to the house to pack up and move our things, she said she was actually considering moving to Havenwood Falls to be closer to me and Camden. But I knew she was torn. There was a gentleman back in New Mexico with whom she'd had a secret relationship, and he wasn't going anywhere.

I peeked out my window and saw Rylan's light click on. Then he opened his curtain and looked directly at me. I waved, and when he waved back, I signaled for him to come over. He acknowledged me with a nod.

My insides twisted in knots. When he disappeared and his light clicked off, I quietly made my way downstairs and threw on my jacket. It was the end of January and about twenty degrees outside.

Slipping outside, I closed the door, and when I turned around, Rylan was standing inches away. He grabbed my neck and pressed his warm lips to mine, stifling my scream.

"What the hell?" I exhaled, breathless. "How did you get here so quickly?"

His head cocked to the side. "I couldn't wait to see you."

"Mmm," I hummed, taking his hand in mine. "Can we take a walk?"

"Sure. Anything wrong?" he asked, his hazel eyes sweeping over me.

"No. I mean . . . I don't know." I looked into his eyes and couldn't help but flash back to the dream, and seeing those eyes without life, his throat ripped out, blood staining his face and the ground around him.

"C'mon, cupcake. Tell me what's on your mind." He tried to smile, but his eyes were studying me, like he knew something was wrong.

I let out a long exhale, my breath commingling with the cold air swirling in front of me. "I had a dream last night. But it wasn't a regular dream. It was different from any other dream I've had. It was so vivid and real, as if I were watching the event happen right in front of me."

His eyes narrowed, and a grin rose on his lips. I knew the dream I had was something totally different than what he was expecting, and it made my chest ache.

"What event were you watching?"

I paused, not sure if I wanted to tell him. But the reason why I couldn't go back to sleep and why we were standing out in the frigid cold this morning was that he needed to know.

"It was about Lars—he . . . he killed you." And although his expression changed to one of disappointment, I proceeded to tell him the entire dream, whether he wanted to hear it or not. Because maybe, just maybe, it could help save his life.

When I was done, Rylan didn't say a word. He stood there, quiet, his eyes staring blankly behind me.

"What are you thinking?" I breathed.

"I don't know," he replied.

I squeezed his hand and made him look at me. "Rylan, you aren't alone. We're—"

"No," he said, firmly. "You and your family are good people. I won't drag any of you into the tangled web that bastard is weaving. He may be a psycho, but he has a plan. It's been his plan since the beginning. To kill my father and his entire pack, including me. He's trying to prove he is stronger than any of us, and wants to punish us all. He thinks the reason my mother rejected him was because of the pack's influence. Like I said —he's a mental case. He believes he needs to fulfill this personal vendetta. And he won't stop until I and the rest of the pack are dead."

My stomach knotted. "Or unless he dies."

His eyes finally met mine, the gold rim around them more pronounced. "Yes. And that's what I plan to do."

It was selfish of me to ask, but I had to. "You don't have to go. You can stay here with me. You're safe here."

Those hazel eyes stared directly at me. "I wish that were true. But there is no safe place for me. Not yet. He'll keep searching until he finds me, and I don't want that bastard anywhere near you or your family."

"Rylan, you helped stop the witch who put Camden under the spell and tried to kill my dad. Let us help you. Please."

His eyes softened, and his arm wrapped around my waist, pulling me closer to him. "You have to understand. Lars gets off on the hunt and even more on the kill. He has no remorse. I won't put your family in danger, after all they've done for me." He wrapped his other arm around me, pulling me tight against his warm body, his calloused hand caressing my cheek. "Especially you. I don't want that bastard near you. I don't want him to know that you exist. Understand?"

I nodded.

Rylan leaned forward and kissed my forehead, then pressed his brow against mine. "I know you want to help, but I can't let you. If anything happened—" He didn't finish, but the sadness in his eyes spoke loud and clear.

There was nothing I could say or do to change his mind, so I remained quiet.

"Hey," he said, trying to break the tension. "I have to work for a few hours at the warehouse, but how about I pick you up for lunch? My treat." His cocky grin was back.

"Sure," I smiled back. "I'll see you then."

Rylan picked me up at noon in the company truck, since I was forbidden by practically the entire family to ride on his motorcycle while it was winter. He took me to Burger Bar, and the lunch crowd was bustling.

As we entered the restaurant, Rylan walked up to a tall, skinny guy with light brown hair, wearing jeans and a T-shirt.

"Hey, Jace," Rylan said, holding his hand out to him. "How are you holding up?"

The boy shook his hand and gave a dimpled smile. "Fine," he said, but his eyes said otherwise. He looked . . . sad.

"If you need anything, let me know," Rylan added, slapping a hand on his shoulder.

Jace nodded and gave a solemn smile. "Thank you. That means a lot."

When we walked away, I asked, "Who was that?"

"Remember the girl, Heidi Bennett, who went missing in December?"

"I remember you mentioning her."

"That's her boyfriend, Jace Edwards."

"Oh," I said, and suddenly felt bad for him. No wonder he looked so sad. He must have been battling his own demons.

As we passed by some of the booths, Rylan stopped again. I recognized one of the boys. It was Kase Kasun, with a few other boys I'd seen at the Festival of Lights a few weeks ago. Most likely football players, because Rylan greeted them with fist-bumps.

"Hey, Eris," Kase said with a tip of his head. "You should meet my sister, Willa. I heard you two have some things in common."

"Yeah, I'd like that." I remembered Rylan mentioning that Kase's twin sister, Willa, was a late shifter, too. And future alpha of her pack.

"I'll let her know. Maybe you and Rylan can come over for dinner sometime soon."

"Sounds good, man," Rylan said, grabbing hold of my hand.

I nodded. "Thank you."

Since I'd come to this town, I'd realized there were so many different species out there. I'd met a vampire, a dragon shifter, an angel, and much more. Havenwood Falls was a place of magic and monsters. Monsters like me and Rylan.

As Rylan pulled me past one of the booths, I spotted Julianna Fairchild, who was in a class I'd just started on Thursday nights at Sun and Moon Academy—an Awakening Lab for supes who had awakened but needed work honing their powers.

"Hi, Julianna," I said, waving. She was beautiful, smart, and voted Miss Teen Havenwood Falls. She was also fae. Her lavender hair was braided down her back and accessorized with a daisy.

Julianna waved back. "Hey, Eris. It's just Jules, remember?" She smiled, then introduced the girls at her booth. "This is Paisley, my cousin, and her friends, Taylor and Makenzie."

"I know Eris," Taylor said. "We, like, met at the clinic when Camden was admitted."

"Yes, we did. It's good to see you again."

Taylor smiled. "Totally."

"How is your brother?" Jules asked.

I smiled and nodded. "He's good. Back to normal, I guess. I'm still trying to figure him out."

"It must be hard," Paisley added, "to adjust."

"It is," I replied. "But it's been good . . . so far."

They all smiled, and Rylan cleared his throat.

"We'd better get a booth before they're all gone," I said. "I'll see you Thursday, Jules?"

"Yeah, see you."

We went inside and found an empty booth at the back, then ordered burgers, tater tots, and milkshakes.

Our time there was mostly quiet, and there was an unspoken tension in the air, knowing danger was close, and Rylan would eventually be going out to look for it. I tried to keep the conversation light, but every time I looked at him, the vision of him dead flashed in my mind.

"How's your burger?" he asked, shoving the last bite of his triple bacon cheeseburger into his mouth in record time.

"It's great," I said with a forced smile.

Rylan reached across the table and took my hand, his gold-rimmed hazel eyes fixed on mine. "Hey, don't worry about me."

"But that's the problem, Rylan. I do worry. Because I care."

His eyes shifted down to our connected hands. "I know. But you have to understand. I've been a loner most of my life, and opening up to someone like you . . . it's not easy for me. I've become a master at hiding my emotions and feelings, because out there, when your entire life is surviving, having feelings or emotions is weakness. So you're gonna have to cut me some slack."

"You're right. I don't know what it's like to live in fear every day, or to have to fend for myself. But I know, without a doubt, that if I ever had a problem or something bothering me, I could go to my dad and he would help me through it, whatever it was. Having someone to talk to is not weakness. It's strength. We are your family now, Rylan. We care about you. *I* care about you. And you have to cut me some slack for trying to make you understand my position. We are a family and a pack, and with that comes trust and strength in numbers."

Rylan let out a deep sigh, then ran his fingers through his thick brown hair. "There were twenty members of my old pack and now there are six. And, even now, it could be less. I would rather walk away now than to drag your family into this mess, knowing that if anything happened to them, their blood would stain my hands."

I closed my eyes. He wasn't getting it. I could see his point, but it seemed he wouldn't budge. My father and uncles had been around for a very long time, and kept very physically fit with their jobs. I knew if they met this rogue shifter, together they would be able to take him down.

"Hey, wanna go?" he asked.

I nodded and stood from my chair. There was no more I could say.

CHAPTER 4

RYLAN

I told Garrick and Vera I was going to spend the night hanging out with Kase and a few other boys from the Havenwood Falls High football team. I hated lying to them, but I had an overwhelming feeling that if Eris knew I was leaving, she'd send them after me.

I hated the look she gave me at the Burger Bar. She was pouring her heart out, trying to get me to open up and see her side, but I still felt like an outsider. I was still on probation, and now, some of my old pack's trash was being dragged back, leaving chaos in its path.

I was a lot bigger and stronger than any of the other male members of the pack, including my dad and Axel, who was my dad's best friend and the most recent alpha, until, as Kiera told me, Lars murdered him, too. I wanted to prove, not only to the Blaekthorns but to myself, that I was capable of taking care of this bastard alone. That I was stronger and smarter than him.

I had no real plan, but knew I needed to get as far away from Havenwood Falls as I could, as quickly as possible, and hopefully put an end to this once and for all.

It was after nine o'clock when I left. The sky was dark, and endless stars sparkled across it. It was a beautiful night despite the horror that lay within it . . . in Montrose.

The look on Eris's face when she told me about the nightmare she'd had was burned in my mind. She was truly concerned, and if premonition was one of her newfound gifts, I'd have to consider it.

Despite the patches of ice still on the roads, I hopped on my motorcycle. Knowing I would be leaving, I winterized it, buying studded tires and installing a windshield. It was my only source of transportation, so I'd have to take it.

The road conditions weren't too bad. Plus, with enhanced vision and reflexes, I maneuvered around the ice patches quite easily.

The road out of Havenwood Falls was quiet and dead. The only sound was the rumbling of my motorcycle and the whipping wind as I sped toward Montrose, and it took a little over an hour to get to the location Keira had written on the paper.

As I pulled into the parking lot of the motel, the hairs on my skin raised. I glanced around. The entire area was eerily similar to the scene Eris had dreamed about and described to me, as if she'd been here.

If she truly had a premonition, then Lars was already here, watching, waiting . . . stalking from the shadows. There were no humans around, and I didn't blame them. This entire area seemed like a slum, a place one would avoid even during the daytime.

I sniffed the air and couldn't catch a scent of anyone from my old pack. Maybe they'd moved on, knowing Lars was on their tail. Keeping my senses on full alert, I constantly scanned the dark areas.

I could feel the wolf inside me, raking its claws against my human skin, ready to break out at any given moment. It was begging to be set free. But I couldn't let it loose yet. I had to keep it inside until the time was right.

He was here. I could sense him, but I didn't want him to run.

If he was here . . . it needed to end here.

I kicked the stand on my bike down and slid off, aware of everything going on around me. Then I heard it. That deep, guttural growl.

The hunter was here, but I was fully aware. I had been given a warning ahead of time. A glimpse into the future. But this situation would have a much different outcome. I'd make sure of it.

Since Eris told me about her dream, I'd run this scenario through my mind a thousand times. I thought I would be more afraid, but as I stood under the starry, crescent-moon-lit sky in front of the motel, the only illumination a single flickering light, I had no fear in me at all. I could only describe what I felt as rage.

This bastard had taken everything from me. He murdered my parents in cold blood, and now he had the balls to hunt me?

I was no longer the helpless little boy he'd seen years ago. I was now in my prime, stronger than ever, and ready to take him on. Alpha or not. This prick would pay.

My skin was tingling, knowing he was so close. I knew where he was. Eris had told me, and his quiet growls confirmed it. He was to my left, downwind.

My girl had given me the upper hand.

The moon wasn't full, but Lars had shifted. I'd heard that he'd sought out dark witches. Maybe they'd given him a way to shift at will too.

I slowly slid from my black leather jacket and laid it on the seat.

The low rumbling from the beast was getting louder, and now, I could hear his claws scraping against the pavement.

I readied myself. I was bred for this. It was in my blood to protect my pack and fight for my life.

I turned to see two red eyes glaring at me.

Then a huge black wolf stepped out of the shadows, lips curled over razor-sharp teeth, foam frothed at the corners of its mouth. He crouched to an attack position, then . . . he charged.

I let the beast inside free and shifted, meeting him head on.

CHAPTER 5

ERIS

I'd just come home from a late dinner at Napoli's with my dad and Camden, when I noticed Rylan's bike was gone.

"Cam, do you know where Rylan went?" I questioned.

His eyes narrowed on me. "Why? Are you keeping a tight leash on him?"

"Camden," my dad said in his fatherly tone.

"No, Eris. I don't know where he is," he sighed. "Probably hanging out with some of the guys, like he did on the weekends before you came to town."

Having Camden in my life as a big brother was still an adjustment. And I could tell it was for him, too.

I had a sinking feeling Rylan wasn't with friends. I couldn't shake the feeling that he'd left and didn't tell anyone. Butterflies were slamming around in my gut, and they wouldn't stop. I had to find out where he was, that he was safe, to ease my mind.

When my dad stopped the car, I hopped out.

"I'm going to visit Aunt Vera," I said, already heading next door. Their kitchen light was on, and I saw a figure moving around inside. They were still awake.

"Sure you are!" Camden teased, and I heard my dad mumble a few words.

I knocked on the door, feeling breathless until Aunt Vera opened it.

"Eris! How are you doing, sweetheart? Come in," she said, grabbing my wrist and pulling me inside. It smelled like a bakery.

She immediately walked over to the stove, slipped on an oven mitt, and pulled out a sheet pan from the oven. "Would you care for a cinnamon roll?"

"I'd love one," I said, sitting at the table. I'd learned to never turn food down from either of my aunts when they offered it, because they would insist, and I'd get whatever it was anyway.

As she took a plate out of the cupboard, she turned to me. "Rylan isn't here, love. He went over to Kase's house to hang out for a while. You know, Sheriff Kasun's son."

"Okay. And yes, I know Kase," I said nonchalantly, trying not to raise my stress levels. But even after hearing her say he was with his friends, I still couldn't settle myself. I couldn't shake the feeling that he had left. I felt it in my bones. It was an uneasiness that wouldn't go away, even as my brain tried to push the thought away.

"So, how was dinner?" she asked, setting the hot cinnamon roll with gooey cream cheese frosting slathered over it and a cold glass of milk in front of me. I breathed in the scents of cinnamon and sugar, and it made my mouth water.

"We went to Napoli's. The restaurant was full, and the pizza was great."

"I love Napoli's. They do have the best pizza."

I agreed, glancing around. "Where's Uncle Garrick?"

"Oh, he's working late at the warehouse. There were a few big orders that came in for next week. He wanted to make sure they were all ready to go."

"Always working." I laughed.

"He is always working, but he loves it."

We chatted about shopping and my homeschool lessons while I finished my dessert and milk. An hour later, I said goodbye, carrying a Tupperware of cinnamon rolls next door to my dad and brother.

Outside, the cold bit my nose and cheeks, and made my breath billow in front of me. I quickly ran toward the warmth of my house and slipped inside.

"Find what you were looking for?" my dad asked, sitting at the kitchen counter with some paperwork.

"Yes and no," I said, sliding the Tupperware next to him.

"What's this?" He peeked under the lid and took in a deep breath.

"Cinnamon rolls. Aunt Vera insisted."

"Is there one for me?" Camden piped in, standing at the top of the stairs.

"Yep. Knock yourself out."

He ran down the stairs, grabbed his roll and ran back up. "I'll tell her thanks in the morning."

I sat on a stool next to my dad.

"You're concerned," he said. He could read me like a book, even when I was trying not to look concerned.

"I think Rylan left Havenwood Falls."

The look on my dad's face showed genuine concern. "Your nightmare. Do you think he went after the shifter alone?"

"I do. He told me earlier today that he doesn't want any of us involved. He feels like this is all on him."

"Did he mention anything to Garrick or Vera?"

"Aunt Vera said he told her he was going to hang out with Sheriff Kasun's son, Kase, and some football boys."

My dad slid off his stool, headed to the phone, and dialed a number.

"Hey, Ric. This is Piers Blaekthorn . . . I'm great, thanks . . . Yes, Camden is doing well. If it weren't for you and the others finding and helping him, we probably would have lost him. Yeah . . . Thanks again . . . Hey, I wanted to ask if Rylan, the kid staying with Garrick and Vera, is with your son Kase?"

I waited, desperate to hear an answer.

"Okay, thanks . . . I'm not sure, but if there is, I'll be sure to let you know. . . All right. Thanks, Ric. I appreciate it . . . Bye."

It felt like forever when my dad hung up and finally gave me the answer. "Kase has been home all night. He's asleep on his dad's couch."

My heart sank. The feeling I'd had in my gut, since I saw his bike missing, was right. Now, hours had passed since he'd left. That meant he was already in Montrose, and . . . I couldn't think about it. I had to remain positive. He was still alive. I had no choice but to believe it.

"He should have talked to us. As a family, we could take care of one rogue shifter together," my dad said.

"I know. But he didn't want any of us to get hurt or killed. He was looking out for—"

"You. He was looking out for you," my dad murmured. "But still." He headed for the stairs. "He should have told one of us." My dad was in his alpha mode, protective.

"Where are you going?" I called after him.

"I'm going to get ready and call your uncles. We're going after him."

"I'm coming with you!" I hollered, making my way to the stairs.

My dad stopped at the top and glared down at me with a look that made me freeze in place. "You are not coming, Eris. You're staying right here with Camden and your aunts, where it's safe."

"Dad."

"Eris, don't argue with me. You're staying." He was using his voice of authority—the voice of our alpha. A voice I had no choice but to submit to.

So I kept my mouth shut and stormed to my room.

"I'll need his location," he said, before shutting his bedroom door.

The location. I didn't have a location. I didn't see the paper Keira had given him. But . . . the dream. In the dream I saw a sign— Montrose Mini Mart.

I quickly flipped opened my laptop and googled the location, then looked for the nearest motel. On the map, there was one motel nearby. I wrote the address down on a piece of paper, and when I heard my dad exit his room, I met him in the hall and handed it to him.

"There is a reason why Rylan didn't tell you he was leaving. A reason why he wants you to stay. I can't let you go, either. Not this time."

"I know." I knew he was right, but I still wanted to go.

"We'll find him," he said, then bounded down the stairs and out the door. I knew my dad and my uncles would be able to take care of themselves. I just hoped—with all my being—that they would make it in time to save Rylan.

Back in my room, I pulled out my Book of Shadows, the one passed down from my great-grandmother. I ran my fingers over the cover, and they tingled as they felt all those powerful spells within.

I wanted to learn all the spells. To master them, especially now that I knew there were other supernaturals in the world, and not all of them good. It was an advantage I was given.

As for the shifter part of me, I still hadn't made the change yet, but I knew it was coming. I could feel the wolf inside, growing in strength, getting ready to be set free.

I wondered when and how it would happen. Would it come with some kind of trigger? Maybe a life or death situation? Or would it happen randomly?

I hoped it wouldn't happen while I was in town shopping or around strangers. And hopefully the tattoo Addie Beaumont had given me when I first arrived would keep that from occurring.

Turning the pages, I came upon a spell—The Five Second Spell. This particular spell could freeze time around the caster for five seconds, and only the one who cast the spell would be able to move, while everyone else was frozen and unaware of anything going on.

The spell, in the wrong hands, could be dangerous. But in the right hands, five seconds could save a life. Or lives.

I memorized the spell and wondered if it would work.

"Hey, Eris," Camden called. "Have you seen my jacket?"

"It should be in the laundry room. On the dryer."

"It's not there," he hollered back. Then I realized I'd thrown it on when I went outside to check the mail this morning. It was lying over my chair. "Eris! I forgot I have to pick something up from the store. Could you please come down here and help me look for it."

I looked at the spell book and knew this would be the perfect time to try it out. I stepped out into the hallway holding the jacket behind my back and looked down to see Camden digging through the dryer in the laundry room.

I quickly recited the spell and . . . Camden stopped moving. He was frozen.

Holy crap! The spell worked!

I quickly tossed the jacket down, and it landed on the couch in the living room. Camden suddenly unfroze and smacked his head on the rim of the dryer.

"Dammit," he cursed as he rubbed the back of his head.

"Your jacket is right there on the couch," I said, pointing down at it.

"What?" He stood and looked at the couch, his brow furrowed. "It wasn't there a few seconds ago."

"Then it must have magically appeared," I said, shrugging.

Inside I was laughing, giddy the spell worked, and it made me want to learn more.

So to keep my mind from going insane until I heard word from my dad about Rylan, I stayed in my bedroom and went through the spell book, learning easy spells that might be helpful in the future.

Camden didn't show any signs of magic, and he was pretty sour about it. Maybe even a little jealous, and I didn't blame him. But my dad explained that in our family, the magic only seemed to pass to the women. He thought that maybe it was a spell by my great-great-grandmother, but he wasn't sure, and said my mom wasn't sure, either.

My stomach twisted inside, as I once again thought about Rylan. I hoped he was okay.

CHAPTER 6

RYLAN

*T*eeth and claws and fur collided in mid-air. Lars was strong, and his unhinged jaws and razor-sharp teeth seemed to be everywhere. He was relentless . . . but so was I.

Knowing what he did in Eris's dream, I kept my head down to block my neck. It seemed tearing out or slicing necks was his modus operandi.

Giant paws slammed into my side, ripping through skin, trying to push me back, but I was just as big and strong as he was. I rammed into him, using my head to push him back. He faltered a bit, allowing my claws to rake down his left shoulder, through fur and flesh.

Ducking, I dodged claws aimed for my cheek. As I turned away from him, he sunk his jaws into my right shoulder. Yelping, I sank my teeth into his back, thrashing my head from side to side until he howled in pain and his jaws unhooked.

As his head whipped back, I swiped my left paw against his face, aiming for his eye. I pushed my claws out, sinking deep into his eye socket. His eyeball burst, fluid spraying as I raked my razor-sharp claws downward.

Lars howled and backed away, part of his eye hanging like jelly. I went to strike again, but a car came down the road, headlights pointed in our direction.

While my attention wavered, Lars took off, running. This prick could not get away.

I gave chase, bounding after him, but he was faster than I'd thought. About a mile down the road, I lost him.

I stood in the middle of a four-way street and caught a faint scent of Lars on the breeze. But then I caught a new scent. An even stronger one—from members of my old pack.

I stopped and sniffed the cold wind. The scent was coming from the opposite direction where Lars had run. The coward. He'd finally met his match, but I knew it wouldn't be the last time I ran into him. He was power hungry and would come for revenge. But for now, I injured him. His healing powers couldn't give him a new eye, and he was now at a disadvantage, being partially blind. I'd go hunt for him after I made sure the others were still alive and safe.

Following their scents, I ended up at an old dilapidated shack that looked uninhabited. Before I approached, I raced back to my bike and shifted, changing into new clothes. I then slipped a gun into my pocket, one I'd had since I was young. It was my father's, and I'd only shot it a handful of times. In my human form, I'd need extra protection in case Lars returned.

Hopping on my bike, I headed back to the shack. As I neared it, I turned off the headlights and called out. "Keira? Keira, are you here?"

A few moments later, two figures exited. It was Keira and her mother Karina. They were dirty, their hair matted and clothes torn. They both ran up to me with tears streaming down their faces.

"Rylan. You came," Keira sobbed, her eyes wide with tears.

"I told you he'd come. I told you," her mom said, visibly shaken.

They looked like they hadn't eaten or bathed in days, so I reached in my pack and pulled out some water and a sandwich I'd made before I left. They gratefully took both, gobbling down the sandwich and drinking the water before saying another word.

"Where's the rest of the pack?" I asked, after I knew they could finally speak.

"Dead," Keira's mom replied, wiping a drip of water making its way down her chin. "We're all that's left."

I suddenly felt like shit. "I'm so sorry," I said, knowing those words weren't enough. "I should have come sooner."

"But you did come. And that's all that matters," Keira replied.

"Are you able to walk? There's a laundromat about a half mile up the road. I didn't see anyone inside, but they should have a bathroom where you can get cleaned up. I don't think Lars will show himself tonight, but if he does, I'll be ready." I held up the gun, and they both nodded.

I could tell they'd been through hell. I couldn't imagine what they had gone through to get to this point. I felt terrible, that since I'd left the pack with my mom and found Havenwood Falls, I'd lived well. Far from the life they had—a life of running and being scared shitless, not knowing when Lars would strike.

I hopped off my bike and pushed it, walking with them until we reached the laundromat. Sure enough, there was a bathroom at the back, and no one out this late.

"Go ahead," I said. "I'll stay here and keep watch."

"You're bleeding," Keira said, pointing at my right arm. Blood had soaked through my shirt. I didn't even notice until she'd pointed it out. It was from the bite Lars had given me on my right shoulder, and another one to my side, where his claws had raked my skin. I could feel the stinging, so I pulled my black leather jacket on to hide it all.

When they went into the laundromat, I took a better look at the wound. The bite marks were pretty deep, and would need attention. What worried me was the amount of blood I was losing. I had to find a way to stop it, but first, I needed to make sure they were safe.

I sniffed the air, but there was still no sign of Lars. When the girls returned, they looked a lot better. They'd cleaned their faces and braided their hair behind their backs. I gave them each an extra shirt I'd packed, not knowing how long I would be chasing Lars. They threw them on and tied them at the front, since they were large and baggy.

"Thank you," Karina said. Because Keira and I were the youngest in the pack, she'd had a part in raising me.

She put her arm around her daughter. They looked so much alike. They had the same caramel-colored skin, curly onyx hair, dark brown eyes, and tall, thin frames.

"You're welcome. There's a mini-mart another mile down the road. I'll give you some money to buy some food and whatever else you need, while I figure out what we're going to do next."

I had hoped there would be another male left, so he could possibly take over as alpha. Because it was just the two of them, I would have to rethink. Maybe they could live a life without a pack. Find a place where they could be safe, and live normal lives.

I couldn't take them back to Havenwood Falls while Lars was still alive. He'd track us all right back to the town and finish what he started. I wasn't going to allow that bastard anywhere near that town, even if it meant me not returning.

As much as I wanted to go back to the life I had, I couldn't. I wouldn't risk the Blaekthorns' lives or what they'd worked so hard to gain. I was all Keira and Karina had now, and felt I was responsible for them until they could make it on their own. It's what my father would have wanted me to do.

We walked to the mini-mart, my senses on full alert, but it seemed as if Lars was truly gone. He was probably trying to figure out what to do with the eyeball hanging out of its socket.

I gave Karina some money and told them to buy whatever they wanted while I sat on my bike and waited. Feeling a little light-headed, I knew we had to find a safe place soon, because I needed to bandage up my wounds and rest. And the motel wasn't exactly a safe place.

Eris was probably worried as shit by now. And the only freaking thing I was worried about was that she'd never forgive me. She'd tried to get me to open up, and I completely shut her down. Her family had taken me in, and I walked out. I wouldn't blame them for hating me.

I glanced at my watch, wondering how much longer Keira and Karina were going to take. Minute by minute, I was feeling weaker. The corners of my vision were darkening, and I was still losing a lot of blood. It was dripping down my fingers and onto the pavement.

Then I took in a deep breath and caught his scent. Lars was back. He was back, and I was in no condition to fight him. I wasn't even sure I could shift.

I looked to the side of the mini-mart and saw one red glowing eye. Then he took a step out of the shadows, his snout soaked with blood and his marred eye patched, confirming he was able to shift at will.

His sharp teeth were bared. He knew he'd injured me, and now he was back for the kill. I reached in my pocket for the gun, but everything around me was a blur.

Keira and Karina exited the mini-mart. Their bag of groceries dropped, some fruit and drinks rolling out into the parking lot. Lars's head snapped toward them, and they froze.

"Get back inside!" I yelled, but they weren't moving. "Karina. Take Keira inside." It was the first time I'd used my alpha authority. Both of their eyes connected with mine. "Now." Karina nodded and pulled her daughter back inside.

Lars stepped out even farther. The hackles on his back were erect.

"You're going to die, pup," he growled.

How the hell could I hear him? I was only connected to and could only hear the members of my own family and pack. Then I heard a wicked laugh. "You've no idea who you're up against. I ripped your father to shreds, slit your mother's throat, and in a moment, you will join them."

"Why? Who the hell made you God, to decide who lives and who dies?"

"Your father stole my birthright. I was rightful alpha," he snapped. "He was a fraud."

"You bastard. You don't know what the hell you're talking

160

about!" I roared, trying to get off the bike, but the world around me was darkening and my legs tingling.

Another growl reverberated through the parking lot. "Ask your father. You'll be reunited with him soon enough."

He took another step toward me, crouched and ready to strike. I was ready to fight to the death and wouldn't give him the pleasure of taking my life so easily.

"See you in hell," Lars roared, rearing back to pounce at me.

Suddenly, tires screeched into the parking lot, then someone called my name. It sounded like Eris's father.

I turned to see a large black truck come to a halt and all three Blaekthorn men jump out. I could feel the strength of their pack—my pack—and when I turned back, Lars was gone.

Piers and Garrick were immediately at my side. Barney was checking the area, while Garrick helped me off the bike.

"What happened?" Piers asked.

"He was here," I breathed and lifted my finger to where Lars was crouched a moment earlier.

"Garrick, stay with him. I'll be back," Piers said, running to the side of the mini-mart and into the shadows. I knew he'd shifted because I felt that raw power of the pack's alpha vibrating through the air.

"Where are you hurt?" Garrick asked, and I pointed to my shoulder. It was an effort to stay awake and keep from blacking out.

He slid my jacket off and took a look at the wound, then let out a few expletives.

"Barney, run inside and get me some alcohol and bandages. As many as you can." Garrick turned his attention to me. "There are a couple of wounds that I'll need to cauterize immediately. Once we get the bleeding stopped, you should be able to heal a lot faster."

"Do it," I said. I'd suffered similar pain in my past. This was just another to add to my list. "There are two women inside. Survivors."

"We'll take care of them," Garrick said, pulling a hunting knife from his pocket before heading to the back of the vehicle. A few moments later, he returned carrying a blowtorch.

"Where'd you get that?" I questioned.

"We're outdoorsmen. This is a convenience," he replied with a wide grin.

Barney came back with the alcohol, so Garrick poured some over his knife and then over my wounds. I bit back a yelp as he told Barney about Keira and Karina. Barney said he saw them near the back of the store, so he went back inside to get them.

Garrick lit the blowtorch and started heating up his blade. When the blade was orange, he gave me a look.

I moaned. "Hey, no pain no gain, right?"

"Yeah, something like that," he said, holding my arm firmly. "This is gonna hurt."

"I know. Do it before—"

He pressed the searing blade to my wound, and a growl ripped from my throat. It sizzled, burning and melting my flesh. A few moments felt like an eternity before he finally lifted the blade.

"The bleeding stopped on this wound. One down, one to go," Garrick said, pouring more alcohol over the knife to clean off the blood. "You still with me?"

I nodded, trying to catch my breath.

Barney came out with Keira and Karina, and they stood in front of us, watching.

"This next wound looks a little deeper." He made Barney press a cloth to the wound while he heated the blade.

The loss of blood already had me weak, to the point of passing out, and I felt like one more scorching blade to my shoulder would do me in. I sucked in deep breaths, trying to stay focused and coherent, when Piers finally returned.

"He's gone," he said. "I tracked him a few miles down, but the wind shifted, and I lost his scent. That bastard must have been moving."

"He'd better, with the Blaekthorn brothers on his trail." Barney laughed.

Piers laid a palm on my left shoulder. "Hang in there, Rylan." I could only nod, trying to keep the pain at bay. "Eris is the reason we're here," he continued, probably trying to divert my attention. "And by the looks of it, we came just in time."

I nodded again, and a smile lifted on my lips. Eris. I knew she would send them. I just hoped she wasn't too upset that I left without telling her.

Pain! Skin sizzled and melted together under the red-hot blade, cauterizing the wound. I was panting now, trying to keep in the moment. But it was too much.

"He's fading," Garrick's voice said, as darkness overcame me.

CHAPTER 7

ERIS

I nearly tripped down the stairs when the house phone rang. Cell phones had no service in our area of town, so we relied on our landline.

"Dad?" I puffed, knowing he would be the only one calling this late.

"We're on our way home," he said, like he would on any normal call.

"What about Rylan?" That was the one question hammering my mind for the past few hours.

"He's with us. We're all fine, but he's unconscious from a bite wound. It shouldn't be fatal. Your Uncle Garrick cauterized the ones that weren't healing quickly enough. We'll have to monitor him tonight."

"What about Lars? The other shifter?"

"He got away. But we have two survivors, a girl and her mother, whom we're bringing home with us."

I wondered if it was the girl Keira, and if Rylan knew if my dad and uncles were bringing them. He'd told me he didn't want them in Havenwood Falls, because he knew they would draw Lars here, too.

"Where will they stay?" I questioned.

"Tonight, they'll be staying with us. Get some extra blankets from the closet, and some clothes. They can stay in the living room tonight, and I'll figure out other accommodations for them in the morning."

"Sure. I'm on it."

I was just glad they were all safe and on their way back.

~

CAMDEN CAME HOME right as I was setting up the living room.

"Sleepover?" he teased as he walked through the door. But his smile dropped and his emotions shifted when he saw my expression.

"Dad found Rylan. He's injured."

"Where is he?"

"He was in Montrose. Dad, Uncle Garrick, and Uncle Barney are with him. They're on their way back now, but are also bringing two members of his old pack. I think it's the girl who met him at the Festival of Lights and her mother."

He nodded slowly. "How bad is his injury?"

"I don't know. Dad said he was bitten and a few of the wounds needed to be cauterized."

"Need help with anything?"

"No. But thanks."

"Okay," he replied. "I'll be in my room. Let me know when they arrive."

"I will." I watched Camden bound up the stairs. It was so odd, after all these years, to finally have a big brother I had forgotten about. But even after all those lost years, we seemed to have fallen effortlessly into our family roles, just as if we had been together since the beginning.

Camden was everything I thought a big brother would be like. Yes, he was protective, but he was also caring and still very sorry for the past and wanting our mother to live, rather than me. And I could tell he was trying to make up for it.

After setting up the bedding in the living room, I paced back and forth and up and down the stairs. It was driving me crazy not knowing how injured Rylan was, or how it happened. As soon as I heard tires on the gravel drive outside, I called up to Camden then ran out into the cold without a jacket. A wall of frigid air slammed into me, but I didn't care. I had to see him.

Uncle Garrick exited the front passenger seat first, and gave me a sad smile. "He'll be okay, but he'll need rest and time to heal."

I exhaled a bit of the building stress as the rear door opened.

Keira was the first to exit, and then an older woman who looked just like her slid out. Uncle Barney hopped out, and he and Uncle Garrick stood on each side of the passenger door. My eyes remained fixed into the dark space, waiting.

Then a soft moan exited the vehicle before he did. Rylan slowly slid out and looked at me, his hazel eyes filled with pain and . . . remorse. He was covered in blood—so much blood. It was smeared on his face and hands and had soaked through his shirt.

I wanted to run over to help, but Uncle Garrick took his left arm and Uncle Barney put a hand on his back for support. He cringed as he took a step.

"If he needs someone to look after him," Camden said from behind me, "I can stay over. Just to make sure he's still breathing in the morning."

"You sure?" Garrick asked.

"Yeah, he helped save me. It's the least I can do."

"Eris, why don't you show the ladies inside," my dad said. "It's awfully cold."

I'd totally forgotten about them standing off to the side.

"Come inside," I said, waving them forward.

They looked at each other first before following me in. I gave Rylan one last glance before I went inside, and he, in turn, gave me a pained grin.

"Keira, right?" I said, extending my hand.

"Yes," she answered, taking mine. "Thank you." She turned to the woman. "This is my mom, Karina."

I shook Karina's hand. "It's nice to meet you. Please, make yourselves at home." I pointed them to the bathroom, where there were clean towels and toiletries set up for them to shower. They were both a little taller than me, but they looked the same size, so I handed them each some new pajamas Aunt Vera had given me, along with some new undergarments. "These should fit. At least until we can get you to town to get some better ones."

"These will be wonderful," Karina said.

"There are food and drinks in the fridge and cupboard. Please, help yourself. We have more than enough." The two of them looked at each other with tears in their eyes. How long had they been on the run? How long had they been out in the cold without a shower, or food, or drink? Things that we didn't pay much mind to were so precious to them.

"You go first, Mom," Keira said, pointing to the bathroom. She nodded and smiled, wiping a stray tear trickling down her cheek.

"Good night, guys," Uncle Barney said loudly. "I'm outta here. Aunt Lydia will bust my balls if I don't get home soon."

Camden ran in and up the stairs. "Gonna grab some clothes."

I peeked outside and watched Garrick and Rylan slowly making their way toward their cabin, Rylan obviously in a lot of pain.

"Did you guys give him pain medicine?" I hollered after them.

"No," Uncle Garrick replied. "He knocked out before we could give him anything."

I headed to the medicine cabinet and found a bottle of extra strength Tylenol, then grabbed a bottle of water and ran out the door after them. I felt like I needed to help, even if it was only offering him pills.

They were almost to their front porch when I reached them. "I have pain meds."

"I'll take six," Rylan said with a grin.

"But . . . six isn't healthy," I said.

"Eris, he doesn't give a damn about his liver right now." Camden chuckled, coming up behind them. "He's in pain. Besides, he's a wolf with a very high metabolism. His kidneys will be fine."

I shook six pills out from the bottle and handed them to Rylan.

His hand was covered in blood, and I wasn't sure if it was his or the other guy's.

He gulped them down with the entire bottle of water.

"Thanks," he said, wiping a drip on his chin. His eyes lingered on mine, and I knew he wanted to talk.

"Tomorrow," I whispered. "After you've rested."

He nodded.

"Ry, you totally need to shower. You look like you've been in a mass murder," Camden jested.

Rylan gave a slight grin. "At least I took the guy's eye out."

"No way," Camden said.

"Yeah, I sunk my claws into his socket and the freaking eyeball burst. Eye juice splattered and eye jelly was hanging down the side of his face."

"Oh, God," I coughed, gagging as I pictured the scene.

Camden laughed. "Dude, that's messed up."

"Yeah, it was disturbingly brutal, but it felt great. And it was payback for the bastard biting me," Rylan coughed. "He would have killed me, but the cavalry came just in time." Rylan glanced at Garrick. "Thanks, again."

"Eris is the one you should be thanking," he said. "It was her premonition and gut feeling that led us to you."

Rylan's gaze turned to me, his expression telling me how thankful he was.

"Hey, Eris," Camden said, before opening the door.

"Yeah?"

"If he needs to be bandaged, I'll call you."

I laughed and turned back toward my house. "Fine."

When I walked in, Keira was hugging her pajamas. She looked so lost and sad and probably didn't have many friends, if any. Maybe I'd take them shopping tomorrow. They both needed some new clothes and winter jackets, so maybe we could head over to Backwoods Sport & Ski. The Kasuns—another pack of wolf shifters in town—owned the shop, so I could probably introduce them.

When Karina exited the bathroom, my dad approached her.

"Tomorrow, I'll have to take you both to get registered. It's something we nonhumans have to do in this town. And you'll each be given a temporary tattoo. It doesn't hurt, but you will be able to control your shifting at will."

"Really?" Keira's voice went up an octave, her eyes wide. "Shifting at will?"

"Yes, at least while you're staying here in the town."

"Okay."

"If you need anything, please let us know," my dad added.

"You're very kind," Karina said, bowing her head.

"Good night, everyone," my dad said, before heading up the stairs and disappearing into his room.

Keira slipped into the bathroom, while Karina got settled into bed.

Inside my room, I felt the stress over Rylan's safety melt away. At least he was here now, and he was safe.

CHAPTER 8

ERIS

*T*he warmth of the sun shining through my window woke me. Glancing at the time, I saw it was eight o'clock. I guess Rylan didn't need help changing his bandages. After changing into jeans and a long-sleeved tee, I threw on a gray hoodie and decided to head downstairs to cook some breakfast.

As soon as I opened the door, I smelled food and heard voices. Aunt Vera and Aunt Lydia were already here, and by the smell, they'd probably whipped up a breakfast to die for.

Heading down the stairs, I noticed the kitchen counter filled with all kinds of breakfast food.

"Good morning, Eris," Aunt Lydia said, with a bright red apron and lipstick on. She and Aunt Vera looked like they could be on the cover of some cooking magazine. How on earth could they look so good this early in the morning? It was a miracle I'd managed to brush my teeth and get my hair untangled.

Karina and Keira were sitting at the table, chatting and laughing.

"Good morning," I said, waving to them.

"Good morning," they replied in unison.

"When did you guys get here?" I asked my aunts. I didn't hear them come in, let alone cook all this food.

"About an hour ago. Your dad called and said the girls were up, so we decided to welcome them with breakfast. Come and eat."

The table was filled with pancakes, sausages, bacon, hash browns, cinnamon rolls, and muffins. Hot coffee steamed from the French press, so that was the first place I went.

"Where's my dad?" I asked.

"He ate and took off. He said he had some work to do at the warehouse, and then he had a meeting with Sheriff Kasun and the Court to discuss the matter about the other shifter."

"Oh, okay," I said, snagging a chocolate muffin and some bacon. My dad had always been thorough. He never procrastinated. He did whatever needed to be done as soon as he could.

"He said he'll be back in a few hours to take Keira and Karina to register and get their tattoos," Aunt Lydia added.

"Hey, Eris, could you run over to my place and see if Camden is up? I tried calling, but it went straight to his answering service. His phone might be dead. If he is, tell him to come and eat before the food gets cold," Aunt Vera suggested.

"Sure." I was eager to check on Rylan anyway.

My heart pattered as I stood outside of Rylan's door. I quickly rapped twice and waited. When there was no answer, I slowly opened the door and peeked inside. Camden wasn't on the floor, so I swung the door open a little wider to see Rylan on his bed, lying on his back.

I looked down the hall and noticed the bathroom door was shut, so Cam must have gone inside. He'd be there for a while, so I decided to go in and check on Rylan.

His shirt was off, revealing his muscular arms, chest, and abs. The blanket covered his navel and everything below. I stepped in and tiptoed over to where he was. The bandage was off and lying on the floor next to his bed. Most of the smaller wounds had already healed. The larger ones were still visible, but the skin was connecting. Then, I noticed one wound that looked like Uncle Garrick had cauterized it. It was bright red and swollen.

I automatically reached over and gently rubbed my fingertips over the skin. It was hot.

"Couldn't wait to get your hands on me, cupcake?" Rylan whispered.

I gasped and snapped my hand back, then saw that crooked grin. That smirk I'd grown to love.

"Yeah, something like that," I exhaled, narrowing my eyes. "I thought you were sleeping."

"I was . . . until you touched me," he said. "I thought I was dreaming." He reached out and grabbed my hand. "I know you're probably pissed that I left without telling you. I'm really sorry."

"Don't," I breathed.

"No, I have to say this," he said, gently squeezing my fingers. "You were right. I should have told you. If I had, Lars would probably be dead, and I wouldn't be injured. But this is what I wanted to avoid happening to your family."

I was upset he didn't tell me, but not enough. I did see his side. He was looking out for me. And my family. "I know. And I forgive you."

"You do?" His eyes narrowed as if he thought I was going to fight him.

"I'm worried about this wound," I said, pointing to the area. "The scar tissue from the cauterization, and the surrounding area is swollen. It's bright red and hot. I think it's infected."

He tried to sit up, but plopped back down with a groan. He was still in pain. "I think I need more pills and water."

Sweat had beaded on his head, so I placed my hand to his forehead. "You have a fever. I think you should go to the clinic."

"No," he said quickly. "I just need rest. The injury is taking a bit longer to heal because it was more severe than the others."

"Then I'm going to get a second opinion."

"Can you come closer?" he whispered, tugging on my hand. "I have something important to tell you."

I took a step closer, until my legs were touching the bed, and bent over to hear what he had to say. His hand disconnected from mine, and in a flash was behind my neck, pulling me closer.

"Rylan," I breathed, but didn't fight it. I'd wanted to kiss him since the moment he returned.

His warm lips met mine, his breath sweet and minty. His fingers gently tangled in my hair, pushing me closer. His kiss deepened. His gentle touch, the way his tongue danced along my lips and raked across my teeth—even injured, he was setting me on fire.

"Well, that's some wake-up call," Cam snickered, making me gasp and pull back.

Damn him.

Rylan smiled and took my hand. "I was just wishing Eris a good morning," he replied.

"Yeah, sure." Cam threw on a T-shirt.

"Aunt Vera and Aunt Lydia cooked a huge breakfast next door. They sent me over to tell you the food is ready and you'd better hurry if you want it warm."

"I'm there." Camden stopped at the door. "Please, no making out until I leave the house," he said, then disappeared.

I turned back to Rylan, and he pulled me back down for one more breathless kiss.

"You're trying to distract me," I breathed, my head spinning.

"Is it working?" Another sly grin.

"No," I said, walking toward the door. "Stay here and . . . maybe put on a shirt." My eyes raked down his chest to his abs, and for a split second, I wanted to see what was below the blanket.

Rylan's hand went to the blanket, and my face immediately heated. "You're welcome to join me," he purred.

I backed up a little farther. "Tempting. But I'm going to go now, and get that second opinion."

"I THINK we need to get him to the clinic. This is infected, and I'm not sure why. He should be healing," Aunt Vera said, looking at the area. Rylan had thrown on a tank top, and I was thankful. "Let me make a call and see if someone can see him."

"No, it's fine."

"Rylan Gilles, you are living under our roof and under our care," she said in a motherly tone.

"Yes, ma'am," he replied.

A few minutes later, she came back. "The clinic is empty right now and Dr. Underwood just came in—that nice man who cared for Camden. So get ready. I'm driving."

Aunt Vera drove, and I sat in the back of her Expedition with Rylan. His face was a little pale, and he was still sweating, even though the air was icy cold.

Inside the clinic, Aunt Vera checked in while we waited.

"Room two, Rylan," she announced.

He stood.

"Do you want me to come with you?" I asked.

A grin. "If you want to. I'll probably have to take my shirt off again."

"Can't you just answer with a yes or no?"

He chuckled. "Come with me, cupcake."

"Fine," I exhaled, and grabbed hold of his hand.

We didn't wait long before Dr. Underwood came in wearing a white lab coat. He greeted us with a firm handshake and a smile.

"What's going on, Rylan?" the doctor asked, standing in front of him.

"I got into a tussle with another shifter, outside of Havenwood Falls," he answered. "My injuries are healing, except one. We think it might be infected."

"All right. I'll need you to remove your shirt so I can take a look."

While the doctor turned his back to put some gloves on, Rylan gave me a sexy side-eyed glance, and a wink, which made my stomach turn and my cheeks blush. I rolled my eyes, but kept them on him as he pulled his shirt over his head with his uninjured arm.

The doctor stepped up to him and held his hand over the infected area.

"There is something beneath the skin that shouldn't be there. That's why it won't heal and why there is an infection. I'll need to make a small incision to extract it."

Dr. Underwood was good. My aunt told me he was fae, so seeing him diagnose what was wrong without even touching Rylan had me in awe.

"Do you know what it is?" I asked.

He turned to me and shook his head. "I won't know until I get in there."

He went to the cabinet and brought back a few things. After dipping a cotton ball into a solution, he rubbed it across Rylan's shoulder.

"This is to disinfect the area," he said, then brought out a small needle. "And this is to numb the area."

He shot liquid into a few areas, and Rylan didn't even flinch. While we waited, he gathered a small incision knife and a long tweezer-like instrument.

He had Rylan lay back, as the wound was near his collarbone. Then he made a small incision, about an inch long. Using the tweezer thing, he reached in and pulled something out, dropping it into a cup filled with solution. He used a few butterfly closures to seal the wound, then placed gauze and held it down with some tape.

Dr. Underwood held up the cup and inspected what he had extracted.

His navy-blue eyes shifted to Rylan. "It looks like a tooth."

CHAPTER 9

RYLAN

a tooth? That bastard's freaking tooth was inside of me?

"Hey, Doc," I said, wondering if he could help make sense of something bothering me. "Is it possible to run a DNA test on that tooth?"

His eyes narrowed and so did Eris's.

"Is there something you'd like to find out?" Dr. Underwood asked.

"Yes, I want to find out if the owner of that tooth is somehow . . . related to me."

"Rylan," Eris breathed, questions swirling in her eyes. "Who do you think he is?"

"I don't know, but he said something to me last night that made me think."

"It is possible to take a DNA sample from a tooth," Dr. Underwood replied. "But I'll need to take a blood sample from you as well. I could have the results back in a day or two."

"That's perfect. Thank you, doctor."

The thought of Lars being related to me soured my stomach.

My father never had any brothers, or never mentioned any. I was born when my grandfather was alpha and was there when he died and my father gained his position.

I just needed to know. I wanted to find out why he would say those things to me . . . that he should have been alpha. Ever since I'd heard those words, my mind had become a whirlwind. There had to be more. A true motive behind all the murderous bloodshed. He was settling a personal vendetta, and I needed to find out the reason why.

After we left the clinic, Eris was quiet on the ride home. I knew her mind was spinning just as much as mine was, but I didn't want to talk while her aunt was in the vehicle.

As she pulled home and exited the car, I grabbed hold of Eris's hand.

"Can we talk?" I whispered.

She nodded, so I led her to the back of the cabins, where the family had built a greenhouse filled with flowers and vegetables. Inside, the greenhouse was warm. Red and white poinsettias were in full bloom.

As we walked down the center aisle, filled with flowers, Eris stopped me.

"Talk to me, Rylan."

I'd been so accustomed to shutting down, quenching all feelings inside to survive. But she, this girl whom fate had brought into my life, was demanding I open up. This was new for me, but I supposed it was a good thing. Because she was good, and was slowly chipping away at my calloused heart.

I wrapped my good arm around her and pulled her against me, because whenever she was close, I felt a little stronger. A little more . . . whole. She didn't pull or back away from me, so I looked deep into her beautiful golden eyes.

"First of all . . . I haven't properly thanked you."

Her eyes narrowed. "For what?"

"Your dream. Or nightmare. It was real. The details you gave me were so eerily similar to the area I was in, I couldn't help but believe everything else. The sign. The motel. The flickering light in the parking lot, and . . . Lars, standing downwind in the shadows. It all happened just like you said." I felt a pang of sadness as I thought of my mother. "I had to believe, because my mother also had the gift of premonition. She had dreamed of this place. And when she died, I followed that dream. It led me here, to Havenwood Falls." I cupped her face in my hands. "It led me to you." I pressed a kiss on her soft, sweet lips.

She stood there, eyes closed, and when they opened, she smiled. I ran my fingers down her soft cheek.

"Because of you, I'm standing here right now." A tear trickled down her face, and I wiped it away.

"What did that monster say to make you consider a DNA test?"

I knew she'd ask, and I decided I wasn't going to hide anything from her anymore.

"He told me that my father stole his birthright. And that he should have been alpha."

Eris shook her head. "That means he has to be related to you . . . to your father."

"I don't know. My father didn't have any siblings. He never mentioned any and neither did my mom. Or my grandparents. Maybe he's just insane. There is a reason why he is alone and not part of a pack. Rogue shifters have reputations for being wild and brutal, and I know that my father was the only one who had right to be alpha."

Eris plucked a flower from one of the pots and ran her fingers against the soft petals. "So, when did Lars show up?"

I had to think back. "After my grandfather died. It was a few weeks after my dad had become alpha. Like I told you before, our pack was one of the strongest, and targeted by rival packs. He claimed he was stronger and should take over. He also claimed he was in love with my mom, but how the hell did he even know her?" The last part I whispered to myself. But it was a good question. How the hell could he love someone he never knew?

"Was he stalking her?"

I thought back to the one time I'd remembered Lars coming into our camp and confronting my father. "The way he and my father talked, it was like they knew each other. And my mother. Lars held out his hand to her, begging for her to come to him. But her only reply was to stand next to my father and take hold of his hand, showing where her loyalty lay. With my father. In the hands of her husband and her alpha.

"That's when I saw the fury in his eyes. The same fury he had when he looked at me that night." I closed my eyes. "He called my father a fraud."

Eris ran her hand down my arm, sending a wave of goose bumps in her wake. "Rylan, are you sure you want to find out who this man is?"

I looked deep into her eyes and asked myself the same question.

"I want to know the truth," I finally admitted. "I need to know if my father was rightful alpha, and why this psycho would claim he was."

Then it was Eris who took my face into her soft, warm hands. "I am here for you, no matter what the report says."

"I know you are," I murmured, kissing her deeply. This girl. This half witch, half shifter who was still trying to find her place in the world, was trying her best to help me, the damaged shifter.

Fate led me to her. I knew it from the first moment I saw her standing in the doorway of the medical clinic. It felt as if her soul called to me, and every molecule in my body answered. I'd never felt more settled. She did that to me. She slowly filled that deep, dark emptiness in my chest with her light.

But with Lars still out there, I had to be extra careful. I would protect her at all costs. And, if it came down to it, I would give my life for her.

CHAPTER 10

ERIS

My dad came home and called a family meeting. He said he'd shared the information about the encounter with Lars with Sheriff Kasun and also with a woman at the Court of the Sun and the Moon. She said she would let the others know.

"All right, I have to take Keira and Karina to register and get their tattoos with Addie. They will be staying with us until we can find them a safe place of their own." My dad looked at Karina, and she nodded, placing a hand over her heart.

"Thank you."

I pulled my dad to the side. "Hey, do you think I can come with you? I'd like to take them to Backwoods Sport & Ski after to get them each a jacket and maybe a few warm things."

My dad wrapped his arms around me. "I'm proud of the woman you're becoming," he said. Then he slipped his credit card in my hand. "Get whatever they need to make them feel comfortable."

"You're the best," I said, hugging him tightly.

"No, you are. Now, let's get moving."

"Always the alpha."

"Always," he laughed.

"I'm gonna head over to my own bed and crash the rest of the day," Rylan said.

"Good," Cam replied. "Because I'm gonna crash on my bed for the rest of the day too."

xxx

The registration and the tattoos were done in less than an hour, and then my dad drove us to Backwoods Sport & Ski.

"This is a quaint town," Karina said. "So much charm."

"It is," I said. "My dad and I recently moved here, too."

"You did? It seems as if you've lived here for a long time."

"Well, it's complicated," I said, and saw my dad's eyes examining me in the rearview mirror. "I'll share the story another time."

Karina smiled. "Sounds good."

My dad pulled up in front of the store and let us out. "I've got to meet with a client about an upcoming order, and then was given the task of picking up dinner at Pyntz Butcher Shoppe. I'll pick you ladies up in an hour?"

"Sure," I said. "How about getting us at Coffee Haven."

"Fine. Go ahead and feed that caffeine addiction."

"Thanks, Dad." I slid out of the vehicle. "Let's go, ladies!"

"Where are we going?" Keira asked.

"Shopping," I said with a smile.

It took a while for me to convince Karina to pick something out, but when I told her that Keira and I would have to choose for her, she buckled.

They each got one warm jacket and enough shirts and pants to last a week. I even talked them into getting some new shoes, as their old ones had holes and weren't fit for the winter weather. Or walking, for that matter.

As we made our way to the register, I noticed how pale Keira had become, as if she'd seen a ghost. Her eyes were wide and frozen outside the window. When I turned to look, a man in a dark, hooded overcoat quickly turned and walked away.

"Keira, who was that?" I asked, but she didn't answer. She was trembling.

Meanwhile, Karina was looking at activity brochures the store offered.

"Hey, is she okay?" the girl behind the register asked. She looked so familiar, with dark, chin-length hair. She was wearing jeans, a T-shirt, and a fleece jacket with the Backwoods Sport & Ski logo on the front.

"Are you Willa Kasun?" I asked.

"I am," she answered with a smile.

"Nice to finally meet you," I said. "I met your brother, Kase."

"Oh, unfortunately," she giggled. "He's my twin brother."

"That's why you looked familiar."

Her brown eyes darted to Keira with concern. "Hey, does your friend need something? Water? A seat?"

I looked at Keira. Her eyes were still focused on the window.

"Karina, I think something is wrong with Keira," I said softly, trying not to make a scene. There were a few visitors in the store.

She walked over and grabbed her daughter's hand. "Keira, what's wrong?"

Keira's attention finally snapped to her mother. "I thought I saw a ghost."

"Oh," Willa chimed in. "And it won't be your last, here in Havenwood Falls. There are quite a few of them lingering about."

"No kidding." I laughed, knowing exactly what she meant.

Karina pulled Keira to the side and spoke quietly with her while I paid.

"You're new here?" Willa asked, swiping the card.

"Yes." I extended a hand to her. "I'm Eris Blaekthorn."

"Blaekthorn? You're Camden's sister?"

"Yes."

"How is he? I heard about the . . . incident."

"Yeah," I sighed. "He's alive and kicking and very snarky."

Willa chuckled. "So he's back to his old self."

"Yep."

She handed me the receipt and the bags. "It was nice to meet you, Eris." She leaned in and whispered, "Kase told me you haven't shifted yet. If you want to talk sometime, just give me a call."

182

"I will. Thank you." She handed me a business card. "I guess I'll be seeing you around."

"I'm sure you will."

Outside, I handed Keira and Karina their jackets and they slipped into them.

"How about we go and get something hot to drink?" I pointed to Coffee Haven. "I think we all need some caffeine."

"Do they have tea?" Karina asked.

"They do."

As soon as I stepped into the coffee shop, I took in a deep breath. Heaven. It smelled like heaven.

We found an empty table at the back, then I got their orders and stood in line. I was desperate to know why Keira was so affected by the guy she'd seen.

Back at the table, I handed them their drinks, and Keira was still visibly shaken. "Hey, Keira. Are you all right?"

She nodded but stayed silent, her hands wrapped around her drink.

"Did you recognize the guy who walked past the window?" I asked bluntly. I didn't want to be left in the dark, especially when my family and I were a part of their lives.

Keira nodded. "I swear it was someone from our pack, but he's dead. We saw his body."

"Whose body?" I questioned.

"Axel's."

The breath caught in my throat. "The last alpha of your pack?"

She nodded.

Axel was Rylan's father's best friend, and the one who took over as alpha after he died.

I took Keira by the hand. "Are you sure it was him?"

She shrugged. "It looked exactly like him. He stared right at me."

"But he's dead, Keira. We saw his body," Karina said.

"How do we know it was his body? It didn't have a head."

"But it was his clothes, and he was wearing the ring."

"You know how easy it would be to plant a body and fake a death, especially if the body is headless? It could have been anyone."

Karina closed her eyes and rubbed her temples. "This is too much. I don't know what to think anymore."

I felt the same way, and couldn't wait for my dad to come and pick us up. Would this madness ever end? There were so many questions blasting in my mind, but one had me frightened.

"Hey," I whispered. "What if Axel got away and Lars faked his death to terrify the pack? And, if Axel is here . . . what if Lars followed him? What if Lars is already here too?"

"Gods no," Karina exhaled.

The mystery was plunging deeper and deeper.

When my dad finally pulled up, I told him everything that had happened. He was our protector and needed to know. On our way home, he had Keira describe what Axel looked like, and then called his brothers for a family meeting.

"Dad, I'm going next door to tell Rylan. He needs to know."

He nodded. "There's a meeting at our place in an hour. I want everyone there. If there is a threat already in the town, we have to cover all of our bases and make sure everyone is safe."

"Okay," I said, then ran next door.

Aunt Vera's and Uncle Garrick's cars were gone, so I lifted the wolf statue on the porch and took the spare key.

Inside, I ran upstairs to Rylan's room and knocked on the door. When he didn't answer, I slowly turned the knob and cracked the door open. His blackout curtains were drawn, making the room completely dark. I couldn't see anything beyond the threshold.

"Rylan," I whispered. "Rylan?"

I pushed the door open further and gasped when I saw golden-rimmed eyes close by.

A hand grabbed my wrist and yanked me inside. Lips crashed against mine as I was flipped onto the bed, and a large, warm body pressed on top of me.

"You dare come into my lair and wake me?" Rylan purred, his tongue swirling against my neck.

Oh, God. He was trouble. So much trouble.

"Rylan, I have to tell you something," I breathed.

"You know how long I've waited to get you alone?" His hands were everywhere, his teeth nipping at my ear and down my neck, extracting a moan. His breath was heavy, his body hot. So hot.

My fingers trailed up his muscular back and tangled in his hair. I wanted him so badly. Wanted his lips, his tongue, his mouth.

As if Rylan heard my thoughts, his mouth crashed down on mine, slow and sensual. I arched into him, and he rocked his hips into mine. Holy hell. This could go too far too fast.

I had to remember why I was here. *Why?*

"Axel," I breathed.

That one word instantly killed the moment.

"What?" Rylan growled, pushing off me.

"Keira said she saw Axel in town," I said, still breathless.

He didn't answer, but then a lamp clicked on, gilding his beautiful face. Dammit, he was so freaking hot.

"Axel's dead," he said, raking his fingers through his hair.

I sat up and adjusted my top. "Yes, that's what she said, but now, she's not so sure."

"Why wouldn't she be sure?"

"Because the body they found was headless. It had his clothes and ring, so they assumed it was him."

Rylan cursed.

"I'm sorry. I just thought you should know."

Rylan exhaled and his eyes softened. "Thank you. Did Karina see him too?"

"No. But Keira looked like she'd seen a ghost."

I couldn't read the expression on Rylan's face. But at this moment, I wished I hadn't killed what we had going. Because for that moment, the weight of the world had been lifted off his shoulders.

"I really am sorry," I said, standing from the bed.

"Come here," he said, his eyes still glinting with gold. As I stepped closer, he wrapped his arms around me. "Why are you sorry?"

"Because I was the bearer of bad news and completely killed our moment."

His hand traveled down my back, resting on my butt. "Oh, we'll have more mind-blowing moments. I'm sure of it."

"Even more mind-blowing than that last kiss?"

"Cupcake, you have no idea," he purred against my ear, sending a chill down my spine.

"Good. Then I have one more message." I grimaced, and he dropped his head and sighed.

"What is it?"

"Family meeting in—" I glanced at my watch—"forty-five minutes."

"I'll be there."

"I'm glad." I wrapped my arms around his bare waist and stole one more breathless kiss before slinking away. I knew if we were alone for any length of time, things would go from hot to inferno in no time.

CHAPTER 11

RYLAN

*T*he entire family gathered in the living room at Piers's house. Even Barney's twins, Weston and Drake, showed up. I hadn't seen them in a few weeks, but they seemed to be getting taller. They weren't very talkative, probably because they were more involved in social media than socially interacting with real people. And they were gamers. Fortnite was their newest obsession, and from what I'd heard, these boys were tearing it up online.

My shoulder was well on the mend. The incision had already sealed together, and the swelling had gone down. Benefits of being a wolf shifter.

The family gathered in the living room, and Eris sat next to me on the love seat, her body pressed against mine. I didn't know what it was about her that drove me crazy. Maybe the fact that she was getting closer to shifting. But everything about her appealed to me. And every day it seemed to get stronger. Her inner wolf was connected to mine, and I knew she felt it, too.

I ran a finger down her arm and watched goose bumps rise. It took everything inside of me not to throw her over my shoulder and drag her upstairs. That, and the fact that her entire family was sitting around me.

Piers immediately took control and discussed the entire

situation. A situation I never wanted them involved in. But they never showed any ill feelings or that they were disappointed in me. In fact, they were more worried about me and Keira and Karina, and were anxious to make sure we were safe and protected.

At the end of the discussion, Piers offered Karina a part-time job as a cashier at the Blaekthorn Lumber & Supply shop, and she graciously accepted. Then Garrick and Vera offered them their spare guest bedroom. It was next to mine, but I didn't mind. I'd lived with them most of my life, and they were happy to have a space all their own. At least, until they could save up enough to get their own place.

After the meeting was over, I pulled Keira to the side and questioned her about Axel. I didn't know how or why he was still alive and walking around Havenwood Falls, but right now, he was considered a threat. Axel was supposed to be alpha. He was supposed to be protecting his pack. If he was alive, well . . . he was better off dead.

After the meeting, the men made sure the area was secure, while the women started dinner. Steaks and ribs were grilling while side dishes were being prepared.

Barney even brought over his guitar and sang some songs around a bonfire. It felt like forever since we'd let go and had fun.

I watched Eris grab a drink from the cooler and make her way around the fire, the flames gilding the beautiful contours of her face. Then, she slowly stalked her way over to me, her golden eyes never leaving mine. If looks could kill, I'd be a dead man.

"Is this seat taken, sir?" she asked. But there was no seat next to me.

"You mean, this seat?" I asked patting my lap. She shrugged, waiting for my reply. "Well, miss . . . this seat is reserved for a special girl."

She smiled and leaned down, her hand on my forearm, her face inches from mine. "And who is this special girl?"

I shrugged. "You might know her. She's amazing. Gorgeous. Smart. Sexy. Witty."

"Hmm," she hummed. "I'm not sure."

Damn her. Those sultry eyes were glimmering in the firelight, drawing me in, deeper and deeper. If her family wasn't watching, I'd grab her and take her back to my room.

Instead, I took her arms and pulled her onto my lap. She wrapped her arm around my shoulder, and I hugged her waist.

The family didn't seem to mind. In fact, they all carried on as if we'd been a couple for a while. Even Piers glanced our way, with no looks of intent to murder me.

I guess I was fitting in. I just had to make sure I followed the rules to keep the peace. And Piers made sure I understood that his daughter was off limits until she was eighteen.

With Eris on me, the tension melted and I found myself laughing. For those few hours, we were ourselves. Enjoying each other's company, good food, and music.

With the strength of this pack—true strength and a real family bond—we didn't have to worry about Lars. He'd be torn to shreds if he came anywhere near this fiercely protective family.

My new family. The Blaekthorn Shadow Pack.

CHAPTER 12

ERIS

He was there. *The black devil, standing in the shadows. His red eyes pierced the darkness, watching, stalking. I looked around for Rylan, but there was no one else but . . . me.*

"Who are you?" I asked, glaring into those demon eyes.

"I see why he chose you," he replied, pacing in the shadows.

"What are you talking about?" I shouted. "Come out here and face me, you coward!"

But he remained deep in those dark shadows.

"The pup thinks he can stand against me? He took my eye, so I'm going to take something even more precious from him. Something he cares deeply about. Something he . . . loves."

Love?

"Such a shame. You're a beautiful girl."

I gasped when he finally stepped out of the shadows. His face was horribly scarred; his right eye nothing but a deep, black hole.

"Stay the hell away from me," I warned as he stalked closer.

My mind was blank. I couldn't remember a spell. Any spell. And the wolf inside me was still slumbering. Dammit. Get up. Get up, you stupid wolf.

"Don't worry, cupcake. I'll make sure it's quick and painless."

"You bastard!"

I turned to run, but he bounded after me, knocking me to the ground. My face and hands raked against the pavement, the wounds burning as he pressed down on my back.

Where the hell was I? There was no landmark around me. Just a dark road and endless trees.

I couldn't breathe. Then I felt sharp claws raking, tearing through fabric and flesh.

"Help!" I screamed. "Help me!"

But no one could hear me. And no one would save me.

I WOKE, gasping for air, still feeling the prickling stings across my back.

I clicked on my light and was in my room, in bed. Sweat clung to me, soaking through my pajamas and making strands of hair stick to my face.

Safe. I was safe.

The phone rang downstairs, sending another shot of adrenaline through my veins. My heart hammered harder and faster as I glanced at the time. Who the hell would be calling at three in the morning?

I opened my bedroom door and clicked on the hall light just as the phone stopped. I exhaled and turned back into my room. But it rang again.

Maybe it was a family member. Or Rylan.

Without another thought, I ran down the stairs as my dad exited his room. He stood at the top, watching me closely, his eyes heavy with sleep.

I picked up the receiver, trying to steady my trembling limbs. "Hello?"

"Eris? Oh, thank the goddess," a familiar voice panted.

"Grandma?"

I looked up to my dad, who was trying to blink himself awake.

"Yes, darling. It's me. I'm sorry for calling so late."

"Is everything okay?"

191

"Yes. Yes, I'm fine," she said, trying to catch her breath. "I just had a terrible nightmare. It was about a demon wolf and . . . he was after you."

Goose bumps rose all over my skin. "Grandma, I just had the same nightmare."

"Oh, my darling Eris," she sighed, "what have you gotten yourself into?"

I swallowed a huge lump in my throat. "I don't know."

"Do you still have the Book of Shadows?"

"Yes, of course."

"I want you to look for a spell, and I want you to memorize it."

"Okay, which one?"

"It's called the Transportation Spell. It can teleport you from one location to another. But you must get it right or you could end up lost in the in-between."

"The in-between? Grandma, I don't know if I can—"

"Eris, listen to me. You are a Witheridge witch and a Blaekthorn wolf. Strength and power are coursing through your veins. Don't ever doubt that power, or yourself. Memorize the transportation spell, and if you should ever need to use it, think of someplace nearby. Someplace safe. Don't travel too far, because the farther you go, the easier it is to get lost."

"Are there any other spells that can kill him?"

"We never use a spell to kill. Those are dark and very complicated, and they require you to give something of yourself. The transportation spell is the easiest to learn, and it can give you a chance to save yourself."

I sighed, overwhelmed. "Can I ask you a question?"

"Of course, darling. What is it?"

"In your dream . . . did I die?" I saw my dad start down the stairs out of the corner of my eye.

She paused, and I knew the answer. I died in her dream.

"It won't happen to you, Eris. Your father and your family will protect you. Tomorrow morning, I'll make my way to you. So stay home. Stay with them."

"Okay," I said, my body trembling. But knowing she would be coming made me feel a little better. "I'll see you soon."

"Oh, and Eris . . . could you please send me directions to where you are? I can't recall how to get there."

"Sure, Grandma."

"Stay close to your family, Eris."

"I will." I hung up the phone and looked at my dad. Overwhelmed with emotion, I broke down and ran into his arms.

"What's the matter, sweetheart?" he asked, stroking my hair.

"I had another dream, and Grandma dreamed the same thing."

"What was it about?"

There was no easy way to tell him. "Lars killed me."

My dad stepped back, and the look in his eyes was one I'd never witnessed before. It was the look of horrible torment. A fear and sadness and rage all wrapped up together, ready to explode. He closed his eyes and steadied himself before gripping my shoulders firmly.

"Listen to me, Eris. You will not die, because I won't allow it. I am your father and your protector, and that bastard will die before he lays a hand on you. I lost your mother, and I swore to her that I would keep you safe. I will not break that promise. Do you hear me?"

I nodded and hugged him, and his large protective arms wrapped around me. I knew he would keep his promise. If he was able to.

Back in my room, I took out my great-grandmother's Book of Shadows and found the Transportation Spell. I repeated it, over and over, until saying the words became second nature. But it took much more than reciting words. It took belief and power to cast a spell.

I slid off the bed and stood in the center of my room. With authority and power, I spoke the words of the spell, three times. As I said the last word, I blinked, and the next moment, I was standing in my bathroom.

It worked! Holy hell, it worked!

I squealed to myself, having added one more spell to my arsenal.

I quickly used the bathroom, then repeated the spell and appeared back in my bedroom.

Oh man. I couldn't wait to use this one on Camden and scare the crap out of him.

THE NEXT MORNING, my dad kept me on a tight leash. I wasn't allowed to leave the house, and there was always someone with me. I begged him not to tell Rylan about what happened, but he said he had to, so he could help protect me. I guess it meant he trusted him, which was a good thing. And it wasn't only him. The entire family knew and had become guards.

But I was more worried about Rylan. The entire reason he left Havenwood Falls in the first place was to keep Lars away from me.

Aunt Vera walked in the door with a Tupperware of fresh baked chocolate chip cookies.

"I know you love these. Eat as many as you like. I won't watch."

"Thanks." I laughed, biting into a hot cookie. It was soft, and the chocolate melted in my mouth. "Where's Rylan?"

"I think he went into town," she said. "He said he'd be right back, then hopped on his bike and took off."

I stopped chewing. My chest felt like a hole had been punched through it. "How long ago did he leave?"

She cringed. "A couple of hours?"

I couldn't breathe. "We have to go find him. What if he left? What if he went after Lars?"

I ran upstairs and threw on some jeans and a jacket.

"Eris, you can't leave. It's too dangerous out there," Aunt Vera begged, chasing after me with her high heels on.

"I have to go," I demanded. "He was there for me when I needed him."

I was about to head out the door when I heard the rumbling of a motorcycle. I flung the door open as Rylan pulled into our driveway and shut off his bike. "Hey, cupcake, where are you headed to?"

194

I didn't know whether to kiss him or smack him for putting me through that stress.

"I didn't know where you were," I said, steadying my breath.

He slid off his bike with a wicked smile. "So, you were going to leave the house and look for me?"

I crossed my arms over my chest. "What if I was?"

"Then you'd be disobeying your father's order to stay home."

I shrugged. "Where did you go?"

He opened the saddlebag on his bike, pulled out a bag, and lifted it up.

"What's that?"

"Some things to kill time while you're on lockdown." He jogged up the stairs and stood in front of me. "You were going to break the rules for me?"

"You would have, for me."

"Damn right I would," he said, leaning over and kissing my lips before heading into the house.

I followed after him. "Wait, what's in the bag?"

He handed it to me, and I opened it up. "Cards and . . . board games? You play board games?" I wasn't sure if a wandering wolf shifter had time to learn or play games.

"Of course I play board games. Remember, I was here months before you."

I lifted a box out of the bag. "Uno and Boggle?"

"I'll have you know, I am the Boggle king."

"Oh, okay," I said, bowing. "Well, it's time to relinquish your throne, sire, because the queen is here."

"On lockdown, I might add," he noted with that wicked grin.

I sighed. "Yeah, whatever."

CHAPTER 13

RYLAN

*W*hen Piers told me about Eris and her grandmother's nightmare, I couldn't help but feel like shit and responsible for everything happening. Had I not come into her life, she wouldn't be in danger.

I'd thought about running again and hunting Lars myself, but decided to take another approach. One Eris would approve of. These were the cards life had dealt me, and now I had to figure out a way to play them the right way.

She made some snacks while I set up the games in the living room. We had fun, the two of us, laughing and teasing and bickering. She kicked my ass in Boggle, which sucked.

Our last card game, I was so way ahead, but she ended up throwing down a winning card, and I swear a few of mine disappeared.

"How the hell did that happen?" I huffed, scratching my head.

Eris threw her hands in the air and squealed, "Five seconds, baby!"

"What the hell is five seconds?"

She winked. "That's for me to know, and you to find out."

"You're cheating," I said, grabbing her by the waist and dragging her to the ground, tickling her.

Then, all of a sudden, she was gone.

"What the—"

"Want a drink?" she said from the kitchen, holding a can of soda, smiling widely.

"You used magic? That's how you won?" I hopped to my feet. "That's low, Eris Blaekthorn."

In a split second, she was standing inches in front of me, making my insides jump.

"Shit. You can't do that to me."

She threw her head back with a boisterous laugh, then wrapped her arms around my waist. "I admit it. I used magic to win." She looked up at me with her beautiful golden eyes and blinked. "Forgive me?"

At that moment I looked at her and knew—I could live the rest of my life with her.

Her hands caressed the back of my neck, pulling me down into a kiss. Her soft lips pressed against mine, her tongue slipping across them, begging for entrance. I obliged.

She was putty in my arms, both of us acutely aware of every place our bodies touched. Waves of heat surged inside me. God, I wanted this girl. As I kissed her again, a pleasurable moan ripped from her throat, and I answered with a soft growl, feral and desperate. My tongue delved between her lips, raking against her teeth, claiming every inch of her mouth.

I pulled away and murmured against her neck, "Forgiven."

She grabbed my ass and squeezed. "Holy hell, Rylan Gilles. You're going to get us into trouble." She ran a finger down my chest, almost too low, while biting her bottom lip. Then she slowly stepped back, pivoted, and swayed toward the TV, turning it on.

This girl would be the end of me.

Vera left to run some errands since I was there, and the rest of them had to work at the warehouse.

"What do you want to do now?" she asked, plopping down on the couch next to me.

"Tell me about your dream." I wanted to know details so I knew what we would be up against.

She lay her head down on my lap and looked up at me. "What did my dad tell you?"

A flicker of rage roiled in my gut. "That Lars killed you."

Her expression saddened, as if she were thinking back to her nightmare. "Yeah, that's pretty much what happened."

"Was it another premonition?"

She nodded. "My grandma called me right after I woke up, at three in the morning, telling me she had the exact same dream."

"Where were you . . . in the dream?"

"I don't know. I was standing on a road, but everything around me was dark. There was no landmark to tell me if I was in or outside of Havenwood Falls."

"And he was there?"

She nodded then turned her head away. "He talked to me. He said that because you took his eye, he was going to take something from you. Something precious. Something you . . . love." Her eyes met mine again. "He called me cupcake."

My body stiffened. "What?"

That bastard. How close was he for him to know my pet name for her? The thought woke my inner beast. I could feel him clawing at my skin, my sight turning red.

"Hey," Eris said, sitting up. She wrapped her arms around my neck and whispered into my ear, "It's okay. You're here with me. He can't touch me if you're here." Her fingers gently stroked down my back, calming the beast inside. I breathed in her scent, instantly feeling the rage melt away. No one else had been able to tame the beast inside. Not like her.

Lars would never touch her. I promised myself that. And I had to find a way to end it once and for all. I had to find him and kill him, even if I never got answers.

This time, it wouldn't be for me or for revenge.

This time . . . it would be for her.

198

CHAPTER 14

ERIS

*T*he entire reason why I didn't want to tell Rylan about the dream was because I knew he'd react and would probably feel like he had to do something to save me. I felt his wolf. I felt its rage, and knew it was seconds from ripping through his flesh.

I had to calm him, and used my inner wolf to speak to his. I put on a movie to try to distract his thoughts, and halfway through, he fell fast asleep. We were lying on the couch, my back pressed against his front, his arms wrapped around me. His warmth seeped through me like a blanket, so I snuggled closer to him.

I listened to the sound of his breath and the steady beating of his heart. A heart that had been through so much hurt and pain. A heart that had been broken and battered, but managed to survive.

I couldn't describe the emotions I had inside. It was a deep admiration, a wanting and yearning to be close to him, to get to know everything I could about him. He was so much more than what he projected himself to be on the outside, and he'd become a master at hiding his feelings.

But I knew I was chipping away at that massive wall he'd built around himself and his heart, and was slowly starting to get a glimpse of the true Rylan. A guy who would leave everything good he had behind, and risk death, to save me and my family.

The phone rang, and when Rylan stirred I carefully slipped from his warm embrace and ran to the phone.

"Hello?"

"Hi, this is Dr. Underwood from the Havenwood Falls Medical Center."

"Hi, doctor."

"I am trying to get in touch with Rylan Gilles. I called Garrick's home, but they said he was probably here."

"Oh, he is. Hold on, I'll get him."

I set the phone down and peeked over the couch. "Rylan," I whispered. "Dr. Underwood is on the phone."

He opened his eyes, sat up, then ambled to the phone.

"Hey, Dr. Underwood. This is Rylan." He turned to look at me. "Okay . . . yes." His voice became low, and his eyes distant. "Are you sure?" His face went rigid. "Thank you, doctor. I appreciate it . . . Bye."

Rylan hung up the phone and ran his fingers through his hair.

"What is it?" I stepped toward him, my stomach knotting, hoping it wasn't the news I suspected.

"He is definitely related to me." He sat down on the stairs, and buried his face in his hands.

"How closely?"

"I don't know. But no one ever mentioned another relative. Not my grandparents, not my parents, and not my pack. And even if he is related . . . why? Why would he kill my father in cold blood?"

I shook my head. "Something must have happened for him to snap."

"I don't think I'll ever find out. Everyone who would know the answer—except Lars—is dead."

"Maybe not everyone."

Rylan glanced up at me.

"If Keira saw Axel, then he must know. You said he was part of the pack and was your father's best friend."

"He could be anywhere."

"If he came to town and stayed for any given length of time, he would have to register. All supernaturals do. And I think that Addie Beaumont would know."

I picked up the phone and dialed the number on the card Addie had given me when she'd given me my tattoo.

When she answered, I quickly told her our situation, and then handed Rylan the phone for him to describe what Axel looked like. Addie told him that he had come into town about two weeks ago, and she gave him his tattoo. He was quiet, but she remembered him telling her he was going to explore Havenwood Falls and was there to camp, and wasn't sure how long he was going to stay.

A car was heading down the pavement, and when I looked outside, I saw my grandma's hatchback heading toward us. "My grandma's here."

Rylan smiled and nodded, and I ran outside to greet her.

She hadn't come as the Grinch, the old woman she glamoured herself to look like while in New Mexico. No, she was the beautiful woman, tall and slender, with long, golden hair braided down her back. She was wearing a white pantsuit with a tan trench coat over it.

She was even more beautiful than I'd remembered, and didn't look like she could be my grandmother. Suddenly, calling her Grandma didn't seem to fit.

"Eris, my darling," she said, spreading her arms wide for a hug. I wrapped my arms around her and was so glad she was here—another layer of protection.

"Grandma, it's so good to see you."

"Well. Let's get back inside. It's freezing out here."

"It's nice to see you, Gertie," Rylan said.

"It's nice to see you as well, Rylan." My grandma turned to me with a smile and wink, making me blush.

"So, tell me what's going on. Why my granddaughter is in danger."

We updated her about the entire situation with Lars.

"Grandma, could you use a location spell on him? Like the one you used to find me here?"

"Yes, but I would need something that belongs to him."

I glanced over at Rylan. "What about his tooth?" He shrugged, then we turned to Gertie. "The clinic has Lars's tooth. They extracted it from Rylan's shoulder and used it to do the DNA test."

"That would definitely work. If we can get it, I can find his location."

Rylan looked up the number and dialed the clinic. "Dr. Underwood said they have the tooth, but he'll only be at the clinic for another twenty minutes. I'm going to run and get it."

I walked up to him. "Please be safe."

"You be safe," he said, kissing my cheek.

"Don't worry. She will be," Gertie said.

Rylan nodded, and headed out the door. He jumped into the company truck and headed down the gravel path.

CHAPTER 15

RYLAN

I made it to the clinic with a few minutes to spare, and Dr. Underwood gave me the tooth. Slipping it into my jacket pocket, I headed back toward the truck. A familiar scent caught my nose. I whipped around to see a man in a dark trench coat quickly dart behind the side of the building, so I gave chase.

As soon as the man saw me, he sprinted toward the nearby woods.

Damn it. "Axel!" I hollered, but he quickened his pace. "Axel!"

He was fast, but I was faster. Right before he hit the tree line, I dove forward and tackled him to the ground. A growl ripped from his throat, and his eyes turned golden. He was going to shift.

"Axel, stop," I yelled, sitting on his back, holding his arms behind him, pressing his face into the ground.

"Get off of me!" he bellowed, trying to buck me off. But he was never as strong as I was, and I held him down.

"Why? Why are you here?" I demanded.

"To watch over them."

"Who?"

"Karina and Keira. They're the last of our pack."

"Why did you fake your death?"

"Because Lars was going to kill me. He picked off the weak,

taunting me. He said I'd be last and he'd make it slow. So I had to fake my death, to survive."

"You're a coward!" I spat, twisting his wrists upward. He wailed in pain. "You're the pack's alpha. They depended on you and you left them vulnerable."

"I know," he said, and stopped fighting me. "But so did you." Those words were a knife to my chest. I let him go, and he moaned, rolling over and rubbing his sore wrists. "You were next in line to be alpha, Rylan. I was just a replacement."

I got up and paced. "My mother asked me to leave with her. She thought if we left, it would save the pack."

Axel looked up at me. His face was gaunt, his eyes sunken in, like he hadn't slept in weeks. "Lars won't stop until every member of the pack is dead."

"Why? Why is he doing this?"

Axel sighed and stood to his feet, scanning the area around him.

"It started way back, when your grandmother was pregnant with your father. A single girl within the pack had also become pregnant, but she told everyone she'd met a man at a nearby tavern, and they shared drinks and spent the night together. When she woke the next morning, he was gone, and left her with child.

"No one suspected anything, because she was young and beautiful and liked to party."

"How was she a member of the pack?" I was curious, because our pack was carefully chosen. A single party girl didn't seem like a choice my grandfather would make.

Axel shrugged. "Her brother was your grandfather's best friend. They grew up together. And when he asked to join the pack, your grandfather welcomed them."

I nodded, and he went on.

"Your grandmother and the girl became friends, having their pregnancies so close. They were always together, and everyone in the pack anticipated their births. They even made bets on who would go into labor first.

"It was a night when the moon was full, when the girl gave birth.

Your grandmother was there to help deliver her baby boy, whom she named Lars. A few days later, your grandmother gave birth to your father—Barin.

"What no one knew, except Lars's mom, was that Barin and Lars were half-brothers. Only days apart, they grew up as best friends. But it was Lars who showed signs of being an alpha, and during their teen years, he had grown bigger and stronger than Barin.

"When they both shifted for the first time, Lars was a foot taller than Barin, but he also started to look an awful lot like your grandfather. When your grandmother brought it up to your grandfather, he denied it. But she couldn't deny the resemblance this boy had to her husband. Your grandmother felt it in her bones, that Lars was his son, so she confronted him once more, and he finally told her the truth.

"Filled with a righteous fury, your grandmother shifted and nearly tore off your grandfather's head. But what hurt her more than the lies and the adultery was that her son's future as alpha of the pack was in jeopardy. Lars was her husband's firstborn, and would be the rightful alpha.

"When Lars found out who his true father was, he coveted the position of alpha. He wanted nothing more than to rule the pack, and the pack had already grown to love him.

"Lars had even found love. A girl who was fatherless and had lost her mother to disease. She was a wanderer, and had found the pack. Lars fell fast in love with her, and in his heart, had already wanted her to be his mate. Yes, she loved Lars, but as a friend and nothing more. He'd twisted their friendship in his mind, and didn't know that Barin also had fallen for the girl.

"Seething with fury and jealousy, your grandmother gave your grandfather an ultimatum. She threatened to leave him and take Barin with her, unless he banished Lars and his mother from the pack forever. The members of the pack would also be given one rule: to never speak of or mention Lars or his mother again.

"Your grandmother wanted to make sure that her son, Barin,

would be alpha. As he rightfully should have been, and not some bastard child.

"Your grandfather had no choice but to agree. He banished Lars and his mother and warned them never to return. When Lars found out the reason for their banishment, he went mad and tore up the camp. What made it much worse was that the woman he'd thought to spend the rest of his life with had chosen Barin to be her mate."

I exhaled loudly. This story was messing with me. My freaking emotions were everywhere. Lars was my uncle, and I couldn't help but feel some kind of pity for him. It wasn't his fault he was born a bastard child and then punished for it. And to think his half-brother stole the woman he loved . . . I could see how that could piss him off. But not enough to murder him and the entire pack.

Axel's eyes shifted around us, like he was looking for danger. But I sensed nothing. Maybe he was so used to being hunted that he couldn't help it.

"Is there more?" I asked.

He nodded. "When your grandfather died and your father became alpha, Lars came back one night and confronted him. Barin tried to be rational at first, but when Lars asked your mother to leave with him, your father snapped and charged after him. He punched Lars in the face, and when Lars threw him off, the pack surrounded him, protecting your father.

"Then you went and stood by your mother and held her hand. And then your mother stepped to Barin's side and took his hand, and Lars finally saw the family you'd become—a family he'd dreamed of having with her.

"Something inside of him went very dark, and he swore, in front of everyone, that they would all die. Because of them, he was stripped of everything—his home, his family, his pack, his love. And now he was out there alone, trying to survive and stay alive.

"Your father, fiercely protective of his family and his pack, demanded he leave and never return, or he would suffer death. The pack stood with their alpha. The same pack that had once loved Lars had now turned their backs on him."

I seriously didn't know what to say. This entire situation was a freaking mess, starting with my grandfather. If anyone was to blame, it was him. He poked his rod into a place he shouldn't have, and because of it, multiple lives were ruined.

"I know you went after the pack in Montrose. It was brave of you, and your father would have been proud." Axel turned his back to me. "I will never forgive myself for what happened to them. I was responsible, and I'm sorry."

He left, and I didn't chase after him, because I needed to get back to Eris.

Axel looked like shit, and I knew it was a physical manifestation of what was going on inside of him. But thanks to him, I knew the truth.

And now, I needed to find Lars.

CHAPTER 16

ERIS

*T*he entire time Rylan was gone, I worried. Yes, his injuries had almost completely healed, but he was in bad shape the other night. And seeing him covered in blood . . . I didn't ever want to see that again.

I set Gertie up in my room, so while she put her things away, I made us something to eat.

And then I heard a vehicle coming down the driveway. I ran to the window and peeked out, glad to see Rylan was back safely.

When he came to the door, I swung it open. A crooked grin rose on his full lips.

"Miss me already?"

"No," I lied. "Just wondering if you got the tooth."

"Liar," he chuckled, slipping a small envelope out of his pocket and handing it to me. When I tried to take it, he held on. "I have some mind-blowing news to tell you."

"That sounds serious," I said, as he let go.

"It is. I think your entire family needs to hear it."

I sighed. "The suspense is going to kill me."

"Where's Gertie?" he asked, his eyes scanning the bottom floor.

"Upstairs. She drove a long way, so I told her to rest."

"Good." He grabbed my waist and yanked me tightly against

him. His right hand cupped my neck as he pulled me in for a kiss. He took me by surprise, but I savored it, sliding my hands under his shirt and over his muscular back.

He flinched under my touch.

"Damn, cupcake. Your hands are freaking cold."

"And your back is warm. So, thanks . . . for the breathtaking kiss and hand-warming service."

"Happy to oblige."

Unwillingly slipping from his embrace, I called the warehouse and told my dad that Rylan had some very important news. He said they were finishing an order, and would be home in half an hour.

xxx

The entire family, including Gertie, Keira, and Karina, had gathered in our living room as Rylan began his story.

He told them about going to the clinic and running into Axel. Keira became ghostly white when he mentioned Axel, but then the entire room was still and quiet as he shared the story about his grandfather, Lars, and his parents.

Even after he was done, everyone was still quiet. But my father stood up and patted Rylan on the shoulder.

"Thank you," he said. "At least now we have a better understanding of where this Lars fellow is coming from. But to tell a pack you'll kill them in revenge is one thing. To actually commit the crime and keep killing and killing . . . that tells me something is not right in his head. I do agree he's had a terrible past, one that could justify him being bitter and enraged, but he took it to an entirely new level. One I'm not sure he can come back from, nor does it seem like he cares to.

"We could attempt to talk to him, but at this point, I don't think he wants to talk. He is so far rooted in his rage and revenge that there may be no hope for him." He turned to Rylan. "I'm saddened to hear the horrors he faced being banished and finding out the truth, and the pain it must have caused. But we are all given choices in life. Paths that will make us better and bring us closer to our end

209

goals. Sometimes, hatred and rage can blur those lines, but if you look close enough, they are still there.

"Lars chose to murder your father, your mother, and all those others in the pack. They were his family—and he still chose to kill them. Because of that, I don't think he can be reasoned with. Because of that, he's a huge threat to my family. Especially my daughter. If that man comes near her, so help me God, I will have no problem ripping out his heart and personally handing it to the devil."

"And I will do the same," Rylan said, proving his loyalty to me and the family.

My father gave him a nod.

"That guy has no clue what he's up against," Camden said, arms folded over his chest.

"A rude awakening," Uncle Barney said.

"Or an early grave," Uncle Garrick added.

Keira and Karina had looks of hope in their eyes.

"If you need us, we can help," Karina said.

My dad smiled at her. "I think you've done more than enough. You've kept yourself and your daughter alive and safe against that madman. Please, allow us to take it from here."

Karina's expression turned to one of relief. They'd been running for too long and were still recovering.

"Thank you," she said.

Aunt Vera walked over to her. "Why don't you come and help us hold down the fort and cook dinner? We'll let the guys handle this one. And they'll be hungry when they get back."

"We'd like that," Karina said with a broad smile, wrapping an arm around Keira, who readily agreed.

Rylan glanced over to me and winked, making my heart patter.

"All right," my dad said, clapping his hands together. "Gertie will be performing a location spell. I'm not sure how it works, but tonight, we will find Lars and end this, once and for all."

Gertie needed a quiet place to do her spell, so my dad, my uncles, Camden, and Rylan stayed while the others, including Keira and Karina, went home. I could tell they were relieved to not be a part of it. They'd run for too long. Now was their time to relax and enjoy life.

Gertie laid a map of Colorado on the floor and placed Lars's tooth in the center. She lit a few candles and while everyone was quiet, she recited a spell while waving her white wand over the map.

The tooth began to roll, and then it stopped—directly on an area where Havenwood Falls would be, only Havenwood Falls wasn't on any normal map.

"What if we use a map of Havenwood Falls?" Camden suggested.

"Do you have one?" my dad asked.

"Yeah. I got one from the Backwoods shop."

Gertie nodded. "Yes, a map of the area would make it a lot easier to pinpoint him."

Camden ran upstairs and right back down with a visitors map. He laid it on top of the other one. Gertie tried the spell again, and this time the tooth rolled right to the edge of the map—maybe a mile from where our cabins were.

"Dad?" My heart was hammering, my stomach knotting.

"He can't hurt you, sweetheart." My dad wrapped his strong, protective arms around me, then addressed the others. "Get ready. Meet me outside in five minutes." Both of my uncles and Camden nodded and left. Then my dad turned to Gertie. "Would you be able to come with us? To pinpoint his location?"

"Of course," she said, gathering the map and the tooth.

"I'm coming," Rylan said.

My dad let go of me and placed his hand on Rylan's shoulder. "Just remember, son—he wants you dead."

"I know. But if there is even a spark of good left in him, I have to try."

My dad nodded. "If he makes any threatening move, I won't hesitate to do what I have to, to protect my family."

Rylan nodded. "I know."

"Dad, since Gertie is going with you, and all of you will be there, I think I should go, too."

"No. You'll stay here with your aunts. They are fierce and can protect you."

"I'll stay in the car. What if he slips through and all of you are out there? Gertie can put a glamour over the vehicle, so he won't even know we're there."

His eyes averted to Gertie. "Can you do that?"

"Of course I can," she said. "Glamours are a specialty of mine. Remember the Grinch?"

"Boy, do I," my dad sighed loudly. For a moment, we all laughed. "Is there a way to put a glamour over the entire vehicle for the entire ride? So he doesn't know we're coming?"

"I can." She didn't even have to think about it. I'd seen Gertie's magic and knew she was powerful.

My dad turned to me with seriousness in his eyes. "You can only come if you promise to stay in the vehicle with Gertie."

"Deal," I said. And that was that.

I gave Rylan a smile, but I knew he wasn't thrilled I was going. Especially after the dream I'd had. But I wasn't alone. Because of that premonition, I would be able to create a new outcome. I just hoped that no one would get hurt in the process.

CHAPTER 17

RYLAN

The ride in the Expedition to find Lars didn't seem to faze the Blaekthorns. It was obvious they'd been in a lot of situations like this one. They were experienced. Probably even more experienced than Lars.

Inside, I felt the tension building. This was it. Live or die. Good or bad. My life, after tonight, would never be the same.

I couldn't help but wonder how broken that man was. Was he damaged beyond repair? I'd done some things I'd regretted in my past, but never like this. Sometimes, you need to kill to survive. But killing someone just because you are pissed at them is not a justifiable reason.

"He's right outside the border of the town limits," Gertie noted. She'd glamoured the car, so no one could see it.

I was sitting in the back seat next to Eris, with Gertie on her other side. Barney and Camden were in the seat in front of us, and Piers and Garrick were in the front. Piers sped toward the location Gertie had given him, his eyes already glowing yellow in the rearview mirror. He was ready for whatever was to come.

"He's close," Gertie finally said, and Piers slowed the vehicle.

I squeezed Eris's hand, and she gripped mine tightly, like she didn't want me to let go. I stared into those beautiful golden eyes and nodded, then she lay her head on my shoulder.

"Stay with me," she whispered into my ear.

"I'll be back," I promised, pressing a kiss to the top of her head.

"Stop," Gertie said. Piers put on the brakes.

"Rylan, promise me you won't risk your life."

"I promise you this: I'll do what needs to be done. Nothing more. Nothing less."

CHAPTER 18

ERIS

We stopped in the middle of a road, and it became hard to breathe. The sides of the road were shrouded in darkness, as were the trees beyond. It was the exact same place as in my dream.

But it was only a dream. This time, I wasn't alone.

"Where is he?" my dad asked.

Gertie swiped her wand over the map. "On the left. Just beyond the shadows. He heard the engine. He knows something is going on."

"Can you put a glamour over us?" Barney asked.

"Not all of you. Maybe one more."

"Then put it over me," my dad said.

"I'll go out and distract him," Rylan added. "That way you can get in a good position to take him out."

"Rylan," I breathed. "You can't."

"I have to," he said, taking both of my hands. "I have to try. Besides, your dad will be there."

"I will," my dad answered. "Just don't get too close to him."

Uncle Garrick patted my dad on the back. "Barney and I will be ready. As soon as anything goes down, we'll be there."

My dad nodded. He knew he could count on them. Then he

turned and nodded to Rylan. Rylan opened the door and stepped out, while Gertie put a spell over my dad. As soon as my dad opened the door and moved away from the vehicle, he disappeared.

My pulse started to race as Rylan stepped away from the vehicle, my eyes locked on the shadows. It was like watching a scary movie unfold in front of me, only this was real.

Then, just like I'd seen in my dream, one red eye appeared, glowing in the darkness.

Rylan walked into the dark road with his hands in the air. "Lars, I know you're out there," he said loudly.

A deep growl reverberated in the air. "You've come to die, pup?"

Rylan took another step forward. "You don't have to do this."

"Shut up!" he roared.

I could hear Lars. "How can I hear him when I'm not in his pack?" I said, mostly to myself.

Everyone in the car turned their attention to me, their eyes narrowed.

"You can hear the wolf?" Uncle Garrick asked, and I nodded.

"Your mother had the same gift," Gertie replied, laying a hand over mine. "She was able to hear wolves from different packs."

There was so much I needed to learn about my new gifts. So much I was learning about my mom.

"Step closer," Lars continued, "so I can take a good look at you before I rip your throat out."

"I know who you are, Uncle," Rylan said slowly and cautiously.

The huge black wolf stepped into the street. His face was marred, a black hole in the place of one eye. Hackles were raised on his back, and lips were curled over razor sharp fangs.

"Don't *ever* call me uncle," he growled. "We are *not* family."

My hands pressed to the glass, silently begging Rylan to back away. Then I watched the horror multiply right in front of my eyes, because six more wolves stepped out of the darkness and stood behind Lars.

And just like that, Rylan and my dad were outnumbered.

Fear overtook me, waking up my inner wolf, begging it to be set free.

Wake up, it screamed. *Wake up!*

"Eris," I heard my grandmother say. I turned to her, and the world around me was suddenly a bright red.

Something slammed into our vehicle. The force was so strong, Gertie whacked her head against the window and was knocked out. Her body slumped to the seat, and her wand dropped to the ground and rolled under the seat. The glamour instantly disappeared, and I heard another growl outside.

Twisting back, I watched Rylan shift, and something inside me stirred. Holy hell, that was hot.

Then my dad suddenly appeared, right behind Rylan. They were nearly the same size. Both huge alpha males.

Without hesitation, Camden and my uncles threw their doors open, immediately shifting before they touched the ground.

It was happening. But not the way it was in my dream. We were changing the outcome.

CHAPTER 19

RYLAN

I could smell them before they showed their faces. Members of my father's pack. Six of them. The bastards.

"Why?" I asked.

Lars snarled. "Because they know who their true alpha is. Their loyalty is to me, alone. They begged me to spare their lives so they could follow me. They wanted me to be their alpha and lead their pack. How could I refuse?"

I growled. "I thought you killed them."

"I did kill those who tried to stand against me. So, in a way, you could call what I did . . . self-defense. After the troublemakers were gone, it was easy for the others to follow me."

Lies. These men were cowards and only joined him to save their own asses.

"How could you kill your own family?"

He growled and snapped his teeth, spittle flying. "I told you. I have no family. Everyone who died deserved to die."

"And what about you? You murdered my father and mother for protecting their family."

"You know *nothing* about me!" Lars roared. He was circling me, and the others behind him were getting closer, braver. I knew then there was no reasoning with him. I tried, but he was too far gone.

"You will die tonight, and everyone who came with you will die too."

A loud crash had me turn around to see the vehicle suddenly appear in the road. Then I saw Eris turn, her golden eyes wide with fear and frozen on me.

"What a delicious treat," Lars taunted. "She'll be mine before the end of the night."

Rage ignited inside, and I shifted, letting my inner beast break free.

This bastard was going to die.

I heard Piers growl behind me, and knew his brothers and Camden were right behind. I didn't care if they outnumbered us. These cowards, who would stand up against me and be party to Lars's plan to murder me and threaten my girl and new family, would die. They were no match for us.

Lars bounded forward like a rabid dog, foaming at the mouth, his one eye filled with so much hate and madness. I charged forward to meet him, dodging his sharp teeth aimed for my face. I caught his left leg in my jaws and snapped them shut. With my forward momentum, I pulled him away from Eris. A flick of my neck sent him tumbling down the road.

I turned back to see the others. The Blaekthorns stood strong against the six others. Those six growled and bared their teeth, but they didn't move to fight.

"Rylan!" I heard Eris scream. I turned back to see Lars bounding toward me. He leapt forward, but I couldn't dodge him fast enough.

CHAPTER 20

ERIS

*M*y heart beat so loudly I could hear it in my ears. Then Lars made his move.

Rylan moved like lightning, swift and smooth, avoiding Lars's first strike. Then he struck, latching onto Lars's leg and dragging him away from us. I wasn't breathing, watching the events unfold.

My dad, uncles, and brother stayed near the truck, protecting me and Gertie, ready to fight the six others who had joined Lars. But the wolves only stood in the road, their eyes on Rylan and Lars, and it appeared they had no intention of fighting.

When I turned back, Rylan's eyes were on them, so he didn't see Lars charging at him from behind.

"Rylan!" I screamed.

He turned as Lars was in the air, and there was no way he could avoid him.

I quickly recited a spell from the Book of Shadows, and the world around me froze.

Five seconds.

A few more spoken words transported me right next to Rylan. I shoved his huge wolf form to the side, and as soon as the world unfroze, we both fell to the road.

A hair-raising growl erupted from Lars as his teeth and claws met nothing but air. He turned, his one evil eye glaring at us, his teeth bared and dripping with saliva.

Rylan was on his feet in a split second, placing himself in front of me, protecting and shielding me from Lars.

Then I felt it. Felt the power of the wolf inside. It had finally awoken.

Lars stepped back, watching me with a sated glint in his eye.

I'd heard the first time you shifted was brutal. The raw intensity of the beast inside dropped me to my knees. I screamed in utter pain as my human body shifted. It felt as if I were dying. And the pain . . . the pain was utterly excruciating. I could barely breathe.

Every one of my bones cracked and snapped into a different form. The flesh—the human flesh—tore apart as the wolf broke free.

I heard my dad calling out to me, but his voice was muted, and I couldn't answer. The agony consumed me.

"I'm here, Eris. He won't hurt you," Rylan said, standing close by.

When Lars moved, Rylan took a step toward him, posturing. A low growl of warning ripped from his throat.

Then, as quickly as the pain of shifting came, it subsided.

I slowly stood to my feet—new feet. Four wolf feet.

Wobbly at first, I quickly felt my body and muscles and tendons strengthen. In my new wolf form, I stepped next to Rylan, and his golden eyes met mine, approving.

A deep, rumbling growl ripped from Lars.

Without warning, Rylan shot toward him. Head down, he slammed into his chest, then swiped a paw across Lars's snout, slicing flesh. Lars roared in pain, but took the blow and steadied himself. His wicked eye watched for the moment to strike. He paced from side to side, that red eye set on Rylan.

"Eris!" My dad bounded toward us, but the six finally attacked, stopping him in his tracks. My uncles and Camden jumped in, but I couldn't focus on them. I knew they'd take care of each other.

Lars charged forward, and as Rylan went to meet him, claws flew and teeth snapped. Rylan got caught in the face and leg, while Lars suffered another harrowing blow to his chest.

Lars struck again and again. His relentless rage fueled his fight. But Rylan fought back, strong and fast, matching the older wolf's strength. Blow after blow, through countless slashes and bites, Lars was starting to pant. He was tiring.

In a last-ditch effort, he let out a deafening growl. His face twisted, and his hind legs pushed forward, shoving Rylan backward. Rylan lost his footing and stumbled back, exposing his neck. Then I watched Lars's eye fix on its target.

As if in slow motion, I watched him pounce, his mouth wide, teeth bared, and his intent obvious. He was going for his throat. He was going for the kill.

All I could do was move. My new strong legs thrust me forward directly into his path, and Lars's teeth sunk deep into my back.

I wailed as pain shot through me, like knives tearing into my flesh.

In a split second, Rylan leapt over us, and in mid-air, sunk his teeth into the back of Lars's neck and yanked him back. Lars yelped and released his grip on me. I hit the ground with a thud. I couldn't move. I couldn't breathe. Warm liquid soaked my new golden fur.

"Eris, stay down," my dad commanded. I looked over to him, still engaged in battle with my uncles and brother. They were all still standing.

I turned to see Rylan land on his hind legs, the back of Lars's neck still clamped tight in his jaws. A raging fire burned in his eyes. I could feel his power pulsing around me—the power of an alpha.

Rylan flipped Lars over his head, slamming his body onto the ground, the air exiting his lungs. Rylan then clamped his jaws around Lars's throat.

"Rylan, stop!" A large man exited from the woods wearing a dark trench coat.

Lars was weakened, his breath slow, suffocating as Rylan squeezed.

"Rylan, don't do this," Axel coaxed, stepping in front of them. "Don't let his blood stain your hands." Axel took a step closer. "Let go."

Rylan's eyes finally met Axel's, his chest panting heavily, then slowly . . . slowly, his jaw dislodged from Lars's neck.

CHAPTER 21

RYLAN

*L*ars was winded, but the bastard was freaking determined. Catching me off guard, he shoved me backward, his jaw open, teeth bared, ready to bite. Before I could right myself, Eris came flying out of nowhere, throwing herself in front of me.

My heart stopped as I helplessly watched his sharp teeth—meant for my throat—sink into her back.

When Eris yelped in pain something inside of me snapped. An anger. An all-consuming rage was set ablaze. He'd touched her. He hurt her. And now he was going to pay.

I jumped over them and sunk my teeth into the base of Lars's neck and yanked back, forcing him to release. And when he did, I slammed his body to the ground. Before he could make a countermove, I sunk my jaws into his throat and clamped down. I wanted him to feel his impending death. To know it was near and fear it, like he'd done to all of his victims.

Then, beyond the pounding rage in my ears, I heard a voice.

"Rylan, stop!" But I didn't want to stop. He'd hurt Eris, and I swore he would never touch her again.

Lars gasped for breath, but I held on, clamping tighter, obstructing his airway.

"Rylan, don't do this," Axel begged, standing in front of me in his human form. "Don't let his blood stain your hands." Axel took another step closer. "Let go."

Bastard. He should have let me have my moment and finish him, once and for all.

But he was right. *Damn it.* If I killed Lars, I would be no better than him.

When Lars went limp, I finally let go and ran over to Eris.

She was lying on the ground, blood coating her beautiful golden fur.

She'd shifted for the first time, when danger had presented itself, and she proved her true strength. But also, as soon as she shifted, I felt an invisible bond, a thread, tighten between us.

She was mine. I'd known it from the start. And no one, including any freaking last blood relative, was going to take her away from me.

I walked up to her and nudged her nose with mine, then said, "I'm sorry." Even though I knew sorry wasn't good enough.

She lifted her head, her golden eyes filled with pain.

"For what?" she exhaled.

"He hurt you. I broke my promise."

She shook her head. "Maybe I wanted to be the hero, for once."

"Rylan!" Camden howled. I turned to see Lars standing back on his feet, foaming at the mouth. But before we could do anything, Axel shifted into his gray wolf form and attacked. He and Lars tumbled off the road and into the dark trees.

Sounds of gurgling and choking, then bones snapping, shattered the night. Then it went quiet.

Axel walked out into the street, blood dripping from his maw.

"It's over. Lars is dead. You're free," he sighed and closed his eyes. "We're all free."

Garrick and Barney ran over to the side of the road and confirmed it.

He was dead. It was over. It was finally over.

Back in our human forms, we made our way back to the vehicle, but Axel stood off to the side.

"Do you have someplace to go?" I asked.

He gave me a broad smile. "Anywhere I want to now, without worry." He pulled his coat around him tightly. "I think I might head north, to Canada. I have a sister there, and a nephew and niece I've never met. I'd like to visit them. And then I'll see where I go from there."

"That sounds nice, man."

Axel looked behind me.

"You've got a good thing going here. I don't blame you one bit for leaving the pack." He gave me a sad smile. "And don't worry about the ones who got away. They're happy to be free. They're probably far away, headed toward other states by now."

I laughed and couldn't help but feel sorry for him. I extended my hand. "Thank you, Axel. You came through tonight."

He nodded. "Thanks for taking care of Karina and Keira. Please tell them I'm so sorry."

"I will."

He turned to leave, but he paused and turned his attention back to me. "Your father and mother would be proud."

For the first time since my parents died, tears slid down my cheeks. "Thank you."

And then he left. I knew it was probably the last time I would see Axel.

Back in the car, Gertie was fine. She had a little bump on the head, but she said it was nothing a few aspirin couldn't take care of. Everyone else had minor injuries and scratches, but it was Eris I was most worried about.

I sat on the seat with her head in my lap, because Gertie put a sleeping spell on her so she wouldn't have to deal with the pain. Everyone in the car seemed in high spirits, especially while Camden was telling his battle story. But I felt numb, thinking back to the moments that brought us here. So much had happened in such a short amount of time that it felt like I was living in some twisted dream.

Then Camden said, "They had no chance with the Blaekthorn Shadow Pack and the Witheridge spells."

"Shadows and spells definitely won tonight," Piers agreed. "And it seems Eris is now a part of both worlds."

"She'll be unstoppable. A force to be reckoned with," Camden said, and everyone agreed.

I smiled at the girl sleeping in my lap. My girl. My cupcake. She was not only beautiful, but she was brave and selfless. In the span of the evening, she'd saved me—not only once, but twice. First, with her magic. And then in her wolf form. God, I'd never hear the end of it.

Eris was wild and untamed, but so was I. We were rule breakers, but only when it served the greater good. And because of it, our lives and the lives of others were saved.

EPILOGUE

ERIS

*T*hings changed after the night Lars was killed. My dad contacted Sheriff Kasun and discussed the situation, and the police took care of the body. My injuries healed quickly, and so did everyone else's. But the excitement came from the fact that I'd finally shifted, and proved to myself that I was a real member of the Blaekthorn pack. It also gave my aunts another reason to throw a huge party and celebrate.

Gertie drove back to New Mexico, after staying a week to make sure I was okay, and promised that by the end of summer she'd come back to Havenwood Falls to live. She wanted to be closer to the family and help me master the spells in the Book of Shadows, strengthening my magical side—the Witheridge witch side. I was looking forward to it.

Karina and Keira made a decision to leave and head back to their home country of Brazil, where most of their family still lived. When my dad presented them with plane tickets, they both cried.

"We could never repay you for your kindness," Karina said.

My father laid a hand on her shoulder. "It's a gift, and we don't want or expect anything in return."

They were blown away at his generosity, and after a few weeks, they were gone.

Rylan also changed after that night. The enormous stress and burden he'd been carrying on his shoulders had been lifted, and it was visibly noticeable. He invited me to most of his Havenwood Falls High activities, even dances, and introduced me to other students who would be attending next year, when I would be entering as a senior.

Rylan and Camden continued to work for the family business. Rylan was saving up enough money to build a cottage on a private piece of the property they'd given him.

We spent a lot of time together that spring, and our relationship blossomed. Rylan graduated from high school. I couldn't have been prouder, watching him walk down the aisle—this cocky guy who had stormed into my life one day and never left.

Because I was still seventeen and he couldn't claim me yet, he gave me a promise ring. It was perfect—a turquoise stone with an infinity symbol twisted on the side of a simple silver band. It was a promise that one day, we'd seal that undeniable bond that had already connected us. Until then, we enjoyed each other's company.

Rylan and I both found ourselves in this magical little town called Havenwood Falls, and had everything we could have ever wanted right around us. Love, family, friends, and . . . each other.

There was really nothing more I could ever want, besides my mom. Although my glimmer had left me—that tiny ball of light that would come and visit me, bringing me peace and warmth during my darkest times as a child . . . the glimmer which I found out was my mom—I knew she was still with me. She'd always be with me. And knowing that made living life so much easier.

～

RYLAN

On Eris's eighteenth birthday, I claimed her. We sealed that invisible bond that had connected us, and it was beyond anything I could have ever imagined. Beyond what either of us could have imagined.

I just wished my parents had met her, because they would have loved her.

The Blaekthorn family had already accepted and supported our relationship. They'd taken me in and treated me like a member of the family.

But it was Eris who had given my life new meaning. She helped me see and understand that my past didn't define me. If anything, it made me stronger.

I welcomed the future and whatever it had in store for me . . . for us. But no matter what it brought—the highs and lows, the good times and bad—I knew, deep down in my heart, that we would get through it together. One day and one breath at a time.

I'd finally found my place in life and a reason to exist. Here, in this magical little town called Havenwood Falls, I'd found home.

ABOUT THE AUTHOR

Cameo Renae was born in San Francisco, raised in Maui, Hawaii, and now resides with her husband and kids in Alaska.

She's a daydreamer and a caffeine and peppermint addict who loves to laugh and loves to read to escape reality.

One of her greatest joys is creating fantasy worlds filled with adventure and romance and sharing it with others. It is the love of her family and amazing support of her fans that keep her going.

One day she hopes to find her own magic wardrobe and ride away on her magical unicorn. Until then . . . she'll keep writing!

ACKNOWLEDGMENTS

Thank you, Kristie Cook, for creating this amazing world, and allowing me to play a part in it. You helped give life to these characters, and then edited and polished their journey. I don't know how you do it all, but you are truly amazing.

FALLING DEEP

J.L. WEIL

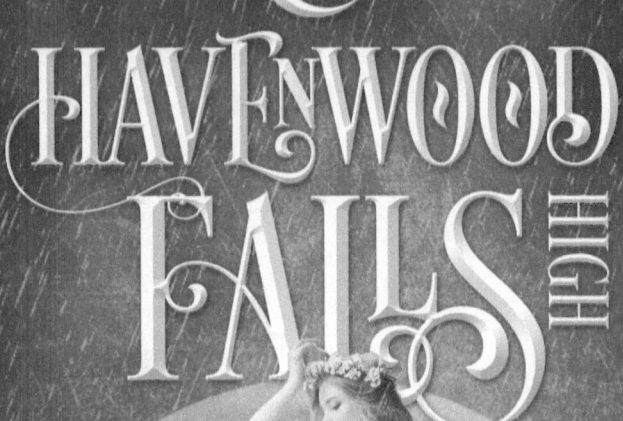

HAVENWOOD FALLS HIGH

Falling Deep

USA Today Bestselling Author

J.L. WEIL

~ A Havenwood Falls Young Adult Novella ~

ALSO BY J.L. WEIL

DRAGON DESCENDENTS SERIES

(Upper Teen Reverse Harem Fantasy)

Stealing Tranquility

THE DIVISA SERIES

(Full series completed – Teen Paranormal Romance)

Losing Emma: A Divisa novella

Saving Angel

Hunting Angel

Breaking Emma: A Divisa novella

Chasing Angel

Loving Angel

Redeeming Angel

LUMINESCENCE SERIES

(Full series completed – Teen Paranormal Romance)

Luminescence

Amethyst Tears

Moondust

Darkmist – A Luminescence novella

RAVEN SERIES

(Full series completed – Teen Paranormal Romance)

White Raven

Black Crow

Soul Symmetry

BEAUTY NEVER DIES CHRONICLES

(Teen Dystopian Romance)

Slumber

Entangled

Forsaken

NINE TAILS SERIES

(Teen Paranormal Romance)

First Shift

Storm Shift

Flame Shift

Time Shift

SINGLE NOVELS

Starbound

Casting Dreams

Ancient Tides

For all the girls who'd rather stay home and read than go to homecoming.

CHAPTER 1

I glanced in my rearview mirror, positive I was being punked. Nope. The boxes were still piled into the backseat of my aging Chevy Malibu. Forget trying to see out the back window. I had my whole life packed up in this hunk of junk.

Kind of sad.

Then again, my life was sad.

I was moving, leaving behind yet another house, another school, and another group of friends.

One year, I told myself. I only had one year left until I graduated, and then I could go wherever I wanted—live the life I chose—go to whatever college would have me. I only prayed this move didn't mess up my chances of getting a swimming scholarship.

I had worked too damn hard at being the best on my team. Correction—*had* been the best, but now that I was gone, the title went to Tiffany Hastings.

My fingers clenched on the wheel.

I'd miss a lot of things about living in Wisconsin, but Tiffany Hastings was definitely not one of them.

In a way, I was glad we were moving if it meant I would never again have to see Brady Cooper, the miserable bum Mom had been married to for the last two years. I wasn't going to miss his sorry face.

Mom had just signed the divorce papers from her third husband. Yep. Third. She wasn't lucky in love, or maybe it was because she only dated douchebags. And before the ink was even dry on the paper, Mom and I had our entire lives jammed into two cars, heading across the country to live in Havenwood Falls with my grandma, whom I called Gigi.

The town's stacked stone sign sat nestled between two flowering bushes, inviting and so cliché. I sank deeper into my seat, feeling anything but warm and fuzzy. "Welcome to Havenwood Falls" was written in black metal lettering.

I snorted. Welcome my left butt cheek. Finding this place had been a joke. I had nearly tossed the GPS out the window after the fourth time it tried to get me to turn around back the way I'd come.

Fortunately for us, Mom had been born here, yet still her sense of direction was crap. It was a freaking miracle we made it at all.

Let the suckage begin.

As I was reciting a list of things I already hated about Havenwood Falls, a streak of black darted out in front of my car, and reflexes kicked in as I slammed my foot on the brake. My poor car started to fishtail, and I knew this wasn't going to end well for either of us—the car or me.

I got one good glimpse of the creature before my car started to spin like a Ferris wheel on crack, and it didn't stop until the Malibu hit the ditch, snapping my head back against the seat.

Son of a—

God, that hurt.

I rubbed the back of my head, praying there was no blood. The last thing I needed was to pass out, and the sight of the metallic sticky stuff would do just that. I could handle lots of things— brussels sprouts, unnatural blondes, guys in thongs—but blood? Nope, no way.

My eyes flew out the window as I suddenly remembered the animal. I searched the road, looking for any sign of the critter. Had I hit it? Was it injured and lying hurt on the side of the street? Was I an animal killer?

Ensue panic attack.

I might be a lot of things, including the new girl, but I was definitely not a murderer.

But it was gone. Just vanished. My best guess? It had taken off into the woods after its brush with death.

Exhaling, I shifted the car into park and got out to check for damage. It wouldn't be the first mishap or dent Betsy had suffered. Betsy was what I called this piece of crap car. A few more dings would probably be an improvement, but really, I shouldn't complain. At least I had wheels to get me around. Not every seventeen-year-old could say the same.

As I glared down the road leading into Havenwood Falls, I realized Mom hadn't even stopped. Go figure. It would probably be a mile or more before she noticed I wasn't trailing behind her.

Fishing out my cell phone from the passenger seat, I sank back into the driver's seat and dialed her number. I left the door open, letting the crisp air of October rush over my face. She answered on the fifth ring.

"Hey, honey, you get lost?" Mom had a naturally husky voice that seemed to draw men to her like ants to a breadcrumb.

"Not exactly. I got run off the road."

"You what?" she shrieked in the shrill voice that always made me cringe. "By who? Another car?"

I rested my head on the back of the seat and closed my eyes for a moment. "Uh, no. It was an animal, I think. I'm going to need to call a tow truck."

"Are you okay at least?" she asked, suddenly getting around to worrying about my wellbeing. Mom wasn't what you would call responsible. She often forgot to turn off the coffee pot in the morning or pack my lunch when I was in first grade. I learned quickly how to take care of myself.

"I'm fine," I assured her. "Just another chapter to add to our adventure." Mom liked to think of each move—or *starting over*, as she so eloquently liked to say—as an adventure. I was tired of adventures and just wanted a place to call home.

"I'll turn around. Give me five minutes." Through the phone, I heard her flip on the blinker.

"Don't bother. I don't want to worry Gigi, and there's no need for us both to wait for someone to show up. I'll call you for directions as soon as my car is back on the road."

"Are you sure?"

"Positive. I'll just look up a towing company on my phone and give them a call. No big deal." So I kept telling myself. *I can handle this. It's time to start adulting.* Which I pretty much had been doing since I was ten. That was when husband number one had decided he'd had enough and split, walking out on us both.

I didn't know my real dad. Never had. One of the pitfalls of being a product of teen pregnancy. Eighteen-year-old prospective fathers don't always stick around.

We didn't need him.

"Okay, honey. Call me as soon as you're back on the road. The house is only ten minutes from where you are," she said. I could tell she was chewing on her lip, her nervous habit.

I assured her I would and hung up, immediately scouring the Internet on my phone for a local tow company. It took forever and a day for the search engine to load, and I blamed the soaring mountains. They were everywhere, and as breathtaking as the view was, my immediate concern was the crappy cell service.

"Come on," I encouraged under my breath, two seconds away from chucking my phone across the road. "Finally," I groaned as a single name and number popped up. *Havenwood Falls Garage & Tow Service.* Perfect. I clicked on the *Call Now* link and waited as the phone rang.

A gruff voice answered, and after I relayed my dire situation in way too much detail, he assured me help would be on the way in no more than twenty minutes. Crisis averted.

Now what to do to kill time? I tapped my fingers on the steering wheel before climbing out of the car. I left the keys in the cup holder and got my first real glimpse of the town I'd be living in for the next ten months. Come graduation, I was gone.

A river ran alongside the road near the base of the impressive mountains, bubbling faintly in the distance. The air was definitely crisp and cleaner as it moved in and out of my lungs. It seemed . . . peaceful, and I didn't know why that surprised me. Across the road was a quaint little neighborhood.

Pulling up the camera on my phone, I angled myself so the mountains were backdropped behind me and snapped a few selfies —okay, twenty, but I wanted to document the moment. My first catastrophe in my new home. Who wouldn't want that memory to laugh about someday?

I liked journals and scrapbooks. It was fun looking back on what was going on in my head or seeing the pictures of my friends. Wisconsin was far away now, including my old life. This marked my new journey aka stuck in hell, but regardless of the bad attitude, I would try for Gigi's sake to make the most of it. No moping around the house.

Fifteen minutes had passed when a truck pulled up, kicking dust in the air as I was snapping a picture of me in front of my poor car, angled so the trunk was sticking up in the air. I spun around and waited for the truck driver to get out. The name of the towing company was painted on the side of his cab. Tucking the loose strands of my honey-blond hair behind my ears, I smoothed the wrinkles from my hoodie. It had been a long drive, and I definitely wasn't looking my finest, but what did I care what some old grease monkey thought of me?

The door swung open and out stepped long legs covered in dark denim, but as the rest of him unfolded, my breath sort of stalled in my lungs. Broad shoulders lifted as he grabbed the side of the door, flashing a bit of defined abs. His jeans hung low on his hips, hugging a perfectly formed butt. My eyes traveled upward to his full, kissable lips, sharp cheeks, and stormy violet eyes fanned by sooty lashes. He looked down at me, the corner of his lip curving.

Holy crap. Nothing about the truck driver was greasy, saggy, smelly, or old.

His unusual and mesmerizing eyes captivated me, drawing me in until I felt as if I was floating in space.

Hot guy alert. Don't freak out. Don't freak out.

What did I do? I pocketed my phone and started rambling. "Thanks for coming. A thing jumped out in front of me, and I had to swerve off the road to avoid hitting it. Not exactly how I pictured my first day here, but maybe the universe is telling me something." *Someone stop me. Now! Before I give him my entire life story.*

"A thing?" he echoed in a deep, firm voice, lifting a condescending dark brow.

Internal wince. Hot guys made me nervous, and I couldn't be held accountable for the nonsense that came out of my mouth. "I'm not sure what it was—wolf or hellhound or bigfoot—take your pick. It was big and hairy."

His lips twitched. "If you say so."

A wave of embarrassment heated my cheeks.

He swept aside the half of his obsidian hair that was long, the other part shaved short. "Are the keys in the car?"

I nodded. "Cup holder."

He brushed past me to open the car door.

Damn. He smelled amazing, like insta-lust in a bottle.

I hated him. And wanted to have his babies at the same time.

"What are you doing in Havenwood Falls?" he asked as he dropped into the driver's seat, snatching up the keys. His eyes scanned the boxes in the backseat. "Vacation?"

"I wish," I groaned. "Divorce."

His questioning eyes found mine.

"Not me," I quickly clarified, feeling utterly mortified. "My mom. We're moving in with my grandma," I informed him, giving him more information than I normally would a total stranger.

"Sorry," he said, a glint of sympathy beaming in his gaze.

I hated being pitied, and my jaw tightened. "Nothing to be sorry for. Brady was a dick." Why was I telling him this?

"You should meet my brother. He takes being a dick to a new level."

I found my lips twitching, even though I didn't want to be amused by him. "And who would your brother be?" I fished. "Just so I can make sure to stay clear," I added so he wouldn't think I was hunting for information, which of course I was.

"I have two, but it's Brysen you have to watch out for. I'm Torent. Torent Stark. And you would be?" His smile reeked of trouble, and not the good kind.

"Mallory Dorian." I couldn't get over how perfectly symmetrical his face was, and I was damn sure his tongue was pierced.

"Who did you say your grandmother was? I probably know her. Havenwood Falls is that kind of town."

Swell. The corner of my lips curved. "I didn't say."

He shifted the car in neutral, and taking the keys with him, stepped out of the car. His full height, which I guessed to be just over six feet, forced me to tip my head back to look him in the eyes. Something about the violet color intrigued me, a glint in the irises that wasn't normal. He arched a brow as he waited for a name.

I had prolonged intentionally. "Layla Whitt."

"Seriously?"

My eyes narrowed. "What is that supposed to mean?"

"Nothing. I just didn't know she had a granddaughter."

He wasn't telling me something, and I wanted to press him. I didn't like secrets, and it had become clear that he was hiding something. "Yeah, well, this is my first time in Havenwood Falls. Actually, in Colorado."

"So you're a . . ." He left the unfinished question dangling as if he was second-guessing himself. Those unusual eyes bored into mine.

"I'm what?" I prompted, watching as he grabbed the hooky-thingamabob from the back of his truck.

He glanced over his shoulder while he secured the anchor under my car, and I caught the flash of a tattoo on his forearm. The movement had been too quick for me to get a clear view, but I was intrigued.

"A sophomore?" he posed.

That was so not what was on his mind. *What gives?* Torent Stark was hiding something, but why? What could he possibly know about me or my family? "No, I'm a senior."

Straightening up, he dusted off his hands on his jeans. "That's got to be rough, changing schools in the middle of a semester."

The sun was at his back, highlighting the sides of his cheekbones. Of all the people to meet first in Havenwood Falls, I had to encounter the most roguish of guys.

I shrugged. When hadn't my life been rough? "It's only seven months. I'll manage."

Something glittered in his eyes. "So you don't plan on sticking around after?"

Were all the people here this talkative? "Just long enough to graduate, and then I'm off to college."

Sauntering back to the truck, he wrenched open the door. "Havenwood Falls might surprise you. Who knows, you might find a reason to stick around." The lopsided smirk he aimed at me made my stomach cartwheel.

Was he implying *he* might be worth sticking around for? How presumptuous. I didn't even know him and wasn't positive I wanted to, regardless of how he made my insides react.

With that carnal grin still playing on his lips, Torent jumped into the truck to hit the button. In under a minute, my car was safely out of the ditch and back on the road. There might have been one or two scratches to commemorate my first day in Havenwood Falls, but I was more concerned about the mark Torent Stark had left on me.

"How much do I owe you?" I asked, tilting my head to the side as he slid out of the truck to lean against the side.

"It's on the house. Consider it a welcoming gift." A breeze blew through from the surrounding mountains, picking up pieces of his wind-tousled hair and sweeping them over one eye.

The urge to reach up and brush the loose strand of hair rose up inside me. I hadn't expected it.

"You really don't have to do that," I insisted, shoving my hands in my pockets before I did something stupid—like touched him.

"I know. But maybe you'll remember what a nice guy I was once you start school."

I gave him a funny look. "Are you saying you're not a nice guy?"

His gaze dropped and ran over my face. Something was there I couldn't quite grasp—a warning? "Definitely not. Welcome to Havenwood Falls, crash car. See you Monday." He dropped the keys into my hand.

Not if I can help it.

Slipping into the driver's seat, I put the keys into the ignition and turned. The car cranked over once before finally starting.

"Thanks for your help," I said, looking up at him with a straight face, the door still open.

He winked. "Anytime."

I didn't plan on making a habit of being rescued by Torent Stark. Something told me to stay far and clear from him. I sat in my car, frowning as Stark got into the truck. I knew guys like him. They were distractions, the kind that got you pregnant before graduation, and that was the very last thing I wanted.

To be my mom.

CHAPTER 2

I pulled into the long driveway lined with aspen trees. The gold and orange leaves made the trees seem as if they were on fire. Fall was in full bloom, colors popping in the flowerbed surrounding the large porch of Gigi's house.

As I opened the car door, the smell of burning wood blew in with the crisp breeze that rattled the leaves overhead. I huddled deeper into my Wisconsin Badger hoodie.

Gigi's house was nestled deep in Havenwood Falls, outside of town. I'd always looked forward to Gigi's visits. Eccentric she was, but it was one of the many things I adored about her. I knew very little about the town where Gigi lived. Odd, considering Mom grew up here, but she didn't like to talk about her past.

Coming home to live with Gigi was a slap in the face, and it took every ounce of willpower Mom had to come back here and ask for help. Pride had made her stay away for seventeen years.

And it only took three failed marriages for her to return home.

Grabbing a box from the backseat, I hiked it up the porch. Gigi and Mom were waiting for me, having heard my car pull up.

"You made it, sunshine." Gigi placed her soft hands on my cheeks, and followed with a kiss. Her silvery hair still shone with highlights of her former color, honey blond like mine. It was long and wavy, framing her oval face. Gigi wasn't like most grandmothers, and it wasn't just that she looked fabulous for her age, with only the lightest of wrinkles crinkling at the corners of her eyes. Her mind was sharp, her tongue was loose, and she had an aura of energy about her.

I adored the ever-loving crap out of her. Unlike Mom, I was ecstatic to see her. Handing the box over to Mom, I gave Gigi a proper hug. "It was no big deal. The guy at the garage pulled out my car, and there was no permanent damage."

"Joshua?" she asked.

I shook my head. "No, his name was Torent."

Gigi's lips twitched, a twinkling moving into her aqua eyes. "Ah, the Stark boy. He's your age, if I recall. The youngest of the three boys."

"He mentioned he had two brothers."

That gleam in her eyes intensified. "Did he now?"

Oh no. I knew that look. It was the one she got when she was plotting something. "Don't start. I'm only here until I graduate, and the last thing I need is you trying to set me up with a guy."

"I agree," Mom added, in case we wanted her opinion. She shifted the box to her hip. The last beams of sun caught the side of her face, picking up the platinum blond streaks she added to her hair. "Mallory is smart. She's going places, going to be someone." Everything Mom had always wanted, when she had put aside her dreams to have me.

"Are you still aiming for that swimming scholarship?" Gigi asked.

I nodded. "If I can keep up my grades, then I have a chance. My coach promised to write a letter of recommendation on my behalf."

"You'll get that scholarship. No one deserves it more than you," Gigi boasted, my personal cheerleader.

"Thanks." I smiled, needing that little boost of confidence.

She draped an arm around my waist. "Let's get you settled in. I've got your mom's old room ready for you."

"Wonderful," Mom said, rolling her eyes.

"Don't worry, Wendy. I had the loft on the third floor made up for you. Lots of privacy." Gigi winked at me.

This would be an interesting year.

∽

STANDING in front of my car, I stared at the three-story red brick building, watching as the hordes of teens rushed into the school through the arched doorways. I took a deep breath. For a flicker of a moment, I contemplated hopping back into my car and driving up into the mountains, away from all my doubts and insecurities. But then I reminded myself: ten months—that was all I had until I got the piece of paper that would allow me to pursue my dreams. I wasn't going to give up on my swimming.

Here goes nothing.

I moved with the crowds, blending in as I made my way to the front office of Havenwood Falls High. It wasn't hard to find. Principal Friske's name was on the door. I gave the woman behind the desk my name, and she handed me a printout of my schedule and locker number with the combination. The basics. Every school had them.

"Books will be handed out in the classrooms," the secretary informed me.

I nodded and took the slip of paper, giving it a once-over. AP Statistics. French III. Physics. AP Lit. Lunch. Blah. Blah. Blah. It was all very similar to my classes in my old school.

Locker number 256.

HFH wasn't difficult to navigate. As I walked down the halls, the upcoming homecoming dance seemed to be a hot topic. I passed a group of rowdy football players chanting "Kase Kasun," who I assumed was a key player.

I found my locker easily. It was the combinations that were always tricky. By the third unsuccessful try, I was about to kick the darn thing when I heard a familiar voice.

"Hey, crash car."

I dropped my forehead onto the locker. *Why?* I asked myself as a swarm of glowing fireflies fluttered in my belly. A body leaned on the gray locker beside mine, and I turned my head to the side to stare at Torent Stark.

Damn.

Why couldn't he have been less attractive than I remembered?

An easy smile crossed his full lips, and the conversation in the hall faded as I gazed into his eyes. They were as bright and mischievous as before. Several of the girls walking by glanced over their shoulders to stare, and who could blame them? Torent had this rock star quality that grabbed everyone's attention, including mine, and I didn't like it.

His jeans hung low on his hips, so when he lifted his hand to run his fingers through his already tousled hair, his black T-shirt tightened against his chest. Torent Stark reeked of danger. I could hear my best friend from Wisconsin, Addison, in my head telling me I needed a dose of danger, that my life was too safe, too boring.

She might be right, but that didn't mean I would fall for the charms of a guy like Torent.

I needed to stop gawking at him and say something that wouldn't sound lame. "Hey."

Yep. Not lame at all.

He plucked the slip of paper from my fingers. "Let's see." His eyes scanned down my schedule. "Wow, crash car. You've got brains."

"Does that intimidate you?" I challenged, lifting my brows. Was I flirting? *Stop it. No flirting allowed.*

A lazy grin curved up one side of his lips. "Nah. I dig brains."

Wonderful.

"Do you need help with that?" he asked, nodding his head at the finicky locker.

"It's all yours," I said, stepping aside to give him a crack. How had I not noticed the little scar on his right eyebrow the other day? It only added to his rebel without a cause persona.

The locker clicked open, pulling my gaze away from his face. "Voilà. It just takes a magic touch."

And I bet Torent had fingers of magic. "Thanks."

"It looks like we have first period together. I'll walk you to class."

"How gallant of you." I shoved a stack of binders and notebooks inside the locker, keeping one of each in my hands before slamming the door shut.

"The car okay?" His lips twitched at the reminder of our first encounter.

My eyes were drawn to his mouth before I forced them to meet his gaze. "For now. I'm surprised it made the trip all the way from Wisconsin," I admitted.

A pretty raven-haired girl sauntered up behind Torent, looping her arms around his waist and resting her chin on his shoulder.

"Who's your new friend?" she asked with a sneer, dark blue eyes assessing me. She made her intentions very clear. Torent Stark was hers.

He has a girlfriend. That was what ran through my head, along with an irrational amount of disappointment. Of course he had a girlfriend. Just look at the guy.

Unless I was mistaken, Torent wasn't pleased with the interruption. The muscle along his jaw tightened. "Mallory Dorian, this is Brooklyn Kendall."

"Pleasure," Brooklyn replied in a condescending tone and quickly dismissed me, returning her attention to Torent. "I missed you last night," she murmured in his ear.

I thought I caught a flicker of annoyance in his eyes, as he unraveled Brooklyn's arms from around his waist. "I had to work."

She huffed, her Cupid's bow mouth turning down into a pretty pout. Brooklyn looked like the girl who was used to getting what she wanted. "Remind me why again? It's not like you need the money."

I felt like an intruder listening in on the conversation, and awkwardness followed.

Buzzzzzzzzzzzzz.

Thank God. Saved by the bell. The first period warning sounded through the halls, giving us five minutes to get to class. I thought about just slipping into the stream of kids moving down the hall, doubting Torent or Brooklyn would notice I was gone.

"You know why," Torent replied, letting a teensy bit of exasperation leak into his voice. "Mallory and I have first period together. I'll see you later."

Brooklyn wasn't going to be brushed off so easily. She twisted her midnight hair around her finger and laid her other hand on Torent's arm. "I'm sure she can get to homeroom without a babysitter. It's not like Havenwood Falls High is a labyrinth."

I was positive I had just made my first enemy, and it only took what, ten minutes? Boom. New record. Girls like her ruined the high school experience. "Seriously, it's fine. I need to learn my way around on my own. I can't have you walking me to every class."

Brooklyn's blue eyes darkened, and not giving Torent a chance to overrule me, I turned and melded into the crowd, but not before I caught a glimpse of the scowl on his perfect lips.

Ugh.

Get him out of your brain, Mal. He's not for you.

~

I SURVIVED the first half of the day with only a dash of humiliation. It could have been worse. And I had only gotten lost twice, but the day wasn't over yet.

The cafeteria was no different than my last high school. Grease coated the air, along with subtle hints of perfume, sweat, and teenage angst. Between the scents and my nerves, I could kiss my appetite goodbye.

A guy with shaggy blue hair sighed and plopped down next to me at the empty lunch table. "God, what I wouldn't do for just five minutes alone in the janitor's closet with that."

I hadn't realized I'd been staring until the newcomer caught me. His gaze, like mine, was fixed on Torent and Brooklyn strolling into the cafeteria as if they owned the place, looking like the perfect high school couple.

"She is pretty," I admitted, never mind that the admission felt like sandpaper in my throat.

He made a face, scrunching his nose. "Honey, I wasn't talking about the she-devil. Brooklyn Kendall is as ugly inside as she is out."

I think I just found my new BFF. My expression must have still held disappointment at seeing how cozy Brooklyn was with Torent.

"Uh-oh. Don't tell me the infamous Torent has already claimed another victim? The guy has been breaking hearts since kindergarten."

I stiffened my shoulders and forced my eyes back to my veggie wrap, reminding myself why I was here. "Definitely not."

"That's what we all say," he said, flashing me an award-winning grin. "Beck Winslow."

I smiled in return. "Mallory Dorian."

His gray eyes twinkled, matching the silver hoop in his eyebrow. "I know who you are. Everyone does."

"Fabulous," I groaned. Torent and Brooklyn had joined a group on the other side of the room, sitting down.

Beck's gaze followed mine. "He does have a very fine ass. If he even thinks about jumping to the other team, I'm throwing myself at him."

I laughed, unable to help myself. Something about Beck and the way he said whatever crazy thing on his mind reminded me of Addison. She would have loved him, blue hair, black earplugs, a touch of nerd, and all.

He lifted a brow. "You think I'm joking."

"Does it matter?" I retorted, picking at my sandwich.

"I knew I would like you." Just as Torent had done, Beck plucked my schedule from atop my notebook, which had been sitting on the table. His eyes read down the column. "Girl's got brains. Thank God you're not another boy-crazed bimbo with big boobs."

"Nope. No big boobs here," I pointed out.

Plucking an apple from his food tray, he grinned. "With that face, who needs them?"

I smiled. It was nice to have a friend, someone I could relate to, and I had a really good feeling about Beck.

He took a bite out of the shiny red apple, eyes returning to scroll down my schedule. "It looks like we're going to be study buddies. Not counting lunch, we have four classes together, including first period with the heart-stealing Torent, I might add."

I groaned. I hadn't noticed Beck during first period, but that was probably because I couldn't take my eyes off Torent. He was definitely not going to be good for my GPA, but as luck would have it, so far, it was the only class we had together.

Beck handed me back my schedule, meeting my gaze head on. "Don't let Brooklyn get to you. Pretty girls threaten her, and by the ferocious scowl she's aiming at your back, she knows she's got competition."

"Good to know. So should I come to school tomorrow looking like a hag to get off her radar?"

Something colorful about Beck delighted me. I couldn't place my finger on it, but it wasn't just his hair color. "On anyone else, that might work, but you've already caught the attention of what she considers hers. HFH's cutie."

Goodie gumdrops. I didn't have to ask who he was talking about. "What's their deal? Is she his girlfriend?" I couldn't believe I was even asking. What did I care if he had a girlfriend?

I don't care.

Yep. It wasn't working.

"What day is it?" he asked, looking thoughtful.

I wrinkled my nose.

He was quick to fill me in on the HFH gossip. "Those two are on again, off again. It's dizzying. Who knows, maybe they're back on, but last I heard through the Havenwood Falls gossip chain, Torent had broken things off."

I nibbled on my lower lip. Interesting.

No! There is nothing interesting about Torent.

Beck leaned down on the table, lowering his voice. "Just be careful with Brooklyn. She isn't afraid to get dirty, and being a

Whitt puts a target on your back even without lusting after Torent."

"I'm not lusting after him," I defended myself, but it sounded weak, even to me. Then it dawned on me that he had referred to Gigi. "Why does my family have anything to do with Brooklyn's dislike of me?"

Now it was his turn to give me an odd sideways glance. His hand reached along the table and grabbed both my arms, flipping them over.

"No hidden tattoos?" he asked, eyes searching over my body.

Okay, this just got weird.

"Should I?" Did I look like a girl who got her body inked?

Releasing both my arms, he leaned back in the plastic chair, observing me with open curiosity. What was I missing here?

"Interesting," he mumbled to himself, his fingers brushing over his chin.

"I'm going to need more than that. What is interesting? Are tattoos like a prerequisite here or something?" I was joking, but a flicker in Beck's face gave me pause.

He laughed in an awkward cover-up kind of way. "No, of course not."

Nice try. What was he hiding? What did tattoos have to do with it? Now that my mind was on alert, I remembered that Torent had a tattoo. And so did Beck. I had caught a quick glimpse of it on the back of his neck, just above the shirt collar.

"You have a tattoo," I pointed out.

His hand moved to rub at the top of his spine. "Yeah, a drunk night regret. I don't recommend it. Puking after having a needle repeatedly stabbed into your neck? Not a fun time."

"Noted," I said, taking a sip of my water, but I wasn't buying the whole I-got-drunk-and-woke-up-with-a-tattoo routine.

And as I went about the rest of the day, I noticed more and more students had them. On their arms, wrists, ankles. I was positive even Brooklyn herself had one. That star-shaped beauty mark above her lip—it was too seamless to be DNA.

For the most part, Havenwood Falls High was like any other school I'd been to. I didn't know why that surprised me. There were the usual cliques, the muscle-bound jocks, the math nerds, the dark artsy group, the all-too-perfect plastics, the dramatic theater kids, and everyone else in between.

And then me.

The shiny new girl—who everyone stared at like I was a sparkling Christmas bauble. I hated the attention.

The bell rang.

It was finally the best part of the day—the end.

CHAPTER 3

*A*fter school, I only wanted one thing—to relax and unwind. Sitting in my car, I flipped the little key card to the Creekwood Country Club in my hand.

"Why the hell not?" I said out loud.

If there was a pool within my reach, I would be in it, and the prospect of a steaming sauna afterward was too much to resist. I stuck the keys into my car and let the engine rip to life—or in my car's case, sputter.

I would have to take it sooner than later for its own sort of pampering, which had nothing to do with a certain part-time mechanic/tow truck driver.

I loved when I fooled myself.

The Creekwood Country Club had all the amenities you would expect—golfing, ski access, a nice restaurant, a full-service spa, and a private lounge with a bar. But it had only one amenity that I cared about—two, if you counted the sauna.

A lap pool was inside a glass enclosure with breathtaking views every which way you looked. It connected to the outside smaller pleasure pool and Jacuzzi. Due to the briskness in the air, I chose to stay inside.

Quickly changing in the lockers, I dropped a towel and my cell phone onto an empty lounge chair. I had the pool to myself, and my excitement went up a notch. It was too early for the older crowd still pushing the nine-to-five, and I seriously doubted the country club was considered a hotspot for the local teens to hang out.

Which made it my perfect sanctuary.

I'd swum varsity since my freshman year, and during the summers, I had worked at the local YMCA giving lessons. It was hard knowing I wouldn't be competing this year, but it didn't mean I had to give it up completely.

As I stared at the calm, crystal-blue water, all I wanted to do was get my butt in the pool and lose myself. I swore, sometimes it seemed as if the water whispered my name, enchanting me.

I slid into the pool and sighed, letting the balmy temperature rush over my skin. There were eight lanes in the lap pool, and I waded over to one in the middle. Warming up with some freestyle laps, I transitioned into the backstroke.

I loved swimming, the feel of the cool water rushing over my face as I glided effortlessly with the waves. It called to me, like a song, and I was powerless to do anything but answer. And then there was the mesmerizing light as it played and changed the deeper I dived.

I'd been swimming my whole life. It was a part of me as much as breathing was, and even when my lungs begged for air, I pushed myself, swimming on through the smooth blue water, strong and sure. Beads of water stuck to my eyelashes as I emerged through the surface, letting the sun warm my golden skin through the glass enclosure, and stared into Torent's stormy eyes.

A little squeak escaped at finding I was no longer alone.

"You scared me," I exhaled, using that as an excuse for the sudden spike in my heart rate.

"So you swim?" he asked, crouching down to the edge of the pool. He was fully clothed in the same black jeans, but had changed his shirt. It was identical to the one he had worn the day we met, Havenwood Falls Garage & Tow Service embroidered into the left breast. I had no clue how, but he managed to make the plain T-shirt sexy.

"There's a lot of things I do. Swimming is just one of them," I replied coolly, feeling pretty smug. I was not going to make a fool of myself around some guy. That's all he was—just a random guy. No one special.

Curiosity spread over his expression as he stared at me with an intense gaze. "You're different than the other girls."

I rested my arms on the edge of the concrete, the tips of my toes barely touching the bottom. "Because I swim?"

One side of his lips curved into a lopsided smirk. "I'm not sure yet. I can't place my finger on it, but there is something about you I find unique."

I could say the same thing about him, but in my case, I had a reasonable explanation. "It's because I'm the new girl."

We studied each other for a deep moment, neither of us moving. Hell, I barely blinked; I was so entranced by the color of his eyes.

He let his fingers dip into the water, nearly brushing my arm. "Maybe, but I don't think that's it."

"Are you always this forward?"

His expression turned impish as he flashed me a pair of killer dimples. "Usually. I'm used to getting what I want."

Was he implying that he wanted me? Well, too bad. I wasn't a possession he could acquire because he got an inkling. I was here to get my diploma and get on to the life I wanted to live. "What are you doing at the club? Stalking me?"

"Just making a drop-off. The shop did some repairs on a golf cart."

"Oh." My eyes glanced over his head to the clock on the wall. I needed to get home. Lifting up on my arms, I climbed out of the pool to see Torent standing and swinging my towel on his finger.

"Hand it over," I said, giving him a dry look.

His eyes swept over me in a slow perusal that did funny things to my belly—warm, gooey things. "Nice set."

And then he opened his mouth and said that. Typical pig. I lifted my brows.

"The swimsuit," he added, grinning like a total shithead.

Oh, he thought he was so witty.

"I'm sure that's what you meant." *Dickhead.* "Shouldn't you be working or rubbing your girlfriend's feet instead of bothering me?" *And ruining the only quiet I've had all day.*

His brow shot up. "You're referring to Brooklyn, I assume."

I wrapped the towel under my arms and tucked the corner in above my chest.

"You have more than one girlfriend. Go figure," I mumbled under my breath.

"I don't . . . have a girlfriend," he added.

I shrugged, dripping water on the concrete floor. "It really doesn't matter to me." *Lies!*

He moved closer and leaned into my space. "Then why bring it up?"

I wanted to duck under the nearest lounge chair and hit my head on the ground. Why indeed had I? Heat gathered in my cheeks, his nearness causing a shiver to roll through me. "I just don't want any crazy jealous girlfriend slashing my tires at school."

Amusing him wasn't what I had in mind, but his lips twitched, and I swore a glint of gold flecks sparkled in his violet eyes. "Brooklyn does have a tendency to overreact, but she isn't mentally unstable."

I took a step back and gathered the rest of my things. "I'll take your word for it. I need to get home."

"Goodbye, Mal." The husky way he shortened my name made my heart sigh, regardless of the fact that I didn't want to feel anything in his presence.

I padded into the shower room, not bothering to shower. I just changed and raced out of the locker room, eager to get home without any other run-ins with he who must not be named. Unfortunately, I bumped into someone way worse.

Brooklyn Kendall and two of her faithful followers.

Someone shoot me now. I wasn't up to having a faceoff with Havenwood Falls' queen bee.

Brooklyn was standing just outside the pool entrance with two other girls, staring at me like the Wicked Witch of the West. Her long glossy midnight hair was pulled back into a ponytail, and her sapphire eyes glared with gobs of hatred.

"Oh, hey." Internally, I cringed. The sight of Brooklyn at the club destroyed its perfect little haven appeal. I had really been hoping for a spot in Havenwood Falls I could call my own, feel comfortable. A pool might not be the right place.

She folded her arms, popping her curvy hip out to one side. "Ladies, let me make introductions. This is Mallory, you know, the new girl."

I stiffened. Would everything out of Brooklyn's mouth always be so snooty?

"Mallory, this is Leena Avon and Cora Sheldon. My squad."

Bitch squad was what she actually meant. The two girls were as flawless as Brooklyn—no shocker—with stunning faces and well put together outfits you only saw in magazines.

Then there was me. Wet hair. T-shirt with damp spots. Ripped jeans. And my favorite worn out Converse. In comparison, I felt poor and frumpy. Brooklyn and me, we weren't even in the same category.

"Nice to meet you," I replied with a smile, doing my best to be nice.

"Wow. That was an impressive backstroke." Leena flipped her dark hair over one shoulder. She was striking, slim, tall, and her skin was a beautiful sun-dusted color of bronze.

"I'll say. A little too good. No one can swim those times without some extra help," Brooklyn sneered.

Was she suggesting I was on drugs? "I don't know what you mean. I used to compete back in Wisconsin. I was the captain of my swim team."

"Cute," Brooklyn replied as if my life story was the most boring thing in the world, next to watching her dog get a bath.

"Do you guys swim?" I asked, attempting to make small talk, seeing as they made no indication of letting me walk past.

Cora shook her bubble-gum pink hair. She reminded me of a Strawberry Shortcake doll. "Not competitively. We just like to hang out at the club."

Brooklyn jabbed her in the side, as if Cora had said something she shouldn't. "I know you're new here and all. Let me give you a friendly bit of advice."

Ha. Friendly my ass. Here it comes. The real reason she stopped me.

The fake smile disappeared from her lips. "It's probably best if you stayed away from Torent Stark. I wouldn't want you to tarnish your family's name. Isn't that right, ladies?"

Cora and Leena nodded eagerly, but I seriously doubted either of them had a single thought for themselves. It was obvious they got all of their direction from Brooklyn, probably even how much sugar to put in their coffee, like little obedient robots.

"What are you talking about?" I prodded. I wanted Brooklyn to know she couldn't intimidate me.

A chilly look entered her eyes. "You haven't lived here as long as we have. The Stark family has a bad reputation—criminals, scoundrels, the usual bad apples."

"But didn't you date him?" I countered, wondering why she would pursue him so hard if he had such a nasty reputation.

"Right, making him off limits." She puckered her glossy lips.

Okay, that didn't make any sense, but I wasn't going to stand here damp, arguing her logic. I also wouldn't let her bully me. Who the hell did she think she was, telling me who I should and shouldn't talk to? Please. I wasn't a member of her *squad* she could order about.

"Thanks for the warning, but I think I can judge for myself who's not worth my time." And Brooklyn was at the top of the list.

I brushed past the bitch squad, leaving all three of them gaping after me. The shock on their faces brought a smile to my lips, but I knew I would pay for it. Regardless of what Torent thought of Brooklyn's character, I didn't trust her. She smacked of revenge.

CHAPTER 4

*T*omorrow was Friday, and that meant I had nearly survived a week at HFH. How hard could the rest of the year be?

Skipping off the sidewalk into the parking lot, I searched for my car, remembering I had parked in the back lot today. Timing was everything when it came to getting a premium spot, as I found out this morning when I'd been running late.

My mind was a million miles away, thinking about school, Addison, and what parties she would attend without me, and I didn't notice the weird angle my car sat at until I was in front of it.

"You've got to be freaking kidding." I stared at my lopsided car and massaged the side of my temple, feeling the headache I'd been fighting all day roar to life. The tire on the driver's side was flatter than my Mom's pancakes. "Son of a bitch," I hissed, sinking against the car.

Of course, I didn't have a spare. Why would I?

I had taken it out to make more room in my trunk for the move. *Smart move, Mallory. I bet you're really regretting that now.*

A chorus of giggles from across the lot caught my attention. Who else would it be but Brooklyn, Cora, and Leena, the three wicked witches. Steam blew out of my ears as my hands clenched together. I was about to go storming over there and grab Brooklyn by her ponytail when I heard a deep voice.

"Hey, crash car, looks like you've got a bit of a problem."

I groaned. Of all the people in the school, Torent Stark was the last person I wanted to see or ask for help.

"I'm going to pop your girlfriend's implants," I growled.

His gaze followed my glaring eye line. "Brooklyn? I told you she isn't my—"

"Save it," I interrupted. "I'm not in the mood for another 'we're just friends' lecture."

"Who spit in your latte?"

"Do you really have to ask?"

He ran a hand through his dark hair.

"I'll take care of her," he said in a short voice that sent a tremor down my spine.

I pulled my glare from Brooklyn to look at Torent. Those gold specks were back. "I'm not sure anyone can control the hurricane known as Brooklyn Kendall."

He leaned one hand on the open car door and the other on the roof, keeping me boxed against the car with his body. "No truer words might have been spoken. But seriously, she'll listen to me."

I ignored the warm fuzzies inside my belly. "It couldn't hurt. But I'm warning you, if she doesn't back down, things are going to get ugly."

"I might just put my money on you." He nodded over his shoulder. "Come on. I'll give you a lift home."

Chewing on my lip, I wondered if it was a good idea for me to be alone in a confined space with him. "What about my car? I can't leave it here."

He had an answer for everything. "I'll come back and take it to the shop, fix the tire, and have it dropped off tonight."

Damn. Why was he being so nice? It was making it really hard to hate him. "You don't have to do that. I can call the garage."

He pushed his hands into his back pockets and rocked on his heels. "And you would still get me."

Right. How could I forget? "Fine. I'd thank you, but I don't want it to go to your head."

"Smart," he agreed, grinning.

"At least you got that right." I grabbed my bag and dropped my car keys into his open palm once again.

Following him to his black Jeep, he surprised me by opening the passenger door for me. Our fingers accidentally brushed as I hopped to get inside. Tiny sparks of electricity ignited on contact.

"Ouch. You shocked me," I accused, sitting in the bucket seat.

"We're electric," he replied with a wicked grin.

A frown pulled at my lips.

"That's totally what I was thinking," I retorted dryly.

He shut the car door, and I watched him go around to the driver's side. My lips formed a tight line as I repeatedly told myself there was nothing special about this guy, that he didn't look every bit as delicious as I imagined.

The engine purred to life, and my gaze dropped to his lips. For each butterfly flutter I felt in my belly, my irritation mounted. So what if his car smelled amazing and I wanted to roll around in it? So what if he made my pulse race whenever he was near?

"This is all your fault," I hurled at him after a few minutes of stewing. We were at the end of the school driveway, getting ready to pull out onto First Street.

"How so?"

I stared straight ahead, watching the road roll by. "Your girlfriend thinks you're flirting with me."

"I am," he said, causing my head to whip toward him. He was grinning. "And she's not my girlfriend."

"Tell that to her," I mumbled, sinking further into the seat.

His fingers held the steering wheel loosely, like he was born to drive. "Oh, trust me, Brooklyn and I are going to have a talk. She has issues with boundaries."

"I'll say," I grumbled. "She cornered me at the club and basically told me she owned you."

That brought a dark scowl to his face.

"No one owns me," he stated with a serious intensity.

I shifted uncomfortably in the seat. For the first time, I could see the danger that lay buried inside Torent. Brooklyn hadn't been kidding about him being dangerous. "Why do I get the feeling there is more to this thing between Brooklyn and me?"

He gave me a slow grin that had my breath catching. "Maybe because you have stellar intuition."

"Are you going to tell me or make me beg?"

"Begging sounds good."

I hit him playfully on the shoulder. "Never going to happen."

He was somehow overwhelmingly close. "Never say never, Mal. I bet I could make you beg."

Holy crap. Was it getting hot in here? Time to stick to the topic, and no more sexual innuendoes in a closed car with Torent. He was too tempting.

"Can you think about something other than sex?"

"I'm a guy. What do you expect?"

"Tell me what you know," I demanded.

He sighed, swinging his truck into the wooded driveway. "I don't know details, only that something happened between her family and yours back in the day. Some kind of beef."

"Beef?" I echoed, staring at the cozy cottage that was now my home. "Gigi is the sweetest woman on the planet. What could possibly cause tension between our families?"

He shrugged, letting the car roll to a stop. "I told you. I don't have details. Brooklyn and I didn't spend a lot of time discussing her family."

Great. Now I had images of him doing *things* with Brooklyn, and it induced an unreasonable bout of jealousy inside me. It was a good thing we were already at Gigi's, or I might have jumped from his moving Jeep. I pulled the door handle.

"I just bet you didn't." Then I hopped out and slammed the door, hoping it would make me feel better. It didn't.

As I started to stomp across the lawn, Torent's laugh reached me, fueling a fresh fit of rage. I gave him the one figure salute. *Take that, Torent Stark.*

His damn roguish laugh only grew louder.

Gah. For good measure, I lifted my other hand in the air, mimicking the gesture.

Behind me, the crunching tires of his truck slowly backed out of the driveway, and I hiked up the porch.

"How was your day?" Gigi asked from the swing. A hint of a smile played on her lips.

I dropped my bag near the front door and slumped down beside her. The wood creaked and swayed under my weight. "Utter shit."

Gigi didn't bat an eye at my language. She was used to much worse from my mother, so I doubted anything I could do or say would surprise her. "Is that why you were giving the Stark boy such a rude finger gesture?"

"Yes, it was." Why did I let Torent get under my skin? I wrinkled my nose. "It was nothing he didn't deserve."

The swing glided smoothly underneath us. "Do you want to talk about it?"

I snorted. "Not in this century."

"DINNER!" Gigi called from downstairs.

Thank God. A distraction I could get behind. Food.

And not Mom's.

Sitting in my room, pretending to do homework, was not going well. Especially when I couldn't get Torent's face out of my head. Those damn dimples.

Dinner at the Whitts' residence was a bit tense. For as long as I could remember, Gigi and Mom never saw eye-to-eye regarding anything.

"So how did the job hunt go, Wendy?" Gigi asked Mom as she passed the salad bowl.

"Are you going to hound me every night?" Mom snapped back.

"I got an A on my Chemistry test today," I quickly interjected, trying to defuse the situation before it spun out of control.

"So you're adjusting well to school then?" Gigi asked, slicing a piece of beef she had roasted in the crockpot.

I shrugged, pushing the salad around on my plate.

"For the most part." I did my best to keep any distress from leaking into my voice.

Gigi picked up on it regardless. Sometimes I thought she had psychic abilities. She had an eerie way of sensing emotions. "Does it have anything to do with the boy?"

"What boy?" Mom asked, perking up at the mention of a guy. Just like Mom. Some things never changed.

"No. Definitely not." *Liar!* my mind screamed.

Mom grinned, lifting her fork to her mouth. "Then why are your cheeks suddenly red?"

Mom was a quandary. One minute she was all, "Stay away from boys, Mallory," and the next, she was picking out which hot guy should be my prom date.

"Because it's hot in here." What a sad excuse. No one would believe that.

"Who is this boy who doesn't have you all worked up?" Mom asked, stabbing a forkful of greens.

"Torent Stark," Gigi answered for me.

"Gigi," I hissed, ready to drop my face into my plate of mashed potatoes.

"Seriously?" Mom asked, raising her brows. "Wow."

I frowned at her from across the table. "Why is that such a surprise? You know his family?"

"Yeah. I went to school with his mom, Raina. I wouldn't have pegged him as your type. He's a little rough around the edges, don't you think?"

"Didn't you know his father as well?" Gigi added.

Mom stared at her plate, looking a bit lost in the past for a moment. "Calmar Stark." I swore she shuddered when she said his name, and the tightening of her mouth wasn't a mirage. "He went to the Academy."

I assumed she meant the private school here in Havenwood Falls. I didn't know much about it, other than I'd overheard Willa Kasun say something about Sun and Moon Academy during lunch the other day.

"Why do I get the feeling you don't like his father?" I questioned.

Her expression turned serious, and it unnerved me. "Just do me a favor. Be careful."

Mom had a reason for running away from this place and never looking back until now. More than ever, I wanted to unearth why. What happened seventeen years ago? I'd always thought it was because of something between Mom, Gigi, and my father, but now I wasn't so sure.

"What exactly should I be worried about?"

Mom waved her fork at me. "Just who you pick as your friends. I don't want you getting mixed up with the wrong crowds."

And just who constituted as the wrong crowd?

"Like Brooklyn Kendall?" I asked, testing the reaction of the table.

Dead silence.

No one moved a single muscle.

Wow. That wasn't exactly what I envisioned happening, and now my curiosity about the past exploded to new levels.

Gigi and Mom shared a look. For once, it looked like they might be in agreement on something. Keeping me in the dark.

"Is that what happened to your tire today at school?" Mom concluded.

Crap. I hadn't meant for this to be turned back around on me. "I'm sure I just ran over a nail. Flat tires happen all the time."

"Not in Havenwood Falls," Mom mumbled under her breath.

What did that mean?

CHAPTER 5

*H*ello, weekend.

It was Saturday, and I had no homework, no plans, and nothing to do, but I wasn't going to waste the day binge-watching reruns of *Vampire Diaries*. Besides, Gigi's TV reception sucked. What was with this place and technology? It was as if it was so far off the grid, nothing worked.

As promised, Torent had my car returned by the next morning, looking good as new. So instead of being cooped up all day, I was going to explore.

It was a beautiful, sunny fall day, one of the few left in October. The air was the perfect sweater weather temperature, and I'd been dying to check out the falls.

Tugging on a soft blue hoodie, I secured my blond hair into a messy bun and tied the laces on my Converse. I tucked my cell phone into my pocket and trotted down the stairs into the kitchen, grabbing a bottle of water and my car keys off the counter.

"I'm going out!" I yelled through the house, hoping someone heard me.

The drive to the falls wasn't far from where Gigi lived. I continued down Blackstone Road, and a tingle danced up my arms, causing my thoughts to travel back to the dinner conversation the other night. I made a mental note to grill Beck on any gossip he might have heard about my family.

I needed answers.

A cemetery sat to the right, and I whipped my car to the side of the road. Not creepy at all. Locking my car up, I hiked across the street. The falls, according to the map, should have been straight ahead through the woods from the cemetery. I didn't claim to be a great outdoorsman, but how hard could it be to find?

After an hour of wandering around in the woods, I knew one thing—I was lost.

"Shit," I swore. No question about it. One glimpse at my cell phone told me I was in deep crap. No service. Of course not.

I'd never been amazing at directions. *Thank you, Mom.* I must have somehow ended up walking too far to the west.

Turning around in circles, I stared through the blue spruces and towering cottonwoods. It all looked the same. I was about to panic when I picked up the sound of running water. I rushed toward the crashing of water, and when the woods finally gave way to a clearing, my entire body sighed.

Water rushed over low cliffs in a trio of falls dropping into a sparkling crystal pool of blue-green that looked like glass. I stood at the edge, breathing in the air flowing around me.

It wasn't as large as I had pictured, not by any means, but that didn't mean it was any less spectacular. The colors and textures of the water and the angle of the light intrigued me.

Mallory.

The water whispered my name. It wasn't an unusual thing. I'd been hearing the call of the lake my whole life, but something unique about the pool of the falls gave me pause.

I saw a flash, a glint shimmering like gold in the sunlight carving through the water, and for an instant, a spark of blue swirled like fairy dust, then was gone.

What was that?

Slipping out of my shoes, I waded into the shallow edge of the lake, dirt and sand squishing between my toes. I gasped at the bite of coldness, but after a moment, it didn't bother me.

Strange.

Most people would think me insane to go into the water at this time of year, but I couldn't explain it. I was compelled.

I let my fingers skim over the surface, feeling the water. An uninterested silver fish swam past me, on his way to the falls, where the water was bubbling. I stepped farther in, the water coming up past my knees, and a gentle hum filled the air. It was as if the lake was saying, *Welcome home, Mallory. What's taken you so long? We've been waiting.*

I blinked, feeling slightly disoriented, but I shook it off, going deeper, toward the spot where I had seen the flash of gold. I'd never imagined when I started the day that I would find myself wading in a lake, seeking out something I couldn't explain, all because of a feeling.

The water was getting higher, to the point I would soon have to dive under. I shivered as the sun peeked through a cluster of branches, again cutting into the water. There it was. The shiny object.

Here goes nothing.

Holding my breath, I ducked under, and a quick gasp escaped. Dang, it was cold, searing my skin in pinpricks. Wasting not a second more, I dove to the bottom, easily spotting the tiny trinket sitting on a bed of sand and shells. A halo of light beamed like a beacon. I reached out my fingers, clasping them around the object, and turned to kick off the bottom. A tide of water rushed over my face, carrying with it a song like a thousand mermaids singing. It surrounded me from all sides, seeming to carry me deeper into the lake.

I should have been scared, freaked out of my goddamn gourd, but I wasn't. Just the opposite. I was glowing, bathed in a soft blue light that carried a warmth of protection, like a bubble. And I found an ease in my lungs, allowing me to breathe underwater.

What the hell?

I paused in the center of the lake, my feet paddling in the water to keep me afloat, and through the blue mist surrounding me were faces—beautiful women who looked like goddesses, draped in crowns and jewels. They were physically there, but as if they were part of the water.

Your time has come, daughter of goddess Styx. Their voices spoke as one unified, powerful voice. *Your awakening is upon you, and we welcome you into the fold, like our mothers before us. We are your sisters, Mallory, and this is our gift to you.*

What gift? The ring I had plucked from the bottom of the lake? This had to be some kind of hallucination, didn't it? Maybe the water was poisoned.

But the *gift* they were speaking of made itself known quickly.

A blinding flash of light exploded in the water. My ears throbbed, and I lost all sense of direction, unable to pinpoint the surface. The lake whirled in a mad blur, an insanity of color and intense coldness.

If this was the kind of gift they were offering me, I didn't want it.

Time didn't seem to exist in the lake, and I thought I might have passed out for a moment or two, but as reality slowly returned, I heard a voice, one I was certain I recognized.

Mallory! Mallory, can you hear me?

Yes, stop yelling. I hear you, I responded, or maybe I had in my head. It wasn't clear.

Mallory! Open your eyes.

Someone shook my shoulders, jostling me, and with effort, I peeled my eyes open. My vision was blurred as if I was looking through layers of gauze, but a dark face eventually materialized.

"Torent?"

In a rush of sensations, the world came flooding back, the sound of the waterfall crashing in the bluffs, the crisp, clear air mixed with hints of evergreens and Torent's cologne, and the coldness that reached deep into my soul.

I was no longer in the water, but on the grassy shore. Torent had pulled me out and was sitting beside me. I was shivering, teeth chattering together.

"W-what happened?" I stammered, searching Torent's face for answers. My heart knocked in my chest at the sight of him dripping wet, his T-shirt plastered against every muscle in his stomach.

"Are you crazy?" he reprimanded, brushing the strands of hair stuck to my face, before framing my cheeks with his hands.

"I saw something in the lake," I chattered, trying to keep my teeth together.

"And you thought it would be a good idea to jump in and get it?" Disapproval dripped in his voice, and it made me recoil.

I tried to scoot away from him, but his fingers slipped from my face to intertwine with my own, keeping me rooted. Dropping my gaze, I stared at our joined hands. They . . . they were glowing, like a mini aurora borealis. Umm . . .

"Why are our hands glowing?" I replied in a daze.

"What?" Torent's eyes moved downward as he noticed the splash of lights in hues of pink, blue, and green, just like the northern lights. "What the—" He released my fingers immediately as if I'd just burned him, extinguishing the light.

A sadness and longing overcame me. I missed it and reached to take his hand again, but Torent stood. I frowned, meeting his eyes.

They were dark, with little flecks of gold. "Oh no, crash car. No touching. Not until I figure out what is going on."

That made two of us. I sighed. "Fair enough. I went in to get this."

Opening my palm, I showed him the dainty gold ring. An engraving was etched into the band, words I couldn't read. They looked ancient. Encrusted into the center was a garnet stone that pulsed with energy. It was mesmerizing. I held it up between my thumb and index finger, watching as the sun bled over the horizon, catching the crystals.

"Is that—?" Torent knelt beside me again to get a closer look. He lifted his hand to take the ring, but the moment our fingers touched,

I was transported to a different time, a different place. The only common denominator was Torent.

In moonlight and shadows of the woods, he kissed me. His lips were soft, and I closed my eyes, falling into the warmth that was all him. My body slipped up against his, quivering as he deepened the kiss, our tongues tangled in a dance. Emotion poured inside me until I ached with it.

Losing the last thread on my control, my hands shoved into his dark, silky hair, and I pulled him closer still. My lips glided over his jaw and down the strong column of his throat to where a pulse beat in time with my own. I flicked my tongue out, feeling the thrill of making it quicken.

Something passed between Torent and me, a power I couldn't explain.

Those crystal-violet eyes fired like flames.

And then it was gone, as quickly as it had manifested.

The vision, or whatever that had been, might have faded, but the feel of his lips, the taste of him lingered, as did the way he made me feel. I stared at Torent, fighting the desire to plead with him to kiss me.

"What are you doing here? Are you following me?" I finally asked when I trusted myself to speak. My voice was raspy, and the sound made my cheeks blush, because I knew he understood why.

"No," he replied, staring at me in a way that made my heart race. "It was a good thing I found you."

He was no longer touching me, and the ring was safely in my palm. I wasn't sure why that mattered. "Okay, stalker."

His lips twitched as he pushed to his feet. "Do I need to remind you that I saved you?"

I followed, standing, and was glad to find my legs were no longer shaking, not after that I-could-live-off-his-lips vision kiss . . . or whatever it had been. There seemed to be a lot of unexplained things happening to me, and it made me wonder if this entire day was nothing but a dream.

"Oh, are you expecting a thank you? For your information, I wasn't in any danger." Or so I thought.

He snorted. "We can argue about that later. First, we need to get warm before we both freeze to death. It's a decent hike, and unless you want to spend the night out here, you need to move your pretty little ass."

The urge to tell him to stop bossing me around rose up swiftly, but I couldn't fault his advice. Cold and wet was not a good combination. The anger was good, though; it kept the blood flowing.

"Do you know where you're going?" I called after his back. He had stepped up onto the embankment and paused, waiting for me to follow. Who would have thought Torent Stark could be a gentleman?

He rolled his eyes. "I've lived here all my life. There is no part of Havenwood Falls I haven't unearthed. How did you even find Peacock Lake?" he asked, giving me a hand up, but he made sure to quickly release me.

We both felt the spark, a thousand times more intense than before, and we both pretended otherwise.

I wasn't going to tell him I had gotten lost and stumbled on it accidentally; then again, maybe I hadn't. Just maybe, this place had summoned me to it.

"This isn't the falls?" I inquired.

He shook his head, dark damp strands of hair stuck to his forehead.

"No, this is Small's Falls. Peacock Lake is rumored to have magical qualities," he added.

I angled my head to the side, arms hugged around my middle to keep warm. "And you believe that?"

"After what just happened, you don't?" he asked, surprised.

Leaves of gold, red, and orange crunched under our feet as we entered the woods. "I don't know. What exactly did happen?"

Torent's deep violet eyes roamed over my face with traces of sympathy, an emotion I hadn't been sure he was capable of. "I think you need to ask your mom."

Confusion set in. "What does she have to do with this?"

"It's time you knew who you really are, Mal. Ask her. There's a reason you were drawn here. I don't think you finding Peacock Lake was an accident. And be careful with the ring. There's something about it that feels . . . off."

What did he mean who I really was?

I pocketed the little gold band, not giving it another thought.

CHAPTER 6

"Where's Mom?" I asked Gigi.

Gigi was in the kitchen, baking a batch of chocolate chip brownies. My favorite. "Out looking for a job, hopefully."

I sighed, sinking into one of the wooden kitchen chairs. My mind was still whirling and hadn't stopped the whole drive home.

Gigi gave me a sideways glance. "Why are you dripping water all over my hardwood floors? Nice T-shirt, by the way. Is it new?"

There she went again with her eerie intuition. She probably knew it was Torent's, so what was the point in lying? When we had gotten into his Jeep, he had thrown me a shirt from the backseat, ordering me to put it on. "I borrowed it."

"Why?" she pressed, beads of worry starting to form in her soft aqua eyes, the same color as mine.

"I went to the falls, or what I thought was the falls. Turns out, I ended up at Peacock Lake instead."

An interested gleam came into her expression before she went back to stirring the flour into her batter. "Did you, now? And did you find what you were looking for?"

The ring was in my pocket, but that wasn't what was on my mind.

"Gigi, I . . ." My voice trailed off. I didn't know how to put into words what had happened to me, not when I wasn't even sure myself.

She set aside the bowl and joined me at the table, taking my hand in her soft one. "It's okay, Mallory. I understand."

I raised my brows. How could she? I hadn't even said anything yet. "Do you?"

"Yes, my dear. This won't make your mother happy, but I can sense the power in you. This is your birthright. You've had your awakening today."

That was what the voices had said. Awakening. "What does that mean? What power? What birthright?"

"This is going to be hard to understand at first, but I want you to keep an open mind. You've always been so good at accepting the unexplained, unlike your mother. She was such a pistol, always challenging everything." She squeezed my hand. "You're a nymph."

I let out a little laugh. "I'm sorry, what did you say?"

"Just take a minute to think about it, really think about you, what calls to your soul. It has always been the water, hasn't it?"

I nodded. But I'm sure there were tons of people who liked to swim. I didn't think that made them mermaids.

"Havenwood Falls isn't just any place. It is a home for many supernaturals, including water nymphs like us," she explained.

Hold up a second. Gigi was a water nymph? Did that mean . . . ? My mouth dropped. How could that be possible? I was beginning to wonder if Gigi was off her rocker. Maybe she was sick. Water nymphs? Really? I shook my head. "That can't be."

She smiled in a reassuring gesture that was calming. "I think you know that I wouldn't make up something like this. Why do you think your mother took you from Havenwood Falls? She got it stuck in her head that she could protect you from this life. But you can't run from destiny, Mallory. And this is yours."

"Is Mom a . . . ?" I couldn't bring myself to say it.

Gigi's lips thinned. "Yes, she is, though she would rather not be."

So that was the big secret Mom had been running away from?

Suddenly all the pieces of my life started to fit into place. Holy fricking Toledo.

"I can't believe it," I groaned, laying my forehead on the table.

"It is a lot to take in," she said.

I lifted my head, trying to contain the storm of emotions swirling inside me. Anger. Betrayal. Confusion. Denial. Hurt. Bewilderment. "Why wouldn't she tell me? Why would she keep it a secret for so long?"

"Your mother's powers have brought her pain, and she wanted to protect you from ever getting hurt, but what she couldn't understand was your path is your own. It isn't your mother's to control or save you from."

I shook my head, still in a daze. "What kind of powers?"

"We don't share the same abilities, other than the call of the water. Our powers are a gift from the goddess and are as unique as our fingerprints. No two are identical."

Did I believe this? Gigi had no reason to lie to me, but still . . . "And there are others like us?"

"Many. And there will be time to learn everything you need to know, but I won't overwhelm you. First, you need to absorb what you've discovered about yourself. Controlling your ability is important. There are classes that can help you, but there is one rule I need you to absolutely understand. The humans can't know what you can do."

This was one of those moments in my life where I didn't know whether to laugh, cry, or run straight for the hills. But I had promised myself I wouldn't be Mom, and that was exactly what she had done.

"I don't even know what I can do," I whispered, staring at the dark grain spots in the kitchen table.

"You will," Gigi assured. "I'm here to help you. Always. But I need you to promise me you will keep this a secret. No one must know unless you're a hundred percent sure they're supernatural."

That might be kind of hard, since Torent more or less had been a witness to my awakening, but he hadn't freaked out. So I couldn't help but wonder. What was Torent? Human or supernatural?

"The Court takes these things very seriously. When your mom called about coming home, I had to ask the Court for permission to remind your mom how to get here."

"Is that why you came to visit?"

She nodded. "It was the only way."

"I have a million questions."

"I know you do, but I think it would be best if you talk to your mom. She has strong feelings about your heritage."

Those feelings had been strong enough to keep me from this place for seventeen years. "Thanks, Gigi, for being straight with me. It's been a very long and confusing day. I'm going to lie down until Mom gets home."

She patted my hand. "Good idea. I'll bring you up a bowl of hot brownies and ice cream."

Because that would make everything better.

I stood up, feeling numb all over.

Gigi wrapped me in a hug. "I'll send your mom upstairs the moment she walks through the door. You should be the one to tell her."

Holy crap. I was a freaking water nymph.

I hurried upstairs to my still unpacked room and immediately opened my laptop. Time to dive into the deep dark web. Or Google, in my case. As expected, it took ten years to boot up. I could have gotten a manicure in the time it took.

Pulling up the search engine, I typed in the words *water nymph.*

As I stared at the computer, it hit me. I wasn't human. How could I have not known my whole life? Tears I didn't want gathered at the corners of my eyes. *Nope. I'm not going to cry.*

The basic info came up. Greek mythology, a nature deity that presided over bodies of water. Okay, the idea of being a deity was kind of badass.

Then I searched *goddess Styx.* The voices in the water had said I was the daughter of goddess Styx. From my mythology class last year, I knew a little bit about Styx, the goddess of the underworld river who was the personification of hatred. That didn't sound promising. As I dug deeper, I found out her parents were Oceanus and Tethys. She became the divinity by whom most solemn oaths were sworn.

I wasn't sure what any of this had to do with me or how much of her power was passed down through our bloodline.

Remembering the ring I had found, I slipped it out of my pocket to examine it. The metal was cool against my fingers as I held it up, twisting it under the soft glow of the bedside lamp. The garnet caught the light, and I swore the stone swirled in a cloudy pattern, but that was crazy. Maybe it was one of those mood rings?

Without thinking, I slipped it onto my finger, surprised to find it was a perfect fit. The whirling inside the ruby intensified, like red clouds during a blood moon. I stared, drawn to the allure it produced. I felt pulled in, and in the clouds, flashes of Torent and me spun inside my head. Steamy. Sexy. Sinister.

I flipped off the ring and quickly dropped it inside the nightstand drawer. Out of sight, out of mind.

Holy crap. I couldn't even process what had just happened. My breath came out in short pants, and my body! My skin was on fire. What was going on? Was this part of my powers, having over-the-top-erotic visions of stupid hot guys? If that was the case, being a nymph sucked.

Before I spontaneously combusted, I dropped down on my bed and closed my eyes. Flashes of being underwater flipped through my mind. If Torent hadn't been there, would I be alive?

Maybe I owed him a thank you after all. If supernaturals were real, then what was Torent?

Definitely not human.

～

Mom and I had our little talk that night everything changed, and I suddenly found myself enrolled in supernatural night classes at Sun and Moon Academy two days a week. I wasn't thrilled about the extra work. It would mean less time for swimming and studying, but I couldn't deny I was a tiny bit excited. As scary as it had been to learn I was supernatural, I was also extremely curious. Knowledge had always been my thing. I liked to learn, and this was no different.

After everything that had happened over the weekend, I needed to unwind, and as much as I loved the water, I wasn't eager to jump in just yet. The Creekwood Country Club had a great space inside a small room of the workout center that was perfect for yoga. I had seen something about yoga classes at the local vineyard, but Beck preferred solo versus group settings. He had convinced me to meet him here after school, assuring that what I needed was the mental, physical, and spiritual discipline of yoga. He was right about one thing. I needed to Zen out more than ever. Plus, I was having the Monday blues.

Starting without Beck, I moved into the resting position of downward dog, concentrating on the ins and outs of my breath. It didn't last more than a minute.

"Nice spandex."

I peered under my armpit at Torent scowling.

"Is there a reason you're interrupting my thirty minutes of peace?" How was this guy everywhere I turned? Was there no place in Havenwood Falls safe from Torent Stark?

His head was angled to the side, and our gazes locked. The depths of his violet eyes glimmered with a magic that could hypnotize. I had no other explanation. "This is what you call peace? I'm still trying to figure out how you're going to get out of that pose without breaking your neck."

I rolled my eyes and dropped down to my knees. "I'm assuming this is about the other day?"

The day I found out I wasn't human. I was still waiting for someone to pinch me and tell me my life had suddenly become a fantasy novel.

His lips spread into a roguish grin. "Nah, I came to appreciate the view."

I ignored the comment, knowing a reaction would only feed his ego, so I took a different approach. "I know I didn't say it then, but thank you for stalking me the other day."

He folded his arms. "Wow."

"What?" I asked, pushing myself to my feet.

"That looked like it hurt. The thank you," he added, in case it wasn't clear, which it had been.

"Shut up. You can be such an ass sometimes, you know that?"

His unusual eyes twinkled. "So I've been told."

And he liked it. "Are you sure it's safe for you to be seen with me here? We wouldn't want to upset the queen."

He winked, taking a step closer to me. "I scoped the place out first. We're in the clear."

My bare feet sank into the foam yoga mat as realization hit. We were utterly alone. "How do you keep showing up everywhere I am? I'm really starting to think you're a stalker."

"The town really isn't that big."

Sad excuse. "So what's the reason you interrupted my practice? I assume there's a reason."

He leaned forward and tucked a stray piece of hair behind my ear. I pretended not to notice how his fingers lingered over my cheek. "Have dinner with me Friday night."

I couldn't ignore the flush that stole over my cheeks. The simple brush of touch ignited a trail of warm embers at the side of my face.

"No," I refused. Me and Torent alone, even in a restaurant, was a dangerous cocktail. It wasn't just his crazy ex-or-non-ex-girlfriend that had me wary of the youngest Stark. It was mostly because I didn't trust myself with him. I could close my eyes right now and still feel what it was like to be in his arms, to kiss him. The vision I'd had at the waterfall had been so real, and yet, it never happened. I wasn't about to tempt fate.

No guys. Remember?

But he was persistent. "We need to talk about what happened."

He wasn't the only one who could be stubborn to a fault. "What if I don't want to?"

"Mallory." He used my full name. Not Mal. Not crash car. Which meant he was being serious.

I sighed. It would be nice to talk to someone other than family, but I remembered the rule. Keep it a secret from humans. I didn't know where Torent stood on the spectrum. Supe or not? "Fine. But no funny business."

"Just so we're clear . . ." He dipped his chin, and the wind shifted directions through the open window, blowing Torent's scent straight at me. I told myself not to breathe, but I inhaled, drawing in the smell of pine and mint. It was all Torent. I wanted to bury my face into his neck, wrap my arms around his broad shoulders, and stay surrounded by his warmth, because lately, I was so cold. "No hand-holding . . ." His fingers laced gently with mine, sending a warm spark down my arm. "No whispering in your ear . . ." He had leaned close, letting his breath fan over my ear. "And definitely no kissing." His lips hovered over mine.

I drew on every ounce of willpower and stepped back, the soft glow that had started to form vanishing. "All of the above counts as funny business."

He gave me a lopsided grin that was all trouble. "If you say so."

Something happened each time Torent touched me, and I was going out on a limb when I added, "Also, one more thing."

He raised a single brow.

I took a breath. "You have to tell me what you are."

He opened his mouth, but then shut it, pressing his lips together. "I'll pick you up at six."

Shit. Please don't let me regret this.

CHAPTER 7

"*D*id I just hear Torent Stark ask you out?" Beck asked, finally showing up. He was supposed to meet me twenty minutes ago.

I wasn't mad and couldn't decide if his being late was a blessing in disguise or a nightmare. "Unfortunately, yes."

Beck scratched his blueberry-colored head. "Strange, because I thought I heard you agree."

I sighed. "I did."

Wearing sweatpants and a T-shirt, Beck dropped his mat to the floor, tsking his tongue. "Girl, you have a death wish. Brooklyn is going to go apeshit."

"Probably," I agreed. What had I gotten myself into? I should have stuck with my initial no, but damn Torent and his violet eyes. And damn those stupid visions for making me wonder if his lips really tasted as hot in person, or if it was just my imagination gone wild.

Beck turned his eyes on me, studying me with a critical gaze. "You look different. What's going on with you?"

"I do?" I squeaked, looking guilty as hell.

Beck's eyes swept over me from head to toe. "Yeah. You're glowing."

"It must be the yoga," I mumbled, shifting my weight to one foot. His intuitive scrutiny was making me nervous.

He wasn't buying it. Beck placed his thumb on his bottom lip. "I've been in touch with all my chakras and never looked that radiant."

"I had a strange weekend."

"That pretty much sums up every weekend here in Havenwood Falls."

"I'm beginning to figure that out."

Beck lifted a brow. "Really? Do you want to elaborate?"

Did I? Beck was really my only friend in Havenwood Falls, but could I trust him to keep a secret of this magnitude? I really, really wanted to tell him, like it was killing me to keep this secret inside me, but I was also afraid. Rule number one: Never tell humans what you were. Right now, I wanted Beck to be supernatural.

"Not yet," I sighed.

Beck struck me as the kind of friend who was okay with me not being ready to talk about what was going on with me. It was one of the many reasons I liked him. He was dependable. I could count on him. I definitely needed a friend like that in my life.

Wednesday after school I was scheduled to get my official tattoo that registered me as a supernatural. My talk with mom had enlightened me on some of the inner workings of life in Havenwood Falls for people like us. I was blown away by what went on in the town right under the noses of everyone else.

I had mixed feelings about being required to get inked, mostly because I didn't feel as if I'd had enough time to digest who I was. My magic was still in an unstable zone, but that was part of the classes at the Academy, to help me learn to control it. My life hadn't moved past the movie quality. None of it seemed real.

But that needle jabbing into my skin . . . that would feel very real.

"Have you picked out what you want to represent you?" Mom asked. She was tidying up the house before Addie arrived. Mom liked cleaning about as much as I liked anchovies. It made her ill, but was the life of a parent.

I gnawed on my lower lip as I wiped down the kitchen table. "I think so."

"Where are you going to put it?" she asked, loading the last of the breakfast bowls into the dishwasher.

"Don't laugh."

"Why would I laugh?"

I gave her a dull glare.

She held up her hands, dripping water all over the floor, and made a cross over her heart. "I swear."

"My ear."

Her lips straightened in a thin line. "That is going to hurt, honey. Like a lot."

Could always count on words of encouragement from Mom. "No pain, no gain."

She returned her hands into the water. "That's my girl. You always were a tough cookie, regardless of your fear of needles."

I put the cleaning supplies under the sink and leaned on the counter beside her. "Can we skip the trip down memory lane?"

The sound of tires crunching over gravel floated in through the open window. Addie had arrived. Mom shut off the water and wiped her hands on the dishtowel. "Can you get the door?"

I nodded and pushed off the counter to make my way down the hall. The bell rang right before I got to the door. *Here goes nothing.* This was it. No denying what I was. With a sigh, I opened the door.

Addie Beaumont was the Court of the Sun and the Moon's business manager. She had pretty light brown hair and warm chocolate eyes behind black-framed glasses. Tattoos adorned both her arms, and her fingers glittered with enough rings for a gypsy.

I instantly liked her, and considering she would be the one holding the needle gun, that was a comforting thing.

"You ready for this?" she asked, the little diamond stud in her nose twinkling.

She followed me down the hall, back into the kitchen. "Is anyone really ready to be assaulted by a rapid needle gun?"

She chuckled, and it was a pleasant sound. "Good point, but I promise I'll be gentle, and it will be over before you know it."

While I pulled my hair back into a messy bun, Mom and Addie exchanged a polite hello. I showed Addie where I wanted the tattoo.

"Really?" she said lifting a brow. "That is totally bitchin'."

I grinned. Hell yeah. I could be bitchin' if I wanted.

Addie set up her supplies on the table and took a moment to sketch the design with a black pen on my ear. This was the easy part. Mom pulled a chair over beside me and held my hand. "Try not to pass out."

"Mom," I groaned, rolling my eyes.

"Could you add a protection charm?" Mom asked Addie.

I glanced over at her, curious why she would ask for protection. What did I need protection from? But I figured now wasn't the best time to grill her for answers, in front of a guest. I didn't want to embarrass Mom, although she had no problem embarrassing me.

Addie gave a short nod. "Of course."

The buzzing of the tattoo gun brought my drifting thoughts to a sobering end. It was the moment of truth.

I forced myself to breathe in and out of my nose like I was meditating.

"Do you want me to numb the pain?" Addie asked, seeing my face pale. The needle dipped in black ink and was hovering to the right of my ear.

I shook my head and squeezed my hands over my knees. "I'm okay." My heartbeat sounded rapidly in my ears.

Addie gave me a soft smile. "Good, now remember to keep still. I wouldn't want to accidentally tat your cheek."

I closed my eyes, and an image of Torent's face appeared, followed by a ribbon of calmness. The first pierce shot a zing through my ear, but it didn't take long for it to go numb. The whole thing took less than fifteen minutes, and I couldn't believe I had made such a big deal about it.

Mom took care of the registry and the supernatural details I knew virtually nothing about while I admired my new piece of body art in the portable mirror. A series of swirls climbed up the lobe of my ear and curved toward the top.

"Let me see," Mom sung.

I angled my head to the side.

"It's official. She's one of us now," Addie said, smiling.

Mom brushed at her eyes. "Yes, she is."

A pang hit me in the heart. It hurt to see her sad, and I wasn't entirely sure why it upset her so much, seeing me embrace my heritage.

Friday night came too quickly. My not-date with Torent.

I stared at the muscles in Torent's arm as he turned the wheel, taking us onto the main road. He was wearing a hoodie with the sleeves pushed up. The black ink of his tattoo was embedded in his golden skin, and I found the sight of the interwoven symbol attractive on him. An urge to trace the lines with my finger snuck up on me, and I had to lace my hands together to keep from touching him.

My eyes moved up to the profile of his face. It was a striking face —cheekbones I could get hung up on, eyes I could lose myself in, and lips I wanted to kiss again and again.

He turned to catch me gawking and let his dimples come out to play. "You don't have to stop staring. I like it."

I snorted. "You would like it." I turned to watch the breathtaking landscape roll by. It was almost as enchanting as the guy beside me. "What does your tattoo mean?" I asked, directing the conversation to a safe topic.

His gaze slid back to the road. It was pretty much a straight shot to town. "What makes you think it has a meaning?"

"Isn't that the whole point of getting one in the first place?" I pressed, unable to believe he got something so permanent for the hell of it, but then again, that was the kind of guy Torent was.

He shrugged. "To some. But for people like us, it is a requirement."

"What do you mean, people like us?" I tossed back with a slight edge in my voice.

The corners of his lips curved.

"Supernaturals," he said, as if it was the most natural answer in the world.

My shock face materialized, and I sucked in a sharp breath, fingers tightening painfully together. So I had been right, but it didn't make my surprise any less real.

"Are you supposed to say that out loud?" I whispered, my gaze darting out the windows.

He chuckled. "No one can hear us, Mal. We're in a car. Okay, that's not exactly true," he backpedaled. "There are some supes who have enhanced hearing, but it is unlikely they're around."

"Should we even be talking about this? Isn't it a—?"

"Secret," he supplied. "Don't worry. You're not going to get in trouble." Swinging his Jeep into a parking space, he shifted it into park.

My eyes narrowed. "And why should I trust you?"

Torent killed the engine and turned to face me, locking his gaze on mine. "You shouldn't . . . but when it comes to your safety, I wouldn't put you in harm."

My heart cartwheeled. Why did he say stuff like that to me?

Together we climbed out of the jeep.

"I hope you like pizza," Torent said when we met at the front of his car.

I scrunched my face. "Is there anyone who doesn't?"

His lips twitched. "I knew I liked you for a reason."

My stupid heart did another acrobatic move. *Big deal. He said he liked you. That could mean a thousand things, including friends,* I reminded myself.

Napoli's was a local pizzeria in a brick building across from the fire station. A large window with a green and white canopy welcomed its patrons. Inside, the place was lively with locals and a few kids from school. Torent gave a short nod in the direction of one table before we were seated.

I slid into the booth opposite Torent, the gently worn leather soft underneath me. It was obvious the town loved this place. The air smelled of gooey cheese, zesty tomato sauce, and garlic. Everything *I* loved. Pizza was life.

"Hey, Zara," Torent greeted the waitress. I recognized her from school. She had amazing olive-toned skin and features that reminded me of an elf.

"The usual?" she directed at him with a cute British accent.

"What do you like on your pizza?" Torent turned and asked me.

I unfolded the menu on the table to keep my hands busy. "The question you should be asking is what don't I like on my pizza."

His smile was lethal. "The usual, thanks, Zara."

Don't get hung up on him.

"Did you take my advice and talk to your mom?" he asked as soon as Zara had left to put in our order, not beating around the bush.

My eyes met his. "It was my grandma who told me."

"And what did she say?" A kind of ridicule dusted his voice, and I wondered why.

Zara returned, setting our drinks on the table. I drew a long sip from the Coke. Was this really the place to have the kind of discussion I agreed to?

"Why do I have to go first?" I challenged, putting the ball in his court. I wasn't ready to reveal my cards just yet. Call me cautious.

"Fine, have it your way, but be warned, you might not like what you learn."

"I can handle it," I assured him, twisting the straw around in my drink. Couldn't I? How bad could it be? Vampire? Werewolf?

He leaned forward on the table, closing us in so we were in our own little bubble. "My father is a higher demon."

CHAPTER 8

"*A* demon," I hissed. The fork and knife in front of me began to tremble, moving toward me on the table. I quickly slapped my hand down over them, feeling a charge of energy in my veins. *Holy crap.* I had done that.

Torent's eyes shifted over the pizzeria, checking to see if anyone was paying us any attention. "You're going to need to work on your control, but it is normal to be unstable at first, so don't freak out."

Who was freaking out? Certainly not me.

"Humans, they don't know about us," he continued. "And we need to keep it that way. It's one of the laws enforced by the Court of the Sun and the Moon."

I stared at him across the table, seeing him in a different light. *A demon,* my brain echoed. I had the hots for a demon. "I'm sorry, what did you say?"

He reclined back into the booth, the corner of his mouth tipping up. "You have so much to learn, crash car."

I sighed, tapping my foot under the table. "This is insane."

"Insane doesn't begin to cover Havenwood Falls."

A group of guys and girls stopped at our table. I didn't recognize any of their faces, but it was clear they knew Torent. Both of the guys were dressed in jeans, white T-shirts, and motorcycle jackets. The two girls were cute. One had lavender hair I would have died for, and the other had deep brown eyes accentuated by bold turquoise eyeshadow.

"Hey, where you been, Stark? You missed our last get together," said one of the guys. He was tall with piercing blue eyes and had a scar just above his right eye that added to his deadly charm.

"Been kind of busy," Torent replied, laying a lazy arm over the back of the booth.

Those roguish blues turned to me. "I can see that. I don't think we've met before. I never forget a pretty face."

Torent scowled. "Mallory, this is River Livingston III, Rowan Bishop, Julianna Fairchild, and Zaltana Purser."

"Hi," I said, at a loss for words. If they knew Torent, did that mean they were supes? I had to bite my lip to keep the question from blurting out.

"What is a nice girl like you doing with the likes of Torent Stark?" Zaltana asked me.

I liked her boldness. "I'm still trying to figure that out."

"Catch up with us later, Pallas," River said to Torent. "And you'd better graduate this year."

He watched as the group moved to a few booths behind us to take a seat. I could easily imagine Torent hanging out with those guys and getting into all kinds of trouble in town.

I lifted a brow. "Pallas? Like the Titan god?"

The corner of his lips lifted a fraction. "It's just a nickname."

Odd nickname.

Tucking my hair behind my ears, I stared at the wrinkles frowning over his forehead. "What did he mean, you'd better graduate?"

He gave a one-shoulder shrug. "Long story short, last year I screwed around, skipped classes, basically blew off my entire senior year of school. I didn't have enough credits to graduate, so I'm stuck doing another semester at HFH."

"They went to Havenwood Falls High?" I inquired.

Torent shook his head. "River and Rowan went to the Academy. The others went to HFH."

"Oh. I'm taking night classes there this week."

The sudden harshness that moved into his face startled me. "Mal, just promise you'll be careful."

His hand reached across the table and covered mine.

I glanced down, seeing the stream of colors starting to take shape as his fingers absently twisted the gold ring I had thrown on at the last second. I wasn't even sure why I wore it, but the metal seemed to warm the second Torent touched me. "Why does that happen when we touch? Is it normal?"

He snatched his hand away before anyone could notice. Those troubled stormy eyes followed mine. "No. Not even by supe standards, but I've been doing some research. You must have gotten some kind of magnetic powers from the water currents, and it reacts to the energy inside me."

The burning sensation that started as a spark in my chest bloomed, spreading throughout my veins. "So you're saying when our powers collide, they give off something that looks like the aurora borealis."

He nodded. "Yeah, I think so."

I shook my fingers, trying to rid myself of the lingering tingle and the urge to reconnect our hands. "Have you ever seen anything like this before?"

The scowl that formed on his kissable lips deepened. "I've seen some pretty remarkable abilities, but no. It could be because I'm involved that makes it more surreal."

I got that.

"None of this seems real," I mumbled.

He lowered his eyes, thick lashes resting over his cheeks. "You're wearing the ring you found."

I shrugged like it wasn't a big deal, and I didn't think it was. "It's pretty. And it fits."

I had also been curious to see if I would have any other flashes of Torent and me doing dirty and wicked things.

"Do you feel that?" he asked, making sure to keep his hands on his side of the booth.

The urge to jump over the table and attack him with my mouth? Hell yes, I felt it, but I kept my composure. This insane pull inside me intensified, and I found myself leaning across the table. His eyes darkened as they collided with mine. The emotion churning in them had my breath quickening.

"Mallory." The husky sound of my name did all kinds of funny things to my belly.

My heart was thumping in my chest as my eyes focused on his. The air between us crackled, and I wanted more than anything to be anywhere but a public place with Torent.

Tearing his gaze from my fingers, he looked at me, and I didn't like what I saw brewing in the violet storm. "There is something about that ring."

For some reason, his tone covered me in a cloud of unease. "Do you want me to take it off?"

"No, I'm sure it's nothing." But the look on his face said the exact opposite.

"You don't really believe that."

His fingers kneaded the muscle at the back of his neck. "I don't know. I have this hunch, but I don't want to jump to conclusions until I ask around. Finding something at the bottom of Peacock Lake is risky."

"Because the lake is enchanted?" I concluded.

He nodded. "It is also fatal to humans. Your mom really never told you what you are?"

Sadness crept into my eyes, and I swallowed the lump of deceit. "No. How could she keep it from me?"

He shifted in the leather booth. "I don't know. But I'm sure she had her reasons, Mal. Probably to protect you from this place."

I fumbled with the edge of my white cloth napkin. "Is it really that bad to be supernatural?"

He bestowed me with a magnetic smirk that seemed to scatter my brain cells. "You're asking the wrong person. I'm a demon. Bad is my thing."

My lips twitched.

"I'm a water nymph, apparently," I said, realizing I hadn't gotten around to telling him.

"I figured as much, but wasn't a hundred percent sure."

"How did you know?" Was that something other supes noticed?

"I've been around a few others enough to pick up the signs."

The pizza arrived, and we tabled the discussion of supernaturals to talk about normal stuff. Turned out, Torent was easy to open up to. I didn't know what it was. Maybe I trusted him, which sounded crazy. I'd only been in Havenwood Falls a short time, and yet, my life had already been turned upside down.

We managed to eat the entire pizza between the two of us. Torent could pack it away, but you would never be able to tell by looking at him. How he remained so fit with an appetite like that I'd never figure out. Just one of those mysteries of life, or being a demon.

He took care of the check, overriding my insistence to let me pay for half. As we walked outside, I made him swear next time it would be on me.

In response, he raised his brows and asked, "So there's going to be a next time?"

I rolled my eyes.

"I haven't decided," I replied and jumped into his Jeep.

A bundle of nerves formed in my belly as we coasted along the road that was now becoming familiar. The butterflies came out of nowhere. Why was I suddenly so uneasy? All evening I'd been relaxed in his presence, and now that we were alone, I found I couldn't calm down. My fingers twisted around the ring.

"There's no reason to be nervous," Torent said as we pulled into my driveway and he killed the lights.

We both unbuckled our seatbelts. "I just learned you're a demon, and I'm not even sure what that means. I have an active imagination, so you can imagine the things that are running wild in there."

"Fair enough." He shifted comfortably in the seat, letting the engine idle in a rhythmic purr. "My mom is human, which makes my demon blood diluted. I don't have the intense power my father does. He can morph into a full-out demon. Don't piss the man off."

I chuckled, but it still had undertones of nerves. There were demons running around, and witches, shifters, and werewolves.

Holy crap.

That animal who had darted out in front of my car . . . it could have been a supe.

"My change is more subtle. I can produce a light called hellfire, and I got the demon eyes and senses."

The more I learned, the more intrigued I was. "Show me the demon eyes."

He lifted a brow at me. "You sure you can handle this?"

I smiled and folded my arms, angling my body toward him in the seat. "Show me," I insisted.

"Okay," he said, and I could sense his reluctance. In the moonlight, the car was dark, but I could see his violet eyes lit up by the dashboard lights. They were as beautiful and mesmerizing as ever, maybe more so in twilight. He took one long blink, and as his long lashes batted open, I gasped.

The entire car was bathed in a golden glow produced by his eyes. The violet color was replaced with vibrant orangey-yellow, like a large cat at night.

He had been expecting me to recoil, be scared even, but that wasn't what I was feeling when I stared at Torent. My hand reached out, tracing the soft lines of his jaw, and something stirred deep within me. My nervous demeanor calmed the moment I touched him.

"They're stunning."

His exhale filled the quiet car, a breath I didn't know he'd been holding. It was followed by a crooked smile on his full lips. Then came the dimples. My heart seemed to stutter as Torent lowered his head, resting his forehead against mine.

"You surprise me," he murmured.

Time seemed to stand still, the seconds stretching out as I stared into his eyes, watching them darken. My hand was still on his face, and I couldn't seem to move it. "Me? I'm the most predictable, boring—"

He kissed me. No, that wasn't quite the way to describe his lips pressed to mine. It was more than a kiss.

He possessed me.

There wasn't a second of hesitation. I wish I could have said the same, but the moment Torent's lips pressed against mine, thought ceased to be available. A shudder raked through his body, and my own answered at the sound of a part growl, half moan at the back of his throat.

I closed the tiny space between us and kissed him with every ounce of fervor in my body. I had no self-control, it seemed. Kissing Torent under the stars was the last thing I should have been doing. My life had enough drama. I didn't need to add to it. And yet, here I was, slipping my fingers into his hair as my body instinctually relaxed into his.

Parting my lips, I deepened the kiss. Something cool and metallic slipped between our tongues as his tangled with mine in a dance as old as time. I could feel myself come alive under his fingers when they dove into my hair. What he made me feel was both thrilling and frightening.

He pulled his lips from mine, tilting his head to the side, and stared at me in wonder. A strand of dark hair fell, teasing his high cheekbone.

"I've never kissed someone with a pierced tongue," I whispered, gazing into his vibrant gold eyes.

A wicked gleam jumped into them. "I'm full of surprises, crash car."

I just bet he was, and if I didn't get out of this car, I would end up in his lap. Kissing Torent in the flesh had been a thousand times more potent than the visions. I didn't know what to make of that yet.

Flashing him a smile, I opened my door and stepped out of the Jeep. "Thanks for dinner. And listening to me." He was the only person besides my family who knew what I was. It had been nice having someone to relate to.

I would never have thought that person would have been Torent.

I just hoped my secret was safe with him.

CHAPTER 9

*H*oly crap. I kissed Torent.

I was having one of those squealing moments, and it felt as if I floated upstairs to my room. The house was quiet, Mom and Gigi in their rooms watching TV or reading.

After taking a quick shower, I texted Beck, letting him know how my not-date with Torent had gone, and climbed into bed. I fumbled with the garnet ring on my finger, telling myself what happened between Torent and me tonight was not a big deal. I wasn't going to let it go to my head. The plan was still in place, and no demon with sexy dimples would derail me.

I fell asleep with a smile on my lips.

That kiss sparked something in my sleep.

HE WAS SLEEPING in his bed, a beam of moonlight slashing across his face. I'd never been to his house, let alone in his bedroom, but I knew, without doubt, this was exactly what it would look like.

What was I doing in his room?

Unable to stop myself, I padded over to his bed and crawled in beside him. What had gotten into me?

But he rolled over in his sleep, and my mouth was on his. The action seemed to have caught him off guard, but only for a second, because then his lips were moving over mine, taking me somewhere wild and electric.

It wasn't enough, just kissing him. I needed more. I needed to go deeper. I needed to taste him, feel him.

My fingers slipped under the sheets, and I moaned, finding he wasn't wearing a shirt. Of course, Torent would sleep in nothing but boxers. God bless him.

I ran my tongue over his lower lip and whispered his name. Torent opened his eyes, and my breath caught. They were no longer a stunning shade of purple, but a fiery gold.

"The ring," he growled.

MY EYES FLEW open as I wrenched upright in my bed, my heart beating rapidly in my chest. I ran my fingers through my tousled hair, the blankets twisted around me.

What the hell was that?

It felt like a ghost had brushed over my soul. I wrapped my arms around myself and stared into the dark. It was then I noticed the ring on my hand. The garnet stone was glowing, pulsing like the beat of a heart.

I ripped the ring from my finger, casting it aside on the nightstand.

ALL DAY, only one word ran through my head over and over again. *Supernaturals.* Something inside me had snapped, and now I couldn't stop staring at everyone, wondering if they were human or something else. It was the something else that was causing me to go crazy.

Oh, I knew what books and movies claimed, but this was real life—my life, and the girl next to me in AP English could be a vampire. The teacher in Physics could be a ghost. And my new best friend, Beck? I was pretty damn sure he was more than the adorable nerd with blue hair.

Maybe if I had wrapped my head around it, I wouldn't be struggling so much, but the truth was, I hadn't. And the other night, I'd been locking lips with a demon.

Never thought that would be something I wanted to do . . . or do again.

Strange thing was, I did, and the dreams I kept having of him weren't helping.

Torent and I hadn't talked much since the kiss, and I told myself it wasn't that big of a deal. I didn't automatically assume he was my boyfriend and we'd be walking hand in hand down the hall, but I had at least expected him to say more than two words to me.

"Earth to Mallory."

I didn't know how many times Beck had called my name, but I pulled my gaze from outer space and looked at him on the treadmill next to mine. We were in the school's gym, getting our cardio on. Or trying to. I had been a million miles away. Why had I let Beck talk me into working out after school when all I wanted to do was go home and not think about kissing Torent? *Because you thought it would be a good distraction.* Joke was on me. "Sorry. Family stuff. I've got a lot on my mind."

Beck's brows drew together. He was barely breaking a sweat, and I hated him for it. "Well, that's not as interesting as what I thought you were thinking about. It was more like you and Torent getting hot and sticky over pizza."

Oh, my god. Did the entire school know we'd gone out? "It wasn't a date."

A hint of a smirk touched his lips. "That's not the word going around school."

"Beck," I groaned, trying to keep my balance on the walking machine. "You promised you wouldn't tell anyone."

He made a zipper motion across his lips. "Babe, these lips are sealed tighter than Fort Knox. It wasn't me."

Wonderful. That would explain why Brooklyn had been glaring

extra hard at me all day. Even now, from across the gym. The damn girl looked good sweating. Her skin glistened. She was wearing a white tank top and a pair of pink shorts.

Is that a—?

Brooklyn had a tattoo.

Shit. Brooklyn was a supe?

My gaze darted back to Beck and the black ink on his neck. God, I was surrounded by supernaturals, and regardless of rule number one, I had to know if he was human or something else.

Didn't I?

"Can I ask you a question?" The words popped out of my mouth before I let myself overthink it.

Not missing a beat, Beck said, "Yes, I think you should have sex with Torent Stark."

I smiled. "Funny. Brooklyn Kendall might behead me. Besides, I haven't decided what I'm going to do about him, but that wasn't what I wanted to ask."

"Fire away."

Our running machines hummed in time together, our strides in unison. "You don't strike me as a tattoo type of guy. Why did you get one?"

Beck wasn't muscular, but he could run. "I didn't have a choice. You know, the rules."

Beads of sweat ran down my back as I gave him a funny look. "Are you saying . . . ?" I swallowed, unable to bring myself to say the word.

His eyes twinkled, enjoying my discomfort. "That I'm a shifter? I thought that was pretty clear."

My eyes darted around the gym fitness room. I was afraid someone might have heard him.

"Not to me, it isn't. This whole new world is confusing." I made sure to keep my voice low.

Holy smokes. My best friend shifted into an animal.

"Right, it's easy to forget you didn't grow up knowing. Why exactly didn't you know?" he asked.

I shrugged. "I honestly don't have any idea. My mom claims it was to protect me, but from what, I don't know. My dad, maybe?"

Beck peered over at me. "Who is he?"

"Another question I can't answer."

"Damn. That sucks, Mal."

"Tell me about it." I adopted my best indifferent tone, but the truth was, the curiosity about who my father was had never dulled, not since I was a little girl. I just did a better job of hiding it from Mom.

"Let's find out," Beck suggested, as if it were a simple thing.

"And how do you propose we do that, besides asking my mom, which I've done a hundred times already. She isn't budging."

"Do you have a name?"

"Yeah."

"And?" he prodded.

"Roth Dorian. I'm not sure this is a good idea," I added, but what was stopping me from taking the chance to find out any information about my mysterious father?

He eyed me. "What could it hurt?"

I hit the decline button on the treadmill, lowering my speed to a walk I could tolerate without my pits dripping. "I don't know, maybe. I actually have something else I wanted to ask you."

Beck lifted his brow as I suddenly had his undivided attention. "This sounds juicy."

I had to tell someone about the ring. Someone other than Torent. "When I was at Peacock Lake, I found something. A ring."

Scowl lines started to form over Beck's damp brow. "The day you came into your powers?"

I nodded. "There's something strange about it."

Beck tugged the plastic key out of his machine and let it roll to a stop. "Anything that comes out of Peacock Lake can't be good. Where is it?"

"I left it at home."

He grabbed a white towel that hung over the armrest on the

treadmill and whipped it across his forehead. "What day do you have night school this week?"

"Thursday," I answered, wondering where this was going.

"Good. I'll meet you there. And bring the ring," he added.

"We're not going to get in trouble or anything?" I was a little taken aback at how forthcoming he was with supe information. He talked about this stuff like we were discussing the weather.

He winked. "Let me teach you the ropes, Mal."

"What kind of shifter are you?" I whispered.

His eyes did a weird glowy thing. Not quite like Torent's, but still eerie. "Wolf." Beck's eyes suddenly changed, hardening. "Don't look now, but I think you're about to get a visit from the bitch squad."

CHAPTER 10

*B*rooklyn sauntered up to my treadmill with her two sidekicks beside her and pulled out the safety key, letting it dangle from her finger as my machine stopped. "Well, if it isn't the late bloomer. Rumor has it you had quite the magical time last weekend."

Did she just make a remark about me being a nymph or was I reading too much into everything she said? It couldn't be.

"What do you want?" I asked her dryly, not in the mood. Way too much crap was going on in my head to deal with her on top of it all.

She stepped up so we were at eye level. I could count her eyelashes, we were that close. "I thought I had made myself clear."

"You're going to have to elaborate. I don't speak psycho ex-girlfriend babble."

She laughed, an evil sound that struck me in the gut. "Is that what he told you? That I was his ex-girlfriend? Torent and I, we understand each other. Where do you think he went after he dropped you off the other night? I can tell you it wasn't home."

I didn't believe it. She was just trying to get under my skin . . . and it was working, but I would keep my cool. I wasn't going to smear the smug smile off her face with the belt of the treadmill. "Why do I care where he goes?"

"Maybe you don't. But you might care about what he is saying about you."

Nope. I wasn't going to take the bait. *Don't do it.* My eyes bounced to her sidekicks, Leena and Cora, before returning to the devil herself. "I can see you're dying to tell me, so just spill it."

Brooklyn leaned forward, closing her hand over mine on the handle of the running machine.

"I know what you are," she whispered. Her hand reached out to grab my wrist, and the little devil shocked me. The jolt was strong enough to make the hairs on my arms stand straight up, and my entire arm jerked.

I kept my face emotionless, not even blinking. "Is that the best you've got?"

It was stupid to taunt her. Brooklyn knew how to wield her powers. Me? I had no clue what I was doing.

She released my hand, blue fire burning in her eyes. "Let's get one thing straight. This isn't just about Torent, no matter how good-looking he is. Our families, they don't mix. Isn't that right, ladies?"

I felt sorry for Leena and Cora. They both did a kind of odd shifting of their feet, but nodded their heads dutifully.

"Is this one of those, the school is only big enough for one of us deals?" I retorted, making a mental note to ask Gigi what was with the Kendall clan. Brooklyn's hatred for me went deeper than boyfriend jealousy. If I was going to survive my senior year, I would need to know what I was up against.

"Torent said you were smart," she sneered.

Torent Stark talked too much. "What is your problem with me?"

"Don't you know? Aww," she moaned like she was petting a kitten. "Did your family keep that from you as well? It must be hard living in the dark while everyone else around you laughs."

All I saw was red, a haze of it filtering over my eyes, with Brooklyn as the target. I was barely aware of the chaos whirling around me. Everything metal in the room began to tremble—weights, screws in the machines, chains hanging from the ceiling. The sounds clattered, but my focus was only on Brooklyn. I jumped off the machine and pounced on her, tackling her to the ground. The other two girls, Leena and Cora, squealed, scampering to get out of our way or risk getting hit.

"Oh, my god," I heard Beck say behind me.

No one talked bad about my family. Brooklyn could take shots at me all day, but bringing Gigi or Mom into it pushed me over the edge. I'd never been much of a fighter, but I also wasn't afraid to stand up to a mean girl.

And she fought like one too.

Grabbing a fist of my ponytail, Brooklyn yanked my head back, and the hissing pain at the hair follicles caused my arm to reach up. My elbow caught her in the jaw as I tried to loosen the hold she had on my hair.

"You white-trash waffle," she seethed, rolling her weight into me.

If I hadn't been so filled with rage, I would have laughed. *Waffle? Really?*

Brooklyn had a good ten pounds on me and managed to pin me to the stinky floor mats, a waterfall of dark hair curtaining around us. Her nails raked over my left cheek, taking a layer of my skin. I hissed.

Before I got the chance to retaliate, Ms. Collins, a PE teacher, secured her arms around Brooklyn's waist and pulled her off me.

"What is going on here?" she demanded.

I shot to my feet, but Beck grabbed me, stopping me from advancing. My breath came out in quick pants, and I touched the side of my face, knowing I was bleeding.

"You're crazy. They should have you caged, you animal," Brooklyn hurled, struggling against Ms. Collins' hold.

"Enough!" boomed Ms. Collins, the muscle along her thick neck popping out. "The two of you, principal's office. Now!" Her finger shot to the double doors of the exercise room.

My face was probably red from exertion, but I could feel it deepening. I opened my mouth to ask if Principal Friske was even in his office after school hours, but wisely snapped it shut. Why make things worse?

"Are you okay?" Beck asked, releasing me.

I stalked toward the exit doors, needing to put as much space between Brooklyn and myself as possible. "Yeah. Angry, but I'll be okay."

Beck followed, and I loved him for it. "That was the single coolest thing that has happened all year."

"I'm going to kill Torent Stark," I growled under my breath as I smoothed my crazy post-girl-fight hair. "How could he tell her about me? I confided in him."

That bastard. I had trusted Torent. Of all people, why would he tell *her* what I was?

Torent Stark was going to wish he had never met me. Demon or not, I would kick his fine ass all the way to China.

"Hey, you don't know that it was him," Beck tried to reason. "Brooklyn is evil. Who knows how many spies she has?"

"It was him. Who else could it be?" I insisted.

Beck strutted down the hall beside me in his blue-and-silver shorts and T-shirt like it was the hottest fashion trend. "Torent has a reputation, but what Brooklyn is implying is out of character, even for him. Why don't you ask him before you chop off his balls?"

I turned to look at him, a wry grin on my lips. "Where's the fun in that?"

I FOUND Torent at the shop after school. My little escapade had earned me a Saturday detention. Joy. I didn't trust myself to confront Torent at school. One visit to the principal's office in a day was my max, and I was mad enough to cause another scene.

He was wearing an old pair of jeans with grease stains that would never come out no matter how many washes it went through. It too had seen better days.

And still, he managed to make the oily getup look hot.

No. He is not hot. He is a jerk.

A distinct scent of gasoline and oil that I found intoxicating wafted in the air. He was bent under the hood of a classic car, wiggling some kind of black hose in in the engine. I stood just outside the open garage, not bothering to say his name or announce my arrival. How could I, when I couldn't take my eyes off his butt?

Focus, Mallory! I took a breath. "How could you betray me like that?" I snapped.

Torent lifted his dark head, peering over at me. For a second, it looked as if he was going to flash those deadly dimples, but when he got a look at my scowl, he obviously changed his mind. "I don't know what you think I did, crash car, but we need to talk."

"Damn straight we do. That's why I'm here," I affirmed through clenched teeth. "Brooklyn was more than happy to fill me in. Why would you tell her what I am?"

He smeared the palm of his dirty hands on the thighs of his jeans. "Calm down. There is a lot of metal in this place, and I really don't want to end up with part of an engine hitting me on the side of the head. So you're not here about the dream?" he asked.

I poked my finger into his chest, not caring if I got dirty. "Don't you dare tell me to calm down!"

"You need to lower your voice," he hissed, eyes darting over the shop. "Before someone hears you."

"Do you think I care?" Yes, I was being completely irrational and over the top. That happened when I got upset. I blamed my Irish blood.

"Mal, I didn't tell her. I didn't have to."

I stared at him unblinkingly. "What is that supposed to mean?"

Torent slipped a hand under my elbow, leading me outside. "I'm at work. I can't talk about this now," he said through his teeth.

Argh! He was so frustrating. There was nothing worse than

ignoring your better judgment and then having that person disappoint you. What had I expected? He had demon blood running through his veins.

"Whatever. I should never have trusted you." I spun on my heels and stomped off to my car, slamming the door shut. Before the engine roared to life, Torent called my name, but I ignored the demon and floored the gas pedal, squealing my tires as I left the shop.

Torent Stark was an asshat of the worst kind.

I should have stuck to my plan. Go to class. Do my homework. Graduate from high school. And then get the hell out of here. My heart wouldn't be hurting as it was. The pain squeezed my chest, making it difficult to breathe. It was better this way, before my feelings got tangled.

I was kidding myself if I thought I didn't already have feelings for Torent.

It wasn't until I was halfway home that I remembered he mentioned something about a dream. I slammed on the brakes and idled in the middle of the road. Luckily, no one was behind me.

"Holy crap," I muttered. No way he could mean the same dream? Right? I was going to hyperventilate.

As prearranged, Thursday after school Beck and I headed over to Sun and Moon Academy. I had two hours to kill before my supernatural evening class started.

"Do you know what we need first?" Beck asked.

I craned my neck to look left and right at the intersection before turning onto the road. "I have no idea, but I assume you're going to tell me."

"Tacos," he announced.

"I think I'm in love with you."

"That's what they all say, and then Torent Stark walks into the room."

I playfully whacked him on the arm. "Stop it. So not true."

Driving down Main Street, I whipped my car into an open spot near where the Tacos for Daze truck was parked. The smell of spices hit us as we made our way down the sidewalk.

"Did you know that the owner, Sky Spill Water, is rumored to be a troll?" Beck murmured into my ear.

"Shut up," I whispered. "A troll? You lie."

He made an X mark over his chest. "Cross my heart and hope to die."

Since school had recently ended, a line had formed. Beck and I got behind a few kids I recognized. They said hi to Beck, before returning to whatever TV show they were discussing.

"You're going to flip over Sky's tacos," Beck assured me.

Sky was wearing a bright Hawaiian-patterned shirt that was making my eyes go loopy. His long gray hair was woven into little braids, and it was all I could do to keep a straight face, thanks to Beck and his troll theory.

My eyes scanned over the menu, and I snickered. "Does he really name all his food after Grateful Dead songs?"

"See, I told you. Troll," he whispered, grinning.

Beck ordered us a couple of Mexicali Blues tacos, which we scarfed down in two minutes flat on the way back to my car.

"I think I could live on those tacos for the rest of my life," I said, climbing into the passenger seat.

"Right?" Beck agreed. "Okay, now that my stomach isn't screaming at me, let me see this ring."

I wiggled in my seat, trying to get my hand into the tiny pocket of my jeans. *Who the hell designs these? And when did pockets become so stinkin' small?* The only thing it was big enough to fit was a ring.

Beck took the little gold band, examining it under the waning sun. His eyes started to glow. "There is definitely something mystical about it. I'd be careful about wearing it until we figure out what kind of powers this trinket holds."

"That's a thing? Objects with magical powers?"

"You bet your fine ass it is. Let's go to the library and dig up some dirt." He handed me back the ring. "Best to keep it hidden for now. In the wrong hands, who knows what might happen."

A shiver rolled through me. What if something had already been unleashed?

It was a bleak thought, but I was afraid there might be a ring of truth to it.

CHAPTER 11

*T*he Sun and Moon Academy library was a book nerd's dream. Rich polished wood shelves lined the walls from floor to ceiling with leather bound books just waiting to be read. Stained glass covered one wall, throwing beautiful colors over the gleaming floors. Two stories above our heads, the ceiling pitched into a dome, adorned with detailed paintings of supernatural creatures throughout the ages.

As if I had stepped onto sacred ground, a tingle of energy rushed over my skin. Silence followed as we moved into the room; the only sounds were Beck's and my footsteps clattering on the floor.

"There is a lot of history in here," Beck whispered. "If there is anything special or supernatural about that ring, it will be in here."

Inhaling the scent of paper and years of magical past, we sat huddled at a table in the corner, a stack of books Beck had collected surrounding us.

"These all have information on magical objects recorded throughout Havenwood Falls' history?" I inquired.

Beck nodded. "There are others tucked inside the Court's private stash, but they are highly guarded. You know about the town's wards, right?"

I plucked one of the books and began thumbing through the pages.

"We actually just covered it in class last week." There were wards that prevented magic at the schools and wards that protected the town itself—like the memory ward that kept Havenwood Falls a secret.

"It's possible this ring has a charm on it. The question is what kind of spell?"

My eyes roamed over the page. "And you think the answer lies in one of these books?"

"Maybe."

I sighed. "It will take all night to get through them all. I have class in an hour and a half."

"How bad do you want to know what the deal is with the ring?" he challenged.

Flashes of Torent and the too-hot-to-handle visions flipped through my memory. "This better not earn me another detention," I grumbled.

Beck gave me a wicked smile. "The image of you tackling Brooklyn is going to stay with me for the rest of my life."

I tossed him a book. "Get to work."

For the next hour, we poured over books older than dirt. If I hadn't been on a mission, the information in some of them would have made great reading. I had so much yet to learn about supernaturals, it almost seemed daunting.

I was beginning to think this was useless. What if the ring didn't have any spell? What if it was just a ring? Nothing more than a pretty bauble a woman lost in the lake? My foot started tapping under the table in restlessness. A low buzzing vibrated in my ears, not pesky like a mosquito, but a gentle hum. The hairs on my arms stood up, but I continued to scour through the books, not giving it a second thought.

I could sense my irritation increasing, but didn't think anything of it until something tiny hit me on the forehead. I jerked. What the—

A silver paperclip had fallen onto my book. Was someone throwing things at me? I couldn't picture the elderly woman behind the desk starting paperclip wars with us. No sooner had the thought flittered through my mind, I was hit with a second paperclip in the arm.

Beck caught the next one in his hand as his eyes shifted to mine. "You need to chill out before we end up with a collection of paperclips stuck to us. What have you learned about your ability?"

Was I doing this?

When it was brought to my attention, I became aware of the hum of energy swimming in my veins.

"Holy crap. Sorry. I'm still figuring this metal thing out." I had a revelation about my powers. Without proper training, I could be dangerous. Paperclips weren't a big deal, but knives, scissors, basically anything metal would be problems I didn't want.

"You're not the first to lose control. It happens to all of us. I once howled at the moon during soccer practice. My dad never pushed the whole sports thing again."

"Ugh. Some days I wish I had never gone into the lake."

"It's your destiny, Mal. I don't think there is much you could have done to avoid it. Fate has a way of catching up to us."

"When did you know what you were?"

"Always. But I grew up here. There are things all locals know, including to keep their distance from Peacock Lake. The waters are poisonous to humans and even some supes. It's your affinity to water that calls you to the lake. The ring didn't just fall off of anyone. Whoever lost it, they were definitely one of us, maybe even a nymph."

Like Mom or Gigi.

Food for thought, not that I needed more to think about. I grabbed another book from the stack, returning to the search for information. It seemed hopeless and a waste of time. We weren't going to find anything in this—

"Holy wereballs," Beck announced in a voice louder than a whisper. "I think I found something. Let me see the ring."

"Ssshh!" came a hissing from the little librarian.

Beck ignored her while I dug into my pocket, producing the inscribed gold band.

"This is it." He pointed to a picture in the book spread out in front of him. I craned my neck over the table as he began reading from the book. "The Teardrop of Desire." He glanced up, capturing my gaze, his eyes sparkling. "Tell me you love me."

"Beck, you're a freaking genius. I love you."

His eyes skimmed over the text below the picture. He swallowed, and I didn't like the serious frown that formed on his lips. "This is bad."

"What?" I shrieked in as quiet a voice as I could manage.

He lifted his head. "Torent was there with you when you found the ring?"

"Yeah, so?"

"Well, according to the legend, the Teardrop of Desire is one link to a magical chain—the Elan Chain. The rings were split up and divided. A witch by the name of Antanasia Gabor was given the Teardrop of Desire by her fiancé. No one knows how it came to be in his possession, but his desire for greed and power was greater than his love for Antanasia. The night before their wedding, he married another in secret, an heiress with a throne, giving Antanasia's fiancé all that he desired. Heartbroken, the witch cast a spell on the ring, offering it to the new bride as a gift. It is said the ring gives the wearer what their heart desires most, no matter how pure or dark, and by any means necessary."

Silenced followed as we absorbed what Beck had just read out loud. I didn't know what I was feeling.

"So, Mal, what do you desire?" He was half joking, but neither of us could deny the ominous undertones in the curse of the ring.

"I don't know . . . that I get out of this town and go to college."

Beck made a snoring noise and pretended to nod off.

I gave his shoulder a nudge. "Funny."

"That can't be what you desire most. What was the first thing you thought of when finding it?" he asked, trying a different route.

I thought back to the lake and the hot vision I'd had when Torent had pulled me out of the water.

"Crap," I muttered. My deepest, darkest desire was to have smoldering sex with Torent.

"Oh, I'm going to like this, aren't I?"

"Beck!" I hissed. "This is serious."

"Torent was with you. There isn't a girl in Havenwood Falls that wouldn't have immediately desired that piece of man-flesh."

"Oh, my god," I groaned, laying my head on the table. "This can't be happening." I quickly lifted my face and looked at Beck. "How do I reverse it or whatever?"

His eyes scanned the rest of the page. "It doesn't say, but it does note that the curse only works when the ring is worn."

Only me. A string of colorful f-bombs rolled off my lips.

I MANAGED to avoid Torent for the rest of the week. One, I was still miffed at the demon. And two, since I unearthed the curse on the ring, I thought it was best I didn't tempt myself. If these feelings I had for Torent weren't real, if they were because of the ring, it would be better if I didn't wear the thing.

The idea of magic dictating my feelings was invasive. Since I found the origin of the ring, I questioned everything, every moment Torent and I had ever shared. Had any of it been real? My night classes and catching up in school helped keep my mind off him.

I walked into Coffee Haven with the agenda of studying and drinking enough lattes to have me peeing coffee for a week. The blueberry scone I ordered was just an added bonus. To die for. Now I understood what everyone at school raved about.

Sunlight streamed through the window, warming my cheeks as I sipped on my coffee, my calculus textbook sprawled out on the table. I attacked the assignment, fueled by sugar and caffeine.

Halfway into my homework, a dark shadow fell over my

notebook. It only took the tingles radiating down my neck to tell me who it was. I didn't bother to look up. "What do you want?"

"Can we talk?" asked a low and husky voice.

My pencil etched a solid black line under problem number thirty-five. "No."

"Mal, you're being unreasonable," he growled in a texture my ears found sexy.

I *was* being unreasonable, but I didn't care. I sighed and finally glanced up, meeting Torent's vibrant gaze. "You betrayed me, or have you so quickly forgotten?"

His eyes held mine with an expression I couldn't decipher. "I did not. I wouldn't do that."

"Says the demon."

"Half demon," he corrected. The chair across from me scooted over the floor and was filled with his tall form as he took the liberty of sitting down.

"That seat's taken," I said, tapping the end of my pencil on the notebook.

His elbows leaned on the table. "Too bad. You're going to listen to what I have to say. Brooklyn is a water nymph like you."

The air halted in my chest.

"She's what?" I shrieked. Of all the things she could be, never once had nymph crossed my mind. I had figured vampire or witch, something hostile.

He leaned over the table with such intensity in his eyes. "Brooklyn, Leena, and Cora, they're all nymphs. Brooklyn has an affinity for water, like you, but Leena's is forests and Cora's is meadows."

I searched his face, sinking into the chair. "And you didn't think I should know this? God, I feel so stupid. She told me you went to see her after you dropped me off."

"She wasn't lying," he mumbled.

"Oh." I didn't know what to say. My heart had just dropped out of my chest.

"It's not what you think," he quickly added.

"And how would you know what I'm thinking?" I fired back.

"Your mind is always going, but it's your face that gives it away. I meant what I said about things between Brooklyn and me being over. I went there to tell her just that." I don't know how or when, but his fingers had found mine on the table. The pad of his thumb was making lazy circles over my hand as if he was compelled to touch me.

I pulled my hand away from his, frowning. "I don't think she took it well."

Something flickered over his face. Irritation? "Brooklyn never does. One of the many reasons we didn't work out."

I averted my gaze down to my notebook for fear of doing something stupid. I had deliberately left the ring at home, but even without the cursed piece of jewelry, I still felt an insurmountable pull to Torent. My body naturally wanted to sway toward him. My fingers itched to touch his face. And the things my lips wanted to do were downright sinful. *Focus, Mal. What had he said? Right, Brooklyn. Water nymph.*

"Wow. I can't believe we're the same species. That doesn't mean we're related, does it? Like third cousins twice removed or some shit?"

"I don't think so. Brooklyn is a descendant of the goddess Aphrodite."

I choked. She would have the DNA of love and beauty. Just another reason to hate her. At least we had different bloodlines. Being related to her would have been a living nightmare. "Does she know you're telling me this?"

He shrugged. "Everyone in the supe world knows. Brooklyn hasn't exactly kept who she is a secret. Just the opposite. She thrives on the attention."

Very true. "What abilities does she have?"

"A wicked shock."

That I could attest to.

"Brooklyn siphons energy from around her. Electricity is readily available, making it easy for her to tap into," he explained.

Since Torent was being so forthcoming, I pushed on.

"Do you know what happened between our families?" I asked.

He didn't immediately answer, appearing to have some sort of internal debate with himself. "Bits and pieces. Something happened between your parents and Brooklyn's before you were born. I don't know what, but it drove a wedge between your families. Your mom used to be best friends with Brooklyn's."

"Really?" It was hard for me to picture my mom being friends with anyone who resembled Brooklyn, especially if she was anything like her daughter.

"I could press her for more details if you think it's important," he added, and my heart fluttered. He had a way of making me feel like he would do anything for me.

I cursed the damn ring. Something told me having that kind of loyalty from Torent would inspire deep emotions. "Because you want an excuse to see her or you want to help me?"

His hand flew to his chest in a wounded gesture. "Ouch. That stung. I'm not an asshole all the time, crash car."

"I don't want to tip her off that I'm digging into our families' past. I'll see what I can find out from Gigi." I absently touched my finger where the band would have been, had I worn it.

His eyes were drawn to the motion, glancing at my hand. "You're not wearing the ring, the one you found at the lake that day."

I shook my head. "No."

Did I tell him what Beck and I had discovered?

He stretched his hand across the table but stopped himself before he touched mine. "I'm good at detecting evil things—demon senses. There is something about that ring that gives me bad vibes."

He must have changed his mind about not touching me. As his eyes moved upward to my face, I felt drawn to him. The pad of his thumb had returned to make lazy circles over my hand, and I leaned forward, unable to help myself.

"We need to talk, but not here. Can you meet me later?" I whispered, making a rash decision to tell him everything.

His lips parted as he leaned forward, bringing our faces close together. "Is this some kind of ploy to get me alone?"

"Yes and no."

"Okay," he agreed, a smirk teasing his lips.

"Tonight."

Mischief flared in his eyes. "I'll pick you up."

I took an unsteady breath. It was settled. I was doing the very thing I told myself I wouldn't do—let my heart rule my life.

Why was it so hard to say no to Torent? I wanted to blame the ring, but was it really a curse that was making me think about the demon every waking moment?

CHAPTER 12

I couldn't believe I was sneaking out to see a boy. A demon, no less! Mom would be so proud.

As the rest of the house slept, I tiptoed around my room, cursing the old floorboards. Through the sheer curtains on the window, a shimmer of moonlight cast ghostly dancing shadows.

I spent way too much time on my appearance. My floor looked like a hurricane of clothes had just blown through. Nothing was ever where it was supposed to be when I needed it, and that included my really good bra, the one that made me actually look like I had boobs.

Torent would be here in fifteen minutes, and I was still running around half naked. No big deal. All I had to do was find those jeans, the ones that made my butt look fantastic.

I stared at my room and declared it a hopeless war zone. Grabbing the first pair I could find, I lay on my bed and wiggled into them. Sitting in front of the vanity, I checked my hair one last time, studying the waves of blond hair framing my face. I swiftly reapplied my mascara and slapped on some lip gloss. Without giving my appearance another thought, I grabbed my phone off the bed, shoved it into the back pocket of my jeans, and snatched the ring from inside the drawer.

Cracking the bedroom door, I peeked down the hall and took a breath. The first few steps I took at turtle speed, deathly afraid the floor would groan under my weight, but the suspense of possibly getting caught got to me, and I raced the remainder of the way downstairs. Of course, the front door creaked like an old woman, but I barreled through, stepping outside.

Torent's Jeep was idling in the driveway, and I didn't have to see inside the car to know he was laughing at me.

I padded across the lawn, and before I got to the car, Torent was waiting with the door open.

"Is it normal for demons to have manners?" I asked, eyeing him.

He chuckled. "I was raised by a demon, but I also had a mother who made damn sure I wasn't a jerk all the time."

I got comfortable inside the Jeep as I waited for him to walk around the car. I told myself not to breathe in the pine and mint scent that was all Torent, but my senses seemed to not listen to my brain. I wanted to bottle the smell and use it as a pillow spray.

He put one hand on the steering wheel and the other on the shifter. "Where to, crash car?"

I blinked, still reeling from the intoxicating aroma of his car. "Anywhere but here."

"Buckle up. Let's see if we can get lost in the mountains."

That was not what I had in mind.

"I'm here to talk, not make out," I stated, making my intention clear.

He backed the car out with a grin on his face that said he didn't believe a word of it. "Who says we can't do both?"

"Torent," I groaned. *Goddess Styx, give me strength.*

"You know, that might be the first time you've said my name. I like it."

"Don't get used to it. I'm thinking jackass suits you better."

His deep laugh filled the Jeep.

We drove away from the center of town to where the road wound upward. The landscape might have been breathtaking, but I couldn't take my eyes off Torent. I really needed to get rid of this ring.

He parked the Jeep, and I struggled for some way to start this conversation. How did I tell a guy he might not really have feelings for me?

"It's so beautiful at night," I murmured, gazing at the bright lights dotting the town below. That was lame.

In the dark, I felt Torent's fingers graze the side of my face.

"Yes, you are," he whispered.

Don't look at him. Don't do it. Too late. My eyes were already moving through the darkness to search out his. "That was super cheesy."

"Doesn't make it any less true." His voice was gruff and sexy, all the things I didn't want him to be. An electric moment sparked between us, and I was stunned by the intensity.

My cheeks flushed, and I was grateful for the cover of night to disguise the heightened color. Drawing my legs up on the seat, I leaned onto the center console. The movement settled me closer to Torent.

Don't kiss him. It's the ring. Remember the ring? It's the whole reason you're alone with Torent Stark!

My brain was such a buzzkill. The only thing I wanted right then was Torent's lips on mine. There would be time to discuss the ring later, after I tasted him, ripped his clothes off, and devoured him.

He leaned near my ear and whispered, "Mallory."

The sound of my name on his lips created tiny coils in the pit of my belly. My tongue darted out, wetting my lips. A shiver rolled through him, and I watched in awe as the purple in his irises melded to liquid gold—his demon eyes.

"Can you control the changing of your eyes?" I asked, completely entranced by them.

"Most of the time, but there are moments they shift of their own accord. Like now." His lips brushed over mine.

I wasn't prepared for the feelings that rocked through me from just a light kiss. My fingers bunched the material of his shirt. "Just. One. Kiss."

His lips curved against mine. "If you say so."

Then he was kissing me, and my brain turned to gooey mush.

I had no self-control when it came to Torent, and I wasn't sure I could keep blaming the ring. Kissing him was the last thing I should be doing, but I didn't want to fight what he made me feel, not when my body was humming.

He tilted his head to the side, putting the slightest pressure on my lips with his tongue. I knew what he wanted. Parting my lips, I sighed at the first taste of him inside my mouth.

Something primitive rose up within me, and if I wasn't careful, this kiss would spiral to the point of no return. I hadn't much thought about the guy I would lose my V-card to, but Torent was as damn good as any.

No!

Your first time is not going to be inside his Jeep. Not happening.

It was far too cliché.

I pushed my hand at his chest, fighting the urge to pull him across the seat. "No more kissing."

"Do you really want me to stop?" he asked, his gold eyes burning bright while his lips cruised along my jaw and to the side of my neck, where the vein pulsed wildly.

"No . . . yes," I corrected and sat back in my seat, giving myself a moment of clarity, but it was short-lived when a burst of swirling colors lit up the Jeep.

"It's amazing, isn't it?" he murmured, twisting our fingers together as the light whirled in the dark.

"That's not the point."

"So tell me, crash car, what is the point then?"

"This." I pulled out the ring. I shouldn't have been astonished to see that the center stone was glowing like fire. It washed both our faces in a radiant red.

"You still have that thing?" His face scrunched up, and he backed away from the ring, leaning against the door.

"Do you know what it is?" I asked, seeing his reaction. It was clear Torent didn't get lovey vibes from the cursed stone.

"It has an aura of dark magic, that much I can tell you. I don't think it is safe for you to have in your possession."

"Beck and I did some research."

"The wolf?"

I nodded. I knew they didn't run in the same circles, but Torent had to have known how close Beck and I had grown. I gave him the rundown of what Beck and I had discovered.

"We need to turn this over to the Court," Torent said, after I finished spilling the details on the ring. "A relic with that much power shouldn't be floating around Havenwood Falls. In the wrong hands, it could be catastrophic."

I agreed.

"Will you take it?" I asked, holding out the ring for him to grab. I didn't trust anyone else.

Torent shook his head as something flickered in his gold eyes. Temptation? "I don't dare touch it. The last thing you want to do is give a demon something that powerful. It would be dangerous for everyone. I won't tempt myself, but I will take you to the Court to turn it over."

Good enough. So I was stuck with it until then. What could go wrong? Famous last words. "Okay. Monday after school?"

He stared at my hand. "Keep it hidden until then."

Because I could see that the ring was making him uncomfortable, I slipped the little band back into my pocket.

"Do you think it's possible that the ring is messing with my emotions?" I asked, chewing on my lower lip. The question made me feel vulnerable.

Torent peered over at me through thick lashes. "Are you trying to blame the ring because you can't keep your hands off me?"

I snorted. "No, that is not what I'm saying. Please. You're not that irresistible."

A sardonic twist curled his lips, and I knew I was going to regret baiting him as my belly fluttered. "Would you like to test that theory?"

Crossing my arms, I said, "I think you should take me home."

Torent had a different idea. "I think we should go skinny dipping in the falls."

"Are you insane? Do you have any idea how cold the water must be?"

"Heat—or cold—is not really a problem for me—demon blood," he answered my question. "And I'm betting your affinity for water allows you to withstand any temperature."

He might be right, but no way was I swimming naked with Torent Stark.

No freaking way!

He started to take his shirt off and . . .

CHAPTER 13

orent was shirtless. Every sensible thought failed me as I felt my resolve weakening. My skin was on fire. Nothing in the world sounded more refreshing than a dip in the water. It was the only way to cool the inferno that had started to spread through my veins.

"Put your shirt back on," I demanded in the weakest voice ever.

Opening his car door, he stepped out, spreading his arms open. "Welcome to the falls, crash car."

"Torent," I growled. "Get back in the car."

His fingers were at the button on his pants. He flipped it through the loop and was about to start on the zipper. "I swear I'm not a bad influence. Come on. Let's go swimming. The water is calling your name."

The thing was, if I closed my eyes, I probably would hear the gentle song, lulling me into the waters. I'd heard the call my whole life. There was nowhere I felt more at home than submerged underwater.

"I hate you," I grumbled. Ignoring his chuckle, I pressed the door handle and let myself out of the Jeep. He had already moved down toward the water, and I followed onto the rocky clearing and nearly sighed. "It's amazing."

The falls might have been prettier under moonlight with a million stars twinkling over our heads. There it was in the center of my chest—that gentle tug, nudging me closer to the water. It grew with each step I took, and I didn't pause until I reached the edge.

Crouching down, I dipped my hand into the water. Tingles skipped over my skin like little beads of electricity.

"What are you waiting for?"

I flipped my gaze over my shoulder, and I probably should have steadied myself first, but I honestly hadn't expected to see a nearly naked Torent standing behind me.

Sweet baby Jesus.

He could have at least warned me. Abs alert. It wasn't like I'd never seen a guy in his boxers. I had Netflix, for goddess's sake. This shouldn't be a big deal.

But I was wrong. Dead wrong.

Torent had an athletic build, not overly muscular, but he definitely kept in shape. It didn't look like he had an ounce of fat on him. I wasn't sure how long I stood gawking, but my cheeks grew warm when I finally became aware.

His gold eyes were glowing eerily in the dark. "Don't get shy on me now, crash car."

As he moved backward into the water, his eyes never left mine.

I needed a moment to get a grip. *What is the big deal? How many times have you worn a bathing suit in front of guys? Why is my bra and undies any different? It isn't.* Except they were lacy, black, and thinner, my mind pointed out.

Lifting my chin, I straightened up and tugged my shirt slowly over my head. A gust of brisk wind blew over my skin, making my nipples pucker. I refused to cross my arms over my chest, regardless of how much I wanted to.

Aware of his eyes watching my every move, a mixture of embarrassment and sexiness danced around inside me. It was hard to decide which emotion was winning.

Mallory.

The water called me, and my attention was diverted. I no longer felt awkward, only a longing I couldn't suppress. Unsnapping the button on my jeans, I wiggled out of them and waded my feet into the water.

Mallory.

The voices called again. Not one, but many, all singing my name like a thousand angels.

I closed my eyes as a surge of power rose from the tips of my toes to the crown of my head, and I stepped deeper into the water. It was indescribable, what I was feeling, as if I could sense every molecule in the water.

"What am I going to do about you?" Torent had lost his smile and was staring at me with a piercing gaze that reached my core.

The water was neither warm nor cold as it glided over my skin. I stumbled for something snarky to say, but the truth was, I didn't know what to do about him either. "It looks like we're in the same predicament."

He went under, and I watched his dark form swim, resurfacing in front of me. Water dripped over his face, sticking to his long lashes. "What are we going to do about it?"

"Not what you're thinking."

"And how do you know what's going on inside my head?"

I dipped my shoulders into the water, letting the waves produced by the falls take me closer to Torent. The ends of my hair haloed around me. "Because you're a guy, and you've got that look in your eyes."

He grabbed my hand, and I let out a little squeal of surprise. He pulled me with him to the center of the pool, my feet treading water as I eyed him.

"What look?" he asked, knowing damn well what I was talking about.

A wave came out of nowhere, pushing me into Torent's arms, and I began to wonder if the water was conspiring against me. I had no other explanation for the sudden gust of water strong enough to throw me off balance. Were my goddess ancestors trying to tell me something?

My hands came up to land on his shoulders lest I risk going under. "Trouble," I whispered.

A long moment passed. His chest rose against mine, sparking almost electric sensations inside me, and when his fingers brushed a piece of hair off my face, that feeling tripled. My power seemed to want to answer his. I leaned my head back, and my breath caught. Above our heads, green, purple, and aqua lights swirled. The aurora borealis we created was floating over the falls.

I thought the view had been breathtaking before. Now, it was like I was living in a fantasy.

The light show above our heads brightened in color.

"A little trouble is good," he murmured.

"Only a demon would say that."

The corner of his lips twitched as his hands roamed to my hips, keeping me from drifting away. In the water, he was no challenge for me. If I had wanted to escape, nothing he could have done would have stopped me. This was my domain. And he knew it.

His lips touched mine, and I breathed in the scent of the falls mixed with Torent's. One of my hands looped around his neck, and the other traced along his jawline, feeling the tiny stubbles of facial hair. My lips parted, inviting him to take so much more, and he responded with a hunger to match mine.

This was dangerous.

Alone.

So few clothes.

And a guy who had the ability to consume me with just a kiss.

Screw it.

I was young.

The moon was full.

And I only lived once.

Wrapping my legs around his waist, I twirled my tongue around the metal stud pierced in his as I captured his moan. His fingers strayed from my hips to cup my backside.

I'd kissed other guys before, but nothing compared to locking lips with Torent. It was like coming home, and what he could evoke inside me was frightening.

Torent broke off the kiss suddenly with a look of murder in his expression. It stunned me at first, before I realized something was wrong. The muscles in his body tightened while he kept me pressed against him.

Over the crash of the falls drifted what I could have sworn were voices and laughter. It couldn't be, not this late, right?

Wrong.

"We're not alone," Torent said, the deep gravel in his voice menacing. "Not that I'm surprised."

Should I be concerned?

His body language made it seem as if something not good might be coming this way.

And he was right.

"Looks like we're late to the party." The intruder's voice made me cringe.

Fuck. Brooklyn.

She sure knew how to ruin a good night.

And the queen bee wasn't alone. She never was, though. A group of kids trotted down the trail behind her, including her two little minions, Cora and Leena.

"What are you doing here?" Torent demanded.

"Just having a little fun, same as you, but we brought party favors." Brooklyn held up two bottles of wine, which was followed by a few chuckles and snickers. "Did we interrupt something?"

I wanted to claw her pretty blue eyes out. She knew darn well she had.

"We were just leaving," Torent said with a frown. He moved away from me, but laced our fingers together and pulled me toward the shore. Under the water, a glow of lights danced. I unwound our hands quickly to avoid any unwanted attention.

"Don't be a party pooper," Brooklyn pouted from the edge of the water. "You've never skipped out on a chance to have fun before."

I tried not to think about how little clothes I had on as we emerged out of the lake, but the whistles from the boys from school didn't help. Torent's eyes began to flash in flecks of gold. I laid a hand on his forearm.

"Let's just go, okay?" There was no need for a fight to break out.

I wasn't sure he heard me, his eyes becoming more gold than purple, but then he turned away from the small group, grabbing his stuff.

I scooped my shirt off the ground and whipped it over my head, not caring that I was soaking wet. Damp clothes were the least of my problems. I wiggled into my jeans, grabbed my shoes, and stormed my way to the car.

"You can be such a witch," I heard Torent growl to Brooklyn as I climbed up the path.

"Coming from you, I'll take that as a compliment," Brooklyn retorted, her voice snapping.

"Are you okay?" Torent asked, sliding into the driver's seat, his keys jingling in his hand.

I nodded. "I'm fine. Just take me home."

Without another word, he turned they key in the ignition and the engine ripped to life. I sat back in the seat, staring up at the moon. I shouldn't let Brooklyn get to me, but she made it so easy to hate her.

I closed my eyes, and when I opened them again, Torent was rolling down my driveway with his lights off. He shifted the Jeep into park. "I'm sorry about Brooklyn."

"You don't need to apologize for her."

"Probably not, but she has a way making a nuisance of herself."

"Thanks for the ride and the . . . interesting night." I reached for the door handle.

His lips curled, and I found that even in my state of irritation, I wanted to brush the lock of hair off his forehead. "Anytime, crash car. Don't forget the ring. Monday after school?"

The ring.

I reached into my pocket to make sure it was still safely tucked inside my jeans. The first string of panic descended when I found both my pockets empty.

No. No. No.

This can't be happening.

Turning in the seat, I combed the leather, before moving to the floor, tearing the inside of Torent's Jeep apart.

Holy crap.

It was gone.

"What are you doing?" Torent's husky voice sounded in the dark. He was watching me with a curious expression.

I spun. "The ring. It's gone," I hissed, panic leaking into my tone.

His eyes narrowed. "What do you mean gone?"

"Gone. As in I don't have it anymore. Do you need me to spell it out for you? G-O-N—"

"You made your point. When was the last time you remember having it?"

"Before you got the bright idea to go swimming at the falls."

Torent's eyes held mine, and we came to the same conclusion.

"Brooklyn!" we both roared in unison.

He forked a hand through his still damp hair. "I'll talk to her."

My anxiety reached new levels. "Is that safe? Who the hell knows what she is capable of, with something like that in her possession?"

"Are you worried about me?"

"I'm concerned about everyone in this town." Myself included. Brooklyn and I had no love lost between us, and with our families' bad blood, I didn't doubt I was one of her prime targets.

I shuddered to think what Brooklyn desired most.

"First we need to make sure she has the ring. I'll go back and check the falls to be safe."

Nodding, I wrung my hands together in my lap. We both knew it would be wasted effort. The ring hadn't grown legs and walked away. His devious ex had swiped it from me.

"Don't worry. We'll find it."

How was he not freaking out? We could have potentially unleashed a psychopath into Havenwood Falls. If Gigi or Mom found out . . .

I was so dead.

CHAPTER 14

*H*alloween had barfed all over the halls of Havenwood Falls High. They seemed to take the spooky holiday seriously. Orange, purple, and black balloons arched around the doorways. The halls were decorated in webs, spiders dangling over our heads. It was kind of cute and made me miss trick-or-treating as a kid. Addison and I had lived only a block away from each other. We strategically mapped our neighborhood to maximize our candy haul, and there would always be a sleepover afterward, staying up late, popcorn, and a scary movie.

I missed her—missed my old life. No demons. No nymphs. No evil ring.

Growing up sucked.

"Are you going to the Haunting on Main Street Wednesday night?" Beck asked. He was sitting beside me in study hall.

Wednesday was Halloween and apparently was a big deal around here.

"Should I be?" I couldn't think about tomorrow, let alone what I would be doing Wednesday night, not with the ring still missing.

"Yes," he hissed back, rubbing at his temples.

"Is you-know-who going to be there?" The last person in the

world I wanted to see was Brooklyn, and if there was a party, I doubted she was far behind.

"Would you believe me if I said no?"

I went back to doodling in my notebook. "I'm busy."

Beck looped his arm through mine, causing my pen to dart across the page. "I'm not taking no for an answer. I need a sidekick, and girl, you're it."

"Are you going to wolf out on me?" I whispered.

He grinned. "Is it a full moon? I can never remember."

You'd think that was something a shifter would remember. "Does this require me to dress up?"

His eyes glanced at my notebook, looking at the hearts scribbled over the paper. "Only if you don't want to be lame."

I groaned.

"Come on, it will be a blast. You can't miss your first Halloween here. We can go shopping after school at Callie's and pick out costumes."

"Fine." I sighed. "But I can't go today." He seemed so excited. How could I disappoint him, regardless that I didn't feel much in the party mood?

"And why is that? No night classes, so a date with Havenwood Falls High's resident cutie then?"

"Hardly." My eyes swept the room before I lowered my voice. "Brooklyn stole the ring."

"She what!" he shouted, earning him a scowl from Mr. Arroyo.

Our study hall teacher was a science nerd. His voice was a tad too high, and he looked like he could use a protein shake with a good dose of vitamin E. Damn. Maybe he was a vampire—a gangly, clumsy one at that.

"Is there a problem, Mr. Winslow?" he asked, raising a brow over his wire-rimmed glasses.

Beck tilted his head to the side. "Depends if boredom is a crime."

"Keep it down. Or I'll be forced to separate you from Ms. Dorian."

J.L. WEIL

"Got it, chief." Beck pretended to open his textbook. "Why am I just now hearing about this? What happened?" he murmured.

I tapped my pen against my cheek. "It's a long story, but the short version is, I snuck out to see Torent over the weekend to tell him what we found out about the ring. One thing led to another, and we ended up swimming in the falls when Brooklyn pickpocketed me."

"Wait. Just. A. Second. Let's back it up to the part where you got naked with Torent freaking Stark."

I rolled my eyes. "I did not get naked with Torent. I was wearing a bra and panties."

He shuddered. "Don't say that word. It gives me the willies."

"Panties," I echoed, because seeing him squirm was too much fun for me to let it go.

He made a disgusted face. "I thought we were friends."

I chuckled.

"What are we going to do now that she has the Teardrop of Desire?" he asked, as if I had all the answers.

"Torent's going to see if he can get it from her. I'm meeting him after school."

Beck scowled. "That sounds like a really bad idea. I'm coming with you."

My head shook. "I don't want to get you mixed up in this. I can't help but shake this feeling something bad is going to happen if I don't find it."

"Yeah, Brooklyn is going to read us all our last rites and then shock us to death."

I mulled over the image he created, and the scary part was, I could see it unfold. "I wish I had never found it."

A body slid into the seat next to mine, and I could tell from the tingles racing down my spine and the glint of excitement in Beck's eyes, Torent had occupied the seat beside me. I don't know how he got away with coming into a class and no one saying anything. I turned to look at him, but found that his violet gaze slid past me to Beck. "Give us a minute?"

I put a hand on Beck's arm.

"It's okay. He knows. I thought we were meeting after school, not during classes," I rumbled as quietly as I could at Torent.

But then he had to go and flash me a pair of dimples that would make a nun's knees weak. "I got impatient. I needed to see you."

My heart galloped in my chest. Why did every word out of his mouth have to induce such strong feelings inside me? With the ring gone, I had assumed this intensity would fade between us. That didn't seem to be the case. "Did you find it?"

If he thought about objecting to Beck being in on our little powwow, he must have changed his mind. "It wasn't at the falls. Someone definitely picked it up."

"You mean she stole it from me. Does she have it?"

"She said she'd never seen a ring."

I snorted. "You don't believe her, do you?"

"I've known Brooklyn my whole life, and I know when she is hiding something. She is definitely up to something."

"Shit."

Torent leaned an elbow on the desk.

"How much did you tell him?" he asked, talking about Beck.

I blinked. "Everything."

Torent leaned in so we shared the same air.

"Everything?" he repeated in a deep voice that oozed sensuality. His gaze held me hostage.

Heat spread over my cheeks as his scent teased me. I wanted to be anywhere but in a classroom. The back of his car. The janitor's closet. Under the bleachers. Dear God, I needed to get myself under control.

Beck took his notebook, fanning himself, and cooed, "It's getting hot in here."

I kicked him under the table as Torent laughed. "What are we going to do? We're not going to get Brooklyn to just hand it over."

It would mean she would have to admit what she had done. And that was very, very unlikely.

"There's a Halloween party on Wednesday night. Go with me?"

"What does that have to do with—"

Now it was Beck's turn to kick me.

I glared at him.

"You'd better say yes," Beck hissed between his teeth. "And I want details."

"Two against one." Torent grinned. "Looks like I win. I'll pick you up at seven. And, crash car, don't forget your mask. We're going to test your inner bad with a bit of B and E."

"Is that some kind of kinky supernatural sex thing, because I think I'll pass."

Both Beck and Torent snickered.

"Mal, I love you," Beck said. "I'll make sure she is properly outfitted on one condition. You swear to me you'll keep her safe."

My eyes bounced between them. "Why do I need his protection?"

They both ignored me. "You have my word. No harm will come to her. We need to get the ring back and turn it over to the Court. I don't think I need to tell you what an object like that can do in the wrong hands?"

And Brooklyn definitely qualified as the wrong hands.

"Will someone tell me what a B and E is?" My voice had grown with mounting irritation, causing a few heads to turn in our direction.

Torent pressed his finger to my lips. He shook his head as his mouth curved in amusement. "Just be ready at seven."

Don't do it, Mallory. Don't give into him.

My eyes snapped downward and I remained silent, studying my open textbook as if it was an advanced reader copy of the next J.K. Rowling book. "Fine. But this better not earn me another detention."

He leaned over and whispered in my ear, "Live a little." The feel of his warm breath on my newly inked ear sent tingles prancing through me.

What was he doing to me?

Screwing up my entire life plan, that's what, and I didn't have the ring to blame.

~

"THERE IS ONLY one place in Havenwood Falls that has what we're looking for. Callie's Consignments." Beck and I were strolling down Main Street with iced coffees in hand.

I took a sip from my straw and nearly moaned. Coffee Haven was godly. "I'll take your word for it."

We walked next door to the quaint little boutique owned by Callie Montgomery. According to Beck, she was a supe. "Don't tell me you're one of those people who hate Halloween?"

The door chimed as we walked inside.

"Actually, I love it. I've just been so preoccupied, I forgot about it."

Beck gasped. "Be careful what you say."

I'd spent so much time dwelling on the ring, battling my feelings for Torent, and dealing with being a nymph, I barely gave more than a passing thought to the numerous other supernaturals in this town.

Take the cute gypsy-demon who owned this shop. Callie looked like she could be a cover model for Free People. Her smile reached her hazel eyes as she greeted Beck and me. You would never know by looking at her that she was anything but human.

We perused the racks, Beck pulling out amazing vintage finds.

"You would look killer in this. I bet Torent would love it," Beck sang, a sparkle in his eyes.

I wrinkled my nose, eyeing the black stretchy material. "No way am I wearing that."

"I don't see why not. It's sexy and perfect for a night of espionage."

"Cat Woman?" The black bodysuit was shiny and looked big enough to only fit one of my thighs. It would leave nothing to the imagination, hugging every curve in my body.

"Exactly. We can get you a tail and cat ears."

I leveled him with a stare.

One side of his lips curled up as he held up the black bodysuit.

"I bet Brooklyn would wear it," he said, dangling it in the air.

I snorted. "My point."

His shoulders sagged, and he turned on the puppy eyes. "Indulge me and at least try it on?" He held out the outfit.

"Augh, if it gets you off my back, fine." I reluctantly took the hanger and marched myself to the back of the shop, all the while grumbling under my breath. What I wanted to wear was a reaper cape to go with my sullen mood lately.

Maybe it was the loss of the ring or not knowing when Brooklyn would strike, but I hadn't felt like myself the past few days, and it was starting to wear on me.

I wasn't in a shopping mood, and I knew Beck only had the best intentions, but I hardly doubted me flaunting my curves would help me. I felt a sense of responsibility to keep the ring from causing chaos. It was my fault the ring was floating around town. If I had never gone into the water, it would still be sitting at the bottom of Peacock Lake.

While my head was whirling with guilt and uncertainty, I stripped down and shimmied into the bodysuit, swearing and grumbling every inch of the way. I turned and studied my reflection in the full-length mirror.

Holy crap.

Is that me?

When did I get hips?

I twisted from side to side, watching the fabric move with my body. It clung to my hips like a second skin. Running my hands over my thighs, I had to give it to Beck. He did have a point. I felt sexy . . . and powerful.

Maybe a little too much.

A gush of energy soared up inside me, and there was nothing I could do to stop it or the stray pins on the floor from flying at me like I was a giant magnet. Three tiny needles embedded themselves into my arm.

"Ouch!" I shrieked, feeling like a human pin cushion.

Beck whipped back the curtain. "What happened?"

I was plucking out one of the pins when he burst in, startling me, and I stabbed the pad of my index finger.

"I poked myself with a needle." I sucked on the end of my finger, drawing in the blood from the tiny pinprick.

"Do I even want to know how?"

"Stupid nymph powers," I mumbled, pulling out the other two pins.

"How's that going by the way? Not good I take it?"

"It feels as if I'm never going to get the hang of my powers." My Awakening Lab night class was supposed to help me hone my abilities, but I was the class klutz. My powers never did what I wanted them to do.

"Don't stress. You'll get the hang of it."

What if I don't?

"Easy for you to say. You've had your whole life to deal with this." I set the pile of pins onto a wooden shelf in the dressing room.

Beck's hands flew to his mouth as his eyes roamed over my scantily clad body. "Holy shit. You look amazing. What did I tell you?"

My face flamed. I had completely forgotten about the cat suit. Turning back into the mirror, I had only one thought.

"It does look good, huh?" I agreed, meeting Beck's gaze in the reflection.

His expression was smug; he was clearly very pleased with himself. "You look fabulous. Brooklyn, eat your heart out. I can't believe you're dating Torent Stark."

I chewed on my lip. "We're not dating."

He pressed his lips together to keep from smirking. "If you say so."

CHAPTER 15

*M*om and Gigi were sitting on the porch swing, sipping hot apple cider as they waited for the trick-or-treaters to come by. The whole house smelled like cinnamon and apples. I snuck a quick glass of cider, crammed down a piece of pumpkin bread with butter, and then walked down the hall in my cat suit, equipped with ears and all.

Outside, the trees swayed with the wind as it blew through, shaking the branches. Leaves of deep orange, flaming red, and honey yellow spun as they danced to the ground, blanketing the grass in color. Someone in the neighborhood was burning leaves, the smell drifting through the trees. Autumn in Havenwood Falls was in full swing.

A part of me missed being a kid, going out around the neighborhood and eating so much candy I nearly puked.

"Why are you dressed like that?" Mom asked, getting up from the swing to refill the half-empty bowl of candy for the little kids.

Gigi smiled at me beside her. "The Haunting on Main Street is tonight."

"They still do that?" Mom asked, surprised.

"Every year. It's tradition," Gigi replied.

"Can't break tradition," I said, grabbing a Kit Kat from the black bucket shaped like a witch's cauldron.

Mom pursed her lips. "Promise me you'll be careful. Halloween in Havenwood Falls isn't your normal holiday. "

I rolled my eyes. "All the freaks come out at night. I got it."

She flicked one of my cat ears. "I don't think you do, but you will."

"What your mom is trying to say is, it's a powerful time of the year. The veil between the living and the dead is at its thinnest," Gigi explained.

Torent's Jeep pulled up before either of them could get into any more detail about the dead. The sight of his Jeep sent my heart racing.

"Is that the Stark boy?" Gigi asked. "You've been spending quite a lot of time with him."

"She has?" Mom queried, raising a brow. "A demon, Mallory? Really?"

I shrugged. "We're friends. Let's not make a big deal about it." I waved to Mom and Gigi as I walked off the porch. "Don't wait up," I called over my shoulder.

The car was filled with the tantalizing scent of Torent, and I couldn't stop myself from inhaling.

"Nice costume."

I let my eyes roam over him. "What are you supposed to be?"

He blinked, letting his gold demon eyes overtake the purple. "A demon."

"Clever," I said dryly. "If I knew dressing up was optional, I would never have let Beck talk me into this."

"Remind me to thank him later." He winked.

I punched him lightly in the shoulder. "Mom and my grandma are keeping a keen eye on you."

The Jeep slowly rolled out of the driveway. "I'm actually shocked your grandmother lets me on her property."

"Why is that?"

"I figured my family's reputation would be enough to have her warn you away. My brothers have only darkened my family's already tarnished name. One of my brothers, Brysen, has been banned from Havenwood Falls by the Court for going full demon in public. Hence he is away at college. The other, Zaren, spent more time in the principal's office than the principal."

I fought the urge to move closer to him in the car, or reach out and run my hands along his flawless jawline. So I clasped my hands together in my lap to keep me from doing something reckless. But damn if I wasn't in the mood to break some rules. Maybe it was the eeriness of Halloween. Or being trapped inside a small space with a guy I hadn't been able to get out of my head since I stepped foot inside Havenwood Falls. But regardless, I was amped up.

"And you're the angel in your family."

He snorted. "Hardly, crash car. We're on our way to break into Brooklyn's house. What does that tell you?"

I dropped my head on the back of the seat. "How did I let you talk me into this?"

Torent flashed me his dimples. "Because I'm cute. And irresistible."

He might be right on all accounts, but this was insane. "You're sure no one will be home?"

"Her parents are working, and Brooklyn will be at the party. Beck is going to text us when she arrives, and then we'll be in the clear. Once we search her room and get the ring, we'll make an appearance at the party." He had it all figured out.

Brooklyn lived only a few blocks from my house, something that didn't make me feel comfortable. Torent killed his headlights as we turned down her street, parking off to the side of her house.

He twirled a lock of my hair around his finger.

"Your Catwoman costume is perfect for what we're about to do," he murmured huskily, his bright gaze holding mine.

I couldn't take my eyes off him, and that urge to be near him quadrupled. I leaned closer, our noses brushing, and for a moment, I wasn't sure if we were going to kiss or get out of the car. From the flecks of gold swimming in his eyes, I was leaning toward lots of bone-melting kissing.

Releasing my hair, he sighed. "You're making it very hard to concentrate."

My lips twitched. "Good."

It was another prolonged moment before he sighed. "It's time for your inner bad girl to shine. Keep to the shadows and try not to activate anything metal."

I rolled my eyes. "If you wanted someone stable as a sidekick, you should have brought Beck."

"Yeah, but he isn't nearly as hot."

I snorted.

We crept up the lawn, sticking to the pine trees. A group of kids passed on the sidewalk, not giving us a second glance. Torent slipped his hand in mine, and for once, I didn't object, but then the sparks of light began to swirl between us.

"We're really going to need to work on your magnetic energy," he whispered, grinning. "We can't have the air glowing every time we touch."

"It takes two to tango," I whispered back. The lights were a product of our joined powers.

"Touché."

Torent guided us to the back of the soft-blue Victorian-style house. All the windows were dark, and I took that as a good sign. I couldn't believe I was doing this. I was an accessory to burglary. How would that look on my college applications if we got caught? My chest squeezed, the beginnings of a panic attack rising within me.

Flattening his palms on the glass pane, he started to wedge the window upward. Taking a quick peek over his shoulder at me, he halted.

"Hey, it's going to be okay," he assured me. "I won't let anything happen to you."

I gazed into his eyes, and a warmth of calm washed through me.

"I'll be in and out so fast, you won't even know I'm gone," he said, trying to put me at ease.

That was unlikely. Somehow I was positive his absence would definitely affect me, but I nodded, leaning against the house while he opened the window wider. He boosted himself up and had one leg inside when my phone started singing.

Shit. Shit. Shit.

Taylor Swift belted from the little speakers, sounding in the silent woods like a bullhorn. I fumbled with my phone, scrambling to turn off the volume.

Torent turned and gave me a dull glare.

Okay. Fine. So I was the world's worst criminal. Sue me.

"Sorry," I whispered. "It's Beck." My eyes scanned over the text.

Abort mission. She's wearing the ring.

Could this night go any more wrong? I tugged on Torent's shirt, pulling him out of the window. "We have a problem. The ring is not in there."

"What are you talking about?"

I flipped my phone around, showing Beck's text.

He rubbed at the back of his neck as his eyes scanned the lit-up screen. "Damn."

"Now what?" I asked, my tone shrieky from the sudden increase in anxiety coursing through my veins.

"I was never good at plans. Come on." He grabbed my hand, leading me away from the house. "We're going to the party."

"She is never just going to hand it over."

"No, but I have many skills. You never know when sleight of hand might come in handy."

I should have known it would be something disreputable. "Are all your skills of a nefarious nature?"

He chuckled, and I took that as a yes.

CHAPTER 16

*T*he celebration on Main Street was at the height of activity. Glowing jack-o'-lanterns were scattered throughout the square. White sheets hung as ghosts in the trees. Spider webs covered the shop windows.

After maneuvering his Jeep around the crowds and parking the car, Torent and I walked down the side alley, toward the sounds of Halloween. Our feet shuffled through the fallen leaves strewn over the street.

"We need to find Beck," I said, rushing to match my strides with Torent's long ones. It wasn't going to be easy, with everyone dressed up.

Just as we were about to cut around a corner, from the shadows emerged a body. I'd never been one for haunted houses or jump scares, and the sight of those glowing eyes coming straight for us had my internal girly shrill rising.

Torent caught the sound of my scream with this hand.

"Shh." His gaze caught mine, forcing me to focus on his face. "It's just Beck."

What? I took another look as a grinning Beck strolled up to me. "God, you scared me," I told Beck.

"So what's the plan? How are we going to get the ring back?" Beck asked.

"We should split up, cover more ground. You go with Beck, and if you see her, text me. You don't confront her alone." Torent gave me a pointed look, waiting for me to answer.

Beck ran a hand through his messy blue hair. "Should we really split up?"

Torent turned to Beck. "You got a better idea?"

"None that wouldn't piss off the Court," he mumbled.

Torent faced me, his hands framing my face. "Promise me you're not going to do anything without me."

He was really worried, which gave me the warm fuzzies, but it also only made the trepidation inside me triple. "Okay, fine. I won't do anything irrational."

Beck and I headed in the opposite direction, and I got an up-close view of the Haunting on Main Street. Strands of glittering lights were strewn in the trees and around the gazebo. The fountain was lit up in purple and orange. Hay bales, pumpkins, and other spooky decorations were hung around the square as speakers pumped the Halloween classics. It was both magical and ghoulish.

We passed a group of superheroes, ghosts, and little princesses as my heels clattered over the brick pavers.

"What was she wearing?" I asked, thinking it would be easier to spot Brooklyn if I knew what to look for. We turned a corner and halted in our steps. "Brooklyn," I said, squinting against the streetlight. "I've been looking for you." Wow. That was easier than I anticipated.

Static crackled in the air, making the hairs on my arms shoot up. She was alone, Leena and Cora not in sight. It was weird seeing her without her two sidekicks.

"Well, you found me," she snarled, her long hair framing her face.

My eyes adjusted, zeroing in on the ring. It sat on her finger, the garnet stone glowing in the dark. Even as I stared at it, I could feel the magnetic pull of its darkness. My hand twitched, dying to touch it, but something about Brooklyn stopped me from ripping it off her finger, a tingle of caution.

She was dressed up as a . . .

A groan escaped my lips.

Brooklyn and I were wearing the exact same outfit. Could this night get any worse?

The answer was yes.

I lifted my phone, but before I had the chance to unlock the screen, Brooklyn snatched it out of my hand, throwing it to the ground.

I stared in shock as the screen cracked, pieces of my phone scattering over the ground.

"What the hell, Brooklyn?" Beck growled. "You just broke her phone."

As I glared into her stormy eyes, I comprehended how much trouble we were in. Something was just not right about them.

"You and I need to have a little chat," she said, taking a step toward me.

Crap on a broomstick.

"Go get Torent," I ordered Beck.

He didn't immediately take off, and I knew he was struggling with the idea of leaving me alone with the she-devil.

"Go!" I hissed. "And hurry. I'll be fine."

He took off, bolting down the alley.

"Love the costume, by the way." I was being a smart-ass, but she deserved it. "I see you helped yourself to my ring as well. I'm shocked it fits."

She looked down at her hand admiringly. "That's the wonderful thing about magical objects. They have a way of forming to their owner."

"Yeah, well, the thing is, I sort of need it back."

Her response was to throw a bolt of electric energy at me. It hit the brick wall just to the right of my face. Wow. I wasn't expecting her to go all commando on me. We'd been in a minor scrap before, but this was different. This time, there was murder in her eyes, and she had delivered a warning. If I didn't listen, she would make this difficult for both of us.

I scrambled to put distance between us. *Just keep her rambling until Beck and Torent get back. How hard can that be?*

"Hold up a minute. Why don't we talk this through?" I said, walking backward. My back hit a brick wall. *Shit.* "Isn't there a no magic rule or something?"

She stalked toward me like a nymph on crack. "You don't even know who you are or what you're capable of."

And no doubt Brooklyn would enlighten me.

"True, but I don't think you need to get bent out of shape about it." Wrong answer.

The air charged again with Brooklyn's electric powers. Shocking was her specialty, and I wasn't keen on finding out how many volts she could shoot into my body.

"Do you think it was a coincidence you found this?" She raised her hand. "It called *you* because it recognized the darkness inside you."

Confusion set in. "What are you talking about?"

She lunged at me, suddenly in my face. Her fingers traced the line of my neck over the rapidly pulsing vein. "You're a descendant of Styx."

I flinched. "And?"

This wasn't a newsflash to me.

She let out a short hysterical laugh, her hand wrapping around my throat. "I can't believe they still haven't told you." Energy crackled over her knuckles. "What your family has kept hidden is that you have darkness inside you. You're dangerous."

That was funny, coming from her, and I hated that inside me, a bell of truth rang. I didn't want to believe her, but I knew my family was keeping secrets.

"You lie," I wheezed, my hands frantically trying to pry her fingers loose.

She slammed my head back against the wall, and black dots swirled behind my eyes. "Do I? You inherited it from your father. It is his darkness that runs in your veins and, combined with the shadows of your nymph powers, makes you unstable."

"Why do you care so much?"

Something other than hate flickered in her dark blue eyes. Sadness? Fear? "Before you showed up, I had my goddess's blessing."

I swallowed hard. "I don't know what that means."

The hatred was back, shining in her eyes, bolder and brighter than before, and for a heartbeat, I thought she might kill me. "My abilities have diminished. Your awakening drained some of mine, weakening my goddess, but strengthening Styx. Your coming back here has reinforced the bloodline and made her more powerful. You took the only thing that mattered from me."

I shook my head. "I swear I didn't do it on purpose. I'm sure we can fix it."

Her laugh was harsh. "You can't really be that stupid. No one tells a goddess to do anything."

Okay. That was it. I'd had enough. I didn't really want to hurt her, but I had to get the ring before it made Brooklyn do something she could never take back.

Lifting my arm, I slammed my elbow into her nose. Blood immediately began to ooze from her nostril. "No one calls me stupid and gets away with it. Now give me the ring before I'm forced to kick your ass."

She took the back of her hand and smeared the red sticky stuff from her face. "This is about to get fun."

Hell no, it wasn't.

Brooklyn's hand snaked out, grabbing a fist full of my hair in the ever classic bitch-hair-pull maneuver. It was effective. I bit the inside of my lip as she spun me around.

"Brooklyn," I shrieked, fire scorching at my scalp. "Oh, my god. Do you hear yourself? Wake up. You're talking about murdering me. Listen to me. That ring is poisoning you. I know, you hate me, and I get it, but do you really want to ruin your life?"

"That night at the falls when I found you with Torent, stumbling

J.L. WEIL

upon this ring was a nice little surprise, and it's going to give me back what you stole from me."

"It's a dark artifact, not a magical matchmaker," I hissed between my teeth, assuming what she wanted was Torent.

Brooklyn looked at me as if she was going to strangle the ever-loving crap out of me. "I don't want the guy. I want your magic."

Imagine that. I opened my mouth to tell her she could have it if she gave up the ring, but I never got the chance.

"Let her go, Brooklyn," a dark voice growled.

Brooklyn spun at the sound of the voice we both recognized. I exhaled, relief pouring from me.

Torent stepped out of the shadows, his violet eyes burning bright with flecks of gold. "I don't want to hurt you."

Beck was standing beside him, his silver eyes luminous and a snarl erupting from his throat, letting a bit of the wolf within him out.

"You're taking her side?" Brooklyn sneered. "First my powers, then you. She's taken everything from me. Why shouldn't she pay?"

Torent's eyes grew gold, radiating in the dark alley like a blazing fire. "Is it worth going to jail for? Being banished by the Court—or worse?"

Her gaze faltered, and I knew I had to make a move or risk getting hurt. Worse yet, she would turn her rage on Torent. The idea of him in danger sent me into a tizzy.

The air shimmered around me in a halo as I let the source of my power build inside me. And then, I let it go. Truthfully, I had no idea what I was doing, which was the worst way to do magic. As the string on my control released, the garbage dumpster in the alley came sailing straight for Brooklyn and me.

"Mallory!" Torent screamed.

He moved like lightning, shooting toward me at blinding speed, and yet, time seemed to slow to an infinite crawl. His arms wrapped around my waist, hauling me out of the way as the dumpster flew past us and smacked into Brooklyn. The force of the metal box tossed her body like a rag doll in the air before she landed with a hard thwack to the ground.

I gasped, lifting my head and peering through strands of tangled hair. My fingers were tingling and my ears ringing with the sickening sounds of metal hitting flesh.

Holy smokes.

"Are you okay?" Torent whispered, his eyes searching over my face.

I leaned my head back against the brick wall and started to breathe again. What had I done?

"Is she okay? Tell me I didn't . . ." My voice trailed off. I couldn't bring myself to say the words. Horror pitted in my stomach.

Beck was crouched beside Brooklyn's unmoving form. He pressed two fingers to the side of her neck. "No, she's breathing."

In that case . . . "Get the ring, quickly, before she wakes up and becomes the Terminator again," I rushed in a panicked string, urging Torent to take action.

Moving to Brooklyn's side, Torent reached for the ring, but he hesitated, glowering at the dark artifact.

"What are you waiting for?" Beck hissed.

Torent picked up Brooklyn's hand, slowly withdrawing the ring. Tense lines etched at the corners of his lips. His gaze was glued to the ring as he rocked back on his heels, still crouched.

"Beck, stay with Brooklyn," he ordered. "We're turning this over to the Court tonight. It's caused enough problems."

That we could agree on.

Torent stood up, staring at the ring with such intensity it gave me pause. A fiery light swirled around his body—demon fire. His eyes were brighter than I'd ever seen them, glowing with a possessive desire. The look on his face frightened me.

And to think I thought the horror was over.

He had warned me once before of the temptation a ring like this would pose for a demon. Seeing it firsthand was not the same as being forewarned.

"Torent," I called his name, hoping to get his attention focused on me. It was a no go. A knot formed in my belly, rolling its way up into my chest. "Hey, it's me." I placed my hand on his forearm.

His lips morphed into a menacing scowl while his eyes flicked up, tracking my movements like a hawk. Such darkness shimmered in them.

I turned my hand palm side up. "I can take it. I should never have asked you to retrieve it."

Not a muscle moved, except for the one in his jaw. It tightened. Beck stood up, shifting his body to stand in front of me, eyeing Torent with unease.

The last thing I wanted was for Torent and Beck to get into a fight, but I didn't know how to stop it from happening. I needed to do something, because things just escalated.

Torent attacked.

CHAPTER 17

Swinging a fist toward Beck, Torent let out a growl that shook his chest. Beck sunk to the ground, narrowly missing being flung across the alley.

"She's mine," Torent said tightly.

In any other situation, this would have called for some serious eye rolling. Now was not the time to get possessive, but the ring had a way of bringing out the absolute worst in people. Dread pitted in my belly. *Now what?*

"No one is contesting your feelings. Why don't you give me the ring?" Beck attempted to reason with the demon.

"You have no idea who you're messing with, dog," Torent snapped.

And just like that, the two went at it. I could never imagine two guys fighting over me, and now that I was seeing it firsthand, I wanted to erase it from my memory. The sounds alone made me cringe. Fists. Bones. Flesh.

No more blood. No more fighting. I'd had enough.

I shot forward, putting myself in between them. "Stop! Enough!"

Neither of them listened to me. Shocker.

Because I was out of options, I used my powers. Again. I focused on two pipes running down the side of the building. They bent at my will, wrapping around Torent to keep him from killing Beck. It was clear who the seasoned fighter was.

Poor Beck.

I had to give my best friend credit. It took balls to go toe to toe with a demon.

Torent's eyes glowed that demon iridescent gold. I stepped up to him.

"I'm sorry," I rasped. "You left me no choice."

"I wouldn't have hurt you," he stressed, almost pleading with me to believe him.

"I know. This is my fault." The ring was clutched in his hand, and I didn't delude myself into thinking he was going to voluntarily hand it over. All I could think about was Smeagol petting his precious from *Lord of the Rings*. Fingers trembling, I took his hand and flipped it over. I kept my gaze fastened to his while I opened his fingers, meeting little resistance. He had meant what he said about not hurting me, and the knowledge made my heart patter.

He closed his eyes, fighting off the power of the ring over his demon. I quickly took the troublesome piece of jewelry and stuffed it into my bra. Torent relaxed his body, resting his head on the brick wall. Using the familiar tingles swimming in my blood, I removed the pipes holding him prisoner. He exhaled, opening his eyes, and I was relieved to see they were crystal violet. No traces of gold.

Beck was near, waiting to see what happened next. His body was alert. Torent nodded in his direction, before looking at me with regretful eyes. "I never would have—"

I stopped him before he could say any more. "It's okay." Any minute, Brooklyn would wake up with a killer headache. "We need to go." For real this time.

Torent ran a hand through his hair, eyes skating over Brooklyn. "City Hall isn't far."

Thank god. Not only was I dying for this night to end, I wanted to lose the boots. Padding down the alley, we left Beck with a stirring Brooklyn. He was going to have his hands full.

The Court of the Sun and the Moon had a secret entrance at the rear of City Hall. Torent knew how to reach someone who would know what to do with the Teardrop of Desire. All we had to do was get there without incident.

It sounded simple enough, but if there was one thing I'd learned about being supernatural, it was that nothing was as easy as it seemed when magic and the unknown were involved. This was my burden. I had been the one who had found the ring, who had unleashed its powers into Havenwood Falls. It was my duty to see it returned into the hands of the Court. I didn't know if I was skeptical or relieved that we managed to make our way across the square to City Hall without incident.

We skirted around to the back of the two-story building, and I tried not to dwell on what Brooklyn had said to me during her enchanted psychobabble, but my mind went there. What if she had been telling the truth? What if I inherited some kind of bad mojo from my father? I knew virtually nothing about him. And Mom and Gigi were definitely not telling me something.

Did I even want to know?

Would it be better if I went on living my life blessedly unaware? Would knowing give it power, bringing forth the darkness?

So many questions. So many uncertainties. So many possibilities.

"Are you sure you're okay?" Torent asked, interrupting my internal rant of panic.

I hadn't noticed the quickening of my breath until now and forced myself to take a deep, even amount of air. We were outside the rear of the building, and my palms had gone damp.

"I'm just ready to get rid of this thing." *And for my life to go back to normal*, I added inside my head. But that wasn't in the cards for me. Not anymore.

I was who I was. There was no running from it.

We paused at a door that looked like nothing more than a maintenance entrance, but the moon and mountain emblem situated above was the only indicator it was something more. This was where the governing body of Havenwood Falls met. It consisted of the leaders from the Old Families, the descendants of the town's founders. I'd never been inside, but I could sense the air of magic that lived within.

Torent turned the handle and waited for me to walk through. I rubbed my hands over my arms, a tremble tickling my spine. We descended a flight of stairs into the City Hall basement and then through a long hallway that opened to a small reception area. It was there that Addie Beaumont, dressed as the sexiest *Star Wars* stormtrooper I'd ever seen, greeted us with her helmet in hand.

"Addie," Torent addressed her by name.

She smiled at him, the stone in her nose twinkling under the light. "What brings you to the Court on All Hallows' Eve of all nights? I was about to hit a party before duty calls at the witching hour." She gave us a wink.

Torent nodded toward me. *My turn.* I dug the ring out of my pocket and twirled it in my fingers.

"I came to bring the Court what I'm fairly certain is a magical relic." The ring was still in my hand, and now that I was here, I was finding it difficult to relinquish it from my possession.

Intrigue brightened in Addie's brown eyes, behind the black-framed glasses. "And how did you come across such an object?"

"At the bottom of Peacock Lake," I retorted.

She lifted a brow. "Let's see this relic."

I opened my palm, showing her the gold band with the crimson stone embedded. Its aura seemed to reach out to me, tempting me to slip it on.

Addie's eyes darkened as she stared intently. "You were right to bring this to the Court. The magic rooted to the ring is dark and powerful, and someone's been trying to collect magical artifacts, especially dark ones. It would be disastrous for our town if the Collector got his hands on this."

The bangles on her wrists jingled as she produced a small velvet-lined box out of thin air. My eyes followed hers to stare at the Teardrop of Desire.

"Mallory?"

It was Torent's silky voice that pulled me from the trance. I glanced up, meeting his worried gaze. Without risking another entrancement, I took a deep breath and picked up the ring, plunking it into the box.

A million pounds was lifted from my shoulders, and I would be happy if I never owned another ring in my life.

Addie quickly snapped the little box closed. "I'll make sure this gets kept somewhere safe. You don't have to worry about it anymore."

I nodded, feeling relieved that someone who was more capable than me had possession of the cursed ring.

"Thanks, Addie," Torent replied, slipping a hand to the small of my back. He applied the slightest pressure, guiding me to move. We'd done what we had set out to do. There was nothing left to say.

We walked back the way we came, climbing the stairs and slipping through the door. Outside, the world was still moving. A group of kids was passing by, laughing and unwrapping candy from their Halloween haul.

Strolling down the sidewalk beside the building, I snuck a peek at Torent, curious what was going through his head.

"That was fun," I stated sarcastically. "Next time you want to bring me to a party, remind me to—"

He moved so fast, I didn't have a chance to prepare myself. One second he was in front of me, and then suddenly he was kissing me as if he was starved for water. I had no choice but to respond, his lips pulling a response from mine.

My mouth parted in a gasp, and being the rogue that he was, Torent deepened the kiss. The cool metal piercing of his tongue brushed against mine, soothing the instant heat. It was a battle of cool and hot inside my mouth, and when he pulled away slowly, my lips clung to his, not ready to end the blissful torture. My hand was curved around the nape of his neck.

"Look." His eyes went upward, mine following. Northern lights lit up the dark alley in the most breathtaking sight.

I doubted I would ever get sick of seeing the electric display of lights.

"It's beautiful," I whispered, disentangling myself from him.

"We did this, together. Our powers, they complement each other —*we* complement each other."

So much for letting my heart rate return to normal—that stupid fluttering was back in my chest. I chewed on my lip. Maybe he was right. Or maybe I wanted him to be right, because my hormones were going batshit bonkers at the moment. "Thank you for saving my life."

"Anytime, crash car. What are boyfriends for?"

"You're not my boyfriend," I clarified, trying to convince myself as much as him . . . maybe more so.

"Really? The way you just kissed me says otherwise," he murmured with a slight curve to his lips.

Damn Torent and his dimples.

~

Thank you for reading!
Torent and Mallory's journey continues in
Ascending Darkness.

~

WE HOPE you enjoyed this story in the Havenwood Falls High series of novellas featuring a variety of supernatural creatures. The series is a collaborative effort by multiple authors.

Other books you might enjoy in the Young Adult Havenwood Falls High series:

The Fall by Kristen Yard
Fata Morgana by E.J. Fechenda
Forever Emeline by Katie M. John
Curse the Night by R.K. Ryals

Stay up to date at www.HavenwoodFalls.com

ABOUT THE AUTHOR

USA Today bestselling author J.L. Weil lives in Illinois, where she writes teen & new adult paranormal romances about spunky, smart-mouth girls who always wind up in dire situations. For every sassy girl, there is an equally mouthwatering, overprotective guy. Of course, there is lots of kissing. And stuff.

An admitted addict to Love Pink clothes, raspberry mochas from Starbucks, and Jensen Ackles, she loves gushing about books and Supernatural with her readers.

She is the author of the international bestselling Raven & Divisa series.

www.jlweil.com

ACKNOWLEDGMENTS

I need to start by thanking Kristie Cook for letting me be a part of this amazing world and community she has created. I feel truly lucky to be one of the authors who gets to write in Havenwood Falls. You put your heart and soul into this project and it really shows.

A HUGE thank you to all the readers who have stuck with me!! It has been a crazy journey. I am so blessed to have such wonderful friends in this author world. Hugs!!

For my Dark Divas. I love you to death. Thank you so much for the best squad in the world. What would I do without you?!

AN EXCERPT

HAVENWOOD FAILS HIGH

Saving Infiniti

ROSE GARCIA

~ A Havenwood Falls Young Adult Novella ~

Saving Infiniti (A Havenwood Falls High Novella) by Rose Garcia

Welcome to Havenwood Falls, a small town in the majestic mountains of Colorado. A town where legacies began centuries ago, bloodlines run deep, and dark secrets abound. A town where nobody is what you think, where truths pose as lies, and where myths blend with reality. A place where everyone has a story. Including the high schoolers. This is only but one . . .

Infiniti Clausman is making the most of senior year. Throwing parties, pulling pranks, and breaking all the rules, she's determined to graduate with a bang! But there's one thing on her senior year bucket list she hasn't been able to cross off yet—falling in love. In fact, she's never even been kissed.

Infiniti hopes to change this when she travels from Houston to Colorado for the holiday break. Instead, she finds her world turned upside down when she discovers all things supernatural exist, time travel is real, and her very life is at stake. Suddenly, that kiss is the least of her worries.

Joe Greg will never forget the injured girl he and Kase Kasun found on the side of the mountain. It was 2012, and he was only twelve, but the image of the wreckage and his interaction with the girl has never left him. When he sees the girl again in 2018, she looks exactly the same. He figures out that she's time-traveled to his present, with a reaper on her heels and a mystery to unravel. Drawn to protect her, he's hell-bent on standing by her side. Even if it means his death.

SAVING INFINITI

Fleet ran his fingers through his dark hair before tilting his head toward the night sky. He eyed the top floor of the Houston skyscraper Tavion had called home since tracking Dominique and her protectors to the oversized Texas city. A cool December breeze swept through the streets, kicking up the stench of trash from a nearby dumpster. Fleet hated all the concrete, all the glass buildings, but mostly he hated taking on the role of being one of the Tainted and on Tavion's side against the Pures. He had accepted the directive for the greater good, but the passing of so many years had started to muddle allegiances in his brain. All sense of right and wrong had started to merge. Too good at his job, he found himself alone and sure of nothing but the perpetual clench in his gut.

Fleet closed his eyes. He tried not to picture the horrible things he had done in Tavion's name while tracking Dominique, but had a hard time suppressing the images. His only solace was knowing that in this life, her final life, Dominique had no recollection of any of her prior lives. Even if it meant forgetting him forever, Fleet hoped Dominique's memories would never return. There was too much pain and suffering for anyone to have to recall, let alone someone he secretly cared about.

Fleet banged his fist against the glass wall of the downtown apartment building. "Get your shit together, man."

Pressing his palm against the cool surface, he held his breath, then let it trickle out between clenched teeth. He had built a brick wall around his true feelings for Dominique and the Pures ages ago, vowing not to let anyone ever see that side of himself, especially Tavion. He had a job to do and was determined to see it through no matter what. To hell with what anyone thought of him.

"Don't let anyone in," he muttered, while strengthening the fortress of his mind. With his vulnerabilities hidden, he turned his focus to Tavion's directive: find Dominique and prepare her for death.

"I got this," he whispered to himself. "I can do this."

With his emotions in check, he jerked the heavy door open. He nodded at the security guard behind the holiday-adorned lobby desk. The guard peered at him from over his computer screen.

"Hey, Fleet. Your boss is in quite a mood tonight." He whistled. "Quite a mood."

Fleet knew exactly what sort of mood Tavion was in. Starving for death and destruction, he displayed hatred like a neon sign. But some days his harsh light shone brighter than usual. Today must have been one of those days.

"Thanks, Sammy."

Sammy said something else about Christmas spirit and holiday joy, but Fleet ignored him. Joy didn't exist for him, hadn't in a long time. And it wasn't likely to ever return.

Pushing the button for the top floor with his key card, Fleet repeated his mission over and over in his mind, drowning out the doubt that lingered in the darkest corners. With a ding, the steel doors opened. He loathed interacting with Tavion and mostly operated on his own, but every now and again Tavion would call him in for a status report.

Fleet steadied himself. He cleared his mind. He stepped into the all-white foyer of the sprawling penthouse. Thick silence and heavy foreboding sucked the air right out of the space. He knew this meeting, like all the others, was going to suck.

Windows lined the long L-shaped living space that looked out on the sparkling buildings of the massive city. The dark sky outside blended in with the shadowy room. Only the soft light from the gleaming neighboring structures gave any indication of life in the space. An oversized brown leather chair facing the view was the lone piece of furniture in the entire apartment. It was Tavion's favorite spot.

Tavion extended his arm over the armrest. He waved Fleet over. "Come."

Fleet's boots thudded against the marble floors, the echo of each step bouncing all around him like a lonely symphony. He took his place next to Tavion and clasped his hands behind his leather jacket. Glancing at Tavion, he saw that he was dressed in his usual black suit. His profile revealed a deep scowl.

"How may I help you, sir?"

Tavion moved his long skeletal fingers to his pale face and started rubbing his chin. "Dominique Wells," he said, letting the *s* trickle out of his mouth as if he were a slithering snake. "I've been thinking of her final life, and the differences here as compared to our other lives, and I do not like it. The events of late do not sit well with me. This year in particular, 2012, is fraught with too many unknowns."

Fleet remembered a time when Tavion's appearance was hardy and robust. Tavion had once stood on the side of right, but over time, a deep-seated hatred toward mankind pulled him away. Tavion detested humans and blamed them for the gradual destruction of the natural world. His departure split the Transhumans into two factions: the good became known as the Pure. The evil became known as the Tainted, and Tavion became their leader. He eventually marked Dominique for death in an attempt to get back at the Pure. With each passing decade, Tavion's hate grew in his heart and in his body, reducing him to his current death-like appearance.

Yet Fleet knew Tavion was right. Things in this life were way different, mainly with the involvement of first lifers Trent Avila and

Infiniti Clausman. Friends of Dominique's, Fleet suspected they'd play a role in Dominique's quest for survival. It seemed Tavion shared the same sentiment.

Testing his theory, Fleet asked, "What do you mean?"

Tavion let out a low growl. "Do not pretend that you know not of what I speak." He stood and faced Fleet. "Or are you keeping something from me?"

Hiding his surprise at the threatening move, Fleet eyed Tavion with matching menace, a look he knew Tavion respected. Tavion resided in perpetual paranoia, forcing Fleet to work overtime to keep Tavion's trust secured.

Fleet raised his chin. "I assure you, I am not keeping anything from you, sir. Nor would I make pretense."

Fleet waited for Tavion's response, wondering if Tavion had somehow discovered the conflict within him. Fleet curled his fingers behind his back, ready to form an energy ball and strike Tavion if needed. Luckily, Tavion's face softened. He placed his hand on Fleet's shoulder.

"My apologies, Fleet. I should not be so angry with you, especially since you are the only one I've been able to count on all these very long years."

Fleet relaxed his fist, but his body remained tense. "It's okay, sir."

Tavion eased back down on his chair. He returned his gaze to the twinkling lights of the downtown buildings. "Dominique keeps eluding us, but I know she's close. I can feel her fear, can practically smell her blood. Her parents cannot hide her forever. Eventually there'll be another break, and we'll find her. In the meantime, I want you to follow this one."

Tavion let loose a dark mist from his palm. It gathered into a swirl, forming a large oval shape. The mist thinned out, revealing an image of Infiniti Clausman, Dominique's neighbor and friend. Petite with small features and long dark hair, she danced around her room while packing a suitcase.

"This first lifer is important," Tavion said. "I can sense it."

Just as Fleet suspected, she *was* important. He thought of the other first lifer.

"What of Trent Avila?"

"Leave him to me." Tavion jabbed his finger at the floating image. "But this one is leaving in the morning with her mother on a holiday trip, and I want you on her heels. You will follow her to Colorado. I want to know everything about her. Understood? What she eats, what she drinks, what she loves, what she fears. All of it."

By the look of her room and the way she carried herself, she seemed like an average teenager of the time—interested in parties, music, and all things superficial. Yet something about her had struck a chord with Tavion. Fleet, too. There had to be more to her, but what?

"Understood, sir."

Tavion whisked the image away. He dismissed Fleet with a wave. "Go."

A sinking feeling grew in the pit of Fleet's stomach as he rode the elevator down to the first floor. He'd never been away from Dominique before. He didn't want to risk Tavion finding her while he was gone, yet he also didn't want Tavion to know about the conflict within him. Should he abandon Tavion's directive? Or should he follow Infiniti to Colorado and trust that Dominique would not be found until he returned?

Back outside, Fleet paced up and down the sidewalk, his mind on overdrive. Everything had repeated perfectly from lifetime to lifetime, but in this life nothing was the same. Nothing! And it was driving him crazy.

"It's better that way," a small voice said.

Fleet whipped around and saw a young girl. No more than five years old, she wore a long white dress that matched her long hair. She studied him with oversized green eyes.

"What's better?" he asked.

"That everything is different in this life."

A million things raced through Fleet's mind. Before he could say anything, the girl went on.

"You need to follow her. She will need you."

"The first lifer?"

"Yes. Infiniti. She will need you in Colorado."

A pink shimmery hue radiated from her body. Recognizing the young girl as part of the spirit world, yet sensing something familiar about her, he peered at her with questioning eyes. He moved closer.

"Who are you?"

The girl lifted her skirt off the floor with dainty hands and gave an old-fashioned curtsey. "I am Abigail. It's nice to meet you." Her innocent face flashed with remorse. "I used to be like you, but then I died. I had to in order to help save Dominique. Her friend is my friend, and Infiniti is important. Everyone in this life is. So you see, that's why you need to follow her. You need to help her."

Fleet latched on to her statement about being like him, but had no idea what she meant. Before he could ask her to explain, she stepped forward. She held out her hand, as if she wanted to touch him, but then dropped her arm. She lowered her head, her shoulders sagged, and she looked as if she might burst into tears.

"I am so sorry about what you are going through. I really am."

He looked about to see if anyone was around to witness the conversation he was having with the spirit girl, but the streets were empty. When he turned back to Abigail, she was gone.

"Hey! Come back!"

Desperate to ask the girl more questions, he waited a few minutes for her to return, but she didn't. He clasped his hands behind his neck. He walked up and down the sidewalk. He had no idea what she meant about feeling sorry for him, but figured it had to do with him joining Tavion's ranks. Shit, even he felt sorry for himself. He eyed the night sky that had begun to lighten to a soft gray. If Infiniti was important enough to garner Tavion's attention, then she probably would need his help.

"Guess I'm going to Colorado."

Purchase *Saving Infiniti* where books are sold.

www.ingramcontent.com/pod-product-compliance
Lightning Source LLC
Chambersburg PA
CBHW021129260626
47169CB00005B/1526